11-94

||||||| ||||| ||||||||| ||||| |||||||| |||
P9-DCM-365

DATE DUE

AUG 1 9 2004			
MAR 1 9 2005			
6-19-09			
	WITHDRAWN		

DEMCO 128-5046

on
R
P
DB

DEMCO

Dream Catcher

OTHER BOOKS BY TERRY C. JOHNSTON

Cry of the Hawk
Winter Rain

Carry the Wind
BorderLords
One-Eyed Dream

SON OF THE PLAINS NOVELS
Long Winter Gone
Seize the Sky
Whisper of the Wolf

THE PLAINSMEN NOVELS
Sioux Dawn
Red Cloud's Revenge
The Stalkers
Black Sun
Devil's Backbone
Shadow Riders
Dying Thunder
Blood Song
Reap the Whirlwind

Dream Catcher

Terry C. Johnston

Bantam Books
New York   Toronto   London   Sydney   Auckland

DREAM CATCHER

A Bantam Book / November 1994

All rights reserved.
Copyright © 1994 by Terry C. Johnston.
Interior illustration & book design by Ellen Cipriano
Map designed by GDS / Jeffrey L. Ward
No part of this book may be reproduced or transmitted
in any form or by any means, electronic or mechanical,
including photocopying, recording, or by any information
storage and retrieval system, without permission in
writing from the publisher.
For information address: Bantam Books.

Library of Congress Cataloging-in-Publication Data

Johnston, Terry C., 1947–
  Dream catcher / Terry C. Johnston.
     p.   cm.
  ISBN 0-553-09669-9
  I. Title.
PS3540.0392D74   1994
813'.54—dc20   *94-11547*
                                                         CIP

Published simultaneously in the United States and Canada

PRINTED IN THE UNITED STATES OF AMERICA

BVG   0 9 8 7 6 5 4 3 2 1

for my lady

VANETTE

who has been with me past the bonds
of time
and once more brought to me
the joy of the present

CAST OF CHARACTERS

Jonah Hook   Gritta Hook
                          Hattie Hook
Jeremiah Hook (Tall One)   Ezekiel Hook (Antelope)
Prairie Night (Antelope's Comanche wife)
Antelope Soldier (Antelope's son)
Good Road Woman (Antelope's daughter)

Shadrach Sweete   Toote Sweete/Shell Woman
Pipe Woman   High-Backed Bull

Danites

Colonel Jubilee Usher   George
Major Orrin Haslam
Baker Cunningham

Shoshone/Snake

Two Sleep

Military

*Colonel Ranald S. Mackenzie

Civilians

Nate Deidecker
*John Doyle Lee
*Brigham Young

Celestials

Bak Sahm   Chung-li Chu'uan

Texas Rangers

Captain Lamar Lockhart—commanding Company C
Deacon Elijah Johns—Lieutenant, Company C
Niles Coffee—Sergeant, Company C
Clyde Yoakam—Second Sergeant, Company C
June Callicott
John Corn
Harley Pettis
Wig Danville
Billy Benton

Ute Indians

Spirit Road

* *historical characters*

Pioche is overrun with as desperate a class of scoundrels as probably ever afflicted any mining town on this coast and the law is virtually a dead letter. . . . It is high time that something should be done, for as matters now stand, the name of Pioche has become a byword for reproach and a synonym for murder and lawlessness throughout the state.

> —*Territorial Enterprise*
> Virginia City, Nevada
> July 1873

> Victorious, you are a king;
> But vanquished, a bandit.
>> —Old Chinese adage

Young man, fit you up a little log cabin, if it is not more than ten feet square, and then get you a bird to put in your little cage. You can then work all day with satisfaction to yourself, considering that you have a home to go to, and a loving heart to welcome you. You will then have something to encourage you to labor and gather around you the comforts of life, and a place to gather them to.

> —Prophet Brigham Young

If a woman marries a chicken, she should act like a chicken; if she marries a dog, she should act like a dog.

> —Ancient Chinese proverb

Hark! listen to the trumpeters!
They sound for volunteers;
On Zion's bright and flowery mount
Behold the officers.

Their horses white, their armor bright,
With courage bold they stand,
Enlisting soldiers for their king,
To march to Zion's land.

We want no cowards in our bands,
Who will our colors fly:
We call for valiant-hearted men,
Who're not afraid to die!

   —Traditional Mormon hymn

Dream Catcher

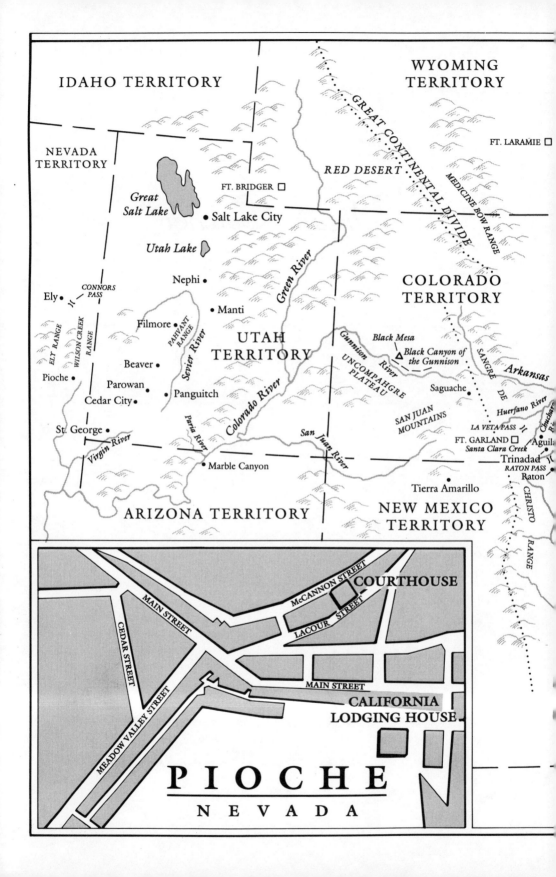

Prologue

Late Summer 1908

S HE REALLY WASN'T here.

This wrinkled, gray-headed, wild-eyed woman of Jonah Hook's. Nathan Deidecker finally realized Gritta wasn't really here.

After so many hours, and all these days he had spent in the shadow of Cloud Peak, in these hills that tumbled beneath the ominous immensity of the Big Horns, Nathan finally accepted that fact as irrefutable.

As if she were in some deep form of concentration, he watched the woman rocking in that chair of hers, its bows continuing to carve themselves down into the rough-hewn pine planks that formed the cabin's porch. Nathan wanted to remember her just as she was—so he could describe her in the most minute detail upon his return to Omaha. There he would have the *Bee*'s staff artist render likenesses of both Gritta and Jonah Hook, those engravings to accompany each installment in the reporter's nationally acclaimed series on the old frontier scouts.

Intending to interview the most unsung of those scouts, the newsman had journeyed west to Wyoming—brought here by a most intriguing, truly seductive proposal by the publisher of Sheridan's weekly. Instead of finding what he had thought would be another interesting Sunday byline, Nathan had bumped right into one of the greatest tales of human endurance, abiding love, and unrequited rage he had encountered in the decade since he had undertaken to write down the stories of the great frontiersmen and army scouts.

It hadn't taken long before his series began to appear in reprint in papers across the country, including the prestigious Chicago *Tribune* and even Bennett's New York *Herald*. But this . . . this had turned out to be a tale altogether more . . . well, more involved. Replete with astonishingly intricate and emotionally terrifying chapters—details he was already crafting in his mind on this unknown character Jonah Hook. Why, Nathan could more than imagine Hook's story exploding across the pages of the nation's greatest newspapers—he could imagine how the East's biggest publishing houses would clamor for him to put Hook's quest down in the pages of a book: a surefire best-seller that would bring Deidecker all the more fame.

Why, to be recognized and whispered about as he strode into Delmonico's, making his grand entrance: escorted by the maître d' to the best of tables where he could easily see and be seen, there to be courted by the power brokers of the East.

Nathan smiled to himself and stroked the head of the old hound that had its muzzle laid in Deidecker's lap.

She doesn't live here, he brooded again. Maybe she never did, he thought as he reluctantly dragged himself from Delmonico's back to the present, back to the summer heat of the high plains. It's likely she doesn't even know what the now is.

He doubted she lived in the present. More probable, Gritta Hook was still tangled up back there some thirty long years ago. And though her body grew older every day, Nathan figured her mind never would. Forever held captive in a long-ago era. Here it was the opening of the twentieth century—and this woman he watched incessantly rocking, forever staring up at the clouds making their shadowy crossing of the great, granite faces of the mountains . . . Gritta Hook was still living in the 1860s. No later than the 1870s.

All Nathan had of her story was what Jonah told him. But where the old scout had ever learned of Gritta's tale, Deidecker could only conjecture. Perhaps she told her husband of her years with Jubilee Usher after Hook had finally freed her.

Gazing again at the old woman in the rocker, he shuddered. Which caused the old hound to raise its head slightly, looking up at the newsman, its head cocked. Nathan went back to stroking the dog's ears as the flies continued to drone in the yard, out there in the nearby flood of sunlight slowly crawling across the yard as that great, brilliant orb continued its incessant whirl toward the west.

The hound let out a sigh, its eyelids drooping as it resettled its great jowls back on his leg, dozing once more.

The very thought of that old woman, taking her revenge.

Across the yard two of the half-dozen horses in the small corral snorted and whinnied, tossing their heads. Beyond them Nathan saw something shimmer, move off in the distance. He realized the animals had taken scent of one of their own kind coming over the crest of the hill to the west. Its smell carried on the breeze. Atop its back, the old man, just then breaking the skyline.

Deidecker wondered if Hook had brought down the game he set out to find that morning in the gray stillness before dawn.

"Jonah's back, Mrs. Hook," he said.

As if he were talking to someone sane, he scolded himself, then watched with intense curiosity as her eyes shifted along the horizon. She had heard him. More than that, Gritta Hook had understood. Yet there was no change in the rhythm of those rocker bows nestled in their grooves in the porch. No measurable movement of her head from where she had been facing when Deidecker spoke. Only . . . only the tiniest shift in those icy blue eyes that, despite all her advancing years, had somehow remained clear of clouding and cataracts.

Now the hound raised its head, nostrils alive, seeming to take in the warm breeze. Then slowly the dog dragged the hind legs under its body and arched up on all fours, stretching languorously before leaping off the porch into the yard, where it trotted away, toward the line of trees that hemmed the base of the long, grassy hill where Jonah Hook was descending beneath the midday sun.

Gone to welcome its master's return.

This time Nathan did more than glance at Gritta. He tried to study her for more than a moment. Could he discern some minute change in that cold blue? Was it only his imagination, his wishful desire—or was there truly some recognition in those eyes, something she refused to show on her face, much less speak of? Perhaps the merest hint of feeling for the man who spent his youth crossing countless miles and endless summers like this one, searching a great, broad, and unforgiving land for her when lesser men would have given up and gone on with their lives.

Don't be silly, he chided himself. This isn't about anything so mawkish. This . . . no, this simply isn't a love story.

Nathan shaded his eyes with one hand, squinting into the brightness of that sun-washed distance.

"If I'm not wrong, Mrs. Hook—looks as if Jonah's coming home with some meat for the table."

Robber jays exploded into flight from a copse of trees near the base of that distant hill as Jonah Hook disappeared from sight. Nathan watched the gray-winged birds arc across the painfully brilliant hues of the nearby tumble of wrinkled slope, then glanced absently at the woman. Surprised, even a little frightened to find her looking at him.

Claws gripped his chest, shutting off his breath. He couldn't remember her ever looking directly at him before. But even if she had stolen a glance at him since that afternoon he had driven the rented buggy into this yard—Nathan could not recall her eyes ever connecting with his as intently as they were now.

Consciously drawing in a breath, Deidecker tore his eyes from hers to gaze out at the shimmering haze of dancing heat still lying between the cabin and the distant horseman. Recalling that he had felt just this way before: frightened, out of place. It had been a few days back when the old man discovered him sitting, rocking, violating Gritta's chair in the cold, murky light of predawn.

The day when Nathan had ridden off with Jonah into those distant hills, toward the high places where the snow never melted. Before he really learned of Jonah's pain. How the father had lost the son. How this old man had paid so great a price, paid in his own blood.

A price exacted not because he had done wrong, not because he was duty-bound to make a blood atonement.

Instead, Jonah Hook's debt was incurred because he was a man who had gone and done what was right: to attempt all that was in his power to put his little family back together.

Nathan figured it had been a price Hook would not have had to pay had the old man just given up, gone to find another woman, made her his wife, had children with her, and buried the past as surely as folks put their kin in the ground and go on day by day.

But right from Deidecker's arrival Jonah Hook had shown himself to be cut of a different cloth. He had been the sort of man who opened up the ground beneath that shady tree near the cabin he built for Gritta and their children in the border country near Indian Territory. Before he set out to put his family back together, Jonah was the sort who had scratched out four long, deep holes in that dark Missouri ground. Such an act was like opening up a great wound in his own heart so it would bleed, so that he could curse his soul to some great and endless perdition until he would allow himself to fill those graves, allow a healing to come upon those holes torn in his heart.

A sudden shudder of sentiment coursed through Deidecker as he began to make out the features on the distant horseman reappearing behind the grassy roll of hills, the old dog loping beside the horse now.

Deidecker had to admit he held feelings for the old man. Naturally curious at first, Nathan had quickly become outright frightened of the angular, wiry, grizzled plainsman. Not that there had been any loss of that initial curiosity. Nor any real diminishing of the fear he felt in the electrifying presence of the man. But both curiosity and fear had been tempered over the hours and meals, days and miles and campfires, spent with Jonah Hook. Coming to learn of the great sacrifice made, the unrelenting pain of the man's quest.

And now finally to admit that Jonah Hook's was in the end a story of love.

So it did make Nathan Deidecker shudder again with a flush of sentiment as he saw the horseman raise an arm to wave.

Turning quickly to glance at the woman, it took Nathan a moment to realize Jonah wasn't signaling his wife. He looked back at the old plainsman. Then something balled in his throat, and he cursed it, scolding himself—it was important to stay objective here, especially here, this close to the last chapters of a story he was sure millions would find so amazing they would doubt that it was true. He had to stay detached.

And as suddenly as Nathan reminded himself of that, he knew it was impossible. Too late already. As much as he would try to write this story dispassionately, it was already a tale of people he cared about.

This old man.

And his silent, emotionless woman.

Grasshoppers fluttered upward into winged flight around the horse's legs as the animal plodded on through the tall, drying grass. Their fleeing raised an oncoming, buzzing rattle atop the light breeze as that sweat-slicked horse and the old hound brought the hunter home from the hills. Behind the saddle hung the headless, gutted carcass of the biggest elk the newsman had ever seen.

"Afternoon, Nate," Jonah said as he eased the weary animal to a halt at the edge of the porch shadow.

"Jonah."

"Well, don't stand there, son," he said with a grin that crinkled his deeply seamed face. "C'mon down from that goddamned shade and gimme a hand."

Nathan bolted to his feet and leaped off the edge of the porch as Jonah slid stiffly from the saddle. Nathan's eyes poured down the length of the old man, noticing how it seemed Hook was splattered with blood all the way from that deep cleft of his neck-wattle clear to his knees. Dried blood caked the crescents of the man's fingernails, streaked clear up to his elbows. Deidecker stared, then suddenly realized the old hunter was studying him.

"S'pose I am a sight, at that, Nate. A city fella like you and all," Hook said quietly. "Elk is a big critter. 'Sides—I always do get a mite wound up in my work. Never you mind: don't let all this blood give you pause, son. C'mere—need your muscle a minute or two." Hook deftly pulled the knots from the last rawhide whang and motioned the newsman alongside.

Deidecker gulped and reached out to seize hold of the forelegs of the skinned and gutted carcass as Hook began to drag it from the horse's rear flanks.

"N-never saw a man so covered . . . what with all the . . . the . . ."

"Blood?" Hook asked, stopping and turning to gaze at the newsman.

"Yeah. To see all that."

With a nod the old man looked himself up and down, then said, "All them years, Nate. Would give a man pause to think back and know all the blood I waded through. Far more'n this."

Deidecker grinned lamely as Hook dragged the elk carcass off the horse and onto their shoulders. "Not hard to imagine at all, Jonah," he grunted under the sudden throw of the weight. "What with all the game you brought down, across all those years searching for Gritta."

Hook stopped, turned slightly. "No, Nate. I wasn't talking about animals. I was talking about the blood of men. Them what hunted me. Them what I was hunting. C'mon." He set off slowly toward the barn beneath the carcass.

"I . . ." And Deidecker's voice trailed off as the weight shifted atop his shoulders and his face was shoved against the skinned carcass, filling his nostrils with the fresh, unmistakable smell of it. Blood and death.

Beside the barn stood a tall rafter beam where hung a block and tackle. The old plainsman came to a halt. Jonah grabbed hold of a hook and savagely drove it through the thick neck muscle, neatly encircling a bone.

"I usually quarter an elk out," Jonah explained, the strain of the morning's exertion beginning to tell around the edges of his voice. "But knowing you was back here to help, I brought it in whole."

Hook slid his shoulder down the carcass as, hand over hand, he took up the slack in the rope gripped in both bloody palms.

Deidecker sensed the weight taken from him as he stood rooted dumbly to the spot, continuing to gaze at the old hunter's bloodstained clothes, the hands and arms caked with the brownish film, at the sweat glistening across the taut, sinewy muscles still youthful despite their years of severe testing.

With a groan Hook straightened and wiped his hands off on those bloody britches, staring back at Deidecker with patient amusement. There in the cool blue shadows of that barn, he smacked the ribs of the elk with an open hand, then nodded toward the creaking, open door, in the direction of the cabin porch in plain sight from where they stood.

"All this time, Nate—she ain't been sure if she wanted me to tell you her story." Hook spoke little above a whisper. "But this morning when I was pulling on my boots, setting about to go hunting—she told me."

"She . . . Gritta?" he stammered, shocked at the revelation. "Excuse me . . . Mrs. Hook spoke to you?"

"Not in so many words, you understand."

Nathan's eyes narrowed, straining to understand. "Then, how?"

He shrugged, scratching the side of his head absently, as if struggling to find an answer for something he had long ago figured out for himself, something that really had no explanation in the ways of logical men.

"The way she looked at me," the old man finally answered. "You spend enough years with a woman, especially a woman what don't talk . . . well—" He sighed, the tip of his tongue poking through a gap in his worn teeth. "A woman who *can't* talk no more. A man spends all them days and seasons, all them years with that woman—way I see it: you get to know her better'n most men would know a woman what talked on and on and on."

"And? She let you know?" Nathan asked anxiously, chiding himself for it almost immediately.

Jonah grinned, his eyes going soft there in the shadows of the barn. "Gritta says she's watched you enough last few days. Figured you out on her own, Nate. So this morning afore I pulled out, she let me know it was all right."

He wagged his head. "All right?"

"What the woman thinks of you."

Deidecker turned now to look across the sunny yard, to that patch of shade beneath the rough porch awning. There in her own shadow he studied the woman, not surprised to find her still staring into the distance of miles and years, that yawning gap between pain and joy known so long, long ago when she had been able to feel something. Staring off into the west with those eyes where nothing seemed to register, as if she were totally unaware that she was the subject of this crucial and most intimate discussion between her own husband and a newsman from Omaha, Nebraska.

For but a moment, nothing more than a heartbeat, Deidecker considered trying to get the woman to talk—to experience the sound of her voice just once before he left this place. After all, hadn't Will Kemper, the old editor of the *Sheridan Press,* whispered in a cryptic hush that Deidecker should *"Find out about the woman"*? This would be Nathan's own personal coup. A career maker.

But as his time with Jonah Hook passed, hour by hour, day by day, Deidecker grew to be less certain. Something just didn't feel right about it.

Then uncertainty became a tangible fear. Fear with a taste all its own.

A cold shiver slipped down Nate Deidecker's spine. For an instant he wondered if it was only sweat—what with his exertion helping the old man in oppressive heat smothering this high land, baking everything into brittleness beneath that late-summer sun.

Then Nate knew better, as the next moment he realized the rocker had stopped.

The woman had turned her head slightly, so she could look directly at him. Her eyes locked on his, those eyes every bit as cold as that chill again raking its shivery fingernail down his backbone as Jonah Hook spoke softly, ominously.

"Gritta figures it's time you heard her story."

Book I

Perchance to Dream

1

IT WAS AS if he were adrift between the two banks of a wide and mighty river.

Sensing himself growing more and more weary as he battled the strong, heaving current. His muscles crying out for him to stop. His eyes blinded, unable to make out the bank far ahead of him. All but unable to see the bank he had left behind.

But it was back there. Jonah knew that. Missouri. The valley farmland outside Cassville. That homestead where he and Gritta had determined to make the rest of their lives count for something. But now it was all behind him. Those four graves scooped out of the rich soil beneath that big, sheltering tree.

One of those holes was yet to be filled.

Weeks ago he had hurled himself back into this current. Once again leaving behind all he had known in that narrow, fertile valley. Here he was kicking at the mighty river again, clawing desperately at the river's overpowering pull.

The last time he had felt this magnetic draw on his lodestone, Jonah had allowed the river to drag him far beyond his goal. The mighty current had flung him south into the scorching land of the mud-and-wattle jacales, on a quest that ultimately led him to the dominion of the Comanche. Far, far from where Jubilee Usher's trail had grown dim, then faint, and finally snuffed itself out.

Not this time.

This time, he swore, he would not let the current of days and weeks, the crushing tidal pull of miles and bruising distance, sweep him along, hurtling him far downstream from his goal. This time, Jonah vowed, he would keep his eye on the far bank. Kicking and clawing with all that he had. Until he made it across the time and miles to Gritta. Or his muscles simply gave in and he was lost beneath the current itself.

He owed his woman no less. No less than his own life in this quest.

Now there were three riders. Eight summers before when he had pushed west from Fort Laramie, Jonah had ridden out alone. Then there were two: an old friend of Shad Sweete's, the Shoshone who stayed on through the seasons, making this search, this fight, this battle his own. Perhaps somehow to heal his own pain.

And now the third: Jeremiah. His firstborn son.

It made Jonah's eyes smart each time he recalled how in that terrible little graveyard he had dug for himself beneath the boughs of a skeletal tree, his oldest son had declared, "I'm going with you, Pa. Even though I ain't a little boy no more—that don't mean I ain't your son."

Damn, but weren't there still some misgivings about bringing Jeremiah along? A long, bloody trail already. But even as hard as it had already been, what lay before him now had all the makings of something far more demanding, far more agonizing, far, far more horrid. Jeremiah might be a young man—even proven in battle among Quanah Parker's Kwahadi Comanche—but no matter what the years had done to put distance between them, nothing could change the fact that he was Jonah's son.

And Gritta was the one who bore him.

"She'll always be my mother," Jeremiah had said there in the gusts of icy sleet beside that dark hole scraped like an evil scar out of the middle of all that snow falling to the ground with a muffled patter. "I owe her just as much as you do, Pa."

So he had asked Jeremiah, "You sure about this, son?"

And the man Jeremiah had become replied, "I ain't asking you, Pa. I'm *telling* you what I'm going to do. With you . . . or without you: I'm going after my mother."

Jonah tugged at the battered brim on his hat to try keeping more of the rain from spilling down the collar of his coat now as they plodded west across Creek country. Reservation ground. Indian Territory. The Nations. Sniffling too, not only from the cold but at the remembrance of how he brought young Jeremiah into his arms there beside Gritta's empty grave, to hug his son fiercely. Gripping on to him like he had never had the opportunity to hold Jeremiah before. As a man. And with his next words Jonah made the vow of a lifetime.

"Son, let's go find your mother."

It was cold, and the sleeting rain slanted down at them in thick, wavering sheets, whipped at them in great, chilling, stinging gobs by a capricious wind. It would take some doing, Jonah realized. This getting to know Jeremiah as a man. Years gone through his fingers, tumbling out of his grasp like that black Missouri soil would spill away from the plowshare as he turned it in the spring. But together they just might have a chance— not only to get to know one another as men, but also to somehow right the wrong done their family.

Family. Now Jonah had family along. Alone no more. His firstborn son on one side. And the aging warrior who had become a brother riding on the other.

Jonah prayed family would make all the difference this time as he flung himself into the mighty, unforgiving river.

The days that surrounded their journey were still short, yet each one lengthening nonetheless, stretching minute by minute imperceptibly as they rode a little south of west out of Missouri, keeping well north of Fort Smith on the Arkansas. Crossing an invisible border into an unforgiving land that tended to swallow whole the white men who dared enter there. Between that Missouri border and Fort Cobb squatting beside the Washita lay a no-man's-land. Since this part of Indian Territory was Creek and Choctaw and Cherokee country, the army had little call to venture in. Rarely was there trouble enough to warrant a soldier patrol. So most authority was civilian, and that authority rested in the hands of the tribes.

While they had been back in southwestern Missouri, heading for that borderland, Jonah tried learning what all that meant.

The Nations had become a cesspool where the worst of white mankind had dumped itself. Horse thieves and thugs, payroll robbers and just plain murderers—all the dregs of so-called civilized society in Kansas and Texas, Missouri and Arkansas, committed their most evil, then scooted across the border into Indian Territory. There to laugh up their sleeves at any and all who sought to dog their trail.

This was a no-man's-land where any man you might bump into on the trail could be the next one to drag a knife across your throat, or slip it between your ribs.

But Jonah Hook was no stranger to this sort of dangerous border

country. For the better part of eight years already he had been riding this
revenge trail. Sucking on his growing, festering rage like a man sucked on a
sore tooth—waiting for the time he could stand the pain no more and was
forced to pull it.

Hook put up his arm, signaling the other two, who came to halt
beside him. Their two packhorses plodded to a stop at their tail roots,
heads hung morosely in the driving rain.

"You smell anything, Two Sleep?" he asked the Shoshone on his left
as he swiped the soaked forearm of his canvas mackinaw beneath his sore,
red nose.

Under the shapeless brim of his rain-battered hat, Two Sleep put his
own chiseled nose to work, nostrils gently flaring as he tested the caliber of
the wind. And what that wind might carry.

He finally turned to Jonah and grinned slightly. "Smoke."

Hook himself smiled as he glanced at Jeremiah. "Give it a try, son."

"Yonder," Jeremiah said, pointing.

With a shiver as more rain spilled down the back of his neck, Jonah
tried to sort out what to do, flicking a look at the menace in the heavy
gunmetal-gray sky hovering overhead, a storm that showed no sign of
relenting. "Don't figure it to be a campfire—not out in this weather. My
gut tells me it's got to be a cabin."

"Cabin, yes," Two Sleep agreed. "I go. You wait with Tall One."

Jonah only nodded as the Shoshone quietly nudged his horse ahead
into the thick stands of hardwood that bordered the Canadian River. At
first, weeks ago, it had sounded so foreign to have the Shoshone call
Jeremiah by that Comanche name. But in time Jonah had come to accept
that it was a sign of respect from one Indian to another, from one warrior
for another.

After all, Jonah's firstborn son had lived more years as the Comanche
called Tall One than he had lived as Jeremiah Hook.

So he waited here beside his son, remembering back to cold, miserable days like this long, long ago in that cabin he and Gritta had raised with
their own hands in that narrow valley. Warmth would radiate from the
small fireplace where she might have some corn bread baking in the Dutch
oven buried down among a blanket of glowing coals. Young Hattie would
be curled asleep on her cot, and newborn Jeremiah would lie nestled in his
hand-hewn cradle an arm's length from their own rope-and-post bed.
Where he stroked and caressed Gritta's naked body beneath the damp
warmth of the blankets, in wonder at the power she held over him.

That remembrance made him cold this time. As if just the remembering allowed the chill of the driving rain to penetrate him to the bone. It scared Jonah. Frightened him: as if he were being told something new and dreadful about the woman. Every dream of her at night, just the merest conscious recall of her touch each day, heretofore had always brought him warmth. But now, this cold.

Maybe she was dead after all.

And he hated himself for feeling that.

Jonah quickly glanced over at Jeremiah, as if his son might truly hear his private thought, when he picked out the sound of sodden hoofbeats moving their way through the soggy timber. It lifted Jonah's heart to have Gritta's boy here with him.

"Cabin," Two Sleep almost whispered as he came to a halt between them. "No horse in the corral. Not a white man's place, looks to me."

"Injuns. Reservation Injuns." Jonah was relieved at that. "All right," he said, shaking some of the rain from his canvas mackinaw, "let's go make ourselves welcome as we can."

And he led them out. Glad in the bedrock of his soul that Gritta's boy was here.

"Better finish them beans, Jeremiah," Jonah said. "You're taking first watch."

Without a word young Hook quickly tipped the old woman's blackened cast-iron kettle over his tin plate and scooped out the last of the sodden white beans with the long-handled wooden spoon, scraping loose that burned layer plastered to the bottom of the kettle.

As he shoveled a warm bite into his mouth, Jeremiah looked over at the old Indian woman seated on the narrow hearth by the fire, her husband's head in her lap. She stroked the man's ashen, wrinkled face with dirty, arthritic fingers as tenderly as a young mother would caress the face of a newborn infant. At times she wrung out the warm cloth she dipped in a foul-smelling bowl and replaced it on the man's shoulder wound. A filthy, bloodstained bandage lay wrapped around the Indian's battered head.

The pair hadn't moved much since Jeremiah's arrival—found much like this by the trio when they rode up to the miserable cabin.

The cold shock startled him. Looking up at the roof in anger,

Jeremiah found it leaking from another crack, forcing him to scoot sideways on the rough bench to escape the cold drip as he wolfed down the last of those beans.

While Jonah and Jeremiah had hung back in the timber with their weapons ready, Two Sleep had approached the cabin door by slipping in where he would not be seen from either of the windows. Finally easing the door open, the Shoshone had found himself staring at the old woman, backlit by her tiny fireplace where she sat at the hearth, an old muzzle loader trembling in her hands. She pointed it at the tall, rain-soaked warrior in the doorway, speaking her smattering of English. Only when she realized the white devils had not returned to finish off her husband did she cease her confused babble. Yet for the longest time she could not take her watchful, suspicious eyes off the solitary white man—Jonah.

Jeremiah chuckled about that again now, wiping his mouth on the back of his coat sleeve. His long, dark hair surely gave him the best of all possible disguises. That and the sunburned skin. Skin from which he had plucked every hair. No white man's whiskers, not even a mustache. Not so much as an eyebrow. For a moment he remembered how he and Hattie and Zeke played Indians when they were younger. A lifetime ago. Played their games not ever having seen a real live Indian—not one of them. Instead they listened raptly to the stories Gritta and some of the other knowing adults around Cassville told. Then made up their own child's play.

What seemed a lifetime ago.

Two Sleep made sense of the old woman's babble—explaining that white men rode through a couple days ago. Horse thieves. When the old man heard them coming, he sent the woman down into the crawl space he had scratched out beneath the hearth long ago. There, the woman explained to the Shoshone, she had waited in the dank, musty dark and listened to the sounds of mocking laughter as her husband confronted the thieves alone.

When the gunfire echoed from out front, she tried to raise the trapdoor, finding that her husband had pulled something over it so that she would not come out and betray herself. It had taken long, hard, straining work to the point of tears to struggle against the trapdoor until the heavy table moved and she was freed.

To find her husband in the yard out front: shot once in the chest, his head bleeding from a blow of some sort. With the last of her strength she had dragged him across the doorsill before pulling down her medicines from safekeeping among the rafters where the spiders haunted the shadows on cold, damp days such as this. She explained that the old man's eyes had fluttered open when she began to minister to him, and he told her there were ten, maybe more, who had come to steal their horses. White devils.

Just like the ones her neighbors to the south told her stories of. The reservation was full of them. White men come to steal Indian horses. Run those horses off to some place where they could sell them to the army.

"You really think there's a chance they'll come back?" Jeremiah asked his father as he pushed himself back and stood beside the plank table. "They got the horses two days ago. Seems to me they'll be a long way off by now."

"A slim chance, son. Better us to be safe."

Taking his narrow-bladed belt knife from its scabbard, Jeremiah peeled loose a wispy sliver of wood from the edge of the bench where he sat to eat his supper of white beans. He stuck the sliver between his lips, intending to use it later to pick his teeth as he sat by the window that faced the open ground out front. Jeremiah figured he would trust in his father's judgment. It couldn't be all blind luck that Jonah had rescued sister Hattie. Something more had led Jonah all these years to hunt down that band of Kwahadi he and Zeke had grown up with.

Jeremiah wasn't really sure where Jonah had come on all his knowledge in the years since his father had marched off proud and ramrod straight to join Sterling Price in throwing the Yankees out of Missouri. But knowledge it was—a real savvy—just the sort of savvy Jeremiah promised himself he was going to learn real quick.

Jonah had led Jeremiah and Two Sleep away from the last open grave on that haunted homestead back in the change of the seasons. When the angry, tormented spring sky acted as capricious as a flighty young girl with her choice of school-yard suitors.

Here beside the window now, Jeremiah remembered the word. April. Late as it was getting, must surely be closing in on the moon that the *tai-bos*—his father's people—called May.

Chiding himself for that, Jeremiah realized he would have to get used to looking at some things like a white man once more. May was coming, if not here already.

But that didn't mean Jeremiah had to look at *everything* like a white man. He doubted he would ever again anyhow. Too much time thinking, too much time damn well *being* a Kwahadi.

Looking at those clouds hung low over the land day after day, he knew only one thing was certain—that sky they had been riding under couldn't make up its mind just what to do: snow, or rain. But the trio kept moving some every day, taking shelter in great copses of trees when they could find no cave out of the wind. At times forced to hunker together under lengths of oiled canvas when they had no other shelter. Moving slowly south of west, marking time and the miles.

They pretty much followed the trail Two Sleep had used to guide them north from Fort Richardson in Texas, northeast through the Indian Nations and on to Missouri. But for some reason in the last few days Jeremiah sensed that his father wasn't retracing their steps back toward Texas. Instead, it seemed Jonah was taking them to Fort Sill.

Word had it that was the place Three-Finger Kinzie was now commander. The soldier chief carried a big reputation now, having waged his own long and private war with Quanah Parker.

Bad-Hand Kinzie, the Comanche called him at times—referring to a wound suffered in the same war Jeremiah's father went off to fight. Kinzie was the same pony-soldier chief who attacked Parker's camp in the canyon at Palo Duro. The same soldier who just last winter sent an offer of peace to Quanah, asking the nomadic warrior bands of the Comanche to come in at long, long last. And declaring that should the gray-eyed half-breed chief not bring in his Kwahadi people—then Kinzie vowed to destroy them.

Perhaps, Jeremiah brooded as he picked his teeth with that bench sliver and watched the long day seep into a rainy twilight, his father was going to that soldier fort to do what he could to save Prairie Night, his son's wife. And Zeke's children.

From the despair. From the hopelessness. From the starvation suffered at the Comanche agency.

How Jeremiah desperately wanted to believe Jonah was going to the Comanche reservation at Sill to do what he could to save his own grandchildren.

2

"THERE IS AN art to your use of the knife," Jubilee Usher instructed the more than half a hundred gathered around him as he pulled his arms free of the long-tailed frock coat of black woven wool, folding it once lengthwise before laying it across the arms of one of his pasty-faced spectators.

As he knelt over the body of the man he had just killed with one of the pearl-handled revolvers he wore stuffed in holsters at the front of his hips, Usher slipped the long skinning knife from its belt scabbard. Grabbing the man's hair and yanking the head back with his free hand, the Mormon zealot suddenly bent over to put his ear near the bloody lips.

"He breathin', Colonel?" came the question from one of those in the ring of breathless gunmen.

"Yes," he answered, his head rising, a twist of a smile curling his lips into a cruel bow. "This will be all the sweeter now."

He let the man's head fall into the dirt and crudely slashed the wool shirt from the man's back until it lay like a dirty scapular fluttering at the victim's waist, only the sleeves still clinging to the man's arms.

Usher was holding court. Instilling in his ranks of roving brigands the most secure discipline a commander in the field can exercise over his men. *Fear.* Sheer, gut-wrenching fear. Jubilee Usher doubted there was another man west of Missouri who surpassed him in extracting such unquestioning obedience. Although from time to time he did so enjoy reminding his

19

crude, Falstaffian army of cutthroats of the need for their unswerving allegiance.

The hapless victim beneath him had made the mistake of not heeding one of Usher's rules of camp, like his predecessor before him sometime last winter—another who showed up for inspection with a dirty weapon, then sought to grin his way out of it. Jubilee always saw they paid with their lives—of more purpose for the moment than they had served in all their miserable existence: their meteoric rise to fame as examples to the rest.

Noticing the dark stain across the pale ground beneath the victim's chest, Usher dragged his dagger across the back of the man's shoulders, then deftly down both sides of the rib cage, finishing with a fourth long incision clear across the small of the back.

"So much for the crude work you are all capable of, gentlemen," he told them, his feral eyes touching a man here, another one there in the front row of the expectant crowd gone silent all around him, many bent forward in worshipful observance. So quiet they could actually hear the gentle breeze nudging the new leaves in the nearby cottonwoods.

"Now for the fine work. Pay heed—for this is nothing short of pure artistry. Nothing at all like skinning game. Nothing like a butcher's game. Pay attention and you'll learn from the master."

As he flicked the tip of the knife beneath a corner of the dying man's skin and pulled up the tiny flap with his left hand, he felt the ring of men lean in to watch this most delicate surgery. Beneath him the victim lay still, his blood and viscera soaking into the soil of Nevada Territory. Closing in on death, he must surely have been oblivious to the man above him slowly working up the flap of skin with sure strokes of the dagger, freeing the flesh from the muscle beneath, inch by bloody inch, until Jubilee Usher finally stood with the prize stretched beneath his hands, turning slowly to show the huge opaque square of fish-belly-white hide he had removed from the victim.

"I've found human skin to make the finest rawhide," Usher told them as he moved around the inside of that circle, each set of wide eyes either locked on him or unable to leave that great flap of reddish, gore-flecked skin.

"You there," Jubilee said, stopping in front of one of them. "Quickly now. Down to the creek and bring me a stone. A round one. About the size of your fist."

"Y-yes, sir."

"No, wait," Usher interrupted the man's departure, glancing at the size of the man's hand. "Make it a stone the size of *my* fist."

Some of those in the crowd snorted, chuckled, even laughed behind their hands.

"Yes, sir, Colonel."

His eyes flicked over them again, finding another likely assistant. "And you—fetch me a stout limb. Bigger round than my thumb, you see. Not quite as big as your wrist. One of those young saplings down by the creek will do nicely."

When the man on the ground groaned, Usher turned, sensing the ring of men lurch back a step or two in their own surprise and fear. He strode over to the body, nudging it with his toe, but his victim did not stir.

"George!" Usher called out.

His black face emerged from the crowd. "Colonel?"

"Bring me that small writing table of mine. The one with the legs."

"Yessuh, I will now."

In but minutes the two returned to the circle, just as Usher's Negro servant was trudging up with the table.

"Set it there, George," he instructed, then laid the large flap of flesh atop the surface of the writing desk. The pliable skin all but covered it.

Taking the stone from the hands of his soldier, Usher laid it near one corner of the skin, then began cutting strips from the skin with his knife.

"Split the end of that handle with your knife for me. Right down the middle about half a foot. Be sure of it."

Usher watched the process, and once satisfied with the man's work, he took the sapling from the soldier and peeled the split end apart. Between them he jammed the fist-sized stone and worked it down into the vee until there were a few inches of the sapling sticking over the top of the stone.

"Excellent. A green hide, men," he told them. "And green wood. Both work the best."

Now he took the first strip of human flesh and wrapped it around the open ends of the split sapling, pulling on the elastic skin as he went, drawing the open ends of the split wood ever tighter around the stone. A second strip of flesh went round and round the sapling just below the stone. Back and forth he worked the two across the stone, forming an X.

"You finish the whole thing with a bit more artistry."

Usher laid the weapon down on the remaining flesh on the writing table, as if measuring several inches out from the edges of the stone, then began to slash a large circular piece from the skin. This he draped completely over the top of the weapon, covering stone and sapling. Pulling it all very taut, he used a last strip of flesh to gather the covering crudely at the base of the stone, again tying off the free ends when he was done.

21

"Now you can carefully warm this over a fire, drying it slowly—ever so slowly, mind you. And the skin will draw up tight as a rawhide drum."

Smacking his flesh-covered sap in his empty left palm, Usher walked slowly round the gaping ring to let them inspect his handiwork more closely. Then he suddenly stopped and stepped over to the groaning victim at the center of that circle.

"But the ultimate proof of your artistry comes in its test as a weapon, gentlemen."

As he finished the last word, Usher began the sap's arc, bringing it out at the end of his arm, only shoulder high, then driving it downward into the back of the unconscious man's head with a sickening crunch. Some blood splattered on his new weapon. The man's legs convulsed. Usher stepped quickly to a new position and swung the sap again, clutching the end of the sapling splattered with gore.

Again and again, and again, he drove the stone into the man's head until there was little but an oozing jelly left of the skull and face, the ground beneath the victim darkening.

"Colonel Usher?"

He turned to find one of Major Haslam's couriers stepping to the inside of the crowd.

"News for us?" he asked, watching the courier's eyes fall to the dead man at Usher's feet, then bound up quickly, noticing the way the courier's Adam's apple bobbed as he swallowed, readying his answer.

"Y-yes, sir."

"My father?"

"No, Colonel. Elder Lee."

"He wants to see me down at the Ferry?"

The man shook his head. "They arrested him."

Something seized inside Usher. "Who arrested Lee? Brigham Young?"

"No. The government. Took him when he visited his family at Panguitch last November."

"November? Why didn't we know?" Usher growled menacingly.

"Word is the government's held him in Beaver all this time we was wintering here in Nevada country."

"Is Young going to protect Lee?"

The man's eyes darted left and right quickly. "Word says he ain't. And that's got some of them folks down in that part of Dixie riled up that the Church is gonna let John Doyle Lee be Brigham Young's sacrificial goat."

"Damn him!" Usher roared. "Like all the rest of the Avenging Angels, I vowed allegiance to Brigham Young. I followed him west. I swore my life to him because I believed him to be the chosen hand of God!"

Then Jubilee's voice grew ominously quiet. "But—we all know that Brigham Young is no longer the chosen Prophet of this Church in the latter day. He is nothing more than a charlatan. And he has the masses duped."

His heart was pounding, his mind working feverishly, dwelling on that old man wasting away in some jail cell, waiting for this trial come eighteen years after the massacre of white emigrants at Mountain Meadows.

From the group came a question. "We gonna go bust him out of jail, ain't we, Colonel?"

"Yeah. No government sheriff gonna stand up to Jubilee Usher's army!" crowed another voice.

Most of them cheered and rattled sabers with war talk until he quieted them, certain of the path he should now take.

"No. We won't bust John D. Lee out of jail, men," he said. "For Brigham Young's days are counted now, don't you see?"

Usher enjoyed the quizzical looks on their simple faces. "Yes! Don't you see? This false prophet up there in Salt Lake City is about to feed Lee to the federal lions as a sacrificial goat to the government. But little does the false prophet know—Elder Lee will in turn be the Lord's own hand of Young's undoing."

"Down with the false prophet!"

"Death to the pretender!"

Immediately he turned at the voices crying from the ring of eager faces. "Yea, I tell you the words fall from the lips of heaven itself: down with Brigham Young! This I swear before you as the word of God Himself: the coming persecution of John Doyle Lee, and the fiery testing of the Church's faithful, will in the end be the pretender's undoing. Yea—the very unmasking of Brigham Young!"

"We're gonna have us a new Prophet!" one of them called out.

And Usher smiled, those great white teeth of his gleaming in the spring sun. "Yes. The hour approaches when we topple Brigham Young from his throne!"

Chewed up by hooves. The trail beneath Jonah's horse and the ground ahead of them, tracked up by more horses than he could count. Only a few of them wearing iron shoes. The rest of the prints were unshod. Injun ponies. The lot of them being driven west by what were likely white horse thieves.

The white devils the old woman had talked of.

With a break in more than a week of rainy weather, Jonah had pushed them hard these past two days since leaving the old couple behind at their poor cabin in the forest. Two mornings since, they had pulled out, leaving behind a couple of presents with the old woman. Hook decided to leave a sixty-six Henry repeater and one of the gleaming, oiled army .44-caliber revolvers, weapons taken off the small band of Mormon Danites Jubilee Usher had sent on his backtrail to kill Jonah seven years before. Hook and Two Sleep had surprised their stalkers, then carried away the Mormons' rifles and pistols, along with their supply of ammunition and horses, leaving the bodies without a decent burial.

"Giving their kind a decent burial is like spitting in the face of God," Jonah had explained to Jeremiah sourly, telling his son about the night he and the Shoshone crept into the Danites' camp back in sixty-eight. "God intended only for decent folks to get a decent burial, to have words said over 'em. Usher's kind gonna rot in hell for eternity."

When presented the gifts, the old woman had pushed the weapons back into the hands of her guests as her husband snored on his pallet by the small fireplace. She tried to explain that she could not accept so great a gift as the rifle, pistol, and boxes of cartridges, powder, and ball.

In sign Jonah and Two Sleep explained that this was not so great a gift as she might think. They told her that these weapons and the ammunition would likely not ever get used, for they had so many others. It was their hope the old couple could defend themselves much better in the future if they did not have to rely on one old muzzle loader. Better to have the revolver and the repeating carbine if horse thieves ever returned.

He remembered how the tears had pooled in the woman's rheumy eyes, creating glistening tracks down the wrinkled face that reminded him of the dark outermost shell of a walnut. How she pulled his face down to hers to kiss him on the cheek. Jonah brushed that cheek again with his fingers now, hoping he had taught something to his son in the giving. In the kindness.

Knowing that in the days and seasons, perhaps years to come—that there was much more Jeremiah was bound to learn just in being beside his father on this trail. Much to learn about the dark side of man. How a man nursed on his own rage, his hope for taking revenge. His dream of retribution.

The sun felt good, warming the left side of his face. It had seemed to take much of the chill from his bones the last two days. This morning they had left behind the south bank of the Canadian River as it cut in a lazy bend back to the north. He was taking them south by west overland now. His nose pointed for Sill.

And then the trail sign. All these tracks beneath him had been made when the ground was damp, muddy. The hooves sinking into the red clay. He tried to imagine the sound of that many horses moving across this ground days before, so many hooves pulling out of the thick gumbo with a sucking sound like peals of muted thunder. But now the ground had hardened for the most part, making rough, tricky going for their five horses having to pick their steps along the churned, pocked trail.

To Fort Sill, where he hoped to hear some word of the band of Kwahadi the soldiers had chased after Captain Lamar Lockhart's C Company of Texas Rangers had attacked them that cold winter morning last February. Zeke's Comanche wife should be among them. With her would be Hook's two grandchildren, fleeing somewhere across the Staked Plain with Quanah Parker this rainy spring. Like a feeble ember left in a fire pit too long untended, Jonah hoped to learn something of that band and the survivors of the army's attack when he reached Fort Sill.

"Pa!" Jeremiah called out.

Instantly turning at his son's voice . . . Jonah's horse misstepped, lurching sideways on the uneven, churned trail across the hardening mud. He yanked tighter on the reins as his weight shifted. . . .

—felt the smack of the bullet an instant before he heard the gun's report. His eye catching a glimpse of the gunsmoke from the trees up ahead.

More than one spurt of gray smoke hung like gauzy streamers in the shafts of sunlight bursting through the new-leafed tree branches.

An instant spray of red, a fine mist settling over the animal's head and the front of Jonah's mackinaw, his vest, the cleanest shirt he owned.

Two Sleep and Jeremiah hollering behind him as Jonah's horse went down, keeling to the side as he pulled the carbine from the saddle boot and flopped to the ground behind the shuddering bulk of the animal.

Glancing behind him as he made himself small, Jonah watched the Shoshone and his boy reach a dense line of trees, still in the saddle, as bullets slapped the branches and trunks around them, the troublesome snarl and whine of lead crying over his head.

"We'll cover you, Pa!" came Jeremiah's reassuring voice on their backtrail.

25

"Cut the son of a bitch down when he breaks from cover!" roared another voice from down the trail in the direction he had been leading them.

Not knowing why, but accepting what he felt—Jonah sensed this was not to be the place where he was to die. Nor was this the time. A man could call it faith. Some might dare call it fate. But this was not the time nor the place.

His destiny lay elsewhere.

When he would finally stand face-to-face with the man who had taken everything from him more than ten years before.

"Cover me!" Jonah hollered to the stand of trees some thirty yards behind him, where the other two had taken refuge.

"Be ready, boys!" that voice called out from the fringe of trees right in front of Hook. "He's gonna break loose soon now!"

"We'll get 'im!"

Then Jonah was up, and his legs were churning beneath him in a clumsy froth as his boots keeled this way and that on the broken, uneven ground. It seemed the gentle spring breeze had knotted itself up into a roar of sound, a furious rush of wind as the air came alive with the snarling keen of bullets.

First one, then another flicked through the flying flaps of his coat as he hurtled from one side to the other, closing in on the trees, hearing the angry voices of the guns snapping and barking behind him.

Jeremiah emerged from the tree line with the next heartbeat, his own repeater notched against his hip. Chambering and firing, chambering another cartridge and firing as fast as he could. Covering his father's retreat.

Jonah's eyes smarted, watching this young man before him put himself in the line of fire. His son, now become a man.

A burning flared through Hook's thigh. The leg went out from under him, toppling him in a heap.

He was rolling, tumbling, his carbine torn from his grasp, flying into the air. And he saw Jeremiah striding forward confidently. Coming for him. Chambering and firing. The muzzle spitting fire with each shot.

Jeremiah was coming for him.

3

A T TIMES LIKE this Bak Sahm felt like one of the many caged canaries suspended from the five long rafters stretched across the low ceiling to his business house in the bustling, bawdy mining town the white barbarians called Pioche.

Sometimes the stench of too many unwashed miners, the odors of dead tobacco smoke, spilled whiskey, and dried urine, were more than Bak could stomach. Yet he escaped—cradling his crippled left arm, pulling the twisted left leg across the uneven floor, slipping back through the curtain hung from the top of the low doorway, there to flee to the sickly sweet-smelling den where three walls were lined with crude, shaky bunks. Twenty-four of them. Thankfully, pushing through the curtain was like passing into another world.

Where he could lay his body out on the thin, grass-filled mattresses, having to do nothing more than inhale the sweet pink numbness of the opium. *His* opium. Here in the gold mountains of Nevada, Bak Sahm was opium king.

Back in China he had been nothing but a dreamer.

Bak had come to the Gold Mountain to catch and ride his dream, the way it was told a man could capture and subdue his fondest, most fervent wish in the ancient dragon myths. Come to this country across the Sea of Lions* to make his fortune in gold before returning home. He: one of the first of the Celestials to make that long journey from China.

* *Pacific Ocean.*

27

Closing his eyes, Bak Sahm inhaled deeply of the pink dream. Trying hard again to content himself though he would never be going home.

Through the thickening haze of floating smoke he saw the flocks of fishing boats bobbing on the currents that washed against the coastal hills flanking the Pearl River estuary. They always sailed in pairs, a net strung between them before the wind that issued from the river's mouth. Dirty square sails rigged on two or three tall masts to capture that wind as men pulled their catch from a jade-green sea, while the rose-hued barren bluffs of the Ladrones stood sunlit in the background. It was there on the muddy terraces that others chose to grow their vegetables on the land rising abruptly from the water's edge.

To the southeast of the Pearl River delta, Hong Kong lay hidden behind the neighboring highlands of Lantao. Even more so than Canton, Hong Kong had become a land of outside barbarians, with its yellow-washed castle of the British governor, its Union Jack flapping above in a Chinese wind, the same flag that fluttered over the residence of the bishop of Victoria and the Catholic cathedral, as well as all those palatial estates where lived the wealthy merchants who looked down on the great green crescent of the bay, safely ensconced hundreds of feet over the squalid life of those bobbing sampans and junks.

Bak Sahm took another deep breath and held the pink smoke in his lungs, wishing no longer to see this vision of how the outside barbarians had taken such control of his country. Wanting instead to see China as it was when he was a child. Before anyone ever told him of the Gold Mountain.

An immense rock formation called the Dragon's Eye guarded the entrance to the rich, fertile Pearl River delta. Farther inland one passed through the Tiger's Gate, where the crumbling walls and overgrown bastions of long-ago fortresses gazed down on the ever-widening river as the Pearl yearned itself to the Sea of Lions. Just beyond the Tiger's Gate the emerald hills receded, and the yellow, translucent rice fields stretched away to the horizon from the east bank. Many countless tiny streams flowing into the Pearl River scratched out their own courses through the delta, dividing the fertile plain into countless islands. Across the river, shadows proved to be more abrupt as the land rose sharply to stand like a threatening landlord over the muddy rice paddies.

Winging him up past the terraced side of the hills, Bak's dream hovered for a moment over the nine-storied pagoda where the holy men rang their bells and said their prayers.

Prayer—it was too late for Bak Sahm.

His sweet pink dream tipped its wing and let him drift slowly back down the slope to the Pearl River flowing in from the east. Yes, Bak thought, smiling as he removed the long, narrow pipe stem from his lips. It is good to go home.

How he remembered the cold of the winters, when the ducks and geese and the wild coots flew in sky-blackening formations, down from the land to the north until young Bak thought the lakes and streams, the rice paddies and the great river itself, could hold no more. The people rejoiced in those hard, cold days, capturing the water fowl with nets to smoke the rich, fatty, delicate meat: stuffing the carcasses with pungent herbs, coating them with mud, then baking the birds in their own earthen shells.

Bak's mouth watered now, as he thought of spring when the land overflowed, when the men still struggled with the land, working the water deep into the soil with their water buffalo heaving before the plows. The women and children came behind, bending, forever bending as they plunged the young rice beneath the cold spring runoff, embedding each plant in the fresh, overturned, moist breast of the earth.

It was not like that in the Gold Mountain. Here the snows melted come the Season of the Snake, but the white demons did not trap the water, using it on their terrace gardens. Instead the torrent rushed unimpeded down from mountaintops standing over the mining town of Pioche, making its way in tiny creeks that merged with streams tumbling ever downward into the rivers falling onward toward the great hot basin. There it seemed what water was not destined to make it eventually to the far sea was quickly swallowed by the thirsty, barren desert that surrounded this high Nevada land. Imprisoning him.

Bak Sahm yearned for the lush, green vegetation of Kwangtung Province, where he had lived for nineteen cold winters near the Tiger's Gate—each day dreaming on what lay beyond the Sea of Lions. Looking back now, Bak felt as if he had lived another lifetime looking for gold in this land of the barbarians, another nineteen winters he spent watching over his shoulder for the mountain ghosts.

Tonight the delicate pink nudge of the opium made him again wish he had kept on digging, scratching, praying for gold. Instead Bak chose to give up on that life of chance and join the hundreds of others when the white demons put out their call for laborers to lay the track for the great *poot poot sh'eh*, the "puffing buggies" that followed the work gangs day after day, inching east out of the valleys, east into the foothills, and finally eastward all the more—up into the dark, cool, treacherous, and forbidding mountains.

It was a cold season, made colder so, so far from the sea. His beloved sea. And so cold it made his bones ache again in the remembrance.

Rubbing his deformed arm, Bak wished they had cut the hated thing off instead of splinting it between long tent stakes after the accident. For days, then weeks, it had lain strapped to his ribs, that splint cradled in a sling, his broken bones calcifying at a grotesque angle, the left wrist frozen with his palm locked up and out as if forever beckoning to others. There was little rotation from the shoulder, enough that he could dress himself.

Although Bak Sahm never did. There were his girls of joy to help him, a different one every day to dress him, bathe him, rub the perfumed oil on the hated arm and leg. He owned this business, his joss house, trading in goods brought all the way in from China, trading in the sweet flight of forgetfulness that opium could give a man, and in the barbarians' whiskey in the saloon where the miners laughed and danced with his girls of joy. Bak owned a dozen of them now.

A high voice inside his head scolded him: why should he brood on what he missed back home? Hundreds, even thousands, of his own had come to the Gold Mountain to work a few years, every man sending home to his family most of his hard-won pay in gold pieces, always dreaming of the day he himself would return to the Pearl River delta, return as hero to be doted over by wife and descendants, revered by many grandchildren, who would feed and dress the old man, clip his toenails, and brush the ancient one's long queue.

True—Bak Sahm had his prostitutes. What need did he have of troublesome children and grandchildren?

He wanted to argue with that high, screeching voice in his head. To ask it why, if he should be so happy with his pink dreams and his whores, why had he been coming here to visit his own opium den more and more in recent months? Hungering for a woman. Not only for her flesh, the smell and taste. Craving more to capture the woman's spirit.

Bak could take a woman's flesh anytime he wanted. Yet for all the women he had taken, Bak Sahm had never had a woman want his spirit to capture hers.

Here the opium helped dull the pain of that gnawing emptiness. This sweet, pink misery numbed Bak Sahm's greatest need.

•　•　•

"*You! The white* man!" the voice called out from a copse of trees less than forty yards away. "We'll let you and them two redskins with you go—just send out them horses. Them's what we want. We get them, we'll be on our way, an' you on yours."

Jeremiah Hook had to grin at that.

He glanced up from checking the crusted bandanna he had tied around his father's leg, finding Jonah grinning too.

"Well, son—guess they figure you to be as much Injun as Two Sleep here," Jonah said.

"Make up your minds! Just a matter of time 'fore we come in an' finish you three off!" a different voice called out to the trio.

"An' what for you gonna die? Them horses of your'n?"

"That's right—they ain't worth getting kill't for."

"All's we want is your horses—"

"And all you'll get is some lead for your trouble!" Jonah snarled back.

For a while that seemed to quiet the bunch that had ambushed them on the trail.

Jeremiah pulled the bandanna tighter, reknotted it over the leg wound. "Looks like it just went through meat, Pa."

"Doesn't mean it can't hurt like hell," Jonah grumbled, shifting his position and eyeing the far tree line, where shadow and sunlight dappled the edge of the small meadow where he had been caught flat-footed.

They had one horse down. The carcass lay still as a stone among the tall grass. Four horses left them. But it would do no good to lose that saddle and his pa's trail gear neither.

"You got any better idea how many of 'em there are?" Jonah asked of Two Sleep.

Dropping his carbine into the crook of his left arm, the Shoshone held up eight fingers. Then with one index finger he pointed here, there, and there again the places in the trees surrounding the trio where he figured the bushwhackers to be lying back in good cover.

Jonah sighed. Studied Jeremiah a long moment. "You do look like an Injun, son."

Young Hook ran his free right hand down the long, dark hair that spilled past his shoulders. "S'pose I do at that." Winking at Two Sleep, Jeremiah said, "Not so bad a thing to be, now, is it?"

"I don't figure 'em to come in blowing this grove of trees apart with lead," Jonah said after a few minutes of quiet, of listening. "They wanted to do that, they've had enough time already to go and rush us."

"They want the horses worst of all," Jeremiah agreed, squinting quickly up into the sun to gauge the time of day. "They won't chance killing any more of what we got left."

"But on the other hand, I don't figure 'em for waiting us out much past dark," Jonah said.

"That's the time to rush us," Jeremiah replied. "But tell me why these fellas want our horses. Them old folks' horses too. They're going to a lot of trouble and taking a terrible chance with us—just for them horses."

With a wag of his head Jonah answered, "Don't know for certain, but I imagine to their kind horse thieving is a helluva lot easier than real work, son."

"What they doing with the horses they steal? Selling 'em?"

"Imagine so. Don't you, Two Sleep?" Jonah asked.

The Shoshone nodded without taking his eyes off his part of the meadow. "Horse always good for trade."

"Always been, always will be," Jeremiah said.

"Up to Kansas," Jonah said. "Maybe take 'em all the way down to Texas." He looked at his son. "I suppose you're about as much a Texan as you are from Missouri, boy."

"No argument there," Jeremiah said. "Me and Quanah. Both Texans."

"That half-breed war chief of the band you was took in by?"

Jeremiah nodded. "He's got *tai-bo* blood in him. Mother's side. But he wants his white mother's folks just leave his Kwahadi alone."

"Ain't gonna happen," Jonah grumbled.

Pursing his lips sourly, Jeremiah had to agree as he inched away from his father's leg. "Don't make it right, Pa."

"Lot of things *are,* and that don't mean they're right, either," Jonah said. "Man figures that out—why, then he can go on to figure out what he can do to make things a little more right."

"Quanah won't never come in, Pa."

Jonah stared at the lengthening shadows across the meadow for a long time before saying any more. "Then I guess that means your brother's wife and her young'uns will be staying out there, wandering with that half-breed's band."

"Them's her people."

"But them young'uns she's got with her just happen to be as much *our* people as they are Kwahadi!" Jonah snapped acidly.

Jeremiah had to agree. "You're right, Pa. Still, it don't change who Zeke's children are with right now. Out there somewhere in Kwahadi country. Running with Quanah's people. Trying to keep their village—the women and children—out of the army's way. Away from the Tonkawa and Lipan scouts."

"They're all running off, busy hanging on to something they got no business hanging on to, Jeremiah," Jonah said. "Like a dream—Quanah Parker's people hanging on to something that ain't no more'n a dream anymore. Their way of living free, roaming the country like they did—it just can't be that way no more."

Swallowing the bitter taste of his father's words, Jeremiah said, "What about you, Pa? What if someone told you years ago that your holding on to your hope of finding us, any one of us—was nothing more than a silly dream? If any man'd told you that, would you just gone and give up?"

He waited, gazing at his father, whose eyes still scanned the distant checkerboard of shadow and falling sunlight. Then Jeremiah asked again, "Well, tell me—would you gone and give up like you're saying them Kwahadi should do?"

Jonah's head slumped a little when he finally wagged it in great weariness. "No. I don't figure I would have give up, no matter what, Jeremiah."

"And I don't think Quanah Parker is gonna give up neither. Don't think he'll ever come in."

"They're gonna have to kill him first, ain't they, son?"

Jeremiah nodded once when his father turned to look at him. "Yeah. They're gonna have to kill Quanah before he gives up."

He felt his eyes stinging a bit as he studied once again the many wrinkles charted around his father's eyes, the deep grooves carving lines of character from the sides of Jonah's nose down past the corners of his mustache and into his dark beard. "Just like you, Pa. You and him a lot alike, way I see it."

Jonah's brow knitted up a bit, testiness in his eyes. "What you mean, I'm a lot like that blood-loving, snake-bellied half-breed?"

He said it softly: "I don't figure you'll give up neither. Way I see it— they'll have to kill you first too."

The sun eventually came down on that long day in their thick stand of trees. Shadows disappeared, and the first evening star had winked into view back in the eastern sky before Jonah turned to Two Sleep.

"You figure a way out of here come dark?"

At first the Shoshone only shrugged in the growing gloom and looked long and meaningfully at the wounded man's leg. "We get out of bad places before, Hook."

"I s'pose we have got out of worse scrapes, ain't we, Injun?"

Two Sleep grinned with half his face, his black eyes shining in the deepening dusk. "Where we go when we make our run?" He pointed back the way they had come.

"No," Jonah said, shaking his head. "I'm going on west. If we gotta go through them sonsabitches killed my horse—we'll just go through 'em."

His lips pressed into a thin line, Two Sleep grew thoughtful for a few moments. "Cover horses' eyes. Cover nose," he said, bringing a hand up to lay over his own nose. "We go," and the Shoshone signed the plains Indian's hand talk for leave-taking, his right palm touching his chest, then brought out quickly until his arm was straight.

"Jeremiah. You heard this Injun. Get us something we can cut up to blindfold the four horses. Cut some strips for their noses."

"I understand the blindfolds, Pa—but why you want to cover up their noses? How they gonna breathe?"

"They'll breathe just fine. Besides, what they can't smell won't hurt 'em. Keep 'em quieter—just like them blindfolds will. Now, get jumping, son. It'll be slap-dark soon enough."

As Jeremiah returned with an old gum poncho and settled back near the two men to begin the work of cutting wide strips from the shiny rectangle, he asked, "What about that saddle and your gear still out on that horse went down on you?"

Jonah shrugged. "No way to get it. Hard as it is to leave it behind, I'll give up on trying for it."

"We ain't got another saddle—"

"I'll ride just fine, son," Jonah interrupted, his voice a harsh whisper.

"We get ready to go, you ride my horse, Pa."

"I ain't about to . . . ," Hook began snappishly, then seemed to think better of it. "You'll be all right with one of them packhorses?"

"I get this done, I'll make a quick job of squaring away what's on one of the pack animals atween the rest. Yeah—I'll make out fine."

"Till we can get me 'nother saddle."

"Maybe over to Fort Sill, Pa?"

Jonah raised his head to look squarely at his eldest son, his eyes seeming to pool in the growing gloom as more stars poked out overhead. "Yeah. I figure on us finding something at Fort Sill, Jeremiah."

4

GRITTA BRUSHED HER grimy fingers across the faded surface of the painted cloth face on the stuffed doll she cradled in her left arm. And softly hummed some wordless song to the babe. Over and over again. Hour after hour.

Day after day. It had been so many seasons now. Winters gone and times for planting lost uncounted. Harvests passed, each one unanswered. But the babe was still with her, with her again at last. Usher had given her a child. For all the unborn life she had ripped from her womb, terrified to have the demon's seed take root and grow within her.

But now Gritta Hook finally had a child to hold, and rock, and croon to.

Jubilee Usher gave her the child so long ago that she couldn't remember now when it had been. At first she thought it was more of the spoils of his evil when he had returned from one of his long forays, bringing her more plunder from his raids. Like the dresses and faded petticoats, or the soft brushes inlaid with pearl or tortoiseshell, pretty things like the hand mirrors, the bright ribbons, and luminescent mother-of-pearl combs that she used to pull her hair back from her face.

But this was different. This gift he brought meant something to her.

Usher had come into the tent quietly, going immediately to sit on the edge of the bed beside her before laying the doll in her arms. Then he pulled Gritta close, his own great arm laid gently over her shoulder as she pressed the babe to her breast and began to weep the slow, quiet tears, her body racked with sobs. Some of those bitter teardrops fell to darken the flat, featureless, faded paint on the face.

Gritta touched her own face now, then picked up an embossed hand mirror and stared at the image gazing back at her from that oval. Studying the babe's face again, she decided this was in fact her child. It looked enough like her. Fortunate that it looked nothing like Usher, the child's father. And she went back to humming those same half-dozen notes again. Up and down an eerie lullaby scale.

Suddenly she held the child out at arm's length. "What's your name?" she asked.

It hurt deep down in the womb of her not to know the name of her own child. Hadn't she given the babe a name of its own? This bastard child, nameless, conceived in evil . . . no matter, she decided. Long ago Gritta had determined that it made no difference that she and Usher were not married. Not after so many endless winters now.

No matter that her babe was a bastard. The child was not to blame. Not even Usher. He was, after all, only a man. And men—they were just what her mother had taught her: lusting after only one thing. She could not blame Usher for his carnal needs.

So instead, long, long ago, Gritta had begun blaming only herself. Not the man who took his earthly pleasures from her flesh. And certainly she could not blame this helpless, defenseless infant who cried in the middle of the night, this babe for whom she would unbutton the front of her dress, pulling aside the chemise and lifting her breast so that the child could nurse. As it suckled her milk, Gritta rocked slowly, humming her lullaby softly to calm the babe, answering its hunger before its cries awakened Usher.

If he was disturbed, Jubilee would flare with anger: roaring and flinging his arms about. Only once had she been so thoughtless that she awakened him when the babe cried out in the night to suckle. Usher had ranted and screamed loud enough to shake the walls of their tent that summer long ago. Ultimately he had ripped the child from her arms, right from the very breast where it lay suckling her milk—and hurled the infant across the tent, where it went crashing into her washbasin, there beside her mirrors and brushes and the beautiful pearl combs.

Shrieking in utter horror, she had flung herself on him, pounding her fists against his chest until drained of the last vestige of her strength, then lay quietly on her back as he pressed his terrible weapon into her once more, panting over her, reminding her that he enjoyed her most when she grew angry at him. When there was some fire in her.

Only when he had finished with her and rolled off to fall back to sleep did Gritta push herself away from the child's father, slipping quietly—oh, so slowly from the side of the bed so as not to move the stuffed tick mattress. And went to comfort the child.

There in the corner of the tent she had sat the rest of the night, her legs tucked to the side, trying not to think on what evil a man's weapon was when it was used inside a woman's body. Invading her the way an enemy army plunged into territory it was about the business of conquering. And once more Gritta had pulled her sleeping gown aside to quiet the frightened, hungry infant, letting it suckle at her full, engorged breast for the rest of the night. As much as it wanted to drink of her warmth, while she promised the babe that she would never allow its father to abuse it again.

Promising herself that she would never again give Usher a reason to enjoy plunging his weapon into her. Gritta vowed never again to grow angry with anything he did or said to her. She could not allow him that pleasure, ever again. She would just lie there, without anger or rage, no tears. For the child's sake.

From now on, she realized as she cooed to the infant, she had to take care of two.

And, Gritta decided, protecting her babe was so much more important than protecting herself. A life so much more important than her own.

"What are you doing, Pa?"

Jonah twisted in the saddle to look back at his son. Behind Jeremiah, Two Sleep reined up and brought his horse around. A look on the Shoshone's face told Hook the warrior understood already.

"Those sons of bitches got a horse from me."

"I know." Jeremiah shrugged, then gestured up the trail where they had been headed in the dark. "And we was going to Fort Sill."

"It's been eating on me," Jonah admitted, the taste of it sour in his throat. "I want a horse back."

"We'll buy another," Jeremiah replied, bareback on one of the packhorses. "Saddle too. Just like you said back—"

Jonah wagged his head. "I want more'n just a horse for the one we lost."

He watched that look of confusion mingled with fear come across

Jeremiah's face. Beside the boy sat the Indian: Two Sleep kept his eyes moving and his head turning as they delayed there in the starlit darkness of Indian Territory. The Shoshone glanced again at Jonah and nodded once. The warrior knew. Things set fine by the Indian.

"We don't have to do this, Pa."

"Yes, we do," he answered softly. "You don't understand yet, Jeremiah."

The younger Hook said, "But—you're saying that maybe I will understand someday."

Jonah shifted in the saddle. "No. That's where you're wrong, Jeremiah. I pray you never will have to understand."

Hook put heels to the horse, reining hard around to the north this time, hearing the two move out behind him. Inching into the darkness, back toward the bushwhackers, road agents, horse thieves, and scum what had shot his horse out from under him and put a bullet clean through the meat of his leg.

Most men would've called themselves lucky with getting out with their lives and the rest of the plunder. But not Jonah. Not by a long chalk. He damned well wasn't satisfied with the hand he had been dealt back on the trail. If Jonah Hook understood anything about himself, it was that he didn't take lightly no more to getting anything stole from him.

Enough already. Damn well enough stole from him already.

This was country he knew better than the Shoshone grown up in the shadow of the Rocky Mountains, out on the central plains. Jonah had been born in the Shenandoah Valley of Virginia. Later planted his roots in the dark loam of southwestern Missouri. Timbered country.

There wasn't enough starshine to pick out much of the land ahead of him, but Jonah felt his way through it well enough. From time to time he glanced at the angle of the tail on the Big Dipper and began working his way around from the north back to the east. He had nothing better to go on but his hunch that the horse thieves would work their way west and north once they discovered the trio gone.

So Jonah picked his way toward the Canadian River, planning to run head-on into the bastards. A stand-up, bold-faced ride-through.

Just like the fight Captain Lamar Lockhart led the men of his C Company, Frontier Battalion, into—that bloody fight over in the White River country of the Texas Panhandle. Pushing through the gate to confront the Kwahadi bold as brass, with not so much as a flinch or second thought to it. Iron-mounted men, some of the very best there was to ride with.

Then Jonah looked at Two Sleep. His brother of the blanket. The goddamned Shoshone who had taken this quest as if it were his own. There likely couldn't be a finer redskin in all the west. Not likely a finer man than that ugly, flat-faced Shoshone.

These horse thieves had taken something of Jonah's—and he aimed to throw down a new hand on them. So by the time the moon was rising, Hook had figured out how to play what cards he had been dealt.

Through the spidery blackness of the leafy trees bordering the river gone silver in the quarter moon's light, he made out the crossing and halted. Turned them aside and moved off downstream until he was ready to give the Shoshone his marching orders.

"Two Sleep," he whispered gruffly as he brought his horse around and back alongside the warrior, who sat inches from Hook. Their knees brushed. "Yonder." And he pointed. Two Sleep looked into the black distance, nodded once. "If I figured right, we come up from behind 'em out of the west. On their backsides. Now it's up to you to find out for sure. Me and the boy'll wait here."

Hook watched the Indian rein aside and disappear into the gloom of the moon's pale light like a limb sucked down into a boggy pool of quicksand. A light fog lay like torn shreds of petticoat along the ground, given enough reflection now with the silver orb's rising toward midsky. The mist swirled softly, rose, then settled and lay still once more through the minutes that ticked away into growing nervousness.

"You think something happened to him?" Jeremiah asked after a long, long time.

Wagging his head, Jonah said, "No. We ain't heard no shots."

"There's more'n one way to kill a man, Pa."

"Don't I know, son. No, the Injun's good at what he does best. Better'n those bushwhackers are in making a creep on someone."

"They nearly finished you off, Pa. Laid a pretty good sneak on us."

"That was different!" he snapped. Then felt sorry for it. Softer, he said, "Don't fret now, boy. Two Sleep and me go back a long ways. Only reason I sent him 'stead of me going myself was this is one thing that Injun's better'n me."

"We gonna know how many?"

"You tell me, Jeremiah—when you went raiding enemy camps with that half-breed's war parties while you lived with them Comanche—did Quanah's scouts know how strong a enemy it was you was facing?"

Jeremiah nodded, some of his long hair brushing the side of his hairless cheek.

"Maybe it's time you started acting more like a Injun again. Not so bad a thing—some of the way Injuns fight. The way they make ready to fight." Jonah stared off into the night, toward the trees where he willed the Shoshone to appear. "Try to feel more of what them Comanche taught you—if you was with them right now, getting ready to make a raid on some Tonks or Lipans."

"You . . . you want me to try being more like, like some Injun?" Jeremiah asked. "After you come to take me and Zeke back?"

Hook could read the startled disbelief pinching his son's face. "Way I figure it, Jeremiah—you spent half your life with me and your mama. The last half of your years with them Comanche. If what me and your mama learned you ain't what it takes to survive sometimes . . . then so be it. You damn well better go and use what you learned from them Comanch'."

The boy shook his head. "Sometimes I just can't figure you—"

"Ain't your place to, Jeremiah," Jonah interrupted in a hushed whisper that nonetheless carried a burnished edge to it. "The way I see it lay, son—them Comanch' can't be all bad."

"Damn—if you don't beat all, Pa. You always said Injuns was savages. 'Cept for Two Sleep, I ain't ever seen you take to a Injun. So just how you figure the Kwahadi ain't all bad?"

When he looked over at the youth this time, Jonah noticed that his son wore a soft smile. "They rescued you from them traders gonna haul you down to Mexico, where I'd likely never'd found you."

"The Kwahadi never hurt us once, Pa."

"You told me so, Jeremiah," he replied finally. Then drew himself up and sighed as Two Sleep appeared right before them at the edge of the dark timber in the moonlight. "Takes a man like me a while to get used to feel beholding to heathen Injuns. But I am, son. I'm right thankful. Not just Two Sleep neither. But to that Quanah Parker too. Just took me a while to get it setting right in my craw, 's all."

He put up his hand to shush any further talk from Jeremiah and waited for the Shoshone's quiet approach. They mulled over things in hushed tones, decided on the approach to their ambush, then pushed off again beneath the climbing moon.

It hung limply at midheaven by the time Two Sleep halted them beneath some bluffs made shimmery with the mercuric light. The Shoshone got down, walked off a ways, and stood with one ear against the side of the rocky wall.

"Not far," he finally said.

"Listen, Jeremiah," Jonah said, putting a finger to his lips.

The youth finally nodded. Hook hoped he had truly heard the faint noise of men crossing the ground above them along the bluff where the main trail evidently led. The plod of many hooves, the squeak of leather. The snort and cough or a noisy sneeze of men on horseback on the move. Men who had no fear they were in enemy territory. Men moving without worry of ambush.

In the dark, Jonah decided, this could work. It had to. He glanced again at the moon. Not all that much light, what with the timber clotting the grassland like drying blood, tall growths of it too. In the dark the three of them could get the horse thieves divided, broken up, whittled down quickly in the sudden confusion and fear.

No man in his right mind likes fighting in the dark. But, Lord knows, Jonah Hook had been doing enough of it.

After signaling Two Sleep to lead out to the spot where they would make their play, Jonah waited for Jeremiah to follow the Shoshone. Then he brought up the rear. And looked over his shoulder one last time. Back to the west.

This was the last time, he promised himself, the last time he would be putting the west on his backtrail. At least until he had Gritta and could turn back for home to what little they had left in Missouri. That—or they buried him out here.

Jonah reined his horse about and prepared to kill them what had taken from him.

"What's it matter, Pa?" Jeremiah asked in a hush, grabbing hold of his father's arm. Still troubled with it. "We got out with our hides. Can't you forget the horse?"

"It ain't the horse, boy!" he snapped a little too loudly. He flicked a look at the Shoshone, who was keeping his eye on the backtrail, moving those dark eyes along the bluff above them where the riders would soon appear.

"But there's more of them than us," Jeremiah said.

Jonah whirled on him, his chest heaving in frustration. "That's the goddamned Comanche in you!"

"Comanche?"

"Yeah! Damned redskins don't fight unless'n they got the odds in their favor!"

Jeremiah swallowed hard, as if choking down his father's rebuke. "Red or white—it don't make any real sense. Just leave it be, Pa. Leave it be and let's get on with what we set off to do."

Hook's eyes narrowed at the dark-skinned youth who sat hatless under the pale light of the moon hung at midheaven, the color of mercury against an indigo sky. "And what'd we set off west to do, Jeremiah?"

"Only one thing: get my ma."

It hit him like the youngster had doubled up his fist and hurled the blow into his belly. Jonah struggled down the acid sting of gall in his mouth, then put to words what he wanted his son most to hear.

"What I'm fixing to do *is* about your ma. And about you. You, and Zeke and Hattie too. I'm gonna make this the last time I wanna explain it to you, son. What I'm set on doing has got to do with the first time anything important was took from me. When Usher took my family. In all that time since I found you gone—I've had me lots to think on. So I went and decided that from now on no one . . . no one at all is ever going to take anything more from me."

"Even . . . even if it means you getting killed before we find Ma?"

His cheeks flushed with anger that Jeremiah could not see it. "What makes you so damn sure I'm—"

"That's what's gonna happen, Pa! You go right on this way: keep butting your head up against the side of the barn like that mean-tempered ol' goat we used to have—you're gonna get yourself killed. Can't you see?"

"No, I can't see, Jeremiah," he said, refusing to listen to anything more. "Only thing I can see is men what took something from me, and I aim in turn to get something back from 'em." He shifted in the saddle, straightening, his shoulders squaring and his body assuming a posture that seemed to say the whole matter was settled for him. "If I get killed here and now—then the good Lord willed that my hunt for your mama should end here."

"So you go and get yourself killed because of your bullheadedness, what comes of me, Pa?"

He rocked forward on the saddle horn, leaning a foot closer to Jeremiah. "Ask yourself that same question, son. What you gonna do I get killed before I get your ma back?"

The young man licked his lips, glanced at the top of the bluff. Two Sleep was signaling them, reining his horse about and moving toward the far stand of trees that was really nothing more than a clot of black shadows in the dim light. "I suppose I'd keep on till I found her."

"Damn right you would, Jeremiah Hook. Now you remember that. Remember that your ma was took from you too. She was *took* from you— and you was *took* from her. And one day soon you're bound to have you the chance to *take* back from them that tore the two of you apart."

Jonah nudged his horse into motion. "You ride with me, son—you goddamned well better never forget that."

5

Hark the voice of one that crieth
In the desert far and near,
Bidding all men to repentance
Since the kingdom now is here.

Oh, that warning cry obey!
Now prepare for God a way;
Let the valleys rise to meet Him
And the hills bow down to greet Him.

T HE STIRRING WORDS of the ageless psalm he had learned at his mother's knee came back to Jeremiah as clear as if he had just heard her singing it to her children gathered near the stone fireplace, rocking in her chair—her babes, the fruit of her loins, seated before her on the hearth. Plain as the cold breeze was in his face this night, Jeremiah heard his mother's soft, crystalline voice in his ear, singing the song first in its original German.

A few scraps, a word here and a word there, were all he could recall of the language of his mother and father's people. Such few words all tumbled up with the Comanche tongue and their songs of celebration and defiance, melodies of victory and courting—everything such a blur beneath this night sky as it churned together inside his heart with all those hymns Gritta had taught her children. Then he tried to remember her face as clearly as he remembered those words.

43

Waiting in the darkness beneath the trees. Hearing the riders coming in the breathless stillness marred only by an occasional gust of fierce autumn wind. Two pistols sweated in his palms. Despite the caliber of the wind, it remained a hot and muggy night for the season. Jeremiah feared dropping the revolvers and wiped the grips on his canvas britches. They still felt new and stiff for as long as he had worn them, back to leaving Texas.

Maybe they still felt strange because it had been so damned long since he had worn white man's clothes. Half his life already.

For an instant he cursed himself for remembering more of the Kwahadi tongue than he could recall of his parents' German. Then realized what he cursed himself for was his fear. Something he hadn't felt when riding out to ambush Tonkawa, or Lipan or the Mexicans. These were *tai-bos,* white men he was preparing to kill.

In all that frantic skirmishing back near the foot of the White River gate when Antelope . . . when *Zeke* was killed at the bottom of a dry wash, Jeremiah could not remember, could not be sure if he had killed any of the Tejannos. Those Texas Rangers who rode in with his father that cold winter day. He didn't think he had killed any of them . . . but in all the dust and confusion and shooting and shouting, no man could be absolutely sure. Maybe he had.

Then Jeremiah figured better for it. He decided a man would know, without uncertainty, when he killed another man. There could be no confusion. Such a thing must surely leave its mark on his soul.

He looked at his father a moment. Jonah had his two pistols drawn, ready. A dull light gleamed from them, captured beneath the starshine. All the men his pa had killed through all these years—surely, each death had left its mark, carved its notch—every last one of them etched like acid on glass, cut into his father's soul. Like scars.

Maybe more like weeping wounds.

The first voices drifted toward them, nothing really more than indistinct sounds floating above the plodding of hooves and the shift of saddle leather atop weary animals.

"Remember, Jeremiah," Jonah whispered. "You take the third and fourth."

Now the approach was more than sound. Shadows, taking shape like a fluid substance congealing to rise from the gloom ahead of them. A glimmer here and there of some chunk of metal—a buckle, a gun's barrel. Perhaps what he saw was the sheen of the moon's light reflected in some man's eyes.

Maybe a man he would be killing, and never really seeing face-to-face. These were white men he was killing. Shooting them, ambushing them the way a white man would. This was not the Kwahadi way of making war. More honor for a warrior to be close enough to see his enemy's face.

As much as his father had talked about it, as much as he had brooded on it, Jeremiah could not figure out what this ambush had to do with a matter of honor. He heard Jonah quietly drag back the double-notched click of the two hammers, working the tumblers and sears, turning the loaded cylinders in the dark.

Nonetheless, what they were about to start had something to do with what Jonah considered defending his honor, more so to do with redeeming that honor.

That was something Jeremiah could understand—for honor was everything to a Kwahadi warrior.

Two Sleep's weapons roared, startling Jeremiah. He shoved the pistols forward over the horse's head as it shied and sidestepped, spooked at the sudden bark of the guns. He could only aim at the dark, forming shadows. His were the third and the fourth.

Tiny white-and-orange lights exploded from the revolvers' muzzles, spurts of brilliant flame, as men hollered, cried out, cursed, and grunted in pain. His father's guns hammered steadily on the far right of him, knocking the third pair of riders from their saddles.

Cries of the wounded, the ferocious whine of lead, the first booms of carbines and scatterguns as the bushwhackers began to return fire. Confusion among them as the first half dozen were knocked out of their stirrups or keeled from side to side clutching wounds, their wild-eyed horses whirling in tight circles, some of the animals heeling back in panic to fling riders off into the black terror of the night.

A moment more and Jeremiah noticed that Two Sleep was gone from his left, the Shoshone's saddle empty. Young Hook feared the worst, his eyes straining now to find his father as more shadows took shape along the tree line, bursting forth from the copse of blackjack oak where the trail emerged into the open at the top of the river bluff. A riderless horse burst past Jeremiah, its wide eyes white and moonstruck as it careened blindly off the sharp edge of the bluff, peeling out of sight into sheer nothingness. Jeremiah never heard the animal land, there was so much gunfire.

Orders shouted at the edge of that clearing: nothing more than pained confusion by those horsemen racing up from the rear when the gunfire started.

How many were there? It seemed like the shadows kept coming and his father kept shooting. And more kept coming—white-and-orange fires and grunts and cries. Jeremiah's fears rattled him—with Two Sleep wounded, maybe dead already. Yet this was what the Shoshone was willing to do: die for Jonah's honor.

It was more than any man had the right to ask of another, Jeremiah decided as he aimed and fired, fired again. The pistol in his left hand clicked empty—without its familiar buck. With the next shot of the right, he found it too was empty. Jamming them into his belt, Jeremiah fought loose the carbine beneath his leg, dragging it free of the saddle boot.

No man had the right to ask another to lay down his life for nothing less than his own honor. Only family. Only blood could demand such devotion.

As the firing withered, dying off in spurts, he found his father on foot, the repeater braced against Jonah's hip in both hands. There was a final explosion of three or more shots from the far line of trees, their bright-yellow flames declaring the gunman's position. Jonah turned on his heel, leveling the carbine at the middistance, and returned four rounds before he levered his last cartridge into the breech.

As Jeremiah reached his father, Jonah quickly pulled a handful of brass from his coat pocket and reloaded the Winchester with a half-dozen cartridges. Allowing himself no more time than those six would take, to be ready if any more of the faceless shadows decided to stay and fight.

"Two . . . Two Sleep," Jeremiah choked, his mouth gone dry, finding the words hard to spit out.

"He was hit?"

He heaved—sucking greedily instead of breathing, finding himself gulping short, labored gusts of air instead of long, hungry draughts. It had never been like this before. Jeremiah was most afraid that it would be like this again, and again. And again until they found his mother.

"Don't know, Pa."

"What you mean?"

"Saw him go down—"

"Where?"

"Not him. Saw his horse. His saddle empty—"

With his empty hand Jonah grabbed his son by the front of his coat. "Where!"

"He was beside me," Jeremiah answered lamely, pointing in the general direction.

"Stay here," Jonah snapped. "Get down on your knees and keep your eyes moving. You'll see better in the darkness if you get down lower, near the ground. Easier to see something moving against the ground than it is to see it moving against them trees off yonder."

"Yes, Pa."

"Reload, Jeremiah," he warned. "This may not be over yet."

His father was swallowed whole by the darkness, leaving the young man to collapse to his knees, stuff hands into his pockets and begin shoving cartridges into the carbine. Then he dragged out the one single-action army revolver he carried in a worn holster and knocked empty brass from its cylinder, then quickly, nervously jammed in fresh loads. Next he pulled the second revolver from his belt to reload it, then sat there clutching them both, crouched over the carbine—his eyes screwging near the ground. Listening, straining into the night.

It grew so breathlessly quiet that Jeremiah became sure he could hear his heart hammering in his ears like one of those old Kwahadi shamans pounding on their ancient drums. How he yearned to hear his father somewhere off to his left. To be reassured, to know for certain that he was not alone.

His eyes widened. Jeremiah was no longer alone.

Not far from where he sat, he saw the shadow slowly rise, like fog from the dark ground. It moved slowly, half crouched, carefully, without a sound. It began to inch toward one of the bushwhackers' horses. The man had to be wounded, the way the shadow was favoring, dragging a leg as he crabbed about at a crouch to catch up the skittish animal, then tried to stuff his left foot in the stirrup.

Jeremiah swallowed, deciding he should shoot.

Then figured the man had been wounded in that left leg, as he struggled ineffectively to haul himself into the saddle.

Jeremiah rose to one knee, holding his left arm out, the revolver following the rise and fall of the bushwhacker's shadow.

For a moment it seemed the man had given up—then he clumsily scooted beneath the horse's neck, still gripping the reins, and came up on the off side of the animal to stuff his right boot into the stirrup.

"Shoot 'im, Jeremiah!"

On impulse the pistol bucked in Jeremiah's hand. He pulled the trigger a second time, the blasts rolling back at him like shards of thunder rocking the far line of trees, then all sound was gone again, sucked right on out of the night by the great depth that lay yawning beyond the edge of the red-earth bluff behind him.

47

He watched the bushwhacker's horse bolt off, without a rider. Its clattering hooves faded in the dark.

"Damn," Jonah muttered in the distance. "C'mon, you damned Injun. We just lost another of them bastards' horses."

"Pa? Pa—that you?"

"We're coming. Hush up and keep your eyes skivvied on them far trees over there."

"You found Two Sleep?"

"He didn't go nowhere, Jeremiah," Jonah growled as the pair came up.

Two Sleep gripped his right arm with his other hand. Even in the starlight Jeremiah could see the dark ooze seeping between the Shoshone's fingers.

"I thought you was—"

"He did his job, son. Just what I asked him to."

The Indian flashed a quick grin at Jeremiah. "Here. Cut piece of my shirt."

"You heard him, Jeremiah. Bandage the man up so we can get moving. I'll go fetch up the animals—"

"Moving?" he asked, stuffing the revolvers away before yanking his knife from its belt scabbard.

"We ain't staying here for long," Jonah said, his eyes roving constantly. "You get the Injun's bleeding tightened down. I'll gather up what horses and plunder they left behind."

"How many we . . . we kill?"

With a shrug Jonah replied, "Not near enough, son. Likely the rest'll come to a stop back down the trail somewhere, regroup and figure out they was bested. Nothing makes a man smart like being bested at his own bushwhacking."

"They come after us, Jeremiah," Two Sleep added. "Jonah, get the horses, the guns—you wrap my arm—we go soon."

And the sooner they did light out would sit just fine with Jeremiah.

"The captain wouldn't know nothing about the fella you was asking after, ol'-timer."

Shadrach Sweete came to a slow halt and turned, his eyes squinting before they landed on the soldier leaning a shoulder against a porch post, back in the cool shadows. Here at Fort Bridger in southwestern Wyoming Territory, the sun rose high and hot this time of year.

Some of the strapping bulk to the old fur trapper had melted away in the last five or six years, but he still carried the heavy bone, and stood ramrod straight, an easy half foot again over six full feet, with nary a bit of slouch to the old shoulders wide as a hickory ax handle where the snowy hair spilled long over the faded oxblood of a calico shirt.

"Ol'-timer, is it? You ain't so young a chicken your own self, walk-a-heap," Shad said with a grin as he came to a stop near the soldier who had been whittling without purpose on a cottonwood sprig.

"Thought that was you," the man replied, folding the jackknife and stuffing it away in his fatigues.

"We know each other?" Shad presented his huge hand.

"Just remember you from Connors's Expedition." They shook.

Sweete's head bobbed a minute as his eyes worked up and down the soldier. "Back to sixty-five. Didn't do a whole hell of a lot of good for all the walking, did we?"

"Didn't do worth a red piss!" the soldier roared, chuckling. "Not the way ol' Red Cloud and his bunch came and jumped down on the Montana Road not long after."

With a wag of his head Sweete asked, "So you figure your post commander wouldn't know anything of the fella I'm looking for?"

"Captain ain't been here long enough. Got to Bridger back to late seventy-three. Hates the place. He bellyaches he's been posted here to die an unnatural death."

"You likely can't disagree with him, can you?"

Shaking his head, the soldier said, "No. This ain't the sweetest of posts."

Shad sighed and stared off across the sunbaked parade a moment. "Suppose I'll push on come morning, can't find out nothing what I need to know."

"You just ain't asked the right folks."

He turned back to study the soldier, wanting to savor that faint twinge of hope. "Ain't that always the case?"

"Now, if you'd gone and come to me about that fella named Hook—I might've had some news to tell you."

"Might have, eh?"

The man nodded, brushing a few cottonwood shavings from the front of his shirt. "To my way of thinking, a fella like that, riding in here all on his own, why—he'd just naturally stand out."

"I'd say your thinking was plumb center."

The soldier nodded. "We see solitary folk come through here from time to time."

"Not like this fella."

"But it's been a damn long time, from what I heard you ask the captain."

"Would've been seven years ago now." Shad stepped right up to the soldier, gazing down at the man when he asked. "You know any man I can talk to was on duty right here at Bridger late the summer of sixty-eight?"

"What we mostly see is trains coming through, you understand," the soldier replied, his eyes not climbing to look at Sweete's face just yet. "If it ain't freight outfits bound north to Idaho Territory, or others on west into Utah, then it's emigrants moving on to California. Still a few going on to Oregon too. Mostly, lots of Mormons. This is the way they all come out of the east. Ain't more'n a hop from here to Salt Lake City."

"That's right where Hook was aiming to go." Then Sweete turned to look off across the parade once again. "I'm mighty dry, soldier. You wouldn't know where a man could buy him a drink, would you?"

The soldier wiped a fingertip across his lips. "Fort Sutler. I'm mighty dry, too—come to think of it. I'll take you there if you'll buy this man a drink."

"For what you know about Hook, I'll buy you more'n just one drink."

The soldier shaded his eyes as he stepped out into the sun and looked up at the taller man. "Why you figure I know something about this fella Hook?"

"Because I never used the man's name when I rode in and was talking to the captain 'while ago." Shad saw the soldier's face go sheepish. He reached out with a big paw, the veins across its back bulging like thin strands of knotted rope, and watched the soldier start to duck. Instead Sweete grabbed hold of the man's shoulder, then patted it. "Don't blame you none for wanting to game me out of a drink for what you do know."

The soldier finally grinned again. "So you'll still buy me a whiskey?"

"Always been good at my word. Let's go find that sutler and see us the taste of his saddle varnish."

Sixty-four winters Shadrach Sweete had walked the face of the earth, and all but the first fifteen of them had been trod out here in the Rocky Mountain west. He had first crossed the wide Missouri with General Ashley in twenty-five when the general led a gallant hundred overland for the very first time to the Shining Mountains, there to trap beaver. Always before, the Americans had cordelled themselves up the river. That mighty Missouri, that is. But Ashley and Henry, the general's partner who ran the galena mines, they fixed on heading overland instead. Not the sort to be stopped by the capricious nature of the Arikarees, a fickle and treacherous tribe who ruled the passage of the upper river, a thievish lot who most often prevented fur-company keelboats from pushing farther north to the land of rival tribes.

Not that Shad could blame the Rees, what with relations between all the warrior clans the way they were on the northern plains.

But the Ashley-Henry overland trek was nothing less than a bold, dramatic act of genius in a time when the first white men were shoving open the door to the far West. Back to twenty-five.

There was more than one man in that courageous band of one hundred enterprising young men who would carve their names clear across the width and breadth of the West. In fact, one of them other young'uns along with Ashley that momentous watershed year came to be Shad's best friend. His name was Bridger.

But by now Ol' Gabe, just like li'l Kit, why—they had both rode on over the Great Divide for the very last time. And again it made Shad Sweete figure he never would know why one by one all his old friends had gone on to the high lonesome before him—why he was left to last winter after winter without them.

There'd never been a friend like Bridger. That pair had fought Injuns together, trapped beaver from the same sets, even married Injun and went to the blanket together. Why, Sweete and Bridger even fought the dag-blamed Mormons together back when ol' Brigham Young decided the Rocky Mountains was simply too small for both him and Jim Bridger to live out here. So Shad and some other ol' hivernants come to help Ol' Gabe stand off a bunch of Brigham's Destroying Angels. Sent the whole bunch of them gunmen called Danites scurrying back to Salt Lake City after a few days of fighting, with their tails tucked between their legs.

It was memories like those that Shad had to keep bringing to mind, he always told himself. Keep thinking on them old glory days—or he'd be apt to forget 'em. Go and forget the days and the faces, the good times and the bad. It wasn't so bad, this pain of remembering.

Like thinking back on his boy. Knowing High-Backed Bull had died as he wanted to die. As proud as any warrior going down protecting his people, the Cheyenne.

Shad was here because of his son. Come here looking again for a clue just as he had years ago—again asking for any word to where he could find another friend. Hook. A friend he had vowed to help before Hook lost his whole family.

After all this time Sweete figured his only real worth was the result of the friends he had, the friends he helped.

Over the years Shad had collected the letters come to Fort Laramie, some of them letters posted from Riley Fordham, out of St. Louis. Later Fordham's letters were marked out to Fort Leavenworth in Kansas. Then there were those other letters from the seminary in St. Louis. Sweete didn't read, so he never suffered any inclination, not the slightest curiosity, to open the letters with their delicate, feminine handwriting scrolled across them, some even sealed with hot wax and daubed with a fancy tusche-mark. By now, though, that red or blue or green wax had grown brittle in the high, dry air of the plains. Most of it flaked off where it lay at the bottom of the pouch where Sweete kept those letters, stuffed down in his saddlebag. Safe, for a day when Jonah Hook could open them, read them—and know of family.

Shad remembered the tight edge of fear on Hattie's face that morning Jonah put his only daughter with Riley Fordham on that east-bound train . . . remembered that pretty oval face poking out the window as the engineer dropped the sand and the big iron wheels spun, spun with a whine again until they took a purchase on the iron rails, steam puffing in clouds above that magnificent, frightening contrivance called a locomotive that would carry Jonah's girl back to safety after Hook, Sweete, and Fordham rescued her from Boothog and his band of Mormons.

It was times like that when Shad brooded on his own daughter, struggling to conjure up Pipe Woman's face. Thinking on the softness of her mother's face too. How he missed Shell Woman. Now, with every day, more than ever.

Come this winter, the toughest season for the old trapper and army scout. Shell Woman was gone now. Buried down in the rocks above the river near their boy. All Shad had left of family now was Pipe Woman, his daughter living with the wild tribes roaming the land of the Rosebud and the Tongue, the hunting grounds of the Little Bighorn and the Powder.

So if any man understood just how Jonah Hook had to feel about his family, it would be Shadrach Sweete. Especially now. After he had lost so damned much himself. When he felt so damned alone.

If it was the last thing that he did, the old man vowed—he would find Jonah Hook.

Find Jonah Hook and finally hand all those letters over to his old friend.

Find his old friend . . . so that at long last Shad Sweete could be there come that day when Jonah Hook rode in for his final reckoning with a bloody butcher named Jubilee Usher.

6

"WHO YOU FIGURE they are?" Jonah asked of the Shoshone. The three of them sat atop their horses, back among a cover of trees near the brow of the rise where they first spotted the distant horsemen.

Slipping down from the bare back of his horse, Two Sleep moved forward cautiously, leaving the backdrop of the trees, careful lest he would cast his figure against the skyline for the men approaching across the wide, grassy swale below. He knelt and studied the heat-wavering distance beneath the early-afternoon sun hung high over the foothills of the Arbuckle Mountains, a collection of low ridges and colorful bluffs in south-central Indian Territory. Then the Shoshone turned his head to speak to the father and son.

"Soldiers, for sure," he declared, then pantomimed with his hands: "Ride in column."

"You want the field glasses, Pa?"

Jonah shook his head. He could begin to make them out more distinctly now. When he had first spotted the horsemen, the riders had been nothing more than a distant, linear mass heaving beneath a stirring of dust that seemed to hover momentarily over the column's line of march before it danced, ultimately to disperse on the errant breeze.

"How many?" Jonah asked; then before the warrior could answer, he added, "It don't matter, Two Sleep. We know they're soldiers. No bushwhackers march column like that."

Hook leaned back from his saddle horn where he had hunched forward to take the weight off a tailbone sore from all its scrubbing on the cantle. In addition, it helped to ease the knot of healing flesh that ran the width of his upper thigh. Jonah was sore and stiff this past week, so much so that he still hobbled about camp every evening when the trio finally dismounted to build a fire and kick out their bedrolls at the end of the day's ride.

"Let's go see what these soldiers know," Hook said.

Where the trail that angled down the ridge entered a broad meadow, Jonah halted them, reining around to help Two Sleep wrangle the eleven saddled horses they had claimed as spoil from the bushwhackers. About the time the animals settled down to cropping at the tall grass, the soldiers entered the meadow.

From the looks of the officer who threw up an arm and signaled his men and a solitary civilian scout to halt, Jonah figured him to be a second lieutenant. On closer inspection the collar of the blue tunic confirmed the man's rank as Jonah angled over and came to a halt.

"Afternoon, Lieutenant."

"Good afternoon, sir." The soldier turned to his scout and the detail's sergeant who rode beside the civilian guide. "Go see what we have here, Carter."

The civilian nodded, eyeing Jonah suspiciously, as the sergeant snapped a salute and set out for the dozen riderless horses.

"You fellas have had a lot of saddles emptied," the lieutenant commented. "Were they friends of yours?"

"Ain't the way it looks," Jonah said, twisting in the saddle to keep an eye on the two who were moving among the dozen grazing horses.

"Not the way what looks?"

He turned back around and spoke to the officer. "Suppose it might seem like there was a bunch of us before—them empty saddles and all. But it's never been more'n just the three of us."

"These horses didn't belong to more of your group?"

"Nope."

Then the lieutenant's face went hard. His eyes moved beyond Jonah, raking the far line of leafy oaks and pecans at the edge of the meadow. "You're trying to tell me there are no more of your group waiting back in the trees?"

Jonah squinted at the lieutenant, quickly appraising the twenty-man detail atop their dusty, restless horses. "There ain't no more of us. S'pose you tell me what's this all about—these questions of yours?"

He turned his head slightly, without his hard eyes releasing Hook. "Corporal—parade dress the detail."

Behind the lieutenant the twenty horse soldiers followed the bark of the corporal's commands, half of their column-of-twos flowing right of the detail's officer, the other half moving to the left until they formed a wide company front, stirrup to stirrup.

For an instant Jonah allowed himself to remember how good it felt to ride with men of honor. So many years now that he had been searching for Gritta, it seemed like that was all he had done in his life. But before him swam the faces of Bible-ranting Deacon Johns and broad-jawed Niles Coffee, shovel-faced June Callicott and the jovial Clyde Yoakam, each one passing before Jonah in but an instant as Hook recalled Captain Lamar Lockhart's final, terse inspection of Company C, Frontier Battalion, Texas Rangers, before he led them stone-faced against Quanah Parker's village of Comanche.

Hooves pounded up behind Hook, yanking him rudely from his reverie. The sergeant passed Jonah on one side, the civilian scout sweeping by on the other. Halting, the sergeant reported.

"Five of 'em carry marks of fresh branding. At least three I think I can identify before army court from descriptions recorded at the fort by the rightful owners."

Jonah watched the civilian's eyes; indeed, the sergeant's and now the young lieutenant's eyes all come to rest squarely on him.

"What have you to say concerning the fact that you have stolen property in your possession, mister?"

Hook saw the lieutenant mouth the words, even heard them clear enough. Yet what was happening had taken on such an unreal quality to it.

"You . . . you t-think—" he started to sputter in disbelief, then began to chuckle.

"In this part of the country, horse stealing has never been a laughing matter," the lieutenant snarled. "What's your name?"

"Hook."

"You have a first name?"

"I do."

And he let the soldier stew.

Finally the lieutenant asked with a crimson face, "Who are the others with you? Those two?"

"My son. And my friend."

"Your son's a half-breed?"

Jonah twisted about to glance at Jeremiah. Sure enough, to a soldier it might be damned easy to take the boy for an Injun. "No, Lieutenant. The young one's a full-blood white boy. Just spent half his life with the Co-manch'. I just found him not too long back."

"You're claiming you rescued him from the Comanche?"

"He did," Jeremiah declared loudly from where he sat among the bushwhackers' horses.

The lieutenant replied with a sneer, "He speaks good English."

"Ought to," Jonah said. "He's as American as you or any of your boys there."

The lieutenant straightened. "Then is the other a real Indian?"

"The genuine article. Snake. I suppose some call them Shoshone. Up by way of Wyoming Territory."

"What are you three doing here in Indian Territory?"

"Heading west for Utah. Looking for my wife. She was took back during the war—"

"And on your way to Utah you just happened to end up with several loose horses, all of which still have their saddles."

He sighed deeply. Figuring he was going to have to tell the whole story soon enough. Figuring the army wouldn't hold it against him for killing some snake-belly bushwhackers and horse thieves what had been troubling old men and women back along the Canadian River.

Jonah said, "Better'n a week back, we come upon some folks what had four of their horses stolen."

He went on to explain about the Indian couple, how the three of them were subsequently ambushed by the horse thieves after leaving the couple's cabin, and briefly how they had surprised the bushwhackers with a ruse of their own. The only detail Jonah omitted had to do with how many they had killed.

"Your claim is that you took these horses from the men who stole them from the citizens of Indian Territory?"

Jonah nodded.

"Those same citizens we are sworn to protect, Mr. Hook. In fact, that's the very reason I'm leading this patrol from Fort Sill."

"Fort Sill? That's where we was headed when we spotted your column coming."

"It was, was it? We'll be more than happy to escort you there our-selves. Sergeant, get us some rope to bind the wrists of our prisoners."

"Prisoners?" Jonah bellowed. "What the hell—"

"I'm placing you three under arrest for suspicion—"

"Like hell you are!" Hook growled, his hand shooting to one of his pistols.

"Detail—ready and aim!"

Jonah's hand froze, just like the moment itself, as those twenty soldiers lowered their Springfields, leveling the carbines at the trio of civilians.

He shook his head. "You got this all wrong. If we was horse thieves and we'd seen you coming like we did, you think we'd just ride on down here to say howdy to you?"

Jonah watched the sergeant approach, dismount, and walk up with the rope in hand. This was damned serious. "Listen, Lieutenant—like I told you, we was looking to ride in to Sill—where we was going to sell the horses to your quartermaster."

"You had designs on making profit by your stolen property?"

"You got the wrong men, soldier!" Jeremiah snapped, his voice booming from behind Jonah. "We didn't steal nothing."

"Corporal, you'll see that a detail is formed up around our prisoners. Let's get them disarmed," the lieutenant ordered. "Also, choose three or four of the men to bring up the rear with the stolen horses."

In bewildered wonder Jonah watched the soldiers fan out, some of them surrounding each of the three riders they had just taken into custody. The rest of the troopers moved easily toward the twelve horses grazing nearby.

"Pa—what we gonna do?"

"It'll be all right, Jeremiah," he hushed his son. "When we get to Sill." He leveled his gaze at the lieutenant and asked, "You are taking us back to Fort Sill, aren't you, Lieutenant?"

The officer nodded, a grin of smug self-satisfaction on his lips. "We most certainly are, Mr. Hook. This detail has turned out most satisfactory. And so quickly too. The colonel will be well pleased with the outcome."

Jonah said to Jeremiah, "It's gonna be all right, like I said. We're going in to Fort Sill with these soldiers and we'll get everything straightened out, son." Again he looked up to speak to the officer. "When we get into the fort, Lieutenant—I want you to take me to see your colonel."

"Why would you want to see him, Mr. Hook? I wouldn't dare trouble the colonel with a routine matter of horse theft."

"This ain't a routine matter, Lieutenant. You see, I know your colonel. Me and the Injun both know your Colonel Davidson."

The lieutenant straightened, the corners of his lips curling up. "Colonel Davidson is no longer in command at Fort Sill," he said, then grinned a bit too grandly. "This territory is now under the command of Colonel Ranald S. Mackenzie."

"Mackenzie?" Jonah asked rhetorically, for some reason feeling he ought to know that name.

"Colonel Mackenzie, commanding, Fourth U.S. Cavalry."

Jonah struggled with it in his mind. "The Fourth?"

"You've heard of us?"

"Can't say as I have, not for certain."

The officer seemed so proud of himself. "Mackenzie's gallant Fourth: the heroes of the Palo Duro Canyon?" he said, removing his slouch hat, which he swept low in a grand arc. "Why—we're the very regiment that drove Quanah Parker's Comanche into the wilderness with nothing but their clothes on their backs!"

She lay beneath the white demon's damp skin.

These American barbarians had so many smells about them. Most of those she lay with smelled of the animals they killed and ate. Not the fowl and fish of her rigid diet. No, these barbarians of the Gold Mountain ate red meat, the animals of these hills and forests, when it could be shot.

Yet it wasn't the stench of dead animals that reeked from the skin of this American ghost. Instead, he smelled as good as any man who had shadowed her with his body. But, she reminded herself, his smell came from a bottle. Those glass bottles that contained either the sweet-scented lilac water, perhaps emerald-green bottles of cinnamon oil, or one of the brown bottles that held the bitter amber of man's whiskey. These white-skinned hill demons all took their life from a bottle.

Her own scent came from the perfumes shipped to her employer, Bak Sahm, who ordered them from Canton. The small porcelain bottles so reminded her of home. A home she now reluctantly admitted she never really had. After every meaningful bath, without fail after every barbarian customer come to shade her with his sweating, heaving body, Chung-li Chu'uan anointed herself anew. And with each fragrance she would remember something in particular about her tiny village of Simsun tucked far away in the Eleventh Province of Ancient Mandarin China, that vivid memory aroused through her nose. If she were aware of anything, Chung-li Chu'uan was most aware of her sense of smell. It had brought her blessings. It had brought disaster.

With the bottle beneath her nose now, her eyes began to sting as she looked out the window, down on Dry Valley Street. She remembered how her older sister had drowned herself and her newborn baby girl in the village well near the center of the cluster of huts that comprised Simsun. How Chung-li admired her dead sister: to choose murder and suicide rather than doom her illegitimate daughter to a life of Mandarin hell. A culture wherein males were praised, celebrated, doted on, educated. Baby girls were a burden. Considered nothing more than another mouth to feed, an existence with no chances for joy—only the certainty that ghosts would haunt the family. Especially for a girl-child without a father's name.

Chung-li fled the despair of Simsun not long after her sister killed herself. Ran away to the seaside at Canton. There she discovered her fifteen summers of life in a distant province had in no way prepared her for the ugly evil that swept her up and carried her away. Onto a ship of the indentured ones, bound for the Gold Mountain four years ago, one of a handful of young girls who were the most special of cargo destined for the First City.* Men from all parts of China, all provinces and villages, both big and small, filled every inch of that ship's hold. With their eyes every one of them showed that they knew why Chung-li was on that ship fighting the waves of the Sea of Lions. They knew that unlike theirs, her passage was already paid.

Chinese women simply did not set out for the Gold Mountain to search for suitors and be married. Women like her set foot on the shores of the Gold Mountain already bought and paid for; a business proposition only.

In those first two and a half years since she had looked upon the hills and streets of the First City, Chung-li had been sold and bartered from joss house to joss house, from one owner to another. Until Bak Sahm showed up in the Second City.+ And found her there. He bought her, as well as three more who worked the houses of joy. Where he got so much money, she would never know. But perhaps she did know. Like so many other Chinese women, she had already paid for her passage many, many times over in the years of her slavery to the needs of men.

Yet the amount of her debt had ceased to matter to her. Some time ago Chung-li had decided she was dead already. Worse off than her sister, who threw herself down the well. Nothing less than a living death here in the land of the American barbarians. It was only fitting that she should

* *The Celestials' term for San Francisco.*
+ *The Celestials' term for Sacramento.*

suffer for all eternity this life of living hell letting the white ghosts shadow her body here in Bak Sahm's California Lodging House.

In the year and a half since he had brought her here, Bak Sahm had never once forced himself on Chung-li. She wondered if it was because he did not find her attractive. There must surely be something wrong with her, she thought again, looking down on the street as shadows lengthened with the departure of the sun. Her employer regularly lay with the other women who worked for him, not just the Chinese but the rest: an odd lot of white demon women, two Indians, and three Mexicans.

Behind his back they all laughed at Bak Sahm; with their cloying words and eyeballs rolling to the ceiling they joked of his leg, his crippled arm—and how in the lamplit shadows of their cribs he made such ridiculous, contorted shadows of himself that danced on the wall when he climbed atop them and began to pant as men always would.

But when Bak Sahm occasionally asked Chung-li what the others thought of him, she lied. Back in Canton she had learned to lie, and to do it so very well. So well that even she did not know at times if she was telling the truth. It no longer mattered anyway. Bak Sahm was due this hurt from those he had money enough to possess. He had earned his pain, in repayment for all the misery he had visited upon her and the rest of them. Indeed, if some small measure of pain would be his lot, it would make her smile.

Downstairs she could hear the noise begin to grow, like a living thing, not unlike the dragons Bak Sahm seemed so obsessed with: the rumble of loud voices, the rattle of bottles and the tinkle of all those glasses thunked on the wood of table and bar, the hammering of dancing boot heels and the wheeze of the tiny hammered harpsichord her employer had hauled all the way from the Second City in the same wagon that brought her across the land of desert to this mountain prison.

On that trip Bak Sahm told her she no longer had to torture herself with the wrappings she had tightened around her feet since that first day in Canton four summers before. He said it made little difference to these white barbarians, such cultural refinement did not matter. The demons of this land had no concern as did the Mandarins for making women's feet smaller than their hands. There would be, he told her, no sense in her binding her feet so the toes curled under and the instep folded in on itself.

Four days later on the trail they took back here from the Second City, he had grown exasperated at something she did. In his sudden anger he whipped his words about her head and shoulders as if they were a nail-studded mace. She winced again and again, attempting to duck out of the way of his verbal anger. But when he was finished lashing her with his words, Bak Sahm ripped the bindings from her tiny feet.

Ah, that pain, that terror, knowing he would not let her rebind them to put an end to the sudden stabs of pain caused by the blood rushing back into the shrunken veins. The throb of every heartbeat slashed with the hot fire of a knife against the bones she had worked so hard to curve downward into a perfect Mandarin arch.

Because he had torn the bindings off and refused her to reapply them for the rest of that horrible ordeal across the desert, Chung-li had not been able to walk for a long, long time. But then, when she had bound her feet, she had not walked very much at all anyway. Women like her were not supposed to in old China. She was a joy girl. Everything would be brought to her by servants of her owner. Food, drink, even the chamber pot. Even her customers came to her bedside. She had no need to travel far, so instructed her first owner, who ordered her feet bound by cultural, if not sexual, imperative.

But this new owner was different. Bak Sahm had watched her hobble on those painful feet for weeks after they arrived here at the California Lodging House. He said nothing, only shaking his head and turning away in disgust, not hinting the least sympathy for what tragedy he had brought down on her head. She knew he expected more of her than he expected of the others—for he hobbled too.

When the customer was finally finished and gone, Chung-li lay for a long time, thinking on her hate for her employer. Slowly she pulled up the bottom of the long silk robe, braided with gold and resplendent with shimmering tassels, brought all the way from China for her by Bak Sahm. Then she quickly dropped the hem, feeling faint. It was a mistake to look at her feet. Instead she hobbled over to the tiny chair by the chest, sat down, and lifted the hand mirror.

Chung-li Chu'uan applied more of the rice powder over her face, dabbed more bright rouge to her cheeks, smeared a shiny crimson to her full lips. As a final dressing she dabbed perfume into her palms, rubbed them lightly, then took a deep breath. Waiting.

It was almost time for more work. Soon another one from downstairs would be brought to her door. Every night since Bak Sahm had brought her here to this place of the noisy white demons, Chung-li had waited. One by one they came to her room, her bed, to her body. Like pilgrims coming to pay homage.

So she waited and suffered—knowing he would walk in the door one day.

Knowing her warrior would one day come to kill Bak Sahm, then take her away.

Where he would take her, she did not care. Only that the man she hated with all her soul would die.

7

HOW COULD QUANAH have trusted the soldiers, when all the *tai-bos'* promises had been broken?

Jeremiah's mind burned with the question as he pressed his face against the bars, straining to peer from the guardhouse window. They had been here two days, told they had to wait before they could see some civilian who was coming down from the Southern Cheyenne Reservation up at the Darlington Agency.

"This fella's going to represent the three of you," the officer of the day told them at long last. "You civilians are going to need someone to speak on your behalf when the army starts its trial of the horse thieves been raiding this part of the country."

But they weren't horse thieves. All they had done was double around to take back what was theirs to begin with. At least that's what his pa had convinced him they were going to do before riding on west to Fort Sill. And now they had made it to the army's post: here to this hot, humid cell squatting under the summer sun that shone down with a growing fervor. The wind didn't move much here, didn't have the chance. And beyond the walls, Big Red Meat's Comanche band was growing sicker every day— forced to pitch their lodges in a swamp where the wind did not move, where the mosquitoes brought sickness, where the water could not flow but lay trapped in stinking bogs.

From his window Jeremiah read the despair, recognized the swallowed rage on the faces of those warriors who dared not approach the soldiers surrounding the mud guardhouse. They were a people that so reminded him of a once-hearty plant: now without sun and water, denied the nourishment of the plains wind—a plant that begins to wither, ready to die.

That third morning a growing commotion brought Jeremiah from the low tick-bunk in his narrow cell. All three went to their barred windows, pressing their faces against the iron, turning this way then that to watch the swelling crowd of soldiers and agency Indians.

Jeremiah knew they had to be Big Red Meat's band of Comanche. Here in what the Comanche called the Moon When the Grass Is Tall, men and women, the children and the old ones, all were gathering in greater and greater numbers, lining the trail that extended past the low fence surrounding the fort. Inside the fort grounds, officers had already formed up their soldiers by companies, both infantry and cavalry. Then as the fort parade grew eerily quiet, everyone could hear the wave of noise growing in the distance, down the post road, taking life like a tangible, locomotive thing headed their way. This noise of celebration and exultation: like the body of a field mouse in the belly of a bull snake—this cheering and *ki-yi*ing of the men, the trilling and keening of the women, the high-pitched yips from the excited children . . . it was coming, slowly coming, this excitement coming toward the fort.

Then Jeremiah saw him, his heart stopping. His friend.

Young Hook turned and blinked at his father but was unable to speak, so he quickly turned back to peer from the guardhouse window. So hard to believe what he was seeing.

How could Quanah trust the white man—the *tai-bos* who had harried him, chased him, put a death warrant on him since the day he had been born near the Cedar Lake far out there on the wild plain?

Then Jeremiah realized, it was not the white *tai-bos* Quanah was trusting, not even the army. Jeremiah understood that his friend, the half-breed Kwahadi war chief who had ruled the Staked Plain for so many Comanche summers, had put his trust in one and only one man. Three-Finger Kinzie.

Not long after bringing his famed Fourth Cavalry here to take command of Fort Sill back in April, Colonel Ranald S. Mackenzie had dispatched Dr. J. J. Sturm with Sergeant John Charlton and two of Big Red Meat's most trusted Comanches to attempt the unthinkable: finding Quanah Parker's Kwahadi. On the far western side of the Staked Plain they finally located the warrior band clinging desperately to their old ways and tenacious in their desire to be left alone. Immediately disarmed by Quanah's warriors, the white men and agency Comanches were led to a lodge where the Kwahadi headmen held three days of intense, heated discussions with the peace delegation.

Sturm carried Mackenzie's two guarantees. First: if the Kwahadi came in, they would be allowed to retain some of their ponies, and none of their leaders would be sentenced to prison like the Cheyenne and Kiowa who had been exiled to faraway Florida. But—if the Kwahadi refused the offer of mercy—Three-Finger Kinzie gave his second guarantee: the soldier chief vowed he would hunt down and exterminate them . . . to the last Kwahadi.

This was the promise of the one who had chased, harried, stalked Quanah Parker for many winters. This was the guarantee of a soldier who was as much a man of honor as was Quanah Parker.

From the far border of trees fully leafed in summer's emerald-green the sounds of celebration grew thunderous. Jeremiah watched the rows upon rows of blue soldiers come stiffly to attention. Into their midst Bad-Hand Kinzie appeared, resplendent in his freshly brushed uniform. He nervously squared his hat, then tugged on his antelope-hide gauntlets as he came to a halt followed by a contingent of officers from his Fourth Cavalry, men who themselves had battled the powerful and wily lords of the southern plains in four campaigns. There beside the tall flagpole that stood at the center of Fort Sill, I. T., Ranald Mackenzie awaited the coming of the Kwahadi. The last, the most mighty of the holdouts.

Cheering, beating drums, and singing their war songs, the Kiowa and Big Red Meat's Comanche throbbed along the edges of the road; they danced through the shadow and sun beneath the leafy trees as the excitement grew. Dogs barked at everyone's heels, howling with the screeching children, who beat on tin plates or hammered on tin cups with peeled twigs.

"Ain't he some sight now?" Jonah Hook asked with deep admiration in his voice. For a moment he looked over at his son, profound respect in his eyes, before turning back to his cell's tiny window.

He rode in, slowly, every bit as proudly as Jeremiah had ever seen the man sit astride his war pony out on the far reaches of the Staked Plain. It made young Hook's heart clutch like the folding of a raven's wing to cast his eyes once again on his friend—the young war chief who had for many seasons assured that Jeremiah and Zeke learned what they needed to become Kwahadi.

Now this morning those two—that man and his pony—looked as one: both wild and free, both bred on the windswept reaches of Comancheria. Horse and warrior.

Right behind Quanah came the first of more than four hundred he was leading in to the agency.

"I . . . I don't believe it," Jeremiah whispered.

"He chose as a free man to come in, son," Jonah said, almost as quietly. "Way I see it. The army didn't drive him in. Hell no. Damn if they didn't try to whip him till he come running in here with his tail between his legs. But—they didn't." There was admiration in Jonah's voice now. "That Comanch' is coming in of his own free will."

Struggling, swallowing hard, Jeremiah tried to say something, to agree with his father, but when the words slipped past the cracks in that sour ball clogging his throat, those words came out a tumble of Comanche.

Jonah turned to stare briefly at his son in confusion; then his eyes softened with realization. "I understand, Jeremiah. You got every right . . . I mean—it's almost like you're two men too. Exactly like that Quanah Parker out there. Both of you: half-white, half-Comanch'."

Through the last of the parting crowd the war chief rode slowly, never seeming to gaze down at the cheering warriors and women, not looking at the little ones who poked their heads between grown-ups' legs to catch a glimpse of this famous warrior. Onto that grassy parade his pony carried him, where Quanah Parker finally signaled the handful of his most faithful warriors that this was where they must stay. From here—he must go alone.

Never did Quanah look at the new gauntlet of gawking, murmuring soldiers or those curious, frightened white women who watched behind the safety of their printed fans or beneath colorful, satin-lined parasols.

Instead Quanah Parker fixed his eyes on the man his Kwahadi had sparred with so many times in the past five summers.

The morning's sun had seared the iron bars until they were hot, yet not so hot that Jeremiah could not press his cheek against them. He brushed some of his long, dark hair from his eyes when the breeze tussled it, and squinted into the bright light as Quanah's bare brown knees tightened against the pony's ribs. Immediately the proud animal halted at the edge of the wide gravel walk that would lead him to the central flagpole. Dropping to the ground, the war chief stood for a moment beside his pony festooned in paint and ribbons, scalp locks and feathers. Stood there just long enough to make Jeremiah believe Quanah might be trying to accustom himself to being the sort of man who stood on legs . . . now that he would no longer be a horse-mounted Comanche warrior: for many generations the true lords of the southern plains.

It was a small thing, this delay, the manner in which Quanah looked down to study his legs, his feet, the ground beneath him—but it proved to be a gesture most significant to Jeremiah as he gripped those iron bars, the young man who had known the Kwahadi chief for half his life.

Then the Kwahadi's eyes came up, and without hesitation Quanah Parker stepped onto the manicured lawn and strode purposefully toward the blue-and-gold, brass-and-braid assembly of officers as some of his warriors began to follow in his wake. But with only a wave Quanah stopped them where they stood, that simple, wordless command instructing them all once more to remain behind among their war ponies.

Silently, and more alone than he had ever been in his life since the day his mother was retaken by the whites, perhaps since the day his father was killed by the Texas Rangers, Quanah Parker walked on, his brass-studded Winchester repeater laid across his arm, clutched there in company with his fan of eagle-wing feathers.

Mackenzie took a step forward, stopped, and turned slightly. Without a word he motioned his officers to remain behind.

Crossing those last few yards of lawn and gravel, the two met beneath that summer sky where the sun climbed hot and radiant with a light that gave a resplendent luster to every color. Over the heads of those two warriors fluttered that red-and-white-striped flag snapping in the clutches of a hot June breeze.

Jeremiah discovered he was holding his breath as the crowd fell silent, as if some great hawk's wing had passed over them all, flew over that gauntlet, swooped above that ring of red and white alike.

He reminded himself to take a breath as the sweat began to stream from his forehead, his eyes smarting. Jeremiah watched as the two old foes simply beheld one another for that long, breathless moment. Here, now at last, come face-to-face. Then something private must have taken place between the two—Jeremiah Hook was certain of it.

If only because Quanah Parker, the last Kwahadi holdout, slowly knelt in the shadow of that great snapping flag of red and white, there to lay down his rifle at Kinzie's feet.

Jeremiah's eyes began to pool, able to contain his tears no longer, when the war chief stood, no longer bearing a weapon, to show the soldier chief that his hands were empty at last. That he had laid down his means of making war at the feet of his old enemy.

The sour ball rushed to the back of his throat as Three-Finger Kinzie's back snapped rigid as a cleaning rod, his right arm folding smartly as the Indian fighter saluted the man he had hunted across thousands of miles, across hundreds of days.

Jeremiah turned, quietly beginning to sob as he slowly sank to the hard-packed floor, his back sliding down the cool stone wall.

Those two warriors having met at long, long last. Kinzie vowing fairness. Quanah trusting in the universal code of a warrior.

"It's all right now, son."

He looked up through the shimmer of tears, seeing his father kneeling a few feet away in his cell, reaching out both his arms through the iron bars. Jonah's own cheeks were wet, his eyes glassy with pools of grief.

"C'mere, Jeremiah. Come to your pa," Jonah choked out the words. "Let me show you it's gonna be all right."

On hands and knees Jeremiah crabbed across the rough clay floor to the bars, letting himself slip once more within the sanctuary of his father's arms, feeling them close protectively about him, pressing himself as best he could into that security of his father's embrace—just to lay his ear against his pa's chest and hear the heartbeat. To feel safe once more after so, so long.

"It's gonna be fine now," Jonah cooed as if his son were no more than a babe in his arms. "There's gonna be peace for some now, son."

He sobbed with the words, "I . . . I love you . . . so much, Pa."

"Gonna be fine, Jeremiah. Looks like I'll finally see my grandbabies. Gonna finally hold Zeke's babies in my arms."

He was still a good Mormon. One of the defenders of Zion. No matter how Jubilee Usher might try to seduce him, again and again.

John Doyle Lee gazed at the sun's last rays settling on the countryside west of Beaver, Utah, where he had been held in a cell since last November, brooding now on the charismatic Usher. Reminded too of how Jubilee had with growing repetition attempted to twist and pervert that zealot's fervor Lee held for his Church. His belief had been his bedrock. But knowing that the sacred Church was Lee's bedrock had allowed Usher to chip away at that strong foundation, to force a crack in what had for a lifetime been a seamless faith.

From the time he was a youngster, Lee had believed in Joseph Smith, the first Prophet of God here in the latter days. Lee was counted among those who defended Zion against the murderous Missourians who killed

Smith. Then, unswervingly, Lee transferred his faith to Brigham Young, believed in the new Prophet's direction—a calling that took God's chosen people west to this land of Deseret.

And now, especially on the eve of this trial for what happened some eighteen years before, John Doyle Lee wanted to believe all the more in Young as his personal Prophet, as Lee's salvation not only in the hereafter, but on earth as well. Surely Brigham would see to it that no one testified against someone so faithful as Lee. Surely John's old friend Brigham would assure that the high offices of the Church were brought to bear for Lee's defense. He wanted so to believe—almost as an article of faith.

The whole thing with those folks from Arkansas crossing through southern Utah back in fifty-seven . . . how Lee and the other good Mormon folk had taken just about all the evil tonguing about their Prophet and their Church from those Gentile emigrants bound for California . . . how Lee and the other church elders had worried over what to do once a band of Indians had the emigrant train surrounded and forted up down there in Mountain Meadows.

With an incendiary shame Lee shook his head—remembering how he and the other elders promised the Fancher party that they would lead them out of any danger from the Indians. But to do that, the emigrants had to lay down their weapons, the men had to march out first, the women and children to follow. And with all those Arkansas folks strung out across the bowels of that valley meadow—their trap was sprung. Lee's elders turned on the men while the Indians butchered the women and older children.

In the end only seventeen small children were spared—survivors who would not remember much of the massacre. Surely, it had been argued that bloody day, those youngsters would not remember that some of their persecutors were white men. God-fearing white men.

Oh, the many times Lee had steadfastly vowed he would not be captured by the Gentiles, arrested by Washington's Federalist government. John knew, deep down he understood, what would happen if he was captured.

"I will not be taken, as I would then be obliged to betray men who did the act through their great zeal in serving our Church, and thought they were doing right."

But here he was in the Beaver jail. Captured at wife Caroline's house. With his trial to begin soon.

"Those men deserved to be punished," Lee said aloud to himself, stepping the four short paces it took to cross his cell. "The emigrants poisoned the springs on their way through our country—laughing about the Mormons they would be killing. But instead the Gentiles ended up killing only a handful of the Indians. That's what sealed their doom."

He sank to the edge of the thin mattress, seeming puny atop the sheet-iron bed. And dropped his face into his hands, sobbing in remembrance. "Oh, the women . . . and children!"

Lee had begged the Pahvants to spare the women and children with the emigrant train. He even had offered to pay the warriors for the life of every woman and child they spared. But in the end the warriors killed nearly all in a great cleansing blood lust.

"And they called me *Nah-gaats.* Crybaby."

Lee rubbed his throbbing temples with his fingertips, the way he had on that day of the massacre. Sobbing as he had done when the echo of the last shot fired into the Fancher party had faded from the surrounding hills.

Rightfully bitter, John realized the only ones who had remained true to him throughout the agonizing ordeal of the intervening years were his own wives and children. Since his excommunication from his beloved Church five years ago, Lee had lived with one or another of the women who stood staunchly behind him no matter what the Church did or did not do to protect him. From the dry, dusty poverty of the willow shanty at The Pools, where Rachel and their children eked out an existence, across twenty-some miles to the low-roofed squalor of the stone house at Lonely Dell, where he visited Aggatha Ann, from the home of Emma or Polly or Ann, Lee moved about in those first weeks that stretched into seasons, then grew into years. He had no Church. It had turned its back on him.

Worse yet: his friend, Prophet Brigham Young, had turned his face from his faithful servant, John Doyle Lee.

Following the massacre, Young put Lee in charge of disposing of the spoil from the Fancher emigrant train—the rocking chairs and the mules, the milk cows and the sideboards, the clothing and what money they had taken off the butchered bodies. The president of the Church had put Lee in charge of getting rid of it all, as if to wash his hands of the stain.

But now, as a final indignity, Young had turned his face from his old friend.

With the rest of the local elders Lee had cooked up their version of the massacre, and they persevered in sticking to that story in those first years, saying they had tried to conciliate the aggrieved Indians, and when they failed, they simply stayed away from the train, justifying their failure to defend the emigrants from overwhelming numbers of warriors.

"We would have been killed ourselves," they excused themselves of blame. "We cannot be held to account for what those Arkansas folks brought down on their own heads."

So John M. Higbee and the other men of Lee's Iron County militia steadfastly held to their story year after year—even after the U.S. government sent a detachment of two hundred soldiers south to Utah's Dixie in fifty-nine to arrest Lee and some others. But the Mormon elders successfully eluded arrest. Lee himself fled north to Salt Creek, then hurried east into the hills where a hideout had been arranged for him. The fleeing elders called the place Balleguard—a sanctuary known only to the couriers who carried messages back and forth between the men and their families, bringing in supplies from Beaver.

When the government could not make its arrests, matters seemed to calm down for some time. But here in the Beaver jail, Lee knew he had only been fooling himself. In all that time, right behind his back, the leaders of his beloved Church had finally crystallized their official policy on the massacre: if there were white men on the scene of the Indian attack on the Fancher train, those white men were acting as individuals—without knowledge or consent of the Church as a whole, without culpability of Church leaders.

As for Brigham Young himself, the Prophet wanted the matter kept locked away. There was nothing to be gained by the constant whisperings and agitation.

"The more you stir a manure pile," Young declared about the massacre, "the worse it stinks."

But Brigham had his foot in it now, Lee knew. Young could not claim ignorance of anything having to do with the Meadows massacre.

Lord—how Lee desperately wanted to believe Brigham Young was God's Prophet still!

Every winter when Young came south to Mormon Dixie to spend out the cold months in St. George, he would have an audience with Lee. How many times in those years since the massacre had Young invited John Doyle Lee to have dinner with the Prophet's family, to sit at the living Prophet's table, to break bread with God's chosen voice? How many times had Young repeated that it was upon the faithful like John Doyle Lee that the Church of Zion had been built?

Yet—now it was Lee who felt like Christ: denied by Young these long years later, just as Peter himself denied Christ three times during that terrible night before the crucifixion.

Lee lifted his tall frame from the tiny bed and stepped to the cell window—drawn by the sound of innocent laughter. Children's laughter. Peering out on the summer day, he could not see them, straining to find those youngsters who made the sounds of such joy. Likely, they played around the corner.

How many now? His mind grappled with it as he stared at the summer sky. Fifty-four as the fruit of his loins. That was a lot of children. All to God's greater glory—borne by seventeen wives. Though not all lived now. And it hurt to remember that some had abandoned him. Denied him. Gone to cling to others when John was excommunicated.

Still, the faithful had remained through it all: the early years of the Church, into the dark days suffered in Missouri, and finally tested in the rigors of that first trek across the plains into this wilderness.

The seed of his loins—the children. Many of them had already blessed Lee with grandchildren. Family: these who were blood of his blood were like a spring in the desert, like water spilling from the riven rock for this old man grown thirsty after a lifetime of faithful duty.

If God demanded John Doyle Lee's head, he decided as he settled wearily to the edge of the iron bed once more, then Lee would turn himself over to God's hand.

How sorely he missed the comforting feel of Rachel's hand in his right now, missed how the little ones clung round his knees when he sat in his chair at the end of a day, ready once more to repeat for them the stories of the faithfuls' exodus from the land of the Gentiles, the coming of God's chosen to Zion.

If God so wanted Lee's life in repayment for some debt the Church owed, the old man was ready to kneel before the throne of his God and offer himself up.

But not for Brigham Young. Never would Lee offer himself up for an old friend who had denied Lee. Not for a Prophet proved a fraud, a charlatan. That denial hurt the most.

Because so many, many times . . . John had denied what he believed to be God's will and instead sworn his unswerving allegiance to Brigham Young.

And for that most serious of transgressions, John Doyle Lee now sat alone in his stuffy cell—without a Prophet he could cling to.

Without a God to answer his prayer.

8

T HESE LEG IRONS hurt the worst of all.

Jonah turned to look back at Jeremiah. His son shuffled up the gravel walk behind him. Two Sleep after the boy. Their wrists cuffed, their ankles encased in bands of iron with a short length of chain preventing any of the three from walking in a normal stride, much less taking off at a dead run.

Hell, he hadn't been forced to endure irons like these back when he was captured, not for those hundreds of miles he was dragged north to Illinois, no chains nor cuffs suffered through the months that became seasons, the seasons into years—one of the many Confederate prisoners of the Yankee army.

Scuffling slowly across the dusty edge of the parade, the three of them had a half dozen around them, guards with Long Tom Springfields at the ready. Infantry, with bayonets, who were transferring the three prisoners from that large, airy room where they had endured their all-too-brief trial before a federal judge and an army prosecutor. Same sort of man, Jonah brooded. Them two wasn't no different from the other.

With a resounding ring of the judge's gavel: found guilty of stealing horses on a government reservation.

His sweaty pink face reminded Jonah of a scalded hog's ass. "You have anything to say for yourself before this court hands down its sentence, Mr. Hook?"

He had raised his head, lifted his eyes to peer at that fat, well-fed

74

government official fanning himself and swatting at flies behind the table at the far end of the long room. Then . . . Jonah finally shook his head and stared out the window.

They could get it over with now for all he cared. So sick of heart, he felt himself emptied of just about everything but hate. Hatred for the Federalists what invaded Missouri so Jonah would march off to war. Hatred for the Federalists who defeated General Sterling Price's volunteers at Pea Ridge and later in Mississippi where they wounded him in the timber near Corinth. Hatred for the Federalists who penned him up like a wild animal, expecting him and the rest to die. Then begged Confederate farm boys like him to wear Union blue and go west to kill red men.

Jonah Hook had nothing left but hatred in his veins for these Federalists who kept him making war when he should have been back in Missouri defending his family and home.

There was nothing left. No Confederacy. No farm in Missouri. No family at all. And now he didn't even have his quest to find Gritta. For so long that was all Jonah Hook had. And now—all that was left was the hate.

"Let the record show that the defendant, Jonah Hook—declared he had no final statement to make," the judge told his army recorder just minutes ago. "Therefore, in the absence of any statement from these defendants . . ."

Jonah had turned to watch the beads of sweat on the man's brow as he declared his findings.

". . . it is the determination of this federal court that the guilty parties will be hanged from the neck until dead."

At the moment Jeremiah gasped in terror, in utter shock and horror, Jonah turned to his son, grasped the youth's hands in his, the lengths of chain that bound their wrists clinking as he pulled the boy close. Unlike these soldiers, unlike that hog-faced, sweating judge, Jonah realized this had to be the greatest terror Jeremiah would ever look in the eye: death by hanging. With a noose strangling the breath from a man's body, that man's soul could not escape from his mouth. His spirit could not fly out of his body at the moment of death—freed from this temporal plane to go on living in the realm of dreams.

So Jonah's eyes stung, beginning to cry even as his lips whispered assurances that somehow things would turn out all right. But his eyes betrayed him as he looked into his son's face. Eyes that told Jeremiah soon enough Jonah Hook would know why God wanted him to suffer. When at last their souls stood before the Almighty.

"Your . . . your mother believed in a loving God, Jeremiah," he whispered to his son. "She'd want you to be strong. To trust."

Jonah himself wanted to believe. Then he looked at Two Sleep, at that impassive face etched with years and miles before they met eight summers before. Perhaps only Jonah could read the eyes—for that was the only place where the Shoshone ever betrayed himself at all.

The judge finished wiping his face with a damp kerchief. "Does the defense have any questions?"

The young soldier rose clumsily from the defense table, a hand pumping aimlessly in the air like a marionette's, spastically. Then the officer appointed to defend the trio shook his head. He could not look any of the three in the eye. "No, your honor. Very good, sir. The sentence is understood."

"Very well," the judge said then, gazing out the window a moment as if regarding something of import. "Sentence will be executed this Saturday—at sunset." He picked up the heavy gavel.

Jonah watched it arc backward at the end of the judge's arm, then fall forward within his beefy grasp.

"May God have mercy on your souls."

And with the loud clap and reverberating echo of that gavel's fall, chairs scooted and boots scraped across the wood floor. It seemed a hundred hands were hauling the three of them up, shoving chairs aside and getting them started toward the door. At the back of the courtroom even more guards waited, formed into an escort that filed with the prisoners through the doors out toward the June sunshine.

"What . . . what day of the week is this?" Jonah asked now of the youngster at his right shoulder.

The soldier turned and replied, "Why, it's Tuesday."

He thought a moment. "Then I got four days to wait."

The soldier tried to smile, offering, "It's that waiting gotta make it worse." There was genuine sympathy in his voice.

"Man gets ready to meet his Maker, he needs time," Jonah said quietly. "Four days . . . it's gonna be enough time."

He bowed his head a little, letting it sag and bob as he shuffled along between the rows of guards. He felt the sun on the back of his neck despite his long hair that draped over his flesh like a thick shawl. He could not turn around to look at Jeremiah anymore. For now, there was nothing to say.

Emptied of all but the hate. His own life gone for naught. He was able to find Hattie. Then he lost Zeke just when he was so damned close. Saving

Jeremiah—only to get the boy hanged at the end of a rope for stealing horses.

What had his life mattered anyway? All the years and winters, the miles and the hunting—just so he could run out of time to find Gritta?

Not that he doubted. Not really. Jonah was sure there was a God, somewhere. He even figured that God watched over folks. But Jonah was just as sure God had failed to watch over his family. Certain down to the empty, hate-filled center of his being that God hadn't held Jonah's little family in the palm of His great hand.

If there was a God who knew what was going on at that moment at Fort Sill, I.T., Hook figured he had never felt farther from God than he did right now.

But—come the setting of the sun on Saturday—Jonah figured he would be even farther still from God than he was at this moment.

Farther from God by that ten feet of rope it took to hang a man.

Bak Sahm hated this time of day more than any other. The sun was coming up. The night was finished. His trade in providing whiskey and his girls of joy to the white barbarians was finished for a few hours.

Which meant he now had to sit alone, unable to sleep—often for days at a time until he collapsed with utter weariness. Here in the corner shadows, at the table no one but Bak Sahm used, he always sat, drinking the strong green tea as the sun's first shafts pierced the smoky windowpanes that reminded him of scales on the dragon's tail. The dragon that kept Bak Sahm awake night after night, refusing to sleep for fear of dreaming of the terrible fire that demon breathed.

Afraid when he went to sleep he would lose control, and want her more than he could stand.

At least now, with morning, he knew she was asleep upstairs. The last customer done and gone—no one left with any of Bak Sahm's girls of joy. Now they would sleep through the day, arise late in the afternoon to bathe, preparing themselves for another noisy night at the California Lodging House.

But in the meantime, even though the trade in whiskey and women waited, the Chinaman would attend to his store right next door. It was there he devoted his attentions during the day, the saloon at night. Across the counter of his crowded shop passed thousands upon thousands of dollars of gold—both coin and dust. If one of the Chinese miners did not have the hard currency to send home to Canton and beyond to the distant provincial villages, Bak Sahm would convert their gold dust. Every one of his customers understood that he took his percentage; it was agreed.

After all, the barbarians' gold was going home to families left behind across the far green Sea of Lions. In the First City an agent of one Tong or another would take his percentage for seeing that the money reached the Pearl River delta, the gold to be converted again upon its arrival in Canton before the Chinese money would begin its climb up the many rivers that converged beneath those green terraced hills.

Bak's fingers traced back and forth over the edge of the playing cards. This was an old deck, but still serviceable. Rarely did he throw anything away.

Sometimes Bak Sahm felt lucky. Like the night he won enough money to buy this saloon from the white demon who owned it before him. Many years gone now. So many that at times he wondered who had really won that single turn of the cards on which they had gambled. Like a prison again, this suffocation became—and he wondered if this place owned him. If he didn't belong to the girls of joy, and to the store, if he didn't belong to the saloon with its whiskey and to the back room with its sweetish clouds of opium.

Still, most days Bak Sahm felt less than lucky. He just worked hard. And kept this saloon going, his store running. Made sure his girls of joy pleased their customers. Certain that the terrible whiskey poured. As long as he did that, the miners would come and he could live out another day like this one just beginning. Praying he could again hold off sleep so the dragon would not come to haunt him.

Gazing at a shaft of sunlight streaking through the window at his shoulder, he was struck with how the opaque shaft reminded him of the sun streaming through one of the translucent sails on the junks that plied the Pearl River. Even the dancing flecks of dust caught in that sunstream reminded him of the distant flocks of water fowl that migrated to the delta every winter, flying down and among and past the tall masts and paper-thin sails of the bobbing watercraft. Ducks and geese were most common, but coots also came to feed in the waterside reeds through the cold months as well.

Then every spring the land would overflow before the men hitched up the buffalo to plant their year's harvest. With their crude plowing complete, the farmers and their wives and children all worked the rice terraces with their hoes. It was a tool made of hardwood, the edge shod with iron, with a handle made as long as possible to increase the force of each blow that pierced the earth as the people moved along together, men and women, young and old, all.

Bak Sahm had liked the mulberry plantations the best. For years now he had wanted something like the mulberry to grow in this climate, at this altitude above the desert—something to remind him of the delta, where each spring they harvested the mulberry shoots. When the shoots were stripped off and stuffed into baskets, those baskets loaded into little boats propelled by paddles to dart back and forth across the canals like tiny insects, the mulberry was taken to the markets, where it was sold to the silkworm farmers.

Sitting back now, with a long sigh Bak ran both his hands slowly down the front of his long silk jacket. It was red—the only color divined to protect him from the dragon's fire.

Just touching the high-collared coat in this way caused him to remember the silkworms' cocoons. When those tiny homes to the worm were ready to be unwound, the cocoons were plunged into hot water for a few minutes to kill the creature inside. Then the empty homes were laid out to dry.

Hundreds, thousands of women were hired by the silk merchants to sit at their windows or sit by their doors and slowly, so delicately unwind the spider-thin thread from the cocoons an inch at a time. At last the silk was hung outdoors on cords to dry in the warming breezes of this very season—the Season of the Snake.

That done, the women took the baskets filled with the dead worms found inside each unwrapped cocoon to feed the fish swimming at the surface of every pond, hungrily awaiting their own rich harvest.

Bak Sahm looked up at the doorway behind which the woman slept. Sensing how she hated him. Knowing how much he wanted to hate her, but could not.

He stared and sipped his tea as it grew cold with the coming of another morning. Feeling just like one of those dead silkworms. How he spun and spun, and spun some more to provide himself a home, some sanctuary from the cold and loneliness.

But for all his labor—it did him no good. One day the dragon would return with its fire. And Bak Sahm's cocoon would unravel.

The dragon would find him cowering inside: a shriveled, deformed worm.

•　　•　　•

She shrieked at him until her throat grew raw with pain, so hoarse she couldn't make any more than a squeak. It hurt so bad in her throat. But nowhere near the hurt she felt deep in her belly.

Jubilee Usher had surprised her this evening with the cunning of his attack. She had been busy nursing the infant at her bare breast, sitting at the side of the bed, rocking gently to and fro as she crooned to the doll with the painted face she held against the dusky rose of her nipple. He had come through the tent flaps to find her feeding their child, when he stopped and stared at her for the longest time.

So long that it made her most uncomfortable. When she turned away to the side, he too had moved so that he could still watch her, gaze down at her breast. Gritta knew what he wanted.

Lord, punish him—strike him now—because she was feeding her child with the milk of her own body . . . and he was enjoying his evil thoughts as he stared at her bared flesh.

When he finally walked over to her and took hold of her naked shoulder, she quivered just as if a cold winter wind had passed her bare breast. A second time he nudged her back onto the bed. Obediently, Gritta lay across the tick, still clutching the babe against her breast. The child clearly was not finished eating. But she would let Usher do his business in her while she went on nursing.

So it surprised her when he did not immediately lift up her dress and rip down her bloomers. Surprised her that he did not immediately unbutton his own britches and pull his hard flesh free so that he could batter her with it. Shaming her as he always did.

No, this time Usher rose from the tick mattress and slowly tied first one of her feet, then the other to the end of the bed as she watched. Next he bound her free wrist to the headrail. Only then did Usher settle back down on the edge of the mattress to seize her other wrist still cradling the nursing infant. Savagely he yanked the arm away from her chest and pinned it up against the top of the bed, where he lashed it securely.

Now she was bound hand and foot, and beginning to sob, begging him to let the child finish its supper.

Gritta was unable to move as he tenderly lifted their child into his arms and stroked its yarn hair, traced the painted pout of the lips, straightened the dingy gray christening gown the doll wore. For those few, confusing minutes she watched him, mesmerized as he cradled the doll, murmured to it as she had always hoped the father of the child always would.

Then he suddenly ran his fingers through the long yarn hair and dropped the child at the end of his arm. Suspended there by a handful of those brown curls. Dangling there, completely helpless. Crying out to her. Screeching for her to help.

That's when she had started screaming, shrieking, keening in horror. Nothing less than terror as he turned and strode through the tent flaps. Disappearing with her infant. She couldn't catch her breath, her heart up against her tonsils. Gasping, choking.

Time and again Gritta tried to collect herself and stop shrieking at the tent flaps—pleading for him to come back with the babe.

Knowing—remembering full well—what had happened the last time Jubilee Usher had taken her children from her.

After Usher's band of gunmen forced Gritta and the children from the valley, they had wandered south by west toward the Indian Nations. Week after week—then it wasn't long before she realized she had not seen her sons for better than a day. Then a second day. And a third. Finally she understood. Jubilee Usher had simply disposed of them. Rid himself of the boys, like some excess baggage.

Another scar formed itself over her heart.

Months later Hattie too was no longer around—gone away with Usher's man named Boothog, a handsome, sinister devil who clearly coveted Gritta's daughter.

The ensuing years turned on their endless seasons while Gritta grew accustomed to being alone. It hurt talking to herself, keeping all the conversations inside. It hurt that no one ever listened. And eventually she stopped talking, even inside.

Until the day the babe came.

How unexpected the surprise had been when Jubilee laid the infant in her arms and she had looked down into its painted face.

For all this time Gritta had been so sure she had been removing every last shred of the demon's seed from her womb with that peeled willow stick she kept so that she could abort herself. Over and over she had recognized the signs—the nausea, the increased hunger, the increasing tenderness of her nipples. After three children and a stillborn, Gritta Hook knew the signs.

So she had aborted every last one of the devil's evil seed herself with the rounded end of that peeled willow twig.

Until she failed, and Jubilee brought the babe to her.

Damp with sweat, she lay there now, twisting, fighting, cutting her wrists and ankles on the coarse fibers of the new hemp rope he had used to lash her to the bed. She had worked herself into a fury, a sobbing, uncontrolled fury. And now Gritta was collapsing. Weak and unable to cry out anymore. Her voice gone, her strength all but used up.

The last rays of the sun were striking the dingy white canvas side of the tent as she quieted, unable to make any further sound. Trembling only. She could not stop shuddering, the cold was so intense within her. Gritta lay there in total abject pain.

First Jeremiah and Zeke. And then Hattie—

Jubilee Usher stepped quietly back through the tent flaps.

Her eyes widened, looking him up and down for some clue as to what he had done with their infant. Surely the babe must be frightened, every bit as scared as was she. And surely the child must be hungry again after its ordeal. It was always hungry. In the middle of the night. Throughout the day it ate. Growing stronger and stronger—so that one day it might escape Usher and his men.

He stood at the flaps, as if concentrating on her ragged breathing, his eyes pouring over her. Then he brought the arm around so she could see the infant.

Her eyes flooding, Gritta began to sob, the sound catching in the back of her tortured throat. And he laid the infant against her, placing its head in the crook of her neck.

She started crying then, able to do little more than rub her chin back and forth over the yarn hair. So relieved, so very happy, the child had been returned to her.

Crying from so deeply within her that she was not aware when Usher untied one wrist, then the other—until the prickly tingle of feeling returning to her hands startled her.

Quickly she clutched the child to her, desperately, twisting up to find he had not freed her ankles. Then raised her eyes in horror to find that he stood at the foot of the bed, removing the last of his clothing.

Those icy blue eyes widened as they fell to gaze at his eager, hardened flesh. How desperate he was to mount her, she thought, seeing the swollen member bob and weave as he kneed down on the mattress between her legs.

It was there he tossed her skirt up and savagely ripped at her bloomers until they hung in tattered shreds about her trembling thighs.

With his flesh cradled in one hand, supporting himself on the other arm, Usher leaned forward and plunged into her with a groan, squirming to seat himself all the deeper. With a final thrust he moaned.

Then began to pump himself in and out of her as Gritta laid the infant against her bare breast and held the nipple against its faded, painted lips so it could suckle.

In his heated fury Jubilee pushed against the child—to move it out of his way. In return she shoved his hand aside roughly as he continued to throttle her with his hot flesh.

Usher grunted and ripped aside the other side of her blouse, tearing it from her shoulder, scratching her bared flesh as he did. Blood oozed to the surface as he kneaded the newly freed breast. She would let him have one of them to squeeze, to suck on, to hurt. But Gritta would not let him have the other.

It was to feed their child.

Tighter and tighter she held the babe against her nipple where it nursed, afraid it would fall from her hold on it for all the pummeling he was giving her. Taking his punishing, how he bit and bruised her, grunting, his sweat dropping on her bare skin as he rutted over her. Flecks of spittle clung to the corners of his mouth as his face contorted.

She knew he was nearing the moment when he would explode. And she knew what always came next.

That first blow hurt, stinging the side of her face where he slapped her hard. But one after another, as the rest rained down on her, Gritta eventually grew numb to his beating. This was what he had to do to find release. What he had to do before he could explode inside her. The only thing that finally allowed him to climax. Beating her bruised face from side to side, side to side, with blow after blow until she sensed him burst free inside her womb.

Usher fell asleep atop her that evening, his weight close to suffocating her. Yet for the longest time she did not move for fear of waking the child that had taken its fill of her warm milk, taken what it needed of her flesh, nourished of its mother's body. Instead Gritta lay there as the feeling slowly returned to her face, sensed the fevered swelling begin, tasted the trickle of warm blood at the back of her throat. From her battered, cracked lips. Seeping from her broken nose.

Still she did not move from beneath him. So afraid of awakening the child.

After so, so long—Gritta's greatest fear was of awakening her sleeping child.

9

T HE WORDS WERE the hardest thing he could remember saying. Never much of one to speak out loud what filled his heart.

"Want you to remember I love you, son," Jonah Hook said as Jeremiah came through the doorway behind him. Into the waning sunlight of that bright summer Saturday on the southern plains. "Sorry things didn't turn out different for us . . . for you."

A mist clouded Jeremiah's eyes as he stopped beside his father, the short chain between his ankles clinking against the leg irons, raising a brief swirl of the yellowish-red dust. "Don't tell me you're sorry, Pa. You got no need apologizing to any man."

Jonah watched two soldiers bring Two Sleep out of the guardhouse into the late-afternoon sunlight, blinking. "After all the miles, Jeremiah— I come to love this ugly Injun like a brother."

He could see the gray-gilled look of fear slowly register across the Shoshone's face as their moment drew near. This thing of suffocation had special significance for Two Sleep, Jeremiah too. To Jonah it was just a nasty way to die. Struggling at the end of a rope, the noose knotted up under the side of his jaw, cocking his head to the side—breaking his neck on the drop . . . if he was lucky.

Leastways, that's the way he heard it was.

If a man wasn't lucky, he'd hang there, his tongue swelling under the hood, his face turning red, then blue, finally just as black as the inside of that hood. His legs would thrash as he kicked and flopped like a fish dragged up on the end of a line. Eyes bugged like a tree toad's, flopping and fighting for air through its gills. Then he'd pass out and the pain would be over. Jonah figured that'd be when he'd piss and shit his pants.

He'd never seen a hanging himself, but he'd heard the stories. All the way back to his boyhood in the Shenandoah.

So he had made sure the guards brought him the bucket a little while ago as the sun began to ease down onto the roofs of the far buildings. Making himself shit and piss. Empty out so there'd be nothing close enough to releasing so as to embarrass himself when that natural part of dying came, there at the end of everything.

Funny, he thought again, what a man thinks on when he reaches the last few minutes before death. Maybe it was always better to have dying come as a surprise. So a man didn't have to worry about soiling himself in front of strangers. Hell if it mattered anyway. Hell with all them what come to watch anyway. They came for a show—but he wasn't about to give 'em one.

As the two infantry soldiers tugged on his arms, Jonah turned away from Jeremiah clumsily and set off in his shuffling walk. Better to squeeze off all those thoughts about the flopping and thrashing. He'd seen enough men doing just that, even though they wasn't hanged by the neck until dead. Men hit in the belly with a big thumb-sized shitload of lead, maybe-so a big minié ball in the lights. Man gets hit in the lights—he really thrashes for a time as his lungs fill up, slowly suffocating him. This way, Lord knows—this hanging seemed a quicker way to suffocate.

There were a dozen of the soldiers in the escort this time, six on each side of the three prisoners. With all of them stiff-backed and sober-faced, they had the trio pretty well surrounded. Not like Jonah and the others were going anywhere. Cuffed and ironed, hobbling along. Just getting up there on that scaffold would be a relief after waiting these last few days for Saturday. Why the judge picked this day, he never figured out.

Must've wanted my soul securely in hell well before it comes Sunday-morning meeting time.

Rounding the back corner of the guardhouse, Jonah saw the first of them. Not the milling knots of soldiers, not even some white women and the few white children did he notice first—it was the overwhelming presence of brown skin. The tanned, seamed faces. The quiet dignity of the naked children who wanted most to be scampering and laughing like the sons and daughters of the white army officers. But instead those little brown ones clung close to the leggings and skin dresses of their parents. Their eyes like big saucers of milk as the gathering began to murmur.

The soldiers' show was about to begin: the escort had been spotted, their three prisoners crossing the last two hundred yards to the tall scaffold.

Comanche. There was no doubt in Jonah's mind who these Indians were. Oh, there might be some Kiowa in there too. But, these had to be the Comanche of Big Red Meat's band. Maybe even some of Quanah Parker's Kwahadi holdouts. Newly come to the reservation, the better part of two weeks ago.

Likely to see their first white man hanging.

Some of them Injuns watching him were the real thing: without peer as horse thieves on the Staked Plain, Jonah brooded angrily as he trudged on, clinking and dragging the leg-iron chain through the dust that rose like talc over his tall hog-leg boots. But the army don't arrest the horse thieves, don't hang them neither. Instead, it gives them brown-skinned horse thieves flour and bacon, blankets for warmth. The same goddamned army what drops a rope around the necks of white fellas like him.

Up ahead an officer was calling out his shrill orders to a detail of infantry. They snapped to attention from parade rest, their Long Toms fixed, with bayonets catching some of the last rays of the sun as it slipped behind the dome of leafy trees. Another order was sung out by a cavalry sergeant—the mounted troopers alert and watchful as they peered over the murmuring crowd who appraised the three prisoners drawing closer, ever closer to the crude scaffold.

He could see it had been made some time back for as many as a half-dozen men, and wondered why the army needed to hang that many fellas at once. The wood was old, weathered, as gray as he felt.

"Pa," Jeremiah said behind him.

Before he could reply, Jonah heard the rustle of movement, sensed the coming of color and the play of light and shadow at the corner of his eye: beyond, behind, obscured by most of the Comanche who crowded the gauntlet along this last hundred yards. Their faces saddened. Someone was coming up behind them—a group of riders.

"I see 'im, Jeremiah," he replied when he recognized that singular pony.

"Quanah."

"The one . . . your chief," Jonah said, knowing already.

Unable to speak, Jeremiah could only nod, choking back the shame he had to feel before the people who saved him, protected him, accepted him as one of their own—now to be hanged before the people who saw him as Tall One.

The Kwahadi leader emerged from the brown gauntlet and dismounted. More than two dozen of his finest dropped to the ground a heartbeat behind him.

Mackenzie was true to his word, allowing them to keep some of their ponies. Magnificent creatures, Jonah decided as he gazed at those Comanche horses. Yet—something was missing that had given this people their startling power; there were no carbines in their hands now. No pistols stuffed into the narrow thongs that lashed the breechclouts at their hips. Instead, only skinning knives—the same weapons used to slash scalps from their countless victims, trophies taken on countless raids across the entire width and breadth of west Texas. Knives . . . and their bows. A daring few conspicuously held clubs at the ends of their sinewy brown arms.

Even though they were heavily outnumbered by the rows of bayonets and the flanks of pony soldiers, even though the warriors had only those few sad weapons to pit against the powerful trapdoor Springfields and longknives and single-action army Colt's revolvers—nonetheless those two dozen warriors steadfastly stood behind their chief as he resolutely stepped into the path of the oncoming scaffold patrol and stopped. The warriors fanned out to either side of Quanah Parker, three deep to block the narrow gauntlet the guardhouse patrol had been threading toward the execution ground.

Parker himself carried no weapon Jonah could make out as the guards closed on the Comanche warriors. No more than ten yards now. The war chief bore no knife, nor a bow and arrows. No club in either hand. Instead, all Quanah had laid across his left arm was what he held in his right hand: the same fan of eagle-wing feathers he was clutching the day he rode in to surrender his rifle to his old enemy.

Anxiously glancing back over his shoulder, through the crowd and over the heads of the uneasy infantry who lined the long gravel path to the scaffold, Jonah saw a wrenlike flurry of activity among the mounted cavalry. Mackenzie's Fourth, these were—in a blue blur of movement. Then he was slammed to a halt against the soldiers in front of him as the guardhouse detail came to a sudden stop.

The detail's sergeant went through two orders of the *Manual of Arms* to bring his soldiers' weapons down from port, ready to use—either with bullets, or with those longknives at the ends of the barrels. For a breathless moment Quanah's warriors stirred uneasily, then settled again as they took courage from the impassive face of their war chief, the Kwahadi waiting for some clue as to when Parker would free them to act.

An uneasy, troubled quiet drifted down over the crowd as many of the children were shuffled out of harm's way, hurried back through the crowd. More warriors appeared, slipping out of the throng along both sides of the gauntlet as the soldiers' eyes widened, faces gone ashen. In utter silence Quanah's reinforcements turned to put their backs against their fellow Comanche—there to face the long rows of infantry who stood at the ready, like two mighty blue walls bordering what few yards remained of the dusty path taking the condemned to the crude scaffold where three new ropes hung knotted. Ready.

"He gonna ... gonna try saving you, Jeremiah?" Jonah whispered harshly, flinging the rasp of it over his shoulder as the guard detail tightened its own noose around the prisoners.

His eyes darting here, then there, across the gathered warriors, the young man answered, "Looks to be, Pa. But since he come to get me— he'll end up freeing all of us."

Then Hook wagged his head dolefully. "God bless him for trying, son—but there ain't enough Comanche here to take on these soldiers. Better'n three-to-one odds. And on the fort grounds too."

"Odds like that never stopped us ... never stopped the Kwahadi before, Pa."

The sharp exhilaration of pride burst through him, the way adrenaline would burn icy-hot in his veins when danger raised its horrid head. "Maybe we can make us a deal—let Quanah have you and the soldiers hang me and the Injun."

Jeremiah lunged up behind his father, his mouth at Jonah's ear. "No, Pa! No deals for me. If these sons of bitches going to hang you and Two Sleep, they're going to hang us all."

Twisting his head, Jonah tried to see his son from the corner of his eye as he said, "Looks like Quanah Parker's gonna have something to say about that—"

"Get me an interpreter!"

Jonah's attention was yanked back toward the Comanche, beyond them farther still to the cordon of blue. The officer barking his order strode right through the midst of his men, both cavalry and infantry, coming to a stop in that dangerous no-man's-land squarely between his soldiers and Parker's Kwahadi.

Jonah figured this had to be the one they called Mackenzie. Young enough to make a lot of generals fret with jealousy because he was already a full colonel, with his own regiment of horse soldiers—already having proved himself one of the most capable Indian fighters in the frontier army. That long bushy brown mustache hung like a shag completely hiding both his lips. Only when he snapped out his commands did he give a glimpse, a flash of tooth.

"Mackenzie?"

With surprise Jonah turned at the sound of Jeremiah's voice. "Hush, son."

"It's all right, Pa," the young man said quietly. Then called out much louder. "Mackenzie?"

"You—the prisoner—what is it you want of the colonel?" a captain nearby hollered at Jeremiah.

"The colonel don't need no interpreter. I know the tongue of the people . . . the Comanche talk. I know Kwahadi."

The captain started toward the trio of prisoners, suspicions written on his face. "Just who the hell are you to know enough of—"

"My son lived with Parker's band half his life," Jonah interrupted with a snarl.

Flicking his eyes arrogantly at the elder Hook, the captain halted by Jeremiah. "You really can interpret their language, son?"

"Give the young man a chance, Captain," Mackenzie bellowed. "Bring the prisoner here."

With a signal the captain ordered four of the guardhouse detail to peel off with Jeremiah. They nudged the younger Hook around the end of the Kwahadi warriors slowly, carefully—the tension twisting back on itself. They moved cautiously for the spot where Mackenzie and his staff waited between the two nervous sides.

Jonah watched the warriors' eyes move, following Jeremiah's progress. It seemed Jeremiah's eyes touched each one of those half-a-hundred warriors too. No words needed here as his boy greeted old friends, mentors. How proud it made Jonah feel, seeing the respect, the worry, the affection those awe-inspiring warriors showed for his son at this moment of ordeal.

"You really do understand Quanah Parker's language, young man?" Mackenzie asked when the detail halted Jeremiah before the regiment's commander. "You can translate what I have to tell him?"

"Yes."

"Spent time among them, is it? Kidnapped—a prisoner?"

"Wasn't captured," Jeremiah offered. "They saved me . . . saved my brother too, from some comancheros. The Kwahadi took us in—we was treated like their own."

Licking his dry lips, Mackenzie nodded once as if to signal his belief in Jeremiah's statement. "Tell them . . . tell Quanah I want no bloodshed here. I want him to call his warriors back and let the execution proceed."

Then Mackenzie seemed to realize that he was talking to one of the prisoners about to be executed and turned to face Jeremiah. "You . . . do understand we must go on with the hanging, don't you, young man?"

"But Quanah don't."

"That's the rub here," Mackenzie replied. "Lots of folks—some of those Comanche women and children gonna get hurt if he doesn't pull back his warriors. Tell him he can't win—"

Then Jeremiah turned away, interrupting the soldier chief's warning, speaking in the tongue that instantly drew the attention of the Kwahadi warriors, quieted the last of the murmurs among the spectators.

In low, hushed tones Quanah and Jeremiah spoke back and forth for several minutes while the infantry anxiously shuffled their dusty boots, the cavalry horses pawed at the ground, and the sun continued its fall beyond the far end of the earth. Summer's shortest night was to arrive in a few days, Jonah knew. But he would not be alive to enjoy it. This, his last sunset. With Gritta out there still. Somewhere. Out there with the man Jonah had sworn to kill with his bare hands.

For a few moments Jonah wished he had never found the boys. Had he not been riding along with Captain Lockhart's company of the Texas Rangers, young Zeke would not have died in that winter-dry arroyo. Chances were good that Quanah Parker's band of Kwahadi would still be packing around those two white boys who had grown up Comanche. Zeke would be alive—happy and content: a husband and father.

And Jeremiah would not be standing here in these last rose rays of the sun, waiting to strangle at the end of a rope.

Cursing himself, Hook felt vile and dirty to his core, able to save only one of the four he had set out to find many years before. Now Hattie would be the last. The only Hook left. Lord, he prayed with what taut fiber was left within him, give Hattie the strength to go on without family—'cause she's a lot better off without a father who brought this misery all down on his blood. Help her find other folk, and get shed of the past, help her leave behind the Hook in her.

As he opened his eyes from his prayer, Jonah found the war chief signaling to the crowd of Comanche. An old man hunched forward in a twisted, shuffling gait, a large leather pouch slung over his shoulder. It rocked gently against his left hip, the fringe along the bottom swaying in time with his ungainly, arthritic stride.

He did not hear the words that Parker spoke to the old man, yet Jonah stood in rapt attention as Jeremiah let his manacled hands hang motionless, his head bent slightly while the old wrinkled one pulled some objects from his bag and began his magic making. With his bony fingers he quickly mixed earth paint and grease, smearing his potent symbols on Jeremiah's forehead, the bridge of his nose, the bones of his cheeks, and finally his chin.

The soldiers, while once anxious and impatient, now watched totally entranced.

When the old man had shaken his rattle all round Jeremiah's head and face, taking special care to touch the young man's throat four times, he stepped back. Quanah stepped closer, reaching to the back of his own head to remove the single eagle feather he wore in a single braid. This he tied in Jeremiah's long, loose hair.

When he stood back, surveying the young man with approval, Parker whispered to Jeremiah, who raised his face to translate.

"Quanah says all is right now. While you're gonna take my life, he and his people have protected my soul."

"What does he mean—all is right now?" Mackenzie demanded, consternation knitting his forehead.

At that moment Jeremiah did not have to explain a thing. All Mackenzie and his soldiers had to do was watch Quanah signal his half-a-hundred warriors back from the gravel path, reopening the long gauntlet leading to the scaffold steps.

"Just what I said, Mackenzie," Jeremiah replied. "Quanah decided there won't be no blood spilled here today."

Still cynical, the colonel asked, "And he's protected you with his hocus-pocus?"

Instead of answering the officer, Jeremiah turned to his father. "I'm ready now. Ready to die with my pa."

Mackenzie sighed with an impatient finality as the last of the warriors cleared the path. "Very well. Sergeant of the guard, proceed with the execution."

Jonah stepped aside to let his son lead them those last yards up to the stout, square beam where the three nooses hung, waiting for the coming shadows of dusk. Jeremiah was the first to trudge up the steps, moving slowly in his leg irons, having to shuffle clumsily, planting both feet on each step.

Then Jonah turned and motioned Two Sleep up the stairs. He hoped that being the last up on that platform, he would be the first to hang. Seemed logical for the moment, since the soldier who stood alone up there by the trap handle was nearest the last empty noose.

Jonah stopped beneath its shadow and stared through the loop of oiled hemp. Praying it would snap his neck clean. Praying he did not dance as most men fear doing. He looked over to see the lone soldier with them on the scaffold step up behind Jeremiah, pulling out the first black hood from under his arm.

Dragging the chain connecting his leg irons, Jonah hurried to reach his son, stood facing Jeremiah. Seeing the tears in the boy's eyes, the fear in his face.

"I'm here with you, Jeremiah. All the way to the end."

"I don't wanna . . . I can't! Not like this—"

He seized the youngster's manacled hands in his, their chains ringing together. "Son—listen to me close: you remember how brave you was when you and Zeke heard white men was riding down on your camp last winter?"

Jeremiah's eyes narrowed. Wagging his head, his voice cracked as he whispered, "I don't understand, Pa."

"You was a Comanche warrior, son. You'd said your medicine that morning and you was ready to go fight—even die—to protect your people."

"Yes, Zeke and me—we both was."

"Can you remember that feeling, Jeremiah?"

"Feeling?"

"How you was brave enough to ride into the mouth of all them guns the enemy was shooting at you?"

He swallowed hard, for the longest time his eyes searching his father's face. "I remember."

"You keep remembering, son." He squeezed Jeremiah's hands, hard. "For the next few minutes you keep on remembering the courage it took for you to jump down into that snowy ravine—ready to fight the white man with your own bare hands."

"That was you, Pa."

"Dammit, Jeremiah—remember the courage it took?"

"C-courage?"

"There ain't no greater courage than what my sons—both of you—had that day."

Taking a deep breath, Jeremiah squared his shoulders, blinking tears from his eyes as they spilled over, coursing down the paint smeared on his cheeks. "Yes. Courage."

"You got even more courage to show this day, Jeremiah. Show them all this is a good day to die."

He pursed his lips a moment, squeezing them into a thin line of determination before saying, "I'll see you again, Pa."

Suddenly pulling his son's arms close, Jonah leaned awkwardly against Jeremiah in the best embrace he could make of it, letting Jeremiah nestle his head against Jonah's shoulder. "Yes, Jeremiah—we will see each other again real soon."

When he finally took a step back, the soldier pulled the hood over Jeremiah's head, slowly enough that Jonah had one more good, long look at his son's eyes. Clear now. Shining with resolute courage.

As Jonah trudged back to the far side of the Shoshone, he reached out momentarily to grasp Two Sleep's manacled hands while the soldier dropped the noose over Jeremiah's head.

The next hood fell past the Indian's eyes, followed by the rope tightening round his neck, drawn snugly at the base of the skull as the soldier went about his work with steely, methodical precision.

A young infantry soldier waiting on the top step handed the executioner the last hood, then turned to leave the platform. Jonah was to be the last. He watched from the corner of his eye as the black, suffocating hood approached.

"Colonel Mackenzie!"

Hook jerked up in surprise at the voice. The entire parade ground appeared to hold its breath, all save for the executioner, who clattered to a halt behind Jonah in the hushed stillness.

"You there! What business do you have with Colonel Mackenzie?" demanded an officer with the colonel, flinging his voice over the murmuring crowd toward a tight band of civilians working their horses through the parting bystanders: man and woman alike, causing no little commotion as well as a great deal of angry cursing from some of those soldiers being shouldered aside by the horsemen.

"I damn well come on the government's business—that's what it is to you, sonny boy!" growled the civilian in a dust-caked, broad-brimmed hat as his weary, lathered horse cleared the edge of the throng and came to an abrupt stop right before Mackenzie and his staff. He leaned forward on his saddle's horn. "I take it you're the commander of the Fourth Cavalry?"

"I am," Mackenzie answered. "And who would you be, sir?"

"A Texan who's come a long ride of many years chasing Quanah Parker." He pointed up at the three hooded men on the scaffold. "So I'll be damned if I'm gonna let you hang that red-skinned son of a devil without me laying eyes on the bastard at least one time while you've still got him breathing."

"In God's name—I'm not hanging Quanah Parker!" Mackenzie gasped in anger.

The civilian shook his head, his back to the scaffold. "Out to Texas— we heard he come in and surrendered. Saw you fixing to stretch a few necks, so I hurried over, thinking it had to be that half-breed devil's whelp."

"Just three horse thieves . . . uh, mister?"

"Captain, it is, Colonel Mackenzie." And that's when the civilian in the big slouch hat turned for the first time to study the platform. Enough to capture a fleeting glimpse of the last man the executioner hooded.

Jonah himself caught just a flicker of the captain's face as the soldier dragged the black sack roughly down over his eyes, causing Hook an instant sensation of suffocation. How he wanted to cry out in despair, but bit down on his tongue—knowing the hood wouldn't muffle his words. The rope dropped over his head as he heard the civilian roar.

"Hold on there just one goddamned minute, Mackenzie!"

"That's Colonel Mackenzie to you!" shouted some angry staff officer. "What jurisdiction do you have—"

"This," the civilian interrupted. "This is all the goddamned jurisdiction I need."

There arose a renewed murmur from the crowd.

"All right, Captain," Mackenzie said. "I'm listening. Suppose you go ahead and tell us what it is that you want us to hold."

"This hanging you're about—that's what in blue hell I want you to hold up!"

Jonah listened, his heart thundering in his chest as he heard the restlessness take hold of the anxious gathering that circled the scaffold, heard the snort of the civilians' horses, and finally some hooves plodding closer. Not just one horse—more . . . maybe as many as a half-dozen horsemen easing up to the side of the tall scaffold.

94

Then more of the soldiers were voicing protest against the brazen civilians, their protests immediately answered with some profane challenges issued by what he took to be more of that band of dusty civilians.

Even more hooves pounded up, all coming to a halt below Jonah's feet. A big band of them, he breathlessly thought. From the sounds of it.

"Lift that goddamned hood, soldier," the captain's voice ordered.

There followed an uneasy moment of eerie silence as Jonah waited under the thick, hot veil of darkness, the sun's light no longer touching the side of his face.

The civilian shouted louder this time, "I won't ask it again, Colonel Mackenzie."

Eventually Jonah heard Mackenzie give the order. "You heard the man, Sergeant. Lift the hood."

As the suffocating cloth came up, Jonah gulped air, not sure if this was an answer to his prayer, or only a cruel, momentary reprieve. Blinking his eyes with the fading brightness of coming twilight, he cleared them of stinging tears, then forced himself to look down at the group of better than twenty-five dust-covered men who sat atop their trail-weary horses at the foot of the scaffold. All had their pistols out, as if to prove they weren't about to be bullied by the likes of Mackenzie's Fourth Cavalry, by damned.

Every last one of them. These—the tried and tested—were there at Jonah's feet, smiling up at him. Faces tanned like saddle leather, those long droopy mustaches and red-shot eyes he had grown so accustomed to over last winter's long, agonizing weeks of search and wait and prayer.

Hook never thought any bunch of iron-tough bravos could look this good to him as he openly began to cry.

"Shit, Jonah," growled Captain Lamar Lockhart, Company C, Frontier Battalion of the Texas Rangers. "What kind of mess you gone and got yourself into this time?"

10

"BEND OVER, WHORE!" the white demon snarled at her. "I want you like a bitch in heat."

He cuffed her again, along the side of her head, where he had hit her more times than she could remember. Chung-li Chu'uan knew Bak Sahm would be angry if this American barbarian bruised her so badly that she was unable to work for a few days.

But as quickly, she silently cursed Bak Sahm. He cared only that she would not bring in money. He was not the sort of man who could ever care on a human level what the customers did to his girls of joy.

Roughly grabbing her at the hips, the man bent her in half and shoved his hard member against her buttocks. He hammered against her unsuccessfully a few more times.

"Spread your legs, bitch. I'm coming in there whether you ready or not."

Reluctantly, she obeyed, sensing him immediately enter. Back and forth he drove, sinking himself deeper with each successive stroke as he began to grunt. With each of those noises of the pig he made as he ground himself into her, the man slapped her upper arms, swearing at her, pummeled the back of her head with the flat of his huge hands, bent against her to rake that big smelly mouth of his along the top of her shoulder.

Whimpering with the sudden fire of pain, Chung-li flinched. Her tensing was instantly answered by another cuff on the side of the head, this time with his balled-up fist. Laughing quickly, the demon fell back to grunting behind her.

She squeezed her eyes shut to all sight, as if attempting to close off all the pain the way she could shut out all light.

Chung-li prayed someone would remember to ship her heart and eyes, the bones of her arms and hands, all of it back home when this white demon finished killing her. Those were the sacred parts of her body that friends were supposed to send home to family in China when a Celestial was killed far away.

Far, far away here in the land of the Gold Mountain.

Silently, she began to sob, choking to keep him from hearing her. A bitter cry—knowing she had no one who would care enough to remove her heart and eyes, to strip the flesh from the bones of her arms and hands, then place them in a sacred red box to send them back to her family. No one.

The crippled one, that Bak Sahm, he would as soon leave her in the alley behind his store. In the alley, to let the dogs eat what was left of her.

Hadn't he already grown so angry many times before, threatening to sell her away to one of these barbarians? He would tremble as he stood cocked to the side, balancing on that one good leg of his, shaking the only arm left him that would move, the only one that would follow his bidding, while Bak Sahm screeched at her—vowing to sell her to one of the smelly cow-eaters.

A person always smelled of what he ate. Maybe even the cow-eater who had her now. Yet this demon could not be one of those who dug in the ground for the gold. Chung-li knew he was different—if only because all the rest were not really mean. They were merely men who took what they needed of her body she kept whitened with rice powder and rouged for her paying visitors, the sort of men who left her be until they needed her again.

Not this one. This barbarian would kill her before he was done.

How she wanted to think on home. It was all she had left, and her heart ached so for it—because she no longer had even a place to return home to.

One night years ago the people of her village had come across the dark land, come for Chung-li's sister, who could no longer hide the child that grew within her belly. The villagers stalked toward their house out of the night as dark as a demon's mouth, their fiery torches dancing in a zigzagging wave against the black flames from a dragon's nostrils. Come to the house where lived the pregnant woman who had no husband.

When the attackers drew close enough, her mother and aunt told all the children to hide where they could beneath the floor. Chung-li found only a place behind a small box as the villagers began to pelt the house with mud and stones. She listened as outside other villagers slaughtered the family's stock: hearing the squeal of the pigs as their throats were slashed, the squawk of their prize rooster as its neck was twisted, the grunted wheeze of their only plow ox as it was gored repeatedly until it fell silent.

Then the first of the buckets of blood was thrown through the windows. Their only door crashed open, and more blood sprayed into the room in a great, arching cascade illuminated by the dancing saffron torchlight.

Suddenly the villagers were in the house, as suddenly as Chung-li realized they would not be content merely with killing the family's animals. They gathered just inside the doorway with their knives and hatchets dripping with blood . . . and she knew they had come to kill her.

For the moment they found the chest containing the clothing and shoes, the combs and brushes that belonged to Chung-li's older sister. Everything came flying out—to be ripped apart and smashed, all that belonged to the pregnant woman.

All of it to the accompaniment of shrill curses laid upon the house and its inhabitants, "Pig ghosts leave!"

Other attackers took her grandmother's newest silk weaving and hurled it into the fireplace, where it smoldered at first, threatening to put out the fire—then of a sudden it was hungrily possessed by the blaze. That done, the villagers turned to breaking every pot and platter they found, scattering the duck eggs Chung-li's mother had been pickling, dumping all the fruits and vegetables, everything tumbling across the floor tracked with crimson sprays, foot- and handprints of blood.

"Broom ghosts never live here again!"

And when they finally left, the villagers took the last of the sugar and the family's bowl of oranges, with that fruit to bless themselves in an ancient ritual after entering such an evil house on that errand of grave necessity.

It was late that very night that her sister went into labor. And as darkness came down on the village the following evening, the woman gave birth to the infant she would kill within moments of its first breath.

A daughter. Its mother mercifully killing it, and herself too. Throwing herself down the village well.

This was no world for a woman. No matter if it was back in

Kwangtung Province. Or this Gold Mountain, where she lived now to pay off her debt to the men who shipped her here from Canton.

Not long after coming to the First City, she had been advised to change her name, to hide who she was from the spirits. To make it harder for the ghosts to find her shame here in the land of the smelly barbarians.

"Take a new name," she was instructed. "Guard your real name with silence."

But she hadn't. Her name was all she had taken with her when she fled China. All she had come here with. She bravely kept her real name, brave—but scared. And so she always walked a crooked path, like the streets of Chinatown in the First City. Crooked walking, false names—it all served a purpose to hide from the ghosts that haunted the unwary in this land of the barbarians.

But the ghosts had not been fooled. They found Chung-li. That's why she was a girl of joy instead of a wife. Instead of a mother. No longer was she someone's daughter, or sister, or niece. In China, or even here—a female was cursed by the spirits.

The white demon flung her away from him as he quivered his last, finally spent inside her. Slapping her buttocks, heaving her onto the bed where she had been supporting herself, he snorted—studying her face. With his softening erection the hairy man settled on the edge of the bed beside her and picked up one of Chung-li's tiny feet. He inspected it casually, sniffed at the bandages, and drew back as if repelled by the odor of the dying flesh.

She thought that strange, since this white demon ate the dead flesh of cloven-hooved animals. Cow-eaters.

Drawing her knees up, she sensed his cruel liquid seeping out of her, growing cold on her buttocks. It was good that it did purge itself from her. Chung-li reached for a red silk gown, the one he had ripped off her back to paw at her tiny breasts, to bite them until she knew he would chew off the nipples, and cried out in great pain. They would hurt her before the night was done. He tore the silk gown from her hands, threw it to the floor.

"You stay naked, bitch!" Then, a moment later, he spoke somewhat softer. "First time I ever poked a Chinee, you know," he told her.

Then he rose to his feet, his erection softened, but still long, wagging as he strode over to the small table where he picked up the glass bottle. Inspecting what he had left of the amber liquid, the demon swilled down a long and healthy draught.

"Chinee ain't no different than a Injun woman," the man continued, and drank between prospering his monologue. "You wasn't half-bad, lil' Chinee woman."

Though her eyes were closed, she heard him return, felt him settle beside her, his weight causing the rope-and-timber bed to groan as he scooted down the full length of her naked body. Chung-li kept her eyes closed, not wanting to look at him again, not wanting to remember his face in the slightest. Wishing he was already gone. No matter how soon he closed the door in his leaving, it would not be soon enough.

She heard the creak of leather, and next felt the smooth coldness of metal on the inside of her thighs. A jarring sensation that he ran from her knee all the way up to where she still dripped his wetness from her. Where that too was going cold.

Cracking open her bruised, swollen eyelids, Chung-li watched the demon stroke the pistol's barrel up and down the inside of both her thighs. He would stop each time he neared the deep cleft he had made moist with his poison. There against her pubic bone he worked the pistol back and forth as she gasped against the weapon's cold hardness.

She kept anticipating the worst, waiting for him to shove the barrel inside her without warning. But instead he withdrew it each time from her cleft, choosing only to drag it back down the inside of her thighs.

"I gotta be going before sundown," he said. "My business is finished here for now."

Very few of the demon's words did she understand. Only the intent, the sinister, soul-shaking power in the voice.

"But I'll be back. Try to make it soon. Maybe when I do, I'll buy you for a whole night, instead of them greaser whores I been buying from your li'l Bak Sahm boss man. I come back and got more time, we'll have more fun, li'l Chinee girl."

By the time he had finished what was left in the bottle of whiskey and clumsily dressed, Chung-li was hurting. Her swollen face pounded with every pulse as he swayed side to side, pulling on his tall boots.

"Want you to remember your night with me," he leaned over and whispered in her ear with a stinking gush of his breath.

She could not see him well, both eyes all but swollen shut.

"Remember my name is Orrin Haslam," he growled as he rolled her over roughly onto her back, then bent his head to gently kiss each of the bloody nipples he had bitten in his mating heat.

"I ain't had near as good a poke from a woman since the colonel brought us back west. Them others—Injun and nigger gals—they really didn't shine next to you, Chinee doll. So I think when I take word back to the colonel that this Pioche is a good place for us to lay low, a place where Brigham Young can't sniff us out—I figure the colonel will want some poking with you himself."

He took his belt knife out of its scabbard and stood weaving over her. For a terrifying moment Chung-li saw the glint of steel, certain he was going to plunge it into her chest. Instead he leaned forward, reached out, and slashed off a chunk of her hair.

"Now, this—I'll show this to the colonel. So he'll believe Orrin Haslam has found a good thing here in Pioche. Found me a Chinee whore he'll wanna try out his own self."

Stuffing the lock of her hair into a shirt pocket, the man reached the door before he turned to gaze at her.

"I'll bet you'll remember me, darling—next time you see me. 'Cause I'll be back with the colonel. And you'll damn well remember the colonel when he gets through poking a good whore like you, Chinee doll."

The white demon opened the door. Notes from the sick, out-of-tune piano floated up from the smoky first floor.

"You think you been handled bad today by Orrin Haslam—why, you just wait till you meet Jubilee Usher!"

"It was this goddamned badge that got Mackenzie to listen, that's what!" Lamar Lockhart explained to Jonah Hook.

It had been more than five hours now since that Saturday sunset, since that black hood had dropped over his head. Since he had felt the first rub of the thick corded hemp drawn tight around his neck. Yet Jonah still occasionally found himself sucking air as if it were the sweetest elixir on the face of God's earth. At times he even stuffed some fingers inside his own dirty collar and pulled—that too a little tight for a man just yanked right out of the hoary paw of death.

"You came to see Quanah himself?" Jeremiah asked. He rose from the ladder-back chair and stepped to the tall, mullioned window that allowed the moon's shine to wash into the adjutant's quarters, where a single oil lamp spread a gossamer glow from a small corner desk.

Jonah watched his son gaze out that window, as if Jeremiah were straining to penetrate the dark of that night and see the Kwahadi village.

"To lay eyes on that Comanche myself," Lockhart agreed. "We got word he'd come in—surrendered his people. Most of 'em anyway. Give up his ponies too, so we was told down in Texas."

"That was something," Niles Coffee offered. He served as sergeant of Lockhart's Company C.

Deacon Elijah Johns nodded his old white-maned head and added, "When them brown-skinned fornicators give up their ponies—you got 'em whipped."

"Only way you're gonna ever beat horsemen the likes of them Comanche," June Callicott said, "is to keep 'em from ever forking legs over a pony ever again."

The Ranger captain's droopy mustache swished like a corn-bristle broom from side to side as he tongued his chew. "Still can't believe we come riding up in time to see you wearing a army necktie, Jonah."

"I suppose you hadn't been curious to see that Comanche with your own eyes after all these years, I'd be watching all this from the pits of hell right now," Jonah once more grumbled his gratitude.

"So you figure the devil's gonna take you?" John Corn asked.

"It's for sure the good Lord won't!" Clyde Yoakam roared, leading some of the others in spontaneous laughter.

"Don't be so sure," Deacon Johns snorted. "For all his sinning ways—Jonah Hook's about as moral a man as they come out here. God bless."

"Thank you, Deacon," Jonah replied. "I owe you, owe you all a great debt, for saving the three of us."

"Weren't us what saved you," Niles Coffee said. "It were the truth what set you free."

Lockhart nodded. "Mackenzie saw the truth in what we told him about you serving with us out to the Panhandle when that band of horse thieves was just beginning to work their evil across the reservations."

Callicott said, "Took us some explaining, but the colonel finally realized the men he was about to hang couldn't be his horse thieves—if you and Two Sleep was with us late last winter out on the Staked Plain."

"By damned," Harley Pettis chimed in, slapping a hand on Two Sleep's shoulder, "this Injun is about the best redskin a Texian can do to ride the river with."

"Suspicious, Mackenzie was for a while," Lockhart added, "what with learning Jeremiah there was running with Quanah Parker at the same time we was tracking his band of Comanche." Lockhart looked over at the youth, who clung by the window, gazing into the night.

"He gonna be all right, Jonah?" asked Billy Benton in something next to a whisper.

Jonah glanced at Jeremiah. "Yeah. Everything all better now that we didn't drop at the end of a rope. Now that we can get on with what we intended to do here at Fort Sill all along."

"What's that?" asked Wig Danville.

"Look over Quanah Parker's people—them what come in with him to surrender," Jonah answered.

"What in God's name for?" demanded Callicott.

"See if we can find Zeke's woman . . . his wife. I want to find my daughter-in-law. Want to see my grandchildren."

Deacon Johns tamped shag-leaf tobacco into the black, crusted bowl of his well-chewed briar pipe and asked, "After you do, what's next under your saddle?"

"Same thing I was doing when I come to the Texas Panhandle and hired on to Company C: go on to find my family. Still got my wife out there."

They were men who would understand. Not a man in that room, indeed not a single Ranger in Company C, was without kin either kidnapped, raped, tortured, or killed by Indians. Not one of them what rode with Lamar Lockhart remained untouched by tragedy. Every last one of them knew real, close, personal loss. They had lived with loss.

So it didn't surprise Jonah when the captain offered, "Why'n't you think about running with us for a while? Pay ain't all that much—"

"But the powerful good company sure makes up for it!" Niles Coffee interrupted with that grin of his as big as the Staked Plain itself.

Jonah wagged his head, as much as he might need the companionship of good men as much as most anything else. "Thanks, fellas. But . . . I see my grandchildren—I'm heading on west from here."

"What's out there?"

"She is. My wife."

The room fell eerily quiet, most of them suddenly shoved back into their own thoughts of family, blood or marrying kin. Not one of them without a painful memory of someone dear to his heart. There was a weighty heft to that sort of pain, a heft that was palpable as the beating of a loved one's heart when they were in your arms. So it was that those nervous men shuffled their boots, cleared their throats, not sure what to say to one another for the moment. Not sure what to say to Jonah Hook.

Lockhart eventually broke the silence. "Anything we can do, you let me know. You send word—anything I . . . any of the boys here can do. Just ask."

Jonah took the captain's hand, sensing a sour ball of sentiment rising in his throat, his eyes stinging. "You all done about all a man could ever ask of another. You saved me. Saved my boy and the Injun from the hanging rope."

"God bless but I never seen the army apologize afore," Deacon Johns said with wonder.

And Callicott agreed. "But Mackenzie bent over backward to apologize. Him returning your goods to you. Even had the surgeon look at the old leg wound for you."

Jeremiah suddenly spun around and spoke to the surprise of the whole room. "Told the sonsabitches my pa was shot by the real horse thieves! But no one at that trial wanted to listen to the truth."

Quickly crossing the floor to the window to join his son, Jonah laid his arm across Jeremiah's shoulder, feeling the youth shudder with pent-up rage. "Truth will always come out, son. Your mother taught the three of you that."

Jeremiah finally nodded, looking into his father's eyes. "You and me—we got to find her, Pa."

"We will, son. Come morning—I'll go with you to look up Zeke's wife. Soon as I get a chance to hold them grandchildren in my lap . . . I'll be ready to ride west again."

Jonah drew his son into a fierce embrace, speaking so the rest of those men in the room heard. "Jeremiah, there ain't yet a rope, or a bullet been made—what'll kill Jonah Hook before I find your mother."

11

THIS WAS SOMETHING he swore he could taste—sour and metallic, something rotting with a cold emptiness.

Jonah swallowed hard, fighting down his own immense sadness at the
despair of these Comanche, forcing himself to look down into all the
empty eyes that gazed up at him as he and Two Sleep followed Jeremiah
through the trees toward the clearing where they entered the fringe of the
outer ring of lodges. Curls of oily smoke rose above the skin-and-canvas
cones on that cool morning air. A breeze danced with the coming warmth
of the sun. It would be hot again today.

But at least the three of them were free.

Again he remembered how Two Sleep had stood by stoically as Jonah
and Jeremiah embraced, once Mackenzie ordered the prisoners freed.
Brought down from the crude scaffold still in their leg and wrist irons by
the soldiers, led off to the post commander's office. And there it was all
sorted through by the colonel and his staff, prodded by the impatient
insistence of Captain Lockhart and the men of his Company C.

There followed those sweet words, ordering the manacles and leg
irons removed, the trio's belongings and animals returned.

"You understand why we're confiscating the horses you stole from the
thieves—don't you, Mr. Hook?" Mackenzie had asked.

"You can take the rest, but I'm due one of 'em, Colonel. One's
mine."

The colonel eventually replied, "To replace what they took from you."

"It's only fair," Jonah had said evenly.

"Yes. It is only fair," Mackenzie agreed. "That, and our apologies for all . . . for the seriousness of our mistake."

"Just want the horse. Only what's coming to me, Colonel. Then I'll be on my way come morning."

At dawn he tried to interest Jeremiah in some of the bread, beans, and bacon the army cooks laid in heaps on their tin plates, served there in the mess hall illuminated at that early hour only by lamplight. But his son took only one of the empty cups a soldier deposited at their end of the long table, clattering his armload of tins atop the pine planks before that same soldier poured some steaming coffee from the huge black pot another old soldier carried up in a cloud of fragrant steam.

"Just some coffee, Pa," the young man said when Jonah told him he should eat before they set out.

He worried again now—it had been so long since he last saw Jeremiah take any nourishment. What with the day of their execution drawing ever nigh, a man naturally lost his appetite. Maybe as far back as Thursday since the boy took in some food. No, Jonah couldn't blame his son for having no hunger still.

Even now—this Sunday morning, Jeremiah had more important things on his mind than bacon and beans and biscuits. They were going in search of family as soon as the sky ballooned with light. Jonah had promised Jeremiah they would seek out the village as soon as the sun began its rise in the east.

This Sunday morning. In so many ways like so many others without number, Sundays he had watched Gritta going through her ritual of preparation to take the children into Cassville for services at the clapboard church. A brimstone Methodist, the minister was. An ardent, fiery disciple of John Wesley. How Gritta loved going to church meetings in town, for this was the first community in all her life where a minister came and stayed. All the rest of the Bible-thumpers, those who had preached back there in the Shenandoah Valley, and those come and gone here in their early years in southern Missouri, they had all been circuit riders. Forced to cover ground, to shepherd many flocks.

So each Sunday Gritta took special care to bathe the children in that washtub there on the hearth by the stone fireplace, then dress each one in the very best they had—for this was truly a church, with a real preacher

106

who ministered to the spiritual, emotional needs of his community—indeed, ministering to the whole county, so it seemed.

How hungry these black eyes that peered up at Jonah in want. Must be how that preacher saw things standing up there in his pulpit, looking down on all the spiritual starvation.

Here he saw the same look in all the eyes. Even the eyes of those ribby, mangy dogs slinking out of the way as the three horsemen moved slowly through the lodges. His nose turned on a gust of breeze. This was a place where the stench clung tenaciously to the ground and refused to leave. Again Jonah was reminded of the wisdom in the nomadic life.

Yet there was no more of that life for these people.

"This ain't Quanah's band," Jeremiah said with some disappointment bordering on exasperation when he reined his horse around and rode back to talk quietly with the two who followed him. He had asked questions in Comanche of a few men—though most everyone in camp regarded young Hook with undisguised suspicion.

"Didn't seem to me like you knew any of this bunch," Jonah said.

"Big Red Meat's band. Seen some of them before, times gone," Jeremiah replied. "When the bands got together for a hunt, or gather up for winter camp."

"Where we find Parker?" Two Sleep asked, acting uncharacteristically impatient.

"Bet the Injun don't feel all that welcome, Jeremiah," Jonah offered.

The younger Hook grinned warmly at the Shoshone. "I understand, Two Sleep."

The Indian answered with a grin of his own. "One Injun to 'nother Injun, Jeremiah?"

He nodded, then jogged his head off in a different direction. "I'm told Quanah's band camped over there. On up the creek, to get as far away as they can from this swamp here—where more and more of Big Red Meat's people been getting sick."

Jonah wagged his head. "From the looks of it, worse thing is these folks going hungry."

"Some'll starve," Jeremiah said, "when the Comanche don't have buffalo to hunt." He sawed his reins around, easing his horse away toward the thick border of trees at the creek's edge.

He knew his son meant nothing personal by it—but Jeremiah's words couldn't help but sting. The boy knew his father had spent a long season hunting buffalo up along the right-of-way owned by K-P Railroad in

Kansas years ago. The work had paid him good money, enough for Jonah and cousin Artus to prosper.

That memory of Artus in those happier days—not the way he had last seen his cousin: burned and bloated, butchered beside the iron tracks punching across the central plains toward the far western mountains. No, more and more Jonah tried to remember family in happier times. How Artus grinned while he gigged a frog of a summer night. How the young-ster's eyes danced when he spoke about one of the girls down the road toward town, the one with brown pigtails and freckles, the one he was sweet on. It was best to remember Artus like that.

There was more than enough sadness to go around in Jonah's life. While he still was able, Jonah vowed he'd keep what sadness he could at bay. Keep it out there beyond arm's length. Just on the fringe of his campfire light. Enough sadness, Lord knows.

Enough to make a man begin to believe he might truly be going slowly, slowly insane.

They had just cleared a thick stand of leafy trees and entered a small, narrow meadow where the wood smoke hung thick above the morning cook fires when the first screech split the air. Jonah tensed immediately, the Shoshone beside him bringing the carbine off his lap.

All about them the clamor grew quickly, talk Jonah did not under-stand: a clipped, guttural tongue—man, woman, and child alike. People crowded forward in brown waves, everyone talking, pointing, clapping hands over their mouths. Many of the men stared in disbelief, others wagged their heads in confusion, a few glared with open haughtiness. And all the while the women increased their trilling ululation, that unrestrained keening.

It seemed every woman's eyes streamed with tears as the gauntlet surged forward to engulf Jeremiah. A hundred or more hands like a field of tall grass strained, reaching out to touch him.

Was it really he? Tall One! Returned home to his family and friends after so long.

"Way they're acting," Jonah said quietly to the Shoshone riding at his side, "you'd think Jeremiah was returned from the dead."

Two Sleep looked at Hook. "He is."

Not too sure what to make of that and the noisy, emotional reception, Jonah followed Jeremiah on across those yards as they reached the center of the camp crescent opening to the east where the sun had climbed above the shortest of the trees across the creek. Ahead of them Jeremiah was led by two younger boys not yet in their teens, each lad with a hand clamped around a length of Jeremiah's reins. Guiding him toward the far end of camp, each boy as proud as if he were leading tribal royalty itself.

The crowd's van ground to a halt, parting slightly as the boys brought Jeremiah up, stopping him before a half-dozen middle-aged warriors, most of them already naked to the waist with the warming of the day.

As soon as he stepped forward, extending his arm to Jeremiah, Jonah knew who the tall war chief was. Not that any man, from Colonel Ranald Mackenzie down to any one of Captain Lamar Lockhart's band of Rangers, had described the Kwahadi chief to Jonah. All through that time Hook had spent on the plains of west Texas, he had never heard of any white men who claimed having ever laid eyes on this Comanche chief, and lived to tell of it.

But no matter that—Jonah knew who this was.

Clasping his forearm against the Comanche's in solemn greeting, Jeremiah slid from the back of his horse, ripping the floppy hat from his head, the better to show that he had not shorn his hair in white-man fashion. They stood before one another, Jeremiah and the war chief. Surprised that he had not really noticed before, Jonah marveled that his son stood almost as tall as Cynthia Ann Parker's half-breed son.

Tall One. They had given Jeremiah a good name, these Kwahadi who took his boys in and saved their lives.

Jonah felt the lump grow in his throat. Thinking just how wrong he had been in cursing these Comanche those many cold nights, vowing revenge those many days he searched for some sign of Quanah Parker's band. When it had been these very same Kwahadi who had saved the lives of his two boys.

Jeremiah turned to him, waved. "Pa, c'mon over here."

Kicking a leg over, Jonah was surprised to find a boy at his side immediately, holding out his hand to take the white man's rein. Leaving his horse in the youth's care, he moved through the parting crowd, then came to a halt beside Jeremiah.

"Pa, I want you to meet the last great chief of the Comanche. This is Quanah Parker," Jeremiah announced as Jonah nervously held out his hand. "Quanah—this is my father: Jonah Hook."

"Jo-nah," the Kwahadi war chief echoed, holding out his own hand, taking Hook's and shaking vigorously.

Quickly gazing over those closest in the crowd, Jonah asked, "Which one . . . which of these fellas rescued you? Become your father, Jeremiah? I wanna meet him."

As he said it, Hook saw something like the black belly of a summer thunderstorm cross his son's face. "It's all right, Jeremiah. I only want to tell the man my thanks for all that he done by you—"

"He was killed, Pa."

"Killed?"

"The morning the white men—you—Lockhart's Rangers and the soldiers from the north—the morning our camp was attacked."

"How?"

"Quanah says he was guarding the retreat of the women and children, staying behind to take the bullets and hold off the soldiers."

"Women and children?" Jonah asked, suddenly remembering. "Do you know?"

"Yes. She's here. Zeke's children too. They come through a hard time of it, Quanah says. But the strong ones held on and lasted."

Hook found his eyes bouncing over the crowd, trying out each of the young female faces, looking for a pair of youngsters about the right age, youngsters who might look a little like their father. Then Jeremiah tugged on his sleeve.

"Pa?"

"What, son?"

"There." Jeremiah said it softly, pointing, as most of the crowd parted while Quanah and some of the older warriors moved the villagers back, opening a path.

He was stunned by how dark she was. How utterly beautiful she was with that gleaming black hair, those almond-shaped, oriental eyes. The full lips that moved slightly as if she were giving quiet instruction to the small boy at her side clad only in moccasins and a breechclout as he clung to her leg, clutching her right hand. Astride her left hip, suspended in the cradle of the young woman's other arm, sat a second child. No more than a year old.

The more he blinked, the worse it became. These goddamned tears stinging his eyes. Likely the bright light from that rising sun didn't help, making his eyes water this way, Jonah thought angrily. Swiping at his drippy, offending nose, Hook cleared his throat as the woman stopped near Jeremiah. The two of them spoke quietly a moment after he knelt to hug the children—the youngsters' eyes wide, plainly filled with confusion. The boy especially, his gaze locked on Jeremiah, as if he ought to know this white man. Then the young boy's eyes found Jonah a few feet away.

Turning his head this way, then that—he studied Jonah hard. Eventually he pulled away from his mother's hand and moved bravely toward the white stranger. Jeremiah followed. Behind him came the woman.

"Pa, this is Prairie Night. She was Antelope's . . . Zeke's wife."

Suddenly very sheepish in her presence, the sight of her brought back to Jonah a flood of memories of Grass Singing and Pipe Woman. Then he remembered and quickly dragged his shapeless hat from his head. The young woman's eyes ran back and forth over his face, studying him, as if finding so much in the father that had been in the son.

"And these two, Pa," Jeremiah said, his hand locked benevolently around Jonah's elbow, urging him forward, ". . . these are your grand-children."

It wasn't like any of the fevered grappling he had experienced in the brush. Not this sweet, delicious coupling with Prairie Night. Not the way it had lasted almost from the time the children fell asleep last night, until now as the early-summer sun was turning the sky to gray far, far in the belly of the east.

Jeremiah had never felt so much a part of this circle of life, a part of family and these people who had been his whole life for many a winter. Season upon season. And through those exquisite moments of sweet torture and sexual bliss Prairie Night had shared with him, Jeremiah time and again entertained the notion of how right it would be to remain behind. Here, where he felt such a sense of belonging.

But each time he cursed himself for that selfishness. He had family still out there. This matter was not finished for any of them. Not him. Not for his father. And surely not finished for his mother.

As much as he yearned to make each coming night just like the one he had enjoyed with Prairie Night within the circle of this dark lodge fragrant with their lovemaking, Jeremiah knew he could not.

And so he tried to explain it to her. Why he was leaving. But would return. It would not be like Antelope's going—for he, Ezekiel, would never return.

More difficult still to explain why he and his father had taken Antelope's body away from the battlefield, realizing now the extent of the terror she must have felt when the Comanche returned two days later to bury their dead and salvage what they could from among the ashes and heaps of black char left in the wake of the pony soldiers. With pooling eyes

Prairie Night told Jeremiah how the People had come back to that cold, lonely place to find the corpses of those few warriors the others were forced to leave behind—each body severely mutilated by the soldiers' Tonkawa scouts.

"Antelope was nowhere to be found," she told him against the reddish glow of a dying fire in her tiny lodge last night.

He had comforted her, and in so doing Jeremiah had found comfort in her. Prairie Night's touch, the way she gave herself to him as if he truly were her husband now. As if, as she reassured him again and again, what Comanche custom dictated could also be much, much more. What she had felt for Antelope, she said she would soon come to feel for Tall One.

She promised to love only him now. Yet Jeremiah was certain she told him that to keep him there, as afraid as she was that he would be taken from her for good, the way she had been abandoned before by Zeke. Realizing that she spoke more out of fear and a desperate need than from love, Jeremiah nonetheless wanted to believe she could love him.

More than anything else, he thought now as she lay sleeping, nestled in the crook of his shoulder, Jeremiah wanted someone to love. More that than someone to love him. Far deeper than that. He had something still within him that made him restless beyond reason to find someone to give his heart and his very soul to—completely, without reservation.

He knew his father loved him. That was without question as far as Jeremiah was concerned. Jonah had come for him. Come for Zeke too. Across all the miles and seasons that became half of Jeremiah's life—Jonah had come on, headstrong and unswayed, to find them. He had no doubt of his father's love.

Even no doubt of his mother's love. As far away as she was now, in miles and time—he sensed something of her inside him each time he thought on her throughout the day, throughout the night. Like this night he spent with Prairie Night. Wondering as he moved in and out of her, feeling, kissing, caressing her breasts and thighs, kneading her round buttocks and biting the curve of her neck where it blended into the shoulder . . . wondered about his mother even then.

Wondering if this magic of man and woman united with such fire so briefly was the selfsame magic that drove his father onward across the seasons and into the wilderness. Jonah could have taken any number of women to be a new wife. But he had not. Something compelled Jeremiah's father, drove him on through the days, on into the unknown.

So now Jeremiah had a better understanding of what it was that pulled his father west to complete this quest begun so long, long ago.

One of her work-toughened hands found his limp flesh, handling it tenderly. He was startled when he quivered slightly at her touch. He had not been aware she was awake.

Prairie Night raised her head and gazed into his eyes as he grew hard, quickly heated for her. He caressed her breast gently, yet most insistently.

Running her lips nearly the length and breadth of his chest, she looked into his eyes again. "You are going," she said quietly. "I know. I must accept."

"If I could stay—"

But she put her fingers against his lips and silenced him. "You cannot stay. Your mother needs you. Not only your father. She needs you to come for her too."

"But your family?"

"Is your family now, Tall One," she replied. "I will hold your promise to return tight, like a fist, here in my heart. Believing that you will come back to us, this family, one day soon."

He let his eyelids close. This was so hard to do, he decided. These choices of the heart. Once more he could not believe how hot he was growing in the palm of her hand as she moved over him, rising above his hips, ready to mount his rigid flesh.

These things that men do out of desperate need, he wasn't sure if he would ever understand. To be pulled apart by two great loves at once— this simply was too hard for him to understand. To have this woman give herself, her heart, to him.

While feeling this gnawing need to follow his father in that quest begun so many years before. Something Jeremiah had to do as family.

She bent over him, her long hair spilling on either side of his face, tickling, her mouth seeking his. Open as it found Jeremiah's, willing to receive.

Moments later when she began to gasp, began to rake at his chest with her fingernails, Prairie Night stammered, groaned, trying to accept.

"I am yours now . . . Tall One. Come . . . please—please come back to me."

12

July 1875

S HE WATCHED THE cloud of rage pass over Jubilee Usher's face as
dark as winter thunder. Darker than Gritta could remember his face
ever becoming.

His eyes glowed like twelve-hour coals burned down to no more than
pockets of searing heat. In a blur his hand caught her by surprise. As she
pitched to the side, reeling, the hammer of his blow resounded like an echo
in her head.

He hadn't hit her with an open hand, as before. This time Usher had
balled up a huge fist.

Now he reached out and dragged her up from the dirt, lifted her
completely off her feet, then savagely drove his fist into her face again.

Black seemed to seep into her like molasses from the crock. Dark,
thick, sticky.

But again he wrenched her off the floor, beginning to grumble his
curses at her. Gripping her shoulders in his two great hands, he shook her
like a limp rag. His face inches from hers, screaming, his rage striking her
like hammer blows.

Across the width of their tent wall he flung her so she landed atop the
trunk, sprawling backward into the small table, where her tin washbasin
spilled over her. Then he headed for her, kicking things aside, clearing a
path to get to her, dragging her by an ankle out of the wreckage, brutally
yanking her up to her feet, only to hurl her back across the tent.

In the numbness and the pain, in her stark terror, Gritta could not make out much of what Usher shrieked at her. Only fragments of words. Shredded remnants, as he was shredding her clothes, ripping them from her.

"Why don't you act like you feel something for me?" he bellowed at her. "Go ahead—hate me! Anything, even hate. Even that! Damn well feel *something*!"

He had her dress and camisole ripped cleanly in two, exposing her fully to his eyes, naked to his fury. Usher lunged for her, tearing aside what was left of the sundered clothing so he could roughly manhandle her small breasts, kneading them so hard she winced in pain.

Gritta swallowed down the ribbons of hurt as he squeezed down on her bruised flesh. So she would not make a sound, she threw her head back, biting down on her lower lip. He saw her prideful act, slowly cocking his arm to backhand her in a blur.

With the strength of his blow her body arched backward, and she felt the inside of her cheek open up, oozing and warm at the back of her throat, wondering—strangely—if he had loosened some of her teeth.

As he fell atop her, she tried arching her back against his weight. He pinned her down, driving two of his fingers inside her without warning. Usher probed and stroked as roughly as any of his men would handle a green-broke colt. The blood at the back of her throat gurgled, but she swallowed down the moan and the warm fluid both, refusing to let him know how he hurt her with his unrelenting cruelty.

What he took for giving her pleasure.

His huge hands encircled her throat, rising over her until she felt him ram his hardened flesh inside her. He choked, shoved, jabbed, all in concert. Feeling her eyes rolling back in her head as she struggled to breathe, Gritta clamped her hands around his wrists, struggling to pull. She did not want to die like this, not with him inside her as her soul departed for heaven. Not wanting to die so dirty, to die with his profane violation of her. Even if her soul spent eternity in hell itself.

With a burst of laughter he took his hands from her throat. Air shot back into her lungs like a heaving bellows. Already she could feel the painful rings of bruise encircling her neck like a stack of nooses.

He continued to laugh and grunt over her, thrusting his hips against hers, jamming, driving her small frame across the dirt floor of the tent with each assault he made within the woman. Roaring just the way he always did when he climaxed in her, Usher's growl became one of unrequited rage. She thanked God that he was done with her so quickly.

But of a sudden he was squatting on his knees between her trembling legs, his softening flesh in his hand, groaning.

In frantic desperation he stroked himself, hard—almost as brutal as he had been with her, trying to restore his erection. Mumbling, he cursed his disobedient flesh. Swore at her.

The passionate betrayal in his eyes plainly told Gritta he blamed her for his failure to satisfy himself in her. So he did what had always worked before: hit her with the back of his hand, punching her with one of those balled fists, torturing her breasts and savagely manipulating her tender moistness with his fingers.

Still the erection did not return.

"You! You did this to me now!" he roared.

She did not know why, but Gritta became suddenly frightened.

"You robbed me of my pleasure—in taking you. In hurting you!"

It did not help when she glanced down at his limp flesh, seeing how he pulled and stroked, all to no avail. Her seeing him so lifeless only drove him to new madness. More desperate still. Then he yanked up her hand, wrapping her fingers around his penis, using her touch to stimulate him. Yet the flesh lay as weak as ever.

Roughly he flung her hand away and clambered to his feet. Dragging his underwear and britches back in place, Usher buttoned them in a furious hurry. Hovering above her, he turned slightly, and the frown disappeared.

Gritta saw what had caught his attention.

He strode over to the corner. From the wreckage where she had stumbled in his beating of her, Usher pulled out their child—that helpless infant with its stuffed body and the painted face.

Whirling on her, he spat, "You care only for this!" and knelt beside her all-but-naked, battered body. "Not me. No, you don't even care for yourself!"

He shot to his feet, towering over her again, holding the infant out at arm's length. "We'll see what you care about now," Usher vowed. "The Lord giveth . . . and the Lord taketh *away*!"

With his empty hand Usher patted his pants pockets quickly, then fumbled over the four pockets of his vest—until he found what he wanted. Dragging out a sulfur-headed match, he taunted her with it.

As painful as it was to move, Gritta struggled onto one elbow, her breath seizing in her throat. Sudden terror clutched her heart in a cage of cold claws. How she wanted to scream—but hadn't allowed herself that release in all these years he had possessed her.

Terror paralyzed her—realizing what he intended to do.

That look on his face, the sickening pleasure in his eyes as he dragged the tip of the match across one of the vest buttons. The lucifer spit a burst of red, then flared in the late-afternoon light: a glowing, dancing head of blue and yellow at the end of the stick.

"The child I gave you—I can take away," he snarled at her, almost too quietly for her to hear.

Beginning to shake her head, Gritta sensed the gall rising, the warmth of the blood bubbling back of her lips. Then she was trembling, unable to move, frozen to the spot as he slowly, tauntingly moved the match ever closer to the infant.

Held that dancing flame beneath the hem of its dirty, discolored christening gown.

Where the blue and yellow caught, sputtered, smoldered a moment before holding on to race up the length of the infant in a veil of yellow flame.

"No!" she shrieked long and loud, lunging for the child. "No, no, no, no!"

With a shocking blow from the back of his right hand Usher drove her back. She stumbled and fell, scrambled to her knees, and fought her own torn dress aside to rush him again.

This time he connected her cheek with his fist, spinning her, dazed and seeing flecks of bright light, back against the wall of the tent.

By the time she shook her head clear, blinked enough to see him across the dirt floor, Gritta saw the child completely engulfed in flame. Usher dropped the infant to the ground.

Mumbling incoherently from her swollen, bleeding lips, she crawled forward on her belly, clawing, hurrying as best she could to reach the babe before it died. Suffocated and burned to death.

But suddenly the back of her head itself seemed on fire.

Grabbing a handful of her yellow hair, Usher yanked her from the ground. Shaking her like a child, he hurled her to the crude bed, where she twisted about, in desperation lunging out for the smoldering, shapeless form engulfed in flame on the ground, oily smoke rising to blanket the top of the tent.

Then he was over her—kneeling at the side of the bed—laughing, grunting in that way of his, his rigid flesh out of his britches once more, peeling her thighs apart roughly and positioning himself for the one thrust that he always used to plant his terrible weapon inside her.

Gritta winced as this demon rammed himself home once again, never tearing her eyes from the last smoking remnants of their infant. She began to gag, her stomach revolting, and turned aside to vomit as he thrust harder still. How she hated him for killing their child.

Now she had crossed a point of no return, able to realize there was something still sane enough in her to recognize she was past all hope of ever being completely sane again. She had crossed a line somewhere just now—someplace where she could never return. And now, no matter how calm and sane she might act outwardly, Gritta realized she was irrevocably crazed.

She did not hate Jubilee Usher.

What she felt for him was something much, much worse. Hate could not begin to describe the black depths of passion she held for this man who had killed their child. Left it to die on the ground as he violated her again.

As if expecting her to create another child for him, with the very real danger that he might take that one from her too. First Jeremiah and Ezekiel gone. Then Hattie torn from her. And now the infant that had suckled so long at her breast. Usher did grant, but more often he had taken away.

Now he was back with a fury, rigid and rutting her—expecting Gritta to make them another child in womb.

She tasted the acid from her stomach as it heaved its last, vowing his demon seed would not take hold inside her, would find no nourishment from her body.

Her eyes filled with tears as she watched the shapeless blackened mass burn itself out on the floor into a pile of char. Vowing to kill herself before she would create any more life that Jubilee Usher could destroy.

The only pleasure that was left her—Gritta realized as he finished atop her, squirming and grunting while he exploded inside her womb—was that she would be able to see the look in Jubilee Usher's eyes as he watched Gritta take her own life.

The sudden rain fell so hard against his hot, parched skin that it felt like he was stabbed with cold needles of pain. Driven straight at them the way the rain was, this storm hurt, battered, beat at a man until he struggled on breathless and weary, cold and without heart.

It was the way of weather out here on the southern plains. He had moved along the faint, trackless traces enough over the past few years to know that. Out here the midsummer's heat and moisture were both roiled about by cold air slipping south, tumbling off the great rolls of northern prairie. Like the dark purple strap muscles along the backbone of a buffalo, low clouds clung to the far western horizon at first. Plain enough to watch it headed their way, the first thin wispy sheets of rain began falling in the distance. As that storm came around and blew into their faces, the veil of rain quickly turned palpable, like the ragged curtains hung in those windows, so like empty skull sockets, back home.

The winds swung around a little more to the north, picking up muscle until the rain no longer merely fell from the sky. It seemed to be coming straight at the three of them. Not that there was anywhere to go out here on this crossing from the Texas Panhandle country, a little north of west toward what he knew was called Colorado Territory. West of that lay the land of the Mormons.

It was the place to start now, almost seven years after he had lost Jubilee Usher's scent among Brigham Young's faithful. A trail gone faint, if not outright vanished in thin air.

But Jonah had learned enough as a boy about hunting, learned enough as a man out here to know that when you were tracking your quarry and you lost the trail, a man always doubled back until he picked up the trail again. He failed at that, then he doubled back again if need be.

Until you felt your way along what trail there was to get a sense of where your quarry was headed, how the critter was moving through the timber and along the side slopes of the hills. Until . . . yes—you were thinking like your quarry . . . and knew where he would go next. Only then could you expect to pick up the lost trail somewhere else down the line. Only then could the hunter count on recrossing the trail of the hunted, miles away.

Maybe even seasons, and years later.

Because it was July here on the southern plains, the rain and the cold brought some relief. They were the better part of two weeks out of Fort Sill now, leaving Haworth's Kiowa-Comanche Agency and Jonah's daughter-in-law. Zeke's young wife. His two small children, one still so small she nursed at her mama's breast.

How goddamned proud he was of his boys. Ezekiel dying to protect his people. His family. And now Jeremiah. Torn as the young man was between his two families: called to go find and put back together the one he was raised with . . . called as well to return to the bosom of a new family he would raise with Prairie Night.

Like Jeremiah, Jonah had taken his daughter-in-law in his arms that dawn they rode away from Quanah Parker's Kwahadi. He had embraced the girl, then remembered young Gritta when they had been married under the shadow of Big Cobbler Mountain in the Shenandoah back in fifty-four. Gritta had been no more than fifteen. Prairie Night no more than that herself.

Then as Jeremiah spoke in hushed Comanche whispers to the young mother, Jonah had swept his toddling grandson off the ground, slipped his infant granddaughter into his other arm, and clutched them to his breast, dearly.

Now in the cold, painful, driven rain of this trackless waste, Jonah remembered how his little grandson had looked up into his moisture-filled eyes with wonder—and ran a tiny, grimy finger down Jonah's cheek, tracing the path of the grandfather's tears.

"Likely he ain't never seen a man cry before, Pa," Jeremiah had explained, slipping up beside his father that morning they had ridden away from the broken hoop of hide lodges. Jeremiah's own arm had clutched the young woman, she clinging to him with both of her arms, refusing to let Jeremiah go.

Here in the wilderness again, he licked the rain from his lips, the ends of his shaggy mustache. Recalling how he had bent his head over his granddaughter's dark, pudgy face, kissing her own little Cupid's-bow lips. Remembering how the girl's eyes widened as he drew back, gazing up at the white man in wonder. Jonah gave the babe over to Prairie Night, then picked up the toddler once more, held the boy out at arm's length, gazing into his face as if to carve every detail of it into memory.

At the last, knowing he could not put it off any longer, Jonah kissed his grandson's forehead, then set him back on the ground at his mother's side. He bent to kiss Prairie Night a last time on the cheek, touched the woman's chin, and turned away.

"Let's go, Jeremiah," he had said, taking the reins Two Sleep handed him. "Before that sun breaks the horizon."

Flinging himself into the saddle, Jonah hadn't looked back. Instead he had sawed those reins hard away, keeping his back on Jeremiah's little family as the two of them rolled their horses and pack animals into motion. Jeremiah would come, but by not looking back, Jonah gave his son the privacy he was due.

They had crossed a hundred yards, then two, before he heard the hammer of the hooves coming up behind them. Jeremiah reined his horse down from the lope on Jonah's offhand side. Not once since had he ever spoken of that painful farewell from the woman—from his own family.

There had been too damned much tearing of flesh from flesh in Jonah's life already. Yet now he had three where before there had been only Ezekiel. With those babes back there among Parker's Kwahadi, Jonah felt certainty that Zeke would live on. In them, and through them. Jeremiah would see to that.

It had taken him all these days to work up courage now to ask, "What . . . what's their names, Jeremiah?"

The younger Hook looked at his father with confusion crossing his clean-shaven face, his soggy hat brim flapping and furling in the fury of the prairie storm.

"Whose names, Pa?"

Jonah swallowed and looked away, feeling the hot sting of tears in his eyes, the cold needles pricking pain across his cheeks battered by the rain. "My grandbabies."

Jeremiah smiled gently.

"The little girl is named Good Road Woman. Because now Quanah's people must walk the white man's road."

"And . . . the boy?"

"Your grandson is called Antelope Soldier."

"Is . . . is he named after his father?"

"Yes, Pa. He was named after a brave warrior."

After a long time in thought Jonah finally said, "Zeke's with us, you know, Jeremiah?"

"I know, Pa. Zeke's with us till the end of this long ride to find our ma—together."

13

" '*V*ENGEANCE IS MINE *saith the Lord, and I have repaid.*' "
John Doyle Lee shifted nervously in his courtroom chair, watching the testimony of one of those elders high in the Church: Philip Klingonsmith, the former bishop of Cedar City.

"It is your testimony that those were the very words Brigham Young spoke upon visiting the massacre site in 1861," the government prosecutor asked, "four years after the Fancher party was murdered?"

"Yes," the big, solid Dutchman answered. Six feet tall and well-muscled, Klingonsmith was nonetheless phlegmatic, and therefore deliberate with his responses, halting to the point of appearing slow. "It was a cold May morning, with ice on the nearby creek," Klingonsmith recalled. "A large pile of stone the army had raised as a cairn had tumbled down some. A wooden cross stood on the top of it, engraved with the words: 'Vengeance is mine and I will repay saith the Lord.' For a long time President Young stood staring at that cross raised on that bloody ground by the Gentile soldiers . . . then he said—'Vengeance is mine saith the Lord, and I have repaid.' "

The prosecutor inched forward from his table, stopping halfway toward the witness chair, which sat beside Judge Jacob S. Boreman's bench.

"What did President Young say after that?"

"Nothing."

"Not another word?"

"No."

"Nothing to explain what he meant by his statement of the Lord taking vengeance?"

"No."

"Did Brigham Young and your party immediately leave the meadow?"

"No."

"If not, what took place?"

"President Young raised his right arm at the tall stone cairn and just pointed. He didn't have to say a thing. In five minutes there wasn't one stone left upon another."

"You tore the soldiers' monument down?"

"Yes, sir. Brigham didn't have to tell us what he wanted done. We understood, every last one of us."

"Just the way you each understood—every last one of you—that Brigham Young wanted that party of emigrants butchered at Mountain Meadows?"

"Objection!"

Lee realized the government was doing its best to prove that the massacre of the Fancher party bound from Arkansas to California was not a random act of violence by the Paiutes of southern Utah Territory. Instead the prosecutors appeared determined to prove that the Church and its leadership were involved at the highest levels. Even unto the Prophet himself.

Lee hung his head as the government's attorney battered away at Klingonsmith—nearly every question eliciting some sort of objection or another from Lee's attorneys. If John Doyle Lee was one of the foot soldiers of God, indeed a foot soldier of Brigham Young himself, then Klingonsmith was one of that holy army's officers.

Some three years after the Prophet's fateful visit to the massacre site, John Doyle Lee had been eased out. In May of 1864 word had come from Salt Lake City that it would be best for Lee to resign his position as presiding elder of Harmony Branch. For most of his adult life Lee had been an obedient servant of the Lord, Joseph Smith, and Brigham Young, both God's Prophets. He remained obedient and stepped aside, thinking that would be it. Losing his position would be all the sacrifice the Church would ask of him to atone for his role in the massacre.

Little did Lee know he would one day be the lamb placed upon Brigham Young's altar.

Year after year had passed, but still the talk continued. Bit by bit more and more damning evidence bubbled up. Public disapproval of those who took part in killing caused one after another of the massacre participants to flee Utah's Dixie. Some went north to Idaho. Others south to Arizona, farther yet to the new settlements Brigham Young wanted established in Mexico. And by 1870 sentiments within the Church itself led to the formal excommunication of Isaac C. Haight and John Doyle Lee.

Yet even this Lee had accepted stoically, believing that once his Church had renounced him, that would be the last of it. Hoping he could go on living his life with his wives and children. To live out the remainder of his years known as the one man among the many who had bravely shouldered more than his load. Asked by the Lord's own messenger on earth to carry that heavy cross.

He had always done what Brigham Young asked. No matter what.

Then less than four years later in 1874, Isaac Haight was surprisingly readmitted into the Church. It wasn't until this past spring that John learned why Haight was so blessed, and why he himself remained beyond the pale of Prophet Brigham Young's forgiveness: Haight had accomplished the unthinkable—transferring the full responsibility for the massacre to Lee, claiming Lee was the leader of those Mormons who murdered the Fancher party.

"Haight's only crime was in not restraining John Doyle Lee," was the Church's new and official position in forgiving and reinstating Isaac Haight. "He had been cut off from the Church on account of a misunderstanding of the president about his course in the Mountain Meadows massacre after which all his former blessings, priesthood, washings, anointings, and endowments were restored fully by the instructions of President Young."

An outcast, a stranger in his own land, Lee continued to suffer in silence. But now it was becoming more than clear to John that the other parties concerned should be brought forward for a hearing, to be forced by the Prophet to shoulder their own sins just as he had owned up to his. As many times as he had prayed over it—Lord knows John Doyle Lee was willing to bear his own responsibility for lives not saved years before—he was not about to submit quietly, carrying all the blame for those others who committed the massacre. Lee had even appealed all the way to the Prophet to be given a rehearing with Elder Erastus Snow, counselor to President Young.

Instead of support from the Church he had served loyally, Lee found an anonymous letter stuffed in a chink at the home he shared with Rachel long weeks later:

John D. Lee
Dear Sir:

If you will consult your own interest, and that of those that would be your friends, you will not press an investigation at this time, as it will only serve to implicate those that would be your friends, and cause them to suffer with, or inform upon you. Our advice is to make yourself scarce, and keep out of the way.

There was no signature on the letter, yet Lee knew it had been a warning from Erastus Snow himself, written upon the orders of no less than Brigham Young.

Ostracized by the last of his friends, excommunicated from the Church to which he still clung, Lee was ordered to the mouth of the Paria on the Colorado River, where Brigham Young instructed him to operate the river ferry. There he built his family a small house, cleared a spot for Rachel's garden, and christened the spot "Lonely Dell." Lonely it was, but here John Doyle Lee prepared to live out the rest of his days in seclusion.

How much pain he had shouldered alone, only he would ever know. Once a man of some note among his people, Lee had owned land, cattle and sheep, impressive houses in several towns, even a mansion of sorts at Washington, Utah. After the Prophet turned his face from him, Lee lived in the wilderness, colossal red walls rising around him, where the silence almost crushed a man's spirit.

At Lonely Dell Jubilee Usher once more found his old friend.

Where Usher first began to speak his blasphemy.

What bitter medicine that talk was to John Doyle Lee—but listen he did to the tall, charismatic, persuasive Danite.

"The Prophet has shown his true colors," Usher repeated. "See how he throws you to the government's wolves, instead of standing strong and protecting all who have defended the Church."

"But . . . I cannot—"

"You can't what?" Usher demanded. "Can't implicate others?"

"I wouldn't think of it."

"Why the devil not? Does the Lord our God mean you to shoulder this by yourself?"

"If not God, then the Prophet himself asks it of me."

"And he is next to God," Usher sneered, "is he not, Brother Lee?"

"Yes. I will obey Brigham Young."

"And obey him you shall . . . until he is proved to be the false prophet."

"No, Jubilee! Don't let me hear you speak your blasphemies! Bad as my lot may be—I will not be the means of bringing troubles upon my own, God's chosen. You must remember: we are people scattered and peeled, a people whose blood was shed in great streams in Missouri."

"Missouri! Missouri!" Usher shrieked. "Great gouts of blood are still to be shed over Missouri, Brother Lee!"

John shook his head in the remembering. "Blood shed only because we worshiped our God in the way He revealed to us."

Usher had looped his great arm over Lee's shoulder. "Is it true the Indians at the massacre called you 'crybaby'?"

"Yes," he admitted to the Danite. "They called me *Nah-gaats.*"

"I say for you to dry your tears and take the Lord's strength to gird your loins for the coming battle," Usher proclaimed.

Lee hadn't known just what battle Jubilee was referring to until now. Hadn't even deliberated on it when he was arrested last November. But now John was seeing the set of things coming clear. To hear these lies coming under oath to God.

Klingonsmith was the first to break the blood pact sworn to by the massacre participants. Likely the Dutchman had struck his deal with the Church, then come forward, presenting himself to the prosecution—offering to turn state's evidence. That Friday morning, the first of Lee's trial, the muscled Klingonsmith had related how the Mormon militia had been mustered and hurried to the scene of the Indians' siege of the emigrant train, testifying that he had seen only men killed from his vantage point when the butchery started.

Then he told how the fate of the Fancher party had been discussed later, even unto the highest levels in the Church, from Cedar City and Parowan to Salt Lake City.

"As if Brigham Young himself knew of the plans to sacrifice the emigrant train?" the prosecutor demanded now.

Klingonsmith chewed on it. "That was our understanding at the time."

"And what of President Young's later involvement?"

The former bishop pulled at his collar. "First week of October—not long after the massacre—John Lee and myself had an audience with President Young. In Salt Lake City."

"What was discussed with your Prophet?"

"The massacre. Mostly the disposal of the emigrants' property."

"Brigham Young decided himself how to accomplish that?"

"Yes—everything but the cattle. President Young said John Lee was a good farmer, the best they came. Said that John Lee should handle dividing up the cattle among us folks down at Parowan."

John looked over the jury box again. Three Gentiles, eight good Mormons, and one Jack—what they called a nonpracticing Mormon. There was no telling how the twelve of them would vote when all the case was tried. Rumor had it that word had come from Salt Lake City: no good Mormon must be found to testify.

Indeed, besides those eight called to jury duty, there were no Mormons to be found in that courtroom.

Lee turned slightly in his chair, steadily growing more uncomfortable in his wool suit, hot as it was this latter part of July. In looking over the near-empty courtroom peopled only by some half-curious Gentiles, there in the last pew at the back against the clapboard wall, John saw him.

Jubilee Usher smiled benignly, his eyes crinkling. His long black hair streamed in neatly brushed plats down the front of his freshly brushed frock coat.

Grinning in that big-toothed way of his.

As if to say to John Doyle Lee that everything was going according to plan.

Usher's plan to shake Brigham Young right down to the Prophet's very foundation.

The Gentile prosecution had taken five days to present its case against his friend John Doyle Lee.

With each day of testimony Jubilee grew more satisfied that the Federalist government had done its best to prove Lee should not have to shoulder the blame for the massacre alone. A damning indictment of the Church and its false prophet. Then the defense team of Wells Spicer and William W. Bishop began to pick away at the tight-knit fabric of the Mormon hierarchy, calling forth those who would show how Church officials had inflamed local passions against outsiders at just the time the Arkansas emigrants rolled through on their way to California.

So Usher had not expected it all to be the exercise in futility Lee's defense turned out to be. Now in the second week of August the jury appealed to Judge Boreman for assistance—they were going nowhere with their deliberations. On the ninth, after five days of argument and stalemate, the jury admitted it could not reach a unanimous decision.

The eight Mormons had voted for Lee's acquittal. The three Gentiles and the Jack voted for conviction.

Disappointed, Usher had pinned his hopes on seeing Lee found guilty. If he was, then Young's henchmen within the Church hierarchy were every bit as guilty. But events hadn't worked out quite that way.

"I am angry now," Judge Boreman instructed the subdued assembly in excusing the jury from its duties. "The previous weeks have been a waste of this court's time. I have no choice but to take this under advisement and schedule a new trial for the defendant—before another jury."

That same Monday evening Usher stood across the street from the Beaver jail and watched as Lee was escorted out to the street, manacled hand and foot as guards herded him into a waiting carriage. The courts were not even going to wait until morning to get their prisoner hurried out of town. Government officers were taking Lee north to the new federal penitentiary in Salt Lake City, where he would await his new trial.

"Right under Brigham Young's nose," Usher hissed as he approached the carriage in the lamplit darkness. And got as close as the armed officials would allow anyone in this emotion-ridden Mormon town.

Jubilee smiled benignly at the two guards who kept him some six feet from the prisoner as the carriage swayed slightly, its driver settling himself atop his seat, taking up the reins to the four-horse hitch.

"Perhaps he'll visit me," Lee said, leaning from the window to speak to Usher as he raised his wrists with a rattle and scratched at his nose.

"Don't dare mention me to the president, John," Usher warned. "Let me be a surprise."

"For now," Lee said.

"And when you return, I'll have you officiate at my wedding."

"The corn-haired woman?"

"Yes," Jubilee answered, his teeth aglow in the flickering light of those lamps held aloft from many hands.

"The same one . . . the sad woman?"

"She is the one given me by the Lord, Brother Lee," Usher proclaimed.

"I will remain steadfast in the Lord," Lee said. "You would do well to do the same, Brother Usher."

"That is precisely why I have undertaken the path my feet now trod."

"But the woman. Back in Missouri . . . you told me she belongs to—"

"She is given to me," Usher snapped, then leaned forward a bit so that he could speak more softly. "Just as the throne of the Prophet is given to me."

"Your words are blasphemy, Jubilee!"

"When will you learn, John? It is not blasphemy to speak the truth about a false prophet who leads our people astray."

"Blasphemy! I cannot hear such talk about President Young . . . blasphemy!"

The carriage lurched away suddenly with a snap of the reins and a creak of the running gear. Usher watched Lee's face framed at the carriage window until it disappeared into the summer night.

"It is not blasphemy," Usher repeated. "This is the will of God!"

14

B AK SAHM WISHED the merchant back in Kwangtung Province
would hurry in sending him the devil herb he had ordered—that
divine mushroom of immortality. It had been more than a year and a half
since he had sent his money to Canton, waiting breathlessly for the mushrooms to come in the shipments that arrived every two months from the
coast.

And every two months Bak Sahm sent gold back to the coast, the
remittances of coolies and Chinese miners trapped in these mountains,
money they had promised to wives and families back home. All over the
west, in Chinese laundries and dry-goods stores, in joss houses and opium
dens and houses of joy—the Celestials turned over most of their earnings
to businessmen who profited in shipping home to China the twenty-dollar
gold pieces from the shores of the Gold Mountain: America.

He ruled what the barbarians called Little China here in this Nevada
town. The most profitable of Bak Sahm's business ventures had to be the
loh kur chigh, the bawdy house where he sold whiskey and the flesh of
women to any man with enough for a drink or the price of a woman's body
in his pockets.

If he had paid more attention to his grandfather when he was younger,
Bak Sahm might have learned more from his venerable ancestor—like
memorizing the finding chant he could use to locate his own sacred
mushrooms. But he doubted these hills produced any of the dream-

inducing mushrooms. Not enough darkness in those forests above the town. This soil was simply not rich enough.

From the window where he sat looking out on Hoffman Street, Bak Sahm looked due south to the far side of town. There below the ridges that rose in bare, gutted steps toward the far mountains sat the immense smelters with their tall stacks belching smoke into the west winds. Just below smelter row lay the string of iron rails and cross ties that first brought him to Pioche—the Nevada Central Railroad.

He cursed the railroads—the *poot poot She'eh*—those smoking buggies that had stolen so much from him. Stolen so many years, along with this useless arm and the withered, crippled leg. More than half his life wasted as a prisoner in the Gold Mountain. Yet he had no one else to blame. Bak Sahm had made himself a prisoner here in the land of the barbarians.

After all, he had come to regard gold and money every bit as highly as the barbarians did themselves.

Never wanting to be a fisherman, much less a farmer, Bak Sahm had always cultivated bigger dreams. Dreams that seemed to feed on him as much as he fed on them. He lived a dream that was consuming him. With the opium now, and the bodies of the women who worked for him—he somehow kept the dreaded dragon at bay. Season by season.

Now the weather was hot again, and he had the girls keep their windows open. Which meant they were all assaulted by the smelters whenever the wind shifted out of the south. This was not at all like Canton with its twisted, narrow lanes of the old city. Here in this season the winds made a man yearn to flee, to head into those mountains, where he found the air sweeter.

But it had been many, many seasons since Bak Sahm had left town. Instead of going where the winds blew sweet, he always slipped into the back of his dry-goods store next door to the saloon. It was there he joined the others in smoking the pipe. Sweet forgetfulness. Enjoying the dreams that let him conquer his own devils.

How he wished the diviner would arrive. Bak Sahm had dispatched a considerable sum of money to the First City, asking to engage a diviner who would come to Pioche, to work in his saloon and entertain his customers. Bak tore his eyes from the murky yellow smudge of smoke clinging low over the smelters, staring down at his right thumb. A good diviner could tell a man's fortune from the whorls in a finger rubbed on an inked pad, then rolled on rice paper. From the pattern peculiar to every man yet dictated by the gods, a diviner would be able to tell Bak Sahm what his fortune would be every morning when he came downstairs for tea and breakfast.

Most of all he wanted to know what would prove to be the best day to approach the woman—to tell her he no longer wanted her to work as a girl of joy. When best to declare himself to her. But that sort of thing was so delicate a matter that he could not trust himself to determine the right timing. Such etiquette had to be divined by the gods. When his fortune stood just so.

Then he would tell her he wanted to make her his wife.

No matter that she said she found him a cruel, thoughtless employer. Why didn't she realize he had to be harder on her than the rest, even the other Chinese?

After pulling on his loose drawers, Bak slipped into a freshly laundered white silk shirt, then finished by selecting the long red pelisse, the gown that reached his knees. He buttoned it all the way to the neck in proper Manchu style. Stockings were next, and finally the soft shoes. Once he had tried the boots these barbarians wore. That was long ago when the hundreds gambled with their lives to lay iron rails through the far, far mountains. But the white demons' boots hurt his feet, and he, like the other coolies, continued to wear what Chinamen wore the world over. No matter the weather. No matter the terrain. No matter the demon country where they found themselves imprisoned.

It seemed like a lifetime since he had tasted a pear, an orange or mango, a peach or plum. Such fruit was found in the rich Pearl River delta. But not here in the land of the barbarians. In his homeland left far behind, the night came down and the quick pulse of the delta slowed, silence covering the water and land, where a barking dog could be heard in twenty villages at once. Here the noise grew louder at sundown when men poured out of mines, came down from the clanging, belching smelters. Night was when Pioche roared.

At first Bak found it hard to be understood in teeming Canton when he had first arrived, come there wanting to travel across the Sea of Lions to this land of the Gold Mountain he had heard so much about. He had journeyed from the farthest reach of the Kwangtung Province, so his Sinhwui dialect was rougher than the purring, pure Cantonese.

But somehow he was understood, and he was made to understand where he was going. Bak got on the boat that guaranteed no return to China. No matter. It had been an evil time for his long-suffering homeland. An era of bad luck had Kwangtung in its grip.

Every field, every stream, every mountain and valley, every well was dominated by demons that controlled the air and water, and the earth itself. Dragons—they alone controlled fire. The fortune and welfare of a man and his family, perhaps an entire village, depended upon propitiating those demons. And if the demons were not satisfied, then that village might be laid to waste by another, rival village. When attacked, the women and children were corralled in a fortified place, the *wai,* in the center of the village, while the boys and men went out to battle the bands of robbers and pirates that raided throughout the delta. Hundreds of men perished in these internecine wars, and sometimes whole villages disappeared.

Bak Sahm wondered if his village still stood. If he still had a family back home.

It was something else that no longer mattered. He would never return home, not with the dragon's curse put on his body. He would be forever ashamed of the arm and crippled leg.

Truly, the dragon did rule the fire.

Bak Sahm had teased the dragon for seasons on end, helping the white demons build their railroads through the high mountains. He had proved himself capable with the barbarians' dynamite, using the magic of the dragon to blast away great chunks of the mountain so the crews of coolies could lay their iron rails.

But he should have realized the dragon never really slept, nor did it ever forgive a mere mortal coming to use its magic for his own. One day, as Bak hung in the basket suspended from a ledge far above him, the dragon drew its revenge.

His work demanded that he be lowered by a crew of twenty men in the basket of woven reeds to plant dynamite after other crews had drilled the holes for his charges. That day, just as he had done countless times before, Bak Sahm lit the fuses and tugged on the message rope to the ones above. That was the order to pull him up from the side of the granite cliff.

But this time the basket rose only ten feet and no more. Ten feet from the hissing, smoking fuses. Desperately he tried to free his basket from the sharp outcrop where it was caught. The crew above him frantically jerked on their lines. Until the dragon roared.

Over and over he remembered tumbling out of the basket as the granite wall came spewing out at him. As if the slippery rock were itself the dragon's own scales and the monster were inside the mountain, come back to life—spitting fire and shaking a mere mortal from its body.

He lay in a crumpled heap at the bottom of the cliff, where the rail lines would themselves be laid a matter of days later. Four coolies got to

133

him as soon as they could, soon enough that they did not have to cut off his arm and leg. Still, the leg did not heal strong, and the bones of his arm mended with a crook, tied as it was against his body.

The dragon had spoken. The monster awakened.

Bak Sahm had looked into the eyes of the dragon and realized he would never put the monster to sleep again.

As long as the dragon did not sleep, as long as it hovered close enough to trouble his mortal dreams, Bak Sahm knew he would not sleep.

Not while the dragon lay waiting.

It was the money he needed more than anything.

Almost as much as he needed the woman.

For Jubilee Usher to topple Brigham Young from his throne, he needed money enough to recruit an army. Money enough to hire the brown-skinned mercenaries. The kind of money it would take to buy the guns his soldiers and Indian allies would need to march into Salt Lake City and wrest control of God's one true Church from the clutches of the false prophet.

All that he had seen dribble through his fingers—like fine sand spilling from his hands—the wealth he had wasted in the last decade . . . oh, that he had all that wealth now in his coming to this fateful moment in the history of mankind itself.

With what his army had taken from those settlers along the middle border during and immediately after the great war back east.

With the many shipments of specie and payroll his guerrilla bands had torn from their military escorts, leaving no survivor to wag a tongue—only evidence that showed the thieves had been Indian: Southern Cheyenne perhaps. Maybe even Kiowa, or the damned Comanche themselves.

With what his murderous legions had earned in Mexican gold, the bounty paid by grateful alcaldes and other government officials for hunting down and killing the Chiricahua and Mimbres, the Apache who floated back and forth across the border.

Usher had always been a man to recognize a profitable business venture when one presented itself. Whether it was a chance to marshal the forces of Zion and protect the eastbound trains returning to Missouri to buy what the faithful could not themselves produce in Utah Territory, or keeping his ear and eye open to learn of both frontier army payrolls and the Mexicans' plea for help.

But out here in southwestern Utah a man would have to lead his mercenaries a long, long way before he could count on running across an army payroll office and escort. And the trade in Apache scalps had all but died off.

While they likely were not exactly behaving like children on Sunday morning, it nonetheless seemed the Apache were no longer acting as bold as they had been, no longer raiding with such bloody abandon. The Mexican hierarchy, from provincial governors all the way down to petty officials, no longer clamored for the services offered by the likes of Jubilee Usher.

Still, he had an army to feed, with new men volunteering or being recruited every week. He had to buy guns and bullets, the better to entice the small bands of Utes and Paiutes in the surrounding area and in the country to the east of St. George, in the hopes of seducing those brown-skins to share a role in his dethroning of the false prophet.

"Colonel Usher." The voice outside the tent made a crack in his brooding. "Captain Haslam has returned."

How Jubilee hoped this would be good news. He glanced at the woman, then flung his voice toward the tent flaps.

"Tell the captain to make himself comfortable at my dining table. Beneath the awning in the shade of the big cottonwood. I'll be there directly."

Then he listened as the soldier trudged away. Soon all he could hear once again that late afternoon was the sound of the buzzing deer flies and the woman's steady breathing. She kept her eyes on him almost all the time now. Watching his every move. He wasn't sure just how long it had been since she had last slept. Maybe she rested after he began to snore at night, awoke before him each morning. She could not go on much longer like this without rest. It had been almost two months since he burned the doll.

Taking her hadn't ever been that good. And pushing his eager flesh inside her hadn't been near as good since. Why did she dredge up such violence within him? Why had the fine line between the brutal violence of his professional life blurred with the violent passions of his most private life?

Rising, Usher stepped over to her, watching her eyes stay locked on his every move, fastened on how his hand came slowly up to stroke her hair. She had learned so, so long ago not to pull away from his touch. Now, instead of turning away, those empty blue eyes merely closed, as if shutting out the sight of him.

It immediately angered him.

The woman did not open her eyes, much less show any fear, when the fingers stroking her hair suddenly gripped a handful of the golden locks and yanked her head back.

How she kept her eyes closed, her face impassive with such pain, he would never understand.

Although he did hear her breath catch in her throat, raggedly—like silk drawn over pumice stone.

He flung her aside, flat on the bed, and whirled away, pushing through the tent flaps into the early September sunshine. Already the days were growing shorter. Autumn was on its way here in these southern climes. Winter would come. Followed by another spring. Then another long summer. By then he wanted to have everything in place for his assumption of the throne.

Next year at the earliest.

Usher strode toward the canvas awning stretched tightly above the table where he took his meals, here in the shade of a huge, rustling cottonwood. The man heard him approach and turned.

"Colonel Usher!" Orrin Haslam said effusively, a smile coming to his clean-shaven face.

"Major."

Usher liked this man, as much as he had liked anyone since Lemuel Wiser. That sudden remembrance of his handsome lieutenant made Usher almost wince with noticeable pain. Not that Jubilee was given to anything near what a man could call sentiment for a fellow Danite, or feelings of camaraderie with other Avenging Angels. No. Instead, Jubilee Usher found the remembrance of Lemuel Wiser painful for one and only one reason.

A remembrance that was irrevocably tied to the woman's husband.

Surely, that farmer man must be dead by now. So many sent against him. None of whom had returned. One of those—just one—must have finished the work begun by Lemuel Wiser.

"Take a seat, Major Haslam."

"Good news is what I have for you, Colonel."

Usher looked up and found George nearby. "Bring us something cool."

"Lemonade?" the old Negro asked.

"Has it been cooling in the creek?"

"The crock's been there since't mornin'."

"Yes. That lemonade will do nicely, George."

He turned back to Haslam. "What did you and your men find out west of here?"

Orrin Haslam smiled even more. "Just like you figured, Colonel. There's mines over there in Nevada. Gold, silver, lead—"

"And mines do mean money, Major," Usher interrupted, with a flick of his hand. He leaned forward on the table and peered at Haslam. "What think you of the potential of the town?"

"There's enough coming out of those mines, enough going across the counters of every saloon and knocking shop—there's enough gold for us to hire on half-a-dozen armies, Colonel."

"The money moves out of this town in well-guarded shipments, I assume?"

"Some."

"Then . . . you've also brought me some idea of a plan you have cooking inside that sinister skull of yours, Major Haslam?"

His head bobbed, eyes narrowing. "Some of them mine owners have small armies guarding their shipments."

"We have our own army, Major."

"Indeed, Colonel. Them escorts is nowhere near as big as what we can muster."

"Then we could have those shipments at our mercy, I take it."

"Just what I was thinking."

"This is good news, Major." He sighed and looked out at the bright sunshine shimmering on the creek where George squatted on the bank to pull forth the earthen crock in which the Negro prepared his seductive lemonade. This southern land the Church faithful called Dixie wasn't much good for anything but the growing of just that sort of citrus. But the lemons would do for now. He watched the old black man struggle back up the grassy, slippery bank with the heavy crock, trudging toward the awning once more.

"I can even draw you a map of the town, where everything is, where the mines all sit along the hills just south of town . . . you start up on the bench—"

"There will be plenty of time for your maps, and for us laying our plans during this coming winter."

Haslam drew back a moment, confusion crossing his face like a pasty-colored cloud. "You . . . you're not fixing to begin working over the place this fall, Colonel?"

"No. We'll use the winter to put our plans in place. And ride out for Nevada come spring."

Haslam clearly did not like that. Perhaps it was the idea of waiting, more waiting. What Usher knew was clearly wearing on those men he had gathered to his cause so far. Or in Haslam's case—it might be something altogether different that so strongly drew the man back to Nevada.

Usher leaned back, tugging at the points of his vest a moment, smoothing it. "There's something I want you to do now that you've found what I sent you for, Major."

"You want me to go back there and scout—"

"No," he interrupted Haslam with irritation, sure now that the major was more than eager to go back to Nevada for the whiskey and the women. "I want you to travel to St. George on a mission of utmost sensitivity."

"St. George?"

"To see the local bishop there."

"What you need me to see him for?"

"To secure his permission to hold a wedding in his Temple."

"A Temple . . . Temple wedding?"

He stared evenly at Haslam. "I will marry the woman as soon as you return from St. George."

"Very good, Colonel. The way it should be for the new Prophet of God's only true Church. A Temple wedding—what a wonderful thing for you. And for the woman, sir."

"By the way, Major—what is the name of this Nevada town where you say the pickings are so good?"

"Not just the pickings, Colonel. It's the whores they got there too," Haslam replied.

Usher glanced at the tent for but a moment, then lightly licked his lips. "The whores, eh?"

"Mexican and Injun."

"If your tastes run to such colors, Major."

"Why, I even had my prick in a little Chinee whore."

"Chinese?" Usher repeated, his interest suddenly piqued. "You did say a Chinese whore?"

"I did. Even told her about you, Colonel. Said you'd likely wanna have some fun with her."

"You didn't mention my name?"

"No, sir. Never. I wouldn't do that."

With a sigh Usher leaned back once again. "Yes, Major. We'll go there come spring. Maybe even for a short visit this winter—just so I can see the place myself before we move our entire base of operations over there."

"I can't wait to get back to that li'l yellow whore."

"You delight in your pleasures of the flesh, don't you, Major?"

"Man's allowed, ain't he, Colonel?"

Playing with a long black curl hanging at his cheek, Usher answered, "Yes. A man is allowed. So—tell me . . . this town where we two will make our army rich, and strong—ready for battle against the false prophet . . . what's its name?"

"Pioche, sir," Haslam said, grinning as if fondly remembering the pleasures of the town. "A place called Pioche, Nevada."

Book II

A Bitter Harvest

15

September 1875

"WHAT THE HELL is that you're eating?" Jonah asked the aging but still muscular man who emerged from the small stone house, his one hand cupping half of some pale-green fruit.

The old one grinned. "Ain't you ever see'd a melon afore?"

"Damn right I've seen a melon before," Jonah replied as he watched the man use his knife to peel off another sliver from the inside of the melon half. "But it's been so long, I wasn't sure just what it was."

Spearing the slice with the tip of his knife, the gray-head stuffed it into his mouth, then used the knife to point at Two Sleep. "What sort of Injun he be?" the man asked, as if the Shoshone weren't there at all, or at least couldn't understand that he was the current topic.

"Snake," Jonah replied, not conscious that his tongue licked his lower lip as he watched the juice bubble up around the knife's edge each time the old man dragged the blade through the melon's pulp. "And he speaks passable English."

Beneath heavy brows the man's eyes lifted from his work on the melon to peer at Two Sleep. "That a fact, now? You speak English?"

"Yes," Two Sleep answered.

"Can't say as I remember running onto a Snake what spoke English very good in all my years."

The Shoshone grunted, "Now you know Two Sleep, old man."

Jeremiah asked, "Got any more of them melons?"

143

The man's eyes rolled over to the third member of the party. "Might have, at that. They come in season just recent."

"How much for a melon?" Jonah asked.

Using his knife to point back up the trail that had just brought the trio down from timberline, the man said, "Looks to be you come over my pass for free, the three of you did."

"*Your* pass?" Jeremiah snorted.

Around a sliver of melon the man replied, "Damn right. I been set up here for few years now. You three standing there on my toll road."

"T-toll?" Jonah asked.

"Folks heading over Raton on their way to Taos and Santa Fe."

Jonah argued, "But we come over from the south side."

The old one heaved the fruit rind toward the nearby trees and gave his knife blade a swipe across some greasy wool britches. "You wanna buy some melons? Or you just wanna pay your toll and be on your way down the trail?"

"Sounds like you're gonna make your money, either way," Jeremiah said.

"Yep," and he watched a rangy cur of a dog get up, stretch, and lope off to sniff at the rind he had tossed away. "Melons are sweet as they come in this country. Got this batch up to Trinidad. North of here. Sometimes the Mex ain't good for nothing—but I gotta say them Mex settlers grow the best melons I ever sank my teeth in."

"How much?"

"For the three of you"—and the man went to figuring, scratching in a meaningful way at something in his beard while he did—"that'll be a dollar apiece."

"How many melons is that?" Jonah asked.

"One each."

"A dollar each or a melon apiece?" Jonah squealed.

"A melon *plus* a ride over my pass—Raton, it's called. Way I figure it, you can head back up this'r road, if you're of a mind to, 'cause I'm the toll master in this neck of the woods."

"A goddamned thief is what you are," Jonah grumbled, twisting in his saddle toward his son. "Dig out some hard money for this melon man, Jeremiah. Seeing him eating got my hungers up."

"Mine too, Pa." Jeremiah went to scratching deep in the pocket of his britches for some coins.

Sliding down from his saddle, Jonah asked, "Besides toll master on this mountain road, what else they call you?"

"Wootton," the man answered. "But some folks hereabouts call me lots of things."

Hook snorted. "Wouldn't doubt it."

"But the name's Dick Wootton."

He held out his hand to Wootton. "Jonah Hook."

Wootton wiped his hand on his britches, then shook before starting to turn toward the open door of the stone house. "Three melons for you boys?"

"Damn right—and we'll eat 'em right here."

Days of summer heat had followed that afternoon of the hard rain, a scorching, hardpan desert heat. As soon as Jonah had spotted the beckoning purple undulation of the hilltops dappling the distant skyline, he had pointed them hard north by northwest. If nothing else, the water they could find among those hills would likely be sweeter than the brackish desert springs.

The water had been a lot sweeter, and colder too, and the shadows stretched a little longer. For days the only shadows of any size they had run across had been due south of their horses' bellies, what with the searing single eye of the sun seeming to travel much of the day at midsky. They plodded on toward the beckoning violet of the distant horizon, where at long last stunted cedar started cropping up, juniper too. The air felt cooler as sundown neared, and tiny streams gurgled in their narrow beds as the trio began their ascent into the rocky hills. It was there they crossed the trail by accident, a well-marked one at that, scoured and rutted over half a century of use. Jonah decided it would be their ticket to follow through the climbing tumble of hills rising progressively into the sky. On the far side Jonah figured they could strike out west once more.

"Trinidad, you said." Hook repeated the name of the settlement Wootton had mentioned as the old man reappeared from the small stone house juggling three melons.

"Twenty mile, not much more," the toll master replied. "Adobe settlement. Mud houses. Lot of 'em."

"Seen enough of mud houses to last me," Jonah said.

"Where away you bound?"

"Utah."

Wootton instantly shivered like a dog shaking water from its coat. He held up the first of the melons to Jonah, when he stopped. "Land of the Mormons. Damn. You boys ain't Mormons, are you?"

"No," Jonah answered sourly, quietly. "We look like Mormons to you?"

Wootton agreed. "You're too damned dirty to be Mormons."

"You a Mormon, ol' man?"

"Jesus goddamned Christ!" Wootton roared. "I'm 'bout as far from being a Mormon as a man can get!"

Jonah took his melon. And Wootton moved on to Jeremiah.

"That'll be three dollar." He allowed Jeremiah to drop the coins into the palm of his hand, then juggled them there while he passed up the second melon.

As Wootton strode over to hand the last of the fruit to the Shoshone still in his saddle, he asked, "You got business dealings with them Mormons?"

"Might say that," Jonah replied, unsaddling and moving over to squat in the shade of a stunted pine. "Get on down off that horse, Injun. We got eating to do before we ride on."

"You boys can't be traders, that's plain to see," Wootton surmised. "No outfits. What sort of business you got out to Utah?"

"We paid our toll, Mr. Wootton," Jonah said as he plunged the thin blade of his belt knife into the middle of the green melon and started drawing it around to split the fruit in half. "We don't gotta tell you our life story to ride this pass of yours, now, or do we?"

"Nothing of the kind."

Wootton disappeared into the dark shadows of the stone house for a moment and reappeared with another melon for himself. "Fella wants to be tight-jawed, that's all right with me, I say. Just figured to pass the time of day while'st you was eating. Didn't mean to give no offense."

Hook looked up at the older man, his long, graying hair spilling well past his shoulders. "Sorry. Didn't mean to give offense, me neither. What business we got is looking for someone in our family. My boy and me."

"Injuns took 'em?"

"No."

"Didn't callate," Wootton said. "Utes ain't that sort—not to take folks. Been over twenty years since they up and killed anyone I heard of. Back to the winter of fifty-four. The settlement up at Greenhorn it was."

"Them Utes the Injuns we'll run into west of here?" Jeremiah asked.

Turning toward the younger Hook, Wootton answered, "Them, and the Paiutes west of them. Some call them bands Pahvants. How far you figure you got to go to find this person from your family?"

"Far as it takes," Jonah replied. "The last I lost the trail, it was in the country between Fort Bridger and Salt Lake City. That fort's the place the army's took over after Jim Bridger let 'em use it to keep an eye on the Mormons years back."

Wootton wagged his head. "Ol' Gabe. Now there was a child made for these mountains."

Jeremiah asked around a chunk of melon, "You knew Bridger?"

"Knew him?" Wootton sputtered, melon juice dripping into his beard. "Trapped with Bridger winters ago. Now, him and Mormons never did mix neither."

"Sounds like you know about the Mormons. So you know about that little army Brigham Young's got him?"

"The Angels he sent to burn and plunder, push Bridger out?"

"Yeah. That bunch called the Danites?"

"Onliest thing I know is what Bridger and some of the boys he had with him said. Just word passed on from mouth to mouth."

"You ever hear tell names of any of them Mormon Danites?"

Wootton shook his head as he scraped some of the melon seeds from his knife onto his wool britches. "Wouldn't know a name if you told me. Or recognize a Mormon on sight if he was to use my road over the pass. Damn, but I'd charge 'em double, I would. For all that misery they brought to Ol' Gabe."

"You know Bridger and his old friends—then I s'pose you might know Shad Sweete."

Wootton's eyes shot up from his carving in the fruit half. "Shadrach Sweete." The old man wagged his head. "Ain't heard his name in . . . damn, if it ain't been a coon's age. How you know Sweete?"

"Same way I know Bridger," Hook replied. "Both of 'em was scouting for the army back to sixty-five."

"Up to Lakota country that was."

"Right. I found Bridger a bit on the quiet side."

"Wasn't always that way. Why, the stories Gabe could tell! Specially the tales he'd spin for the greenhorns. Them two was peas in the pod. You could always count on Shad Sweete to be a windy feller. Always will be. I expect he ain't changed. He still living, that is. Where's he running these days?"

Jonah shrugged, then said wistfully, "I was hoping to run onto him somewhere here in the mountains."

"Likely you'll have to go back up to that Lakota country to find that ol' nigger. Think he took him a Cheyenne woman."

"He did. But you ain't heard nothing of him recent?"

Wootton shook his head. "Shining times is long gone, friend. The days of Jim Bridger and Shad Sweete, the high times of Dick Wootton too. All . . . long gone now. No, I ain't heard tell of Shad in more years'n I'd care to admit. But that don't mean nothing necessarily. This ain't his country. My guess'd be you'd find sign of him far north of here. Back toward that Snake's country." He pointed his knife at Two Sleep, who was just then prying his melon into halves, inspecting each half, then bent to sniff at the fruit.

"What you think of that, Two Sleep?" Jeremiah asked.

The Shoshone licked the side of one half. Then shrugged and put his knife to work.

"You looking for Shad too?" Wootton asked. "Or you looking for that someone in your family out to Mormon country?"

"Heading first to Mormon country," Hook replied. "Been seven years now since I seen Shad."

"Where was that?"

"Back to Fort Laramie."

"Seven years a long time for someone old like Shad and me," Wootton snorted. "Wouldn't surprise me if that child's gone under."

"Shad?"

He nodded. "What with all the hell them Lakota and Cheyenne been raising up there last few years. Ain't at all peaceable country like this here."

"How's the Injuns—them Utes and Paiutes you was talking about?" Jeremiah inquired.

"Damned peaceable," Wootton answered. "They stays on their reservations and don't make no ruckus at all."

"Twenty miles you said?" Jonah asked.

Wootton nodded downhill. "To Trinidad. Yep."

Wiping his mouth with the back of his hand, Jonah peered up at the sky, then asked, "Late as it's getting to be, you mind us making camp here for the night?"

Wootton's countenance brightened noticeably. "Why, no—I wouldn't mind at all. Three weary wayfarers to spend the night makes no never mind to me. Besides—any friend of Shad Sweete's is a friend of mine."

"Maybe you can tell me some stories about your days long ago with Shad."

Wootton rose slowly on knees that crackled. Jonah could tell that the old man's bones must hurt him. The toll master scratched again at his beard, then pulled something away from it between two fingers. He cracked the louse between his teeth, then tossed the tiny vermin aside.

"Damn tootin', neighbor—I'll go get the missus warming up some victuals for us while we smoke a pipe and get down to swapping yarns on ol' Shad."

"Would you like to light a candle, *señor?"*

Jonah raised his head, startled at the voice, finding the priest in his long black robe at the far end of the crude bench. Then he looked up again at the tall crucifix of Christ above the altar and nodded once.

"Por favor."

As he moved from the front pew toward the altar, the dark-skinned priest said, "I speak English."

Jonah creaked to his feet from the hard timbers where he had knelt, praying. "That's good, Father. My Spanish is not so good. Not near good as your English."

Taking up a long taper, the thin-faced priest lit it and turned, waiting for Hook to approach the altar, where only about half of the tiny red candles flickered in their rose-hued glasses.

As he took the taper from the priest, Jonah looked toward the shadowy back of the small church, finding Jeremiah leaning against the back wall. The young man would come no farther through the midst of the crude, hand-hewn benches, no closer to the red candlelights twinkling on the altar, no closer to that effigy of a bloody Christ.

Jeremiah wagged his head at his father before turning to slip out the open half of the heavy double doors suspended in their massive cottonwood arch. He would feel uncomfortable here in this church, Jonah knew. It had been a lifetime since his mother had taken her children to Sunday services. There for all those years, Gritta had steadfastly visited church meeting with the children every Sunday morning. But ever since . . . ever since Jubilee Usher it had likely been a different story. Jonah realized it had been more than half Jeremiah's life since his son had been to church.

Hell—Jonah thought now as he turned back to look at the priest, gaze over the other candles lit in prayer—it's been every bit that much longer since I entered one of God's houses.

Twilight had begun to streak the whitewashed adobe walls of Trinidad, painting them with hues of violet by the time the trio had come down the north slope of Raton Pass and crossed the Purgatoire River.

"The Picketwire," Wootton had told them. "Spanish that be—for 'purgatory.' You know what purgatory is, don't you, Jonah Hook?"

Damn right he knew, Jonah thought. If any man knew what that no-man's-land was between heaven and hell . . . then he immediately tried to drive the thought from his mind as he chose a candle on the topmost row, those nearest the bloodied feet of that carven wooden image, a deep crimson painted on the nailed feet, slashed in the figure's side, stark against the pale skin of the pierced hands.

This one's for Gritta, God, he prayed. Just like I was saying when this priest here asked if I wanted to light a candle. This is the way folks do things down here—so I'm saying my prayer with this candle. Asking you again what I ain't asked you in a long, long time. I just can't remember how long it's been since I last prayed to you.

But—even though I ain't come to you in all that time—I'm still asking you to keep watch over her. Wherever that bastard's got her. Where he's took her.

Jonah handed the taper back to the priest, who snuffed out its tiny flame between two fingers.

"I will go now," the Mexican said quietly, stepping down from the altar where he had waited beside Jonah. "If you need something . . . need to talk—you can find me near."

"Me and the others will just be pushing on when I'm done here," Jonah tried to explain lamely.

"*Sí.* You are not from around here," the priest replied. "You and your friends are wanderers. Pilgrims, maybe."

"Maybe. You might say. I just . . . it's been a long time since I been to church. But I wanted to . . . seeing there's someone I had to pray for real bad."

"God will hear, *señor.* Trust in him—God will hear."

Jonah watched the priest step away, dragging his loose-fitting sandals that allowed his brown feet to peek from the bottom of his black robe slurring the plank floor of the little church.

How I want God to hear me, Father. To keep watch over my Gritta till me and Jeremiah can find her. Till I can square things up with the one what took her from me.

He knew she was alive—had come to believe that she was alive every bit as much as he could reach down and touch his own body, as much as he could feel the fatigue and miles, the years and winters draining through him, making him sense more of a sodden heaviness than he thought possible.

But he knew Gritta was still out there, alive. Waiting on him.

As if weakened, his legs began to buckle, his knees gone to water. Jonah did not fight it. He knelt before the altar, accepting that this was natural to prostrate one's self before one's God. Resting his clasped hands on the edge of the altar where the candles glowed, Jonah let his head fall forward, where it rested on his wrists, as he continued to brood on the road behind him, to imagine that road still remaining before him.

And if you got a blessing left over after keeping Gritta safe as you can . . . then I'm asking you to help me, God.

Help show me the way to go.

Help me, God. Help me find her quick.

And give her the strength to hold on till I can come to her.

That ain't too much to ask—is it, God? Just . . . just see to it Gritta holds on.

16

"MY GOD AIN'T the same as your God, Father," Jonah said.

The priest nudged another piece of fragrant cedar kindling into the small adobe fireplace squatting in the corner of the tiny cell he kept at the back of the church.

Hook sat on the floor, looking from time to time at the rattle of the low door where the wind rose and fell, howling and hissing around the cracking timbers. Beyond, in a small creaky stable, Two Sleep and Jeremiah had chosen to remain with their animals and the priest's old burro instead of joining Jonah and the blackrobe as night and autumn's storm quickly descended on southern Colorado Territory.

Somewhere off in the darkness of the rest of that village, the strings of a guitar were being plucked in some plaintive call. Familiar enough, the lover's song reminded Jonah of all those seasons spent moving from one poor Mexican village to the next. Looking into a myriad of weary faces, forced to ask the same questions at every stop—seeking the comancheros, who were first rumored to be at one place, then another. Finally seeking the *ricos*, who funded comancheros' trade with the Kiowa and Comanche in cattle, in horses, in human misery.

"There is only one God," the priest replied, his voice thick with fatigue. He spoke Jonah's language unexpectedly well, going on to explain that in country such as this, a man might well minister to as many who spoke English as those who spoke Spanish.

152

"If there's just one God," Jonah asked while the priest lit another of the candles in that room beneath a ceiling darkened by the smudge of many dark nights like this, "how come there's so damned many folks claiming their God's the one and only? So many folks saying they got the only way to worship the only God?"

Each wick in the priest's poor lantern candles floated across the surface of a small cup of animal fat. From the smell Jonah figured it was pork renderings, a fragrance that made him think back on the pigs they'd had at home. The remembrance hurt: there no longer was any home for him. Only those graves dug near that cabin falling into ruin. No more fields. No more milking cow or breeding pigs. No more family gathering inside those walls come twilight.

The priest lit another of the floating candles. Its fragrance added to the cedar glowing in the squat fireplace in the corner. So much like the smell of frying bacon, it made Jonah's stomach grumble in hunger. He hadn't eaten since leaving Dick Wootton's toll house that morning.

"The Lord God our Christ long ago warned that there would be many who came in His name," the priest said as he snuffed out the thin shaft of kindling he had lit at the fireplace, then used to light the candles, flickering now against the walls, bare but for the painted figure of another crucified Christ.

Jonah stared at the carven image. Trying to grasp the intangible, struggling to conjure up the priest's God from that dead figure still nailed to the cross after all these centuries.

"What brings you here, *señor*?"

Hook turned, struck at the directness of the question. "I don't know why I come into your church. Maybe just to find a special place to pray for someone. I ain't no . . . never been one of your kind. Hell, I never was a churchgoing man. Not like . . . not like someone else in my family."

"No, *señor*," the priest said, "what brings you to Trinidad?"

He shrugged self-consciously, amazed with himself at the mistake, at how he had just blurted things out to the black-robed man of God. It was like he was in the presence of something bigger than himself—like Jonah couldn't keep from saying things that tumbled off his tongue.

"I'm headed—we all three are headed west. Coming from Indian Territory and Texas. Pushing west for Utah."

"That would explain why you believe my God is very different from your own."

"Come again?"

The priest poured some water from a crock pitcher into a small brass kettle, then hung the kettle on a trivet that he swung over the flames. "You are Mormon, yes?"

"No," he answered quickly. Jonah found it downright scary that anyone would figure him to be one of them that had taken so much from him. "Ain't never been."

"I thought you would be going to join their church communities in Utah. Find your place among those people."

"Don't figure on ever being one of them."

"But you said you have a mission to go to Utah."

"Yes." But he decided he had to keep it closed off from here on out.

From a small set of shelves the priest took down some tin boxes and from one spooned out some ground tea into the two china mugs he wiped clean with a musty cloth draped over the back of the only chair in the cell. "Do you know anything about them? These Mormons?"

Jonah looked at the priest in surprise. "I don't have to know anything about them to do what I gotta do."

"Then . . . it sounds to me like you are on a very serious mission, *señor*."

"You might say that."

"A mission of killing?"

He studied the priest's back for a long time, then eventually answered, "There ain't no other way out of it now. Yes."

"There is always some way besides the killing."

Instead of replying Hook just watched the side of the priest's face as the man put away his tiny container of tea and took down a small tin of sugar. In some ways the priest looked as if he could be no more than forty years old, but in other ways he just *felt* to Jonah as if he were at least twenty years older than that.

He stirred some sugar into one of the china cups. "These Mormons— they claim my church is the whore of Babylon."

"The whore of what?"

He wagged his head, offering an apologetic grin. "It does not matter that you understand that word. It is just that I have always believed that my church—the first Church founded by Christ—should find ways to reason with all others that have come after it."

"Yours was the first church?"

The priest nodded.

"Must be something wrong with your church, then, if folks had to go out and come up with all their own churches."

154

"Perhaps," he answered. "Something wrong that my church did not see in itself."

For some time Jonah sat immersed in his thoughts. It was warm here. He glanced at the door once more as the wind rose, rattling the wood against the iron hasp, wondering why the Indian and his son had not wanted to join him here. Then he looked again at the crucifix, and back to the priest, who had settled into the only chair in the tiny cell.

"Why the Mormons call your church a whore?"

"They believe we are apostles for the devil."

"Apostles. Like . . . messengers?"

"Like that, yes."

"Is that why so many other churches come after yours, the first church? Because all your priests, all your believers are messengers of the devil?"

His eyes held the soft light of those flickering, fragrant candles, patience a tangible thing. "If Satan were to seduce a man of God, to trick that man of God into leaving God's holy church and go about forming another church based upon sinful and separatist teachings—what do you think Satan wants that man of God to believe?"

Talk of such philosophical things always seemed to hurt Jonah's head. His life was made of simple things: hunting so he could eat, building a fire so he could stay warm, keeping his eyes and ears open so he could stay alive. This, why just to think about—

"If Satan wants to take over the minds and hearts and souls of those people who are truly looking for God," the priest continued, "don't you think he is going to appear before them as a prophet of God Himself, rather than cloaked in his own demon clothing as the Fallen Angel?"

Jonah rubbed his temples. "Father—I'm just a simple man. I don't know nothing about fallen angels and Satan and prophets."

"But you will. And you must learn. For in going into the land of the Mormons—you are entering the land of a good people. Good people who have been led astray by no less than the devil himself."

"I don't have no call with that church of theirs. My business is with a man."

"Is he a Mormon?" the priest asked. "Isn't that why you are looking for him in Utah?"

"I'm looking for him there only because that's where I lost his trail last time I hunted him."

The frayed hem of his robe dragged the earthen floor as he knelt to pull the kettle from the flames. Folding a piece of coarse cloth, the priest carried the bale over to the small table, where he poured the steaming water into the two china cups. Setting the kettle aside, he stirred both with the same spoon and handed Jonah his fragrant tea.

"Smells good, Father. Been a long, long time since I had anything like this."

"Coffee may be a necessity of life," the priest said. "But tea—yes, this is truly one of life's celebrations."

In taking his first sip Jonah was instantly struck with the remembrance of times gone, of Gritta's kitchens in the Shenandoah and in that Missouri valley, kitchens warm and steamy with her baking and frying, resplendent with smells so heady a man felt compelled to linger. It was Gritta who first shared tea with him. And he had not had any since, not since—

"North of here you will cross the Apishapa River."

"North of here?"

"You are wanting to get to Utah, *señor*?"

"I follow the Apishapa west?"

"No. Cross on. Keep on north."

"How will I know the Apishapa?"

"You cannot mistake it," the priest replied. "To the west are the Spanish Peaks. *Wah-to-Yah*. A pair of them."

"But I keep on north?"

"*Sí*. Then you cross Cucharas Creek. You can ask locals if you are not sure."

"How far?"

"About the same from here to the Apishapa."

"After I cross the Cucharas?"

"North to Huerfano River."

"That's when I go west?"

He nodded. "One of two ways. Southwest over Sangre de Cristo Pass. Or north by west to Medano Pass."

"That's the one I want," Jonah said, then took a sip of the hot tea. "It will get me there quicker."

"It will. On the far side are the sand dunes. Go around them. Do not try to go through them, *señor*. They do not last forever—so go around them."

"How far to Utah?"

"Still very far. From the sand dunes you must keep to the creeks that will take you north by west. To Saguache. From there you will climb up to the Blue Mesa. That will take you down into the Black Canyon."

"Blue Mesa . . . Black Canyon," he said, his head ringing with it all. "I want to get it right."

The priest turned quickly, setting his cup down and pulling at a small leather satchel leaning against the wall beneath the table. "I will draw you a map, *señor*."

"Why—why do you do this for me?"

"You go to find someone in Utah you told me. *Sí?*"

"Yes," Jonah answered as the priest pulled paper from the satchel, along with a quilled pen and a small bottle of ink, which he opened.

"It is family?"

"Yes. But I didn't tell you—"

"It does not matter, *señor*. You see, I still believe we are all family in the eyes of God. No matter how we worship Him. Even if a man does not worship Him. The only ones who are lost from our family of God are those who have listened to Satan and worship the Fallen Angel—fooled into thinking they are worshipping God instead."

"Just what you think the Mormons are doing?"

"If a member of your family was lost among Satan's messengers, would you not want all the help others could put in your hands to find that person?"

"I never once turned down any help."

After moving one of the candles closer to his work, the priest bent over his paper. Across it Jonah could hear the quill scratching in the midst of the sounds of the distant village settling in for the night. And the sounds of the crackling cedar and juniper in the fireplace that had bullied the chill from this tiny room at the back of the adobe church where the wooden figure of a dead Christ hung from those three nails on a bloody cross.

"We are all one family, *señor*," the priest continued as he drew his rivers, scribbled in squiggles for his mountain ranges. "If we do not help one another set our feet on the right paths to righteousness, who will show us the way?"

"You just show me the way to Utah, Father. I'll let righteousness and the Mormons and the devil himself be damned. I'm only going there to find my wife."

The priest stopped drawing of a sudden, turning to gaze at Hook with the deepest pity in his eyes. "Your . . . wife."

Jonah's own eyes narrowed. "It's her the Mormons took. A thieving, murdering band of 'em."

For some time the priest stared at the small crucifix on his wall. Finally he explained, "Winters ago there was talk—and only talk—from travelers from the south and west, some folks gone down to Mexico and across the Apache country."

"What sort of talk?" Hook asked, leaning forward a bit anxiously, regarding the priest over the edge of his china cup.

"They spoke of a band of Mormons. Like an army. Tales of a tall, long-haired man who leads this powerful army, so goes the story."

"An army," he repeated, gazing now at the floor, the weight of the word striking him like a hot coal in the middle of his ice-cold chest.

"It was a tale I don't know the truth of, *señor*."

"Like a . . . a legend?"

"Yes. Perhaps nothing more than myth."

"Legends always have some grain of truth in them, I learned long time ago."

With a sigh the priest nodded. "Maybe so. It was said that one day this army appeared out of nowhere. Behind their imaginary leader they marched wherever they wanted. Took what and who they wanted. And then, one day, they just disappeared. No one has heard any word of that man and his army in a long time."

"They . . . they ain't heard nothing of 'em no more?"

With a wag of his head the priest turned back to his paper. "I hope this map I draw for you will lead you where you want to go, *señor*."

He wiped his palms down the front of his dirty britches self-consciously, feeling struck with so much more than his own naked poverty here in the face of this poor man of God. "I don't have no way to thank you, Father."

"I have found that every man has his own journey—that journey to find what he seeks most. For most they end up seeking God Himself."

"And for the rest of us?"

"For the rest," the priest explained, "it is a person they seek."

"Nothing against your God, Father . . ." Immediately he felt blasphemous. "Don't mean nothing against God. But it is a person I'm seeking."

"Your wife."

"Like I said."

"No, *señor*. The truth that lies at the end of your journey. It is not your wife your heart seeks."

"What the hell do you know about truth—"

"As much as you love your wife, it is hate that fills your heart all the more."

Tears of anger welled within him. "Damn you! Loving her is all that's kept me going!"

With a wag of his head the priest said, "I think in this that you are wrong. The truth is that it is the hate poisoning your heart that has kept you going all these years. Not the love for your wife that remains in some corner of your heart. Instead, what carries you on is the hatred for the man who took her from you. That is what feeds you most on your lonely journey."

"I am not lonely. I got two others. A friend and the woman's son with me."

"No matter that you have an army of your own with you when you find the man who leads his army—you have always been alone on this journey. You started alone. You will always be alone. And you will end your journey alone."

Jonah felt the sting grow at his eyes, sensed his throat constrict around the words "Until she's free—"

"You won't be, *señor*."

17

"THEY'RE SPINELESS BASTARDS!" Jubilee Usher roared. "Every last one of them. Not a man among the bunch has the nerve to stand up to that false prophet!"

Orrin Haslam stood nearby, watching Usher pace back and forth over the ground between the table beneath the canvas awning and Usher's large tent.

Jubilee stopped before his lieutenant, grabbing Haslam's coat in one hand. "You're certain you talked to them all?"

"Every last one of them," Haslam answered. "No one's going to give you permission for a Temple ceremony."

He let his grip go, smoothing Haslam's coat. "Yes, of course. What if Brigham Young was to find out? God's own anointed Prophet!"

"I was thinking when I was on the trail back, Colonel—can't we bring you one of them here?"

"What for?"

"To perform the wedding."

"Haslam, dear man. If you were to convince one of St. George's leaders to accompany you here, even at the muzzle of your guns, it would still not be a Temple wedding, you idiot!"

"But, Colonel—"

"I mean to have myself a wedding in one of the Church's Temples— right under the nose of Brigham Young. To bind my wife to me as that false

160

prophet has bound all of his wives to him for all of eternity. I will have no less, Haslam."

"We could push on north."

"Where?"

"Nephi is the next-closest Temple."

Usher considered, then shook his head with determination. "No. There's no reason for me to believe it would be any different in Nephi than it is in St. George. We will have the ceremony performed for my bride and me in the Temple at St. George."

"It's his winter home, Colonel." Haslam explained what Usher already knew.

Jubilee whirled about and came inches from the man's nose. "When is he expected in St. George?"

"By the end of October. First of November, usual. Depending on how fast winter starts to set in, so I've heard."

"It's been mild weather so far," Usher said, turning away and speaking more to himself. "I suspect we have time to take a few days in preparation, a few more in travel south to St. George—how far is it?"

"From here?"

"Yes. How long did it take you?"

"About sixty miles, give or take, from Cedar City."

"Three days' travel for the wagons, barring bad weather."

"You're taking the whole bunch, Colonel?"

Sweeping some of the long black hair back over his shoulder, Usher answered, "No. Only a small force. Enough to act as an armed escort. In case of any unforeseen problem along the way. But not enough to attract the wrong sort of attention, mind you."

"We get to St. George, then what?"

"Then what?" And Usher chuckled, whirling about to gaze at the tent flaps behind which waited his bride. "Then we have ourselves an audience with the bishop of St. George, that's what. We bring him and what local elders we need to preside for the whole ceremony . . . and we have ourselves a blessed wedding!"

"Nothing going to stand in your way, is there, Colonel?"

"Major Haslam—I can't think of anything short of God Himself that can stop me marrying my bride."

"Glory be to His name!"

"Yes," Usher replied lustily. "Glory be to God's name!"

•   •   •

161

It always grew cold here in the Season of the Boar. Bak Sahm dragged on another layer of clothing. The padded, quilted coat and those quilted pants.

Yet every morning he awoke colder still, taking longer and longer to make himself warm after climbing from his bed. He knew the cold rested in his bones.

The dragon was slowly changing him into a serpent from the inside out.

Only then would the dragon see fit to come do battle with him.

"Yes, she really hates you."

So said the girl who was brushing his long hair that morning. She pulled and struggled the brush through it before she began to plait the long hair falling from the crown of his head into a tight queue, just as she did once a week when Bak Sahm took his bath. How he loved the smell of the English lavender soap. It was one of the few barbarian customs he allowed himself. Once more, as he did each week just after bathing, Bak hoped to find himself more presentable to her. Although he never admitted to anyone that was why he went through this indulgent ritual.

Instead he maintained the aloofness of the employer, coyly asking about his status with each of his other girls from the different one he selected to brush and plait his freshly washed hair each week. This way, with a new girl chosen each week for this familiar, almost intimate talk, Bak could disguise his desire for the one, by lumping her with all the rest.

It had been many weeks since he had last chosen that one to perform this ritual brushing for him. Or the manicure and the care for his feet. Such residual decadence of Manchu culture still alive here in the land of the Gold Mountain.

"And you hate me too," he said, making it sound like a statement with such defined shape to it.

"Of course," the prostitute answered. "All of us hate you."

He had to devise a better way to ask it. "Do any of you hate me more than the others?"

"No," she said finally as she tugged so hard on the long black hair that she hurt his scalp as she pulled the plait into a silken braid. "We all hate you the way all girls of joy hate their employer."

"This is so," he replied as her hands came away from his head, and he was disappointed that the touching was now at an end. She came around his chair, head dutifully bowed, and stopped before him.

She said respectfully, "It has always been so. It must always be."

As he looked at her face, seeing it again without a fresh application of the rice powder, he was reminded of this woman's plainness. And so reminded of the other's beauty that stirred him to great distraction.

He gestured. "Go to the bed."

Her eyes flicked there and back, some confusion in them.

"Yes," he answered her unspoken question. "Lie on my bed."

Without meeting his eyes again, her head bowed, she asked, "Do you want me to remove my clothing?"

After his eyes had looked her up and down, he said, "No. I want to take your robe from you."

She wore only her nightdress, a silk robe pulled over that. She had not dressed for the day, nor had she combed her hair and applied her makeup. It did not matter, he decided. He would have her anyway. Like taking one of the girls he had dreamed of bedding back in Sahn Kay Gawk—that tiny, sleepy village tucked away in the shadowy part of the Pearl River delta. "The Corner of the Mountain Where the Water Falls" was the name of his village.

How many times when only a youth had he dreamed of taking one of the plain-faced, mud-caked village girls and pulling her behind a rick of hay, into one of the oxen stables, and showing her how big his penis had become just in imagining it pumping in and out of her moistness. Instead Bak Sahm always pumped his hot and hard flesh in and out of his hand, having to content himself with only dreaming of the plain-faced, hard-working field girls, while telling himself that one day he would have better than they could give him. One day he would earn himself a porcelain-faced, sweet-smelling Manchu doll who answered his every whim, one who did not smell of ox dung, a rouged woman who did not laugh behind her hands at him whenever he stumbled over words in trying to speak to her. One day, he had told himself, he would surely have a woman who wanted Bak's penis in her as much as he wanted to plant it there.

Bak Sahm gently pulled apart her silk robe, then the folds of her sleeping gown so that he could cup the small mounds of her breasts in his hands.

One of these days he would learn the right finding chant. There were those who learned a finding chant so that they were able to find lost things. To locate valuable possessions—misplaced, hidden, frantically searched-for things.

Bak Sahm wanted a chant to help him find what he longed for most. It was not something he had once possessed then misplaced. No, he had never had what he wanted most to find.

"Do you want my hands on you?" she asked him softly.

"If you want them here on me."

When she loosened the knotted braid that held the padded drawers around his waist and found him already much excited, Bak Sahm pushed her roughly back onto the bed and climbed between her legs. She kept hold on him with one hand, her eyes closed, slowly stroking him while he pulled her robe and gown aside, exposing her bare thighs. Seeing the tiny patch of black hair over her mound made him stop a moment.

"There is nothing more you want from me before you enter?" she asked.

He looked up at the young woman's face, then over her bare breasts, small as they were, but firm, their nipples rigid beneath his hurried stimulation. Then finally he gazed down to where she kneaded him there between her legs, near that dark thicket where he wanted most to be buried.

Shoving her hand aside, Bak mounted her with no more ceremony, finding her unprepared for the savageness of his entry. Her gasp, her whimper of pain only made him all the more brazen. Just to be done with this one, for she was not the one he wanted.

The one he desired more than anything was like a ghost to him. This was the only way he could temporarily exorcise her. If only for a few moments as he climbed the steep slope of the mountainside rising above the dark and fertile delta. So green and cool. Reminding him of home, and contentment.

She lay unmoving beneath him as he spent himself in her. Without wanting to touch him, the woman only let him touch her. She took no part in this except to act as a vessel he filled from time to time. Bak knew that about her. And once more felt ashamed for his weakness before her. Instead of contentment he felt cold all too quickly.

He had wanted those few moments of flesh to touch his soul. Wanted a few moments of warmth, but was forced to steal them like some poor blinded beggar stumbling along with his hand out, the high-pitched cant of his voice so desperate to all who passed him by.

He lay atop her as long as he could before fearing that his good right arm was falling asleep. Bak Sahm rolled off, staying beside her without passion, forced to touch the woman only because of the narrowness of his tiny bed. As his breathing became more regular, he felt the woman slowly pull her gown closed and slide gently from the edge of the mattress. His sleep-filled mind listened as her feet slurred across the floor. She quietly turned the door latch and left him alone in the room.

Alone once more with himself and his return to the slopes of those mountains looking down on the Pearl River delta. In climbing up that long, dreamy slope he finally came to the shady entrance to a cave, startled to find a little girl sitting there at the great entrance playing with three beautiful pearls.

Bak Sahm stopped back in the trees, afraid he had been seen, trying to hold his breath so she would not hear him. But when the wind came up at his back, the girl smelled his presence and quickly scrambled to her feet, fleeing into the cave as Bak lunged from the trees, calling out for her not to be afraid of him.

As she disappeared into the cave's dark interior, he saw the girl place the exquisite pearls into her left ear. Skidding to a halt there before the cave's yawning mouth, Bak sensed fear mingled with excitement at the prospect of entering the forbidden place the entrance represented.

Of a sudden the whole world grew bright, and hotter still than the most miserable day of summer. He was hurled backward by a great and hoary blast of foul air blown from the cave's mouth. As he picked himself up, he watched the dragon's head emerge, seeing it was a female—for its nose was straight, and without a horn. This one was *ch'i-lung*, hornless. And behind its evil left eye, in that ear sat the three pearls.

"You have eaten the child?"

Another searing blast of fire issued from the dragon's mouth, the wall of heat flinging Bak Sahm back even more toward the timber. Then he realized the dragon was the child in disguise. And knew he had been fooled by appearances once more.

Sliding on his side, thrashing his legs against the ground, he scooted backward toward the trees as the dragon slinked its long body from the cave's mouth. This was the pearl-guarding beast, the one the Celestials called the "stag of the sky." It kept a man's riches from him until he was content with what he had and hungered no more.

How could he? Bak asked as he felt the cool swarm of the undergrowth surround and accept him. A man had to be suicidal to want for anything more, since the dragon would sacrifice that man for his lust—whether he craved gold, or fishing boats, or a silkworm farm . . . or even a woman to fill his aching void. No man would dare flaunt himself before the *ch'i-lung*, the hornless dragon who kept riches and happiness just beyond the grasp of a hungry man.

If he could only avoid its searching eyes, just beyond the dragon's power of smelling humans, if Bak could do that until winter came . . . then he knew the dragon would sleep in its pool during that season of drought. Until then Bak would have to lie here beneath the leaves and tangle of vines, hoping the dragon would not be able to smell his human smell— only the fragrance of the flowers and pods and leaves where he hid himself.

And in the spring the hibernating dragons would arise to do battle with one another after the long, dry season of winter.

There was great discomfort here on the rocky ground. He turned carefully, sure not to make a sound as the dragon roamed the edge of the thicket, trying to sniff him out with its powerful nostrils where the noxious smoke still curled up in ghostly black columns. Bak Sahm was lying on a bed of stones, as if this ground had been the belly of a creek or stream long ago. And beneath his shoulder Bak found one of the stones his people spoke of as a "dragon's egg." Indeed, it did have a small crack in it already.

Legend told him that when that rock split completely, thunder and lightning would issue forth, the sky brightening like day as his ears were punished by the great celestial claps of noise. Rain would then pour forth from the crack in that stone just before the infant dragons would burst free from the egg, their leathery wings slapping the air around them as they climbed into the sky with a shrieking roar.

No bigger than a worm, or a lizard, would they be when born—but Bak would have to realize he had unleashed another dragon on the world.

He stared, sensing the egg tremble in his palm, watching the tiny crack grow larger. Hearing the large female dragon at the edge of the timber. Her earsplitting roar was like the crash of rocks that came when the mountain of the dawn split to give birth to the sun at the far end of the earth.

If he could only be like the old woman in the legends who found three dragon's eggs and carried the tiny ones to the edge of the river, where she released the newborn creatures. For her faithfulness to the dragon young, the woman was given the power to foretell the events of man. With her new-won powers, she became a high priestess, called "Dragon Mother" by all in her province. And whenever she washed her clothes at the riverbank, all the fish, who were loyal subjects of the dragons, danced and sang for her, telling her what was to happen to all those who desired most to know the future.

Bak Sahm stuffed the quaking egg inside his jacket, securing it within a fold where it would not come loose as he crawled back through the thicket, away from the roar of the female dragon, far from the heat and sulfurous stench of her flaming breath.

Back, and back some more he pushed with legs beneath the suffocating tangle of vine and weed, threading himself over the rocky ground until he felt himself slipping. Bak reached out to grasp a vine. But it tore from his hand as he slid faster and faster. The dragon's roar faded farther and farther away as he tumbled down the slope until he careened from the cliff and was falling through the air.

All sound gathered at the back of his throat but could go no farther. His weakened leg was no longer of any use to him, his only good arm had nothing now to clasp on to. Down, down he spun wildly.

And crashed against the rocks at the bottom of the valley.

Slowly, Bak Sahm blinked himself awake on the floor of his room, his mind more racked with pain than his once-broken body. His dream fall was like the dynamite explosion, the great tumbling spill from his basket as he flew away from the hot, fiery blast that split rock from rock, a landslide from the mountain slope.

To find himself just like this, lying motionless, unable to move at will, his heart pounding, his breath heaving.

Reaching inside his quilted coat, Bak found he had at last brought the dragon egg out from the land of his dreams—knowing that to have his own demon was the only way he would be able to do battle with the dragon when it finally showed itself.

It would not be the hornless *ch'i-lung*. Not when the beast was finally ready to devour him. It would be a large male dragon. A *k'iu-lung*. Its face dominated by a great horn that undulated as it beat its leathery wings against the sky.

Bak Sahm would know its eyes when he finally saw the dragon that would come for him. He had seen those eyes before in the fiery moment the dynamite had exploded below him in the basket. He would remember those eyes for as long as he lived.

Every man was given his moment to stand before the gods and tell what he had proved of his life.

And now Bak Sahm had his dragon egg. One day soon he knew he would no longer be victim.

One day he would possess the hornless *ch'i-lung*. He would possess his dream woman.

18

"I HOLD THE Melchizedek Priesthood," Usher told the half-dozen Saints before him. "God Himself calls upon you to perform this most sacred and high ceremony for me."

Most of the six high priests overseeing the St. George Temple did not train their eyes on the tall, long-haired Danite commander. Instead their attention remained locked on the two pistols Jubilee held on them. Those pistols, and the other weapons held by the twenty men on either side of Usher.

When Orson Hyde swallowed, his Adam's apple bobbed like a piece of fruit in a washtub filled with water, shooting to the surface, bouncing each time the bishop sought to find words to fill his mouth working like a steam piston. Only nothing came out for the longest time.

When he finally found his voice, Hyde said, "We've been . . . I was told you are charged with apostasy."

"Apostasy!" Usher roared. "Me? An apostate to the one true Church of God? Guilty of conduct in violation of the law and order of our Church?"

Bishop Hyde nodded once, his eyes flicking down once more to the guns Usher held.

Jubilee lunged a step forward, stuffing one pistol into its holster across his left hip. "Who accuses me?"

"P-president Young."

He savagely wrenched Hyde's coat lapel into a ball, seething. Then thought better of it. Smoothing the wool cloth, Usher smiled benignly. "The penalty for that would be excommunication."

"Y-yes."

"But Brigham hasn't excommunicated me yet," Usher said, his feral eyes crawling over the rest of the Temple leaders. "Has he?"

"No. There's only been talk."

"For some time now," Whitney Pratt said.

Quickly, Jubilee's gaze shot to the other Church leader. "What else have you heard from the presidency about my apostasy?"

"Only . . ." And then Pratt stopped, his own frightened eyes glancing over the others. Hyde nodded, as if to permit Pratt's telling of it. "Only that you stood accused by President Young of leaving the Church."

His burst of laughter caught the elders all by surprise. Nervously they shifted their feet, licked their lips, once more looked round at the big muzzles of those pistols and rifles being held on them.

"Apostasy is the most serious offense a Saint can be charged with," Jubilee said when he abruptly ended his laughter. "But to be an apostate— I would have to be wrong, wouldn't I, Brother Pratt?"

"I don't know what you're—"

"The point is that I have not left our beloved Church, my brothers," Usher interrupted, pounding the empty, open hand on his silk brocade vest. "It is here in my heart that the Church forever rests. On this rock of true faith."

"President Young has said—"

He pointed a long finger out at the end of his arm, silencing Hyde when he roared, "It is Brigham Young who should stand trial before us all! In the years I have been away from Zion, he has led the faithful further and further astray!"

Hyde's face grew red as he stammered, "D-dare you speak of the one, true Prophet—"

"Damn you!" Usher interrupted again, but this time dangerously quiet, his words issuing forth as a menacing snarl.

"You were a member of the highest priesthood," Enoch Higbee said. "If you will not repent of your continued apostasy against the one true Church, against its one true Prophet . . . then according to Church doctrine—Jubilee Usher—you will be cast into the outer darkness with Satan and his fallen angels, where there will be only weeping, wailing, and the gnashing of teeth."

169

"For years I have held Temple Recommends," Usher began. "None of you can dispute the place of my family in the early Church."

Hyde shook his head. "No. No man can dispute the fidelity of your family to our faith."

"Then you must realize that it is your bound duty to perform this ceremony for a member of our priesthood."

"I cannot, in any way, consider you still a part of the Melchizedek," Bishop Hyde said.

"Why don't you call me Brother Usher?" Jubilee asked. "Why not call me Elder Usher?"

"You have apostatized," Enoch Higbee repeated.

He turned on the priest. "You! I am sure you must have something to do to prepare for this sacred ceremony."

Higbee shook his head emphatically. "I won't have anything to do with your blasphemy."

Usher turned slightly. "Brother Haslam?"

"Yes, Colonel," Orrin Haslam said as he stepped forward.

"Take Elder Higbee here to a private room and see if you can convince him that he is doing the right thing, the only thing, in marrying me to my God-given wife in this Temple ceremony."

"You can't take me—"

Haslam motioned four of his gunmen forward. All of them seized Enoch Higbee and dragged the struggling priest from the room as the other five watched, frightened into silence. But their eyes told the story. Usher enjoyed finding the unabashed fear discolor their faces.

"I want it clearly understood that I am not against shedding blood on this holy ground," Usher said.

"If you killed here," Hyde said, then swallowed with that bouncing Adam's apple, "it would be near the greatest sin before the eyes of God."

"Did Abraham not stand on holy ground—before his God—the one true God—when he performed his ancient sacrifices?"

"You can't possibly compare yourself—"

"God told Abraham to sacrifice his only son!" Usher roared. Then he leaned over the shorter Hyde, his voice almost at a whisper when he asked, "So do you think that I, Colonel Jubilee Usher of the Order of the Sons of Dan, would stop short of shedding blood in the name of the one true faith?"

Bishop Hyde blanched, his eyes squinting in a mixture of fear and revulsion. "No. I don't think you would stop at anything. Even unto killing all of us."

With a smile Usher glanced dramatically at the door where Haslam's men had dragged Enoch Higbee, then said, "But if I killed *all* of you, there wouldn't be anyone qualified to perform this sacred wedding ceremony for me—now, would there?"

Whitney Pratt stuck a finger inside his tall collar, yanking it away from the abundant flesh. It seemed a little too tight on his turkey-wattle of a neck. Bishop Hyde nodded to him with permission to speak. "When . . . when do you want to have us prepare for . . . to perform this wedding for you?"

Usher watched how the other three grew most uncomfortable when Hyde and Pratt agreed at last to doing what this uninvited guest demanded. His eyes raked them harshly. "Do any of the rest of you wish to join Brother Higbee?" And he waited.

They shook their heads reluctantly.

"You will help Elder Pratt and Bishop Hyde perform the wedding for my chosen bride?"

The four nodded.

"Good," Usher declared smugly. As he looked over his shoulder at the fifteen Danites who remained in the room with him, Jubilee instructed, "I want two of you to go with each one of these priests as they and their assistants prepare the Temple for my wedding. You, there—go out to the ambulance and help George bring in my bride. Find a comfortable place for her to wait. Somewhere warm. There was that small room off the front entrance."

Usher watched the soldier nod, turn, and leave the room.

"So, Bishop Hyde," Jubilee gushed as he turned back around, putting his second pistol away and tugging again at the bottom of his vest, smoothing it to look his best on this, his wedding day. "I'll wait right here for you to come fetch me. When you're ready to start."

Hyde's lips moved, mouthing silently for a moment before he said, "Just because this will be a Temple ceremony does not confer God's blessing on your wedding."

Jubilee watched the bishop turn and start away between two of Usher's men.

"Make no mistake about it, Elder Hyde. My wedding will have God's blessing. And you will be sure that my wife has *your* blessing, won't you? But even more important than your good wishes for my betrothal—I will soon have the throne of power in this one, great Church . . . before another year is out."

•　　•　　•

It was as if the scales of dark, radiant earth were peeling off one at a time, spilling from the earth ghost's head—a monstrous visage like a dark, gleaming raiment. Those falling scales resembling long, curly hair that swirled in a resplendent mist. Showering streams of rich, fertile earth caught the dancing light, cascading from both sides of the earth ghost's smooth head where the two horns emerged, jutting from the cruel brow just above a pair of evil eyes luminous with the fires said to burn in the pits of the earth itself.

Chung-li Chu'uan knew the earth demon was the most powerful of all ghosts. It hovered over her, singeing the very air around her—its steamy breath pregnant with moistness out of the bowels of the earth. But, miraculously, heat was all she felt. Not the tongues of fire from its mouth, nor the destruction wrought from its piercing gaze. Only the cremated stench of this beast's breath.

The earth ghost was, after all, what fed on the bodies of the dead who had been planted beneath the ground.

With a start Chung-li awakened suddenly, shivering uncontrollably, finding her sleeping gown damp. Frost crusted the inside of the room's one windowpane. Morning would soon arrive: the sun's pale light approaching from the east beyond the hills, coloring the crystal swirl of window frost into a reassuring hue of golden rose.

Chung-li hated these morning dreams. They were always the sort that haunted her the rest of the day. Clung to her like a sinister spirit until the night returned and she must again face her fear of closing her eyes.

Still, this was different, far different. This morning was the first time she had been visited by the earth ghost. And it frightened her beyond any fear she could remember.

Chung-li could understand if she had seen the earth demon breathing fire that night following the terrible beating she took from the white barbarian. But that had been back in the Season of the Snake. Why now? When it was almost time for the fourth full moon to arrive since he had brutally violated and profaned her?

"Did you really love yourself so little that you could end your own life?" she said aloud with a puff of breath-frost, trembling still, thinking on her eldest sister as she pulled her damp, cold gown back over her bruised breasts.

Thinking hard on that eldest sister giving birth to the girl-child of a man whose name remained a secret, then plunging to find death at the bottom of the village well.

To be a woman was her sister's only sin. To give birth to a daughter in a time of little food had brought about her total ruin. In the darkness of her tiny room Chung-li admitted she would never possess the courage of her sister. Chung-li could not end her own life.

What was better? Life suffered in Mandarin China? Or life endured here among the white demons in the Gold Mountain, her body sold every night by her employer?

In China her sister could not dare utter the man's name—for to do so would be one more admission of his existence.

Chung-li's body was bought every night by the simple men who scratched holes in the mountainsides, slave work for the big mining companies perched south of this town high above the desert. So different was this place from her home in China. So far from her life there.

Yet there was nothing to return to there.

And nothing to walk forward to here in the land of the white barbarians.

Like Chung-li, her sister ultimately had no other choice. The nameless man had commanded her to lie with him, ordering her to spread her legs and let him enter. She had been his desire, his secret longing made real.

More obscene still: perhaps that man had even been with the other villagers when they stole out of the night with their torches and burned the family's few special possessions, splattered blood about the house, butchered the family's stock in their pens outside. Perhaps he too had put on a mask like the others who came in the dark, like those come to shame the whole family for the terrible evil of their eldest daughter.

Women were truly a curse in the eyes of the gods.

Chung-li's sister had been brave enough to kill herself. Brave enough to take her newborn daughter with her too—moments after birth. Before the child was even given a chance to suckle.

What courage! What love that must have taken to shut off the life breath of one's own girl-child. To save it from a life filled by pain and torment.

Chung-li was not near so brave.

Men were blessed by the gods. Given dominion over women like Chung-li. Men like Chung-li's employer.

Who had that secret man been, the one who led her sister to kill herself? Was he someone she met in the fields every day? Or had she first seen him in the marketplace, where he made her believe his eyes that she was something special? He could not have been a stranger. In their village there were no strangers. Her sister had known the man who shamed her.

And he had known of the dark-night raid on the house. The burning, the blood splattering, the killing of all the animals. Nothing less than the wholesale exorcising of the evil ghosts evoked by the evil daughter—the attempt to clean the stain from both the family and village, from both the fields and the nearby stream. All of it tainted by the bastard child growing in the young woman's belly.

Had the man worked the adjoining field, gazing at Chung-li's sister with such longing all through the day? His stares making her uncomfortable at the first, then later coming to feel flattered that he chose only her to look at.

Or had he been one of the merchants who sold cloth? Or tea in the marketplace? Perhaps some strange and mystical item imported from far-off lands—like this Gold Mountain? In that close-knit village Chung-li's sister would have to have some form of contact with him other than merely obeying his command to lie down and spread her legs for him.

As Chung-li used to do for her employer. How glad she was that he had not demanded that service of her in a long, long time. It made her skin crawl like the march of a thousand centipedes to think of his grotesque, distorted body climbing atop her, pumping away as she squeezed her eyes shut, trying to force away the image of a deformed manhood part crookedly and painfully working in and out of her.

But lo, those many times before she had obeyed her employer. Just as Chung-li's sister had obeyed the man in their village back in China. Chung-li imagined that it was probable her sister had been flattered by his demand to lie with him at first. Yet soon she likely grew terrified. As frightened as Chung-li had been of her employer's demands. Every bit as frightened as she was when she had awakened this morning from her first earth-ghost dream.

It signaled such import. The appearance of this most powerful of all demons presaged great doom in one's life.

Without a choice Chung-li had always obeyed her employer. Even here in the Gold Mountain women did as they were told without fail. No matter the cost.

Better that Chung-li's niece had died with her mother at the bottom of the well.

"If you tell anyone ... if you tell your family, tell your sisters," Chung-li uttered the cruel words quietly now, lying there in her cold bed, mouthing the threat the man would have made to her sister back in China so many years before, "I will not stop at beating you. I will come to kill you. But first I will make you watch me strangle the child that grows in your belly. Only then will I kill you. No matter that you hate me—you must be here to lie with me again next week. On this same day. At this same hour. Next week. Each time I will lie with you."

Chung-li shuddered. It must have been just like living here in her employer's house of business. Working, eating, and sleeping here where the sad, deformed man lived out his day too. For so long she had been able to separate this lying with men from the rest of her life, to separate out this spreading of her legs for their pleasure and not hers. It was really of no importance, she came to believe so long ago—only a matter of lying back, spreading her legs, and letting the men do the rest. Some wanted her to stand. Or bend over the bed. Or have her touch, fondle, stroke them with her hands until they groaned, became white-eyed, and finished in a hot explosion all over her wrists.

Ever since being brought here on that ship to the land of the Gold Mountain, Chung-li had always been able to separate that evil from the rest of her daily existence.

So now there were two demons seeming to clog her bowels with their darkness. Four full moons ago there had been the white demon who beat and sodomized her mercilessly, laughing at her pain. And there was her employer who had not protected her from his terror. Bak Sahm had shown how little he cared for her even as a valued possession that made him money.

The tears came slow, warm on her cold cheeks. She hurt so badly because of the aching void in her womb, the terrible emptiness in her own heart.

Her sister had probably told the father of her unborn child that she was pregnant with his baby. So it was probably he who had organized the villagers' raid on the family.

Chung-li bit her lower lip, hard. Hard enough a sting that it brought new tears to her eyes.

She dared not speak to her employer. She was not as brave as her sister had been, to declare herself before the man who took what he wanted from her and gave nothing back.

She vowed she would never speak to her employer of her despair, and pain, and hopelessness.

She would never be brave enough to do that.

19

WHAT AIR BRUSHED her cheeks inside this huge stone building wasn't fresh, crisp, and clean, nothing like the autumn air outside, where she had been kept waiting in the ambulance. Nevertheless, in here it was cool—cool enough to remind her of fall days back in her childhood, playing among the shadows cast by Big Cobbler Mountain on the floor of the Shenandoah Valley. So little to care about back then.

There was damned little for Gritta Hook to care about any longer.

The door closed behind her, and she was left alone with George. Usher's Negro servant shuffled uneasily toward the table in the center of the small, bare room. Gritta's eyes moved over the walls, naked save for the multitude of hooks all hung at eye level. Below each set of two hooks sat a small wooden box with a hinged lid. At the outer edge of that lid was nailed wood trim to form a lip.

"The colonel said I was to see to you getting ready for your ceremony," George eventually said, breaking the eerie, shadowy silence.

Gritta turned, finding the Negro at the corner of the table, a folded piece of cloth across his arms.

"You to take off your clothes and hang 'em on one of them hooks," he explained, his eyes showing how anxious he was. "Your coat and dress hang, he told me so. And the rest goes in one of them chests, the one right under your hooks. Your boots set on top of the chest when you all done. I think I got it right, ma'am."

She saw how his yellowed eyes caressed her a moment, but not with any desire. Instead it was the old man's gentle way of apology. She was young enough to be his daughter. Gritta knew that George knew that she knew. As cold, and lost, and scared as she felt inside—she realized that he must oftentimes suffer the same fear with all that Usher put them both through. Precious little remained in her for feelings. What was left she had to admit, if they were not the darkest of emotions, they were nothing more than the shreds of all that had made her life worthwhile before. Emotions in a tatter, torn asunder. Nothing strong enough to make her care any longer. At least not enough to do something about anything at all.

"Your coat, ma'am?"

Gritta turned and slowly pulled the long blue coat from her shoulders, feeling a sudden sense of lightness as it came from her arms. Jubilee had brought it to her two winters before. Army wool. Brass buttons. Long enough to reach her ankles; her arms swam helplessly in the sleeves. But it was warm for the long rides, long periods of enforced inactivity in Usher's ambulance. Winter was coming. So she was thankful for the coat. Such a little thing to be so grateful for.

But there was little else to give thanks for.

After hanging the coat on one hook Gritta slipped each of the tiny buttons from its hole all the way down the front of her dress. It fit her, one of the few out of all that Usher brought her over the years. And its sapphire-blue color made it a real favorite of hers. As she had countless times before, she stepped out of the dress, then hung it from a second hook.

Her hand stayed there, frozen in the cool darkness of the candlelit room, where she held on to the dress, gripped the hook in the other hand. Staring at it.

Gritta whispered, "Hook."

"Ma'am?"

Wagging her head as if scolding herself, Gritta turned around to face George and stepped toward the table where he waited with that bundle of cloth over his arm.

"Your other clothes," George said. "The rest of 'em, ma'am."

She looked down at herself, the camisole, the sets of fluffy slips.

"I'll lay this here," he told her, his voice suddenly grown even tighter with anxiety. He laid the cloth on the corner of the table and turned his back to her. "You just get the rest of your clothes off like the colonel wanted."

One by one Gritta stepped from her petticoats, folding each one separately and stacking them neatly for the chest in the gentle light of the yellow candles that fluttered in the breeze she stirred up. At the end she released the buttons on the camisole and pulled it from her breasts, off her arms, and folded it. Now she stood naked in the coolness of the room, all but for the wool stockings and the lace boots.

Her nipples grew rigid in this interior, stone coldness, her skin tingling, goose bumps dappling across her breasts and belly, down her arms. She hunched her shoulders instinctively as she pulled the folded cloth into her hands. Unfurling it, Gritta found it to be much like a long white poncho, with a hole in the center. She pulled it over her head, sensing its caress of her tender, rigid nipples. Although it was open down either side, the garment did take some of the cold from her skin.

"You dressed, ma'am?"

Instead of answering, Gritta stepped around the edge of the table, stopping right in front of him so that she could present herself to George.

"All right," he said quietly, the tip of his tongue darting to his lips nervously, his eyes seeming as pale yellow as a pair of egg yolks skillet fried as they flicked over to the door. Then he looked down at her feet. "Your boots, ma'am. Them and the stockings. They gots to come off too. I'll put everything else in the chest yonder."

When he moved around the table to scoop up her undergarments, Gritta saw them on the table.

There beside the candlesticks. A small box of the lucifers used to light the candles. For the longest time she stared at them. From time to time her eyes climbed, as if to be reassured by the flickering dance of the yellow-blue flames at the apex of each beeswax candle. Then she would stare some more at the open box.

Enough there for her to take some, and no one would know anything was amiss.

Gritta started to put a hand out, set to take some into her hand when George turned. Her arm dropped to her side.

"Your boots? Want me help you with 'em, ma'am?"

Instead of answering, Gritta went to one of the chests and sat down, loosening the laces on each boot, then pulling the calf-high wool stockings from her legs. Those she draped over the top of the boots she set squarely in the middle of the chest lid where her undergarments were stored. Then she stood.

"Looks to be you's ready," George said, almost too quietly.

He stepped closer. She could see the yellow hue given to the whites of his eyes, close enough now to smell the breakfast on his breath. "Myself: I only got to marry once't in my life, ma'am. Ol' Saracy—she was the preacher in our plantation camp. She was the one married me and Josey. We jumped the broom together. Both done jumped that broom, and Saracy said her powerful words over us . . . making us two together for all time until the kingdom come."

He glanced away for a few moments, blinking. And she could see the moisture welling in those yellowed eyes. Something powerful in his remembrance.

"Josey and me was together till she was big with child," George explained. "Then the master up and sold her and our baby, it was still in her belly. Sold Josey and some of the rest when times was getting hard just afore the war. Folks coming into Missouri from all over hell and gone—come riding in to shoot and kill, burn our fields and stock too. Folks from Kansas they said. Folks what didn't believe in owning slaves," and he looked back at her, his cheeks glistening with the tracks of his tears.

"They took my wife . . . but I stayed on. I promised the Lord I wouldn't leave. I'd stay there until I could go and buy Josey back one day when the war was over."

He dragged the veiny back of his black hand beneath his nose, a thin glistening track strung over the knotted ropes of muscle, sinew, and vein. Then snorted. "It weren't long after I heard word come from up north Missouri that Josey been killed in a soldier fight—killed by cannon fire from one army or t'other. Didn't know which't. Folks what told me didn't know about the baby. Not word one of my baby."

Swallowing with difficulty, George coughed around what sounded like a sour lump in his throat. "That's about the time the colonel come through with Major Boothog and theys men. I was first up to the colonel's horse, grabbing on to the man's leg and thanking him for coming to free us poor niggers. But he just looked down at me while'st all the shooting was happening—said he wasn't there to free no damned niggers. He just come with his men to get food and wagons, horses and guns. Anything he could sell.

"When the shooting was over—every nigger what tried to help protect the white owner folk on that place was dead. The white women was screaming most horrible in the house . . . and the colonel's men was coming and going from the house and the slave cabins. Colonel even had one of them house girls tied belly down over the hitching rail out front of the porch, cut her dress off so she was nekked to her ankles—screaming like murder as them white men hurt her something bad, one after t'other. Colonel said he give her as a special present to his men.

"That's when he turned round to find me staring at that high-yellow gal's creamy skin, just the way the colonel likes his coffee—and he asked me if I wanted to have me some of her when all his boys was done with her. I shook my head.

"Later on he asked me if I wanted to come or stay. I didn't know, just standing there watching the killings and the looting and the burning, and the way the colonel's men hung round that coffee-skinned gal and all the rest of them women like flies to a honey-lick, waiting their turn, then a second turn, and a third too, some of 'em.

"I tol't the colonel I had to go. Had to go somewheres now. So he said to come with him. He climbed down from his big horse and put his arm round me. Told me I'd allays be safe from then on out. I allays been safe, ma'am. Onliest time I ain't safe is when I deserve a whupping. Them whuppings is for my own good."

George's eyes fell to the floor. A tear pattered the dusty toe of his scuffed, worn-out boot. "I s'pose it's like your whuppings, ma'am. They allays for our own good."

When he looked back at her face, George blinked his eyes clear of tears. "Let's go show the colonel his bride."

Bride. She sensed something special in that word.

As George cupped her elbow gently and led her to the door opposite the one they had come in, Gritta was overwhelmed with the memories that single word brought her. Sweet youth and heart-pounding excitement, fear and anticipation for a man's mouth and his embraces and all that tingle she felt down below when she was with her betrothed. Try, she told herself. Remember. Then of a sudden she turned and glanced one last time at the wall where her coat and dress hung on those hooks. Out like arms from either side of her garments spread rows of them. What was she trying to tell herself? Trying to remember?

The Negro opened the door, where four men waited beyond. Three of them Gritta recognized as Usher's own. The fourth, who immediately stepped before her, she did not know. Reaching out, the stranger took one of her hands and helped her through the door. His other hand, however, shot up to stop George.

"There's no niggers allowed in here," he said gruffly, the sternness in his voice mixed with genuine fear. "He'll . . . the nigger's gotta wait back in the room where he was."

"G'won, George," one of Usher's trio said with a nod of his head.

"Yeah," agreed a second, who stepped forward and gently nudged the old Negro back through the doorjamb. "We'll come to fetch you when it's time."

Gritta watched him go. Watched the look in those old yellowed eyes that reminded her of Luke when he'd grown tired of a long day racing the timbered hills, more the look in old Luke's eyes when he'd been bested by some critter out there in the woods and he'd come limping home, ear nearly chewed off, his muzzle in bloody shreds or poked full of porcupine quills, maybe favoring a paw where a bit of bone lay exposed within some angry flesh and the bloodied, tangled fur.

The door closed behind her.

Holding a single candle, the stranger led her away from George, away from her clothes, down a dark hall, where it grew even cooler. She knew her nipples were hardening once again. She could sense the goose bumps growing, up and down her legs. Her feet were bare padding across the cold stone floor. Behind her marched the three, Usher's men. All of them carried candles, their glow flutted along the dark walls. In the dancing light as she passed, Gritta thought she saw mural scenes painted on the walls, but could not really be sure, the way the light danced. Perhaps they were only her imagination.

No sense anymore of what was real, what was not. It had all been a loss to her for a long, long time now.

She was led through another door and there turned to the left, where she was taken to a booth with walls of canvas. She was surprised to find two women there. How she wanted to speak to them—it had been so long since she had really been this close to another woman. But they kept their eyes away from her face.

Gritta grew frightened that she had done something wrong, since they did not look at her, kept their heads down. From two earthen bowls of water they took hand cloths, squeezed them out, and parted the open sides of the garment.

The cold water shocked her skin.

"You are washed to be free from the blood and the sins of this generation," one of them said quietly, almost whisperlike.

Back and forth they immersed the cloths in the water, continuing with her ritual washing as they recited their part of the script, along with its proscribed prayer, ceremonially cleansing each part of her body. Were it not for the cold water, this sponge bath would have been a magical experience for Gritta, with these monotone invocations of God's blessing on this newcomer to the Saints' sacred Temple.

When they had finished bathing her from neck to foot beneath the long garment, one of the women ritualistically proceeded to Gritta's head.

"That your brain and intellect will be clear and active."

From there it was on to the eyes, the ears, and nose—explaining how she must see, hear, and breathe only the righteous.

When the pair was finished, they took two steps backward out of the candlelight and the stranger took hold of her elbow once again, turning her, leading Gritta to another booth across the room, where another pair of women emerged from the darkness into the candles' light to begin their prayers. But this time they did not wash Gritta. Instead they poured oil from large clay urns into their hands and anointed all parts of Gritta's body, in the same order those parts had been washed. With each anointing came a new invocation.

Finished, they too stepped back into the shadows, and her guide led her to a third booth. Here a lone woman came forward, her arms held out, some folded cloth draped across them.

"Remove what you wear, now that you have been washed in the blood of the Lamb. Now that you have been anointed in the name of the Holy of Holys."

The solitary woman helped Gritta pull the white drape over her head, disposing of it somewhere behind her in the darkness. Then she dressed Gritta in the cloth she had over her arm.

"This is called a garment. It is a most sacred shield. Only those wearing garments can present themselves for Temple ceremonies," the woman explained as she draped Gritta in it, tightened the cord around Gritta's waist.

"It represents the garment God gave our father Adam in the Garden of Eden. Unless you defile it, this garment will be a shield and protection for you against the power of the devil—the power of the Destroyer himself . . . until your work on earth is complete."

She smoothed it out from Gritta's waist, tugging it here and there to make it fit just so. "From this day forth you are to wear this Temple garment in place of your ordinary underclothes. You are to wear this for the rest of your life here on earth. To protect you against the Destroyer. To protect you until you become a god in heaven."

Gritta watched as the woman's face faded, disappearing backward out of the candlelight into the shadows at the back of the booth. Her guide took her arm once more and turned her around. He leaned forward, whispering in one ear.

"Your husband for eternity has chosen a new name for you. It is a name you are not to reveal to anyone until you are asked in the ceremony that is to follow. Do you understand?"

Gritta nodded once. Her eyes narrowed, not understanding why she had to have a new name. Then her expression relaxed, for it suddenly struck her, making sense. Hadn't she been lost before? True—she didn't remember much about what had gone on years ago. So this was her new life, and it mattered not that others had called her Gritta . . . what a blessing that she would be christened with her real name again. Find out here just who she was.

"Your husband has chosen your new name to be Joy," the guide explained, leaning forward to whisper in her ear again. "Will you remember your new name?"

She nodded again.

"Good. You will be asked your new name at a certain place in the Temple ceremony and when you are sealed to your husband for eternity. There will be no other men in your life after this ceremony. That is why your name is changed for him. Why he chose your name. For now and evermore you will belong to him, and him only. Sealed to him in death. Sealed to him in life everlasting."

Leaning back from her ear, the guide took Gritta's wrist and led her from the opening of the booth at the far end of the room, where candles lit a door oiled in a dark mahogany. There the man knocked and the door was immediately opened from the other side.

"You are about to enter the Creation Room," the guide explained, holding up a hand to prevent Gritta from entering too soon. "In here you will witness a play reenacting the creation of the world. You will hear the voice of Elohim—the father of Jehovah. The voice of Jehovah—who is actually Jesus the Christ. And you will hear the voice of Michael—the fallen archangel who at one time ruled all of heaven with Elohim and Jehovah—but then descended into the bowels of the earth, into the lake of fire."

She was the first to be passed through the doorway. Into a room so totally dark it was frightening. Hands reached out of the blackness and took hold of her arms, urging her slowly forward. As Gritta shuffled one small step after another into the cold void, she felt the guide moving right behind her, sensed his breathing as well as those on either side of her.

Suddenly she was stopped. A moment later a deep voice began to speak from somewhere in the distance across the room, the words piercing the darkness. She was supported by those around her as the voice rumbled mightily from the walls and the ceiling of the black chamber.

"The earth was void of light. All creation was yet to come. Elohim, the very father of our god Jehovah . . . Elohim the creator, also known as Adam, found need in his heart to make this world, one world among many worlds.

"Jehovah was given birth to join his father, as was the archangel Michael. Together Jehovah and Michael stood on either side of Elohim and determined they should create from void. To bring life from the nothing. This holiest of holy trinity of gods created the stars scattered across the firmament. Our star was born."

Across the room someone struck a match. It flared, caught, danced upward in its spiral of yellow flame as an unseen person held the match to a candle. In front of the candle was a large circle made from a sheet of transparent yellowed paper. Behind the candle hung a round reflective mirror to radiate the saffron light.

"Behold the sun! Behold! Our sun is given life by the gods!"

For the moment she did not much care to pay such close attention to that booming voice across the room. Instead Gritta stood transfixed, staring at the candle and its reflective orb—something that truly reminded her of a small, radiant sun.

Suddenly she promised herself she would remember to get her hands on some of those matches back in that room where she had undressed and George had told her of his marriage.

Gritta did not understand why the old nigger told her of jumping the broom with a slave girl. Why tell her about marrying when she was changing clothes and changing names and being shown how the world was started—not created by God . . . but started by someone called Elohim and Jehovah and the devil archangel too. All of them having a hand in it.

No matter, any of that world making. She determined she would wear what she had to wear. Say what words she had to say. Repeat what she was told to repeat. And respond to her new name.

Take an oath to any or all of their gods.

After all, she was far past heavenly forgiveness.

Her soul fallen far, far beyond God's blessed redemption.

Anything she would do, anything at all, she would do . . . just so she could get back to that room when she was finished here in the darkness.

A voice boomed from the darkness, "Life was given to the moon!"

Where she could get her hands on some of the matches.

"The stars flung across the universe itself!"

Then there would no longer be any darkness for her, Gritta thought. Just get her hands on those matches, and she would never be frightened of the dark again.

20

Late October 1875

"SEALED — MAN AND wife—for all time."

Gritta heard the words, looking into Jubilee Usher's face as he stood before her, holding her two hands in his.

But those words made little sense.

"Sealed together for all time. Soul to soul, throughout eternity. So it is the will of the gods."

The candlelight flutted against the walls of this magnificent inner room where she had been led near the end of a long journey of many stops over many hours, coached to perform one confusing ritual after another at every one of the stations that prepared her for a final, grand entry into this ornate Temple decorated with its deeply mystical symbols—for it was here that Gritta Hook finally rejoined Usher.

She cursed herself for the tepid degree of security that her return to him gave her.

How twisted all life must have become if she feared these strangers who spoke in riddles and singsong ritual, preferring instead what profane normalcy she had grown accustomed to with the cruel master of her life.

"Celestial marriage stands as one of the eight pillars of our beliefs," a voice droned on and on, from one of those gathered at the long low altar draped in a blood-red velvet where she stood with Usher. "Marriage is the sole pillar that grants woman her rightful place at the side of her god."

Walking down the carved steps into the huge baptismal pool earlier hadn't been frightening. She had been baptized before: once in childhood and . . . a second time just before she was . . . married.

Numbly, Gritta gazed about curiously as voices continued to mesmerize her with their haunting quality. This . . . yes, this felt to her like a wedding now. What with the long row of men arrayed near Usher. She turned now and glanced at the four women who stood off to her side. The speakers, five or six of them, formed the main arch of the crescent at the long altar, near the place where Usher held her hands. He too spoke from time to time. Nothing that she could understand. Most of the day had a dreamlike quality to it. But then, long, long ago Gritta had come to accept that if she was meant to understand something, then she would understand.

This was a mystery she could not grasp. The sort of dream that was lost upon awakening.

Two women and two men had awaited her in the baptismal pool, the whole room gloriously lit by candles and lamps burning against the walls that were brightened, made active, by their heroic murals.

"Come, my sister," one of the men said as he took Gritta's hand and led her down into the pool, where she stood in waist-deep water with the rest of them.

She knew what they wanted of her. It was time for the Holy Ghost to take over her body once more. Although she was willing to cooperate, Gritta still doubted the Holy Ghost would visit her this baptism. There were some who were just too far lost to be found.

The elder had taken both her hands into one of his, then raised the other to heaven as he closed his eyes and spoke most solemnly.

"Sister Joy, by virtue of the authority vested in me from the one, true holy Church of God, I baptize you for the remission of all your sins. In the name of the Father, and of the Son, and of the Holy Ghost. Amen."

There it was again—talk of the ghost. But as the others in the pool came close, joining her so they could lower her backward into the water, Gritta sensed a vacuousness within—missing that recognition of the Lord's spirit come thundering through her body as it had before. Instead she felt only the cold of the water, the hands upon her, and the peace that came with knowing that she had to endure only a little while longer before she would have in her hands the means of her own redemption.

"Let these two marry according to the holy order of God."

She turned back to the speaker at the altar now, feeling Usher caressing her hands in his.

"May man and wife begin to lay the foundation of a little family kingdom which shall no more be scattered upon the face of the earth, but dwell in one country, keeping their genealogies from generation unto generation, until each man's house shall be multiplied as the stars of heaven."

Usher turned slightly, holding out an open, upturned hand. One of those nearest him placed a ring in his palm. He slipped it on Gritta's finger.

"Verily," the speaker continued, "verily I say unto you: that whosoever you seal on earth shall be sealed in heaven. And whatsoever you bind on earth, in my name, and by my word, saith the Lord, it shall be eternally bound in heaven."

She looked down at her hand. Up at his face. Then back to that ring on her finger. Some of it was clear enough that it scared her down to the soles of her feet: all day she had been instructed, baptized in a new Church, and now joined to the master of her life. Sealed for all time.

"Obedience is a virtue, we have been taught," she heard another speaker say, this time a woman who stepped up to stand near the couple. "Obedience to your husband is the highest virtue before God. Rebellion from your husband is the sin of witchcraft."

A second woman came up as the first finished, then said, "God commanded lineage of Abraham. God commanded obedience of wife Sarah. So it was that Sarah presented the servant Hagar to her husband, thereby to be his wife. And from Hagar's loins sprang the peoples of many nations."

"Therefore," said the central man, dressed in a long robe, "if any man espouse a virgin, and desire to espouse another, and the first gives her consent—and should he espouse another and another—and they all are virgins, and have vowed to no other man, then that man is justified in sealing himself to all. He cannot commit adultery with that which belongeth to him and to none else. If he have ten virgins given unto him by this law of God's Church, this man cannot commit adultery, for every last one of those women all belong to him under the eyes of God. They are given him by God, and he is justified in the eyes of the Lord."

"The Virgin Mary," said a second woman dressed in a long white gown, "was the lawful wife of God the Father. After the resurrection He intends to take Mary to wife again, as one of His own wives, to give birth to and raise up immortal spirits throughout the rest of eternity."

"It is this same way with men who would one day be gods," the priest declared. "Men are the only saviors of their wives. Unless a woman please her husband, and is obedient to him in all ways, and unless that woman was saved by her husband from eternal damnation and ruin, she will not be saved come Judgment before the seat of God."

Now Gritta grew confused again, listening to all this talk that, to her, had little to do with marriage. If they were joining her to her master in the state of holy matrimony, then why all the rest of this?

Gritta was still as lost now as she had been earlier in the day, after she had entered the Creation Room—where one of the characters played the part of God, called Elohim by those who illuminated sun and moon and stars. Elohim's voice had called upon her to take a sacred vow of sacrifice to the Church. Should she be found guilty of profaning her vow—the penalty would be death.

Without explaining how her penalty was to be carried out in words, the priest drew a finger from his left ear quickly—savagely—under the jaw and across the throat to the other ear.

Then with the heavens created and illuminated, Gritta had been taken to an adjoining room said to be the Lone and Dreary World, where the characters enacted another vignette. She watched as Satan held a confusing dialogue with Adam, introducing to that first man on earth a figure dressed all in black—a character Satan said represented the preachers of all the world's churches.

To this preacher Satan offered, "I will give unto you five thousand dollars to preach to this man."

"I require more," demanded the preacher. "I have spent many, many years in preparation for my ministry and have gone to seminary to learn the will of God. You must give me more money before I will preach to all mankind."

"If you do well in preaching to this man and all those to come after him," said Satan, "I will give you more."

The preacher then turned to Adam, saying, "Good morning, sir. Do you believe in a god who is without a body, without parts or passions? A god who sits on top of a topless throne? A god whose center is everywhere and whose circumference is nowhere? A god who fills the universe . . . yet is so small that He can dwell within your heart?"

"I cannot comprehend such a god," Adam admitted.

"That's the beauty of it," the preacher exclaimed, performing for Gritta, his sole audience. "Perhaps you believe in hell—that great, bottomless pit which is full of fire and brimstone, the pit into which the wicked are cast and where they are continually burning and yet are never consumed?"

"No, I cannot believe in that either," Adam replied.

After more dialogue that made nothing but fun of the preacher and what doctrines he espoused, a woman stepped forward out of the darkness behind her to wrap a colorful sash around Gritta's waist. Another woman came forth to place a white cloth cap on Gritta's head, as well as a green apron emblazoned with embroidered fig leaves.

"What is your name?" one of the women whispered in Gritta's ear.

She remembered what she had been told, and said, "My name is Joy."

"The penalty for disobedience," the other woman asked in a whisper, "is death." She drew a wooden knife across Gritta's belly to symbolize disembowelment.

From there her guide led her into the Terrestrial World for more instruction, then on to another room for the Law of Chastity, on to the Sign of the Nail, the Law of Consecration, and the Patriarchal Grip. The procession of names and characters and sanctified instruction all seemed like an endless labyrinth. Soon enough she grew physically as well as mentally numb. Her feet felt like chunks of ice as she was finally brought to a room called Through the Veil, where she stood on one side of a tall curtain that separated the Terrestrial World from the Celestial World.

"What is your name?"

"My name is Joy," Gritta replied, praying she would be allowed to sit and rub her feet at last.

A hand came toward her through a hole in the curtain.

"Shake it," one of the women behind her whispered. "As you've been shown the secret handshake."

Finally she was allowed through the curtain into the warmly furnished Celestial Room, where she found Usher awaiting her. From there he led her and the others into the Temple itself, where he held her arm as she commanded her frozen, plodding feet to climb the steps to the long, low altar drenched in the blood-hued velvet drape that hung from all sides, reminding her of deep, rich lamb's blood dripping from a sacrificial stone altar.

At the very start of things in this great hall they allowed her to kneel on one of two soft pillows bound with white silk edging. Usher knelt on the other there before the altar with her as both men and women began a new and different ceremony in the flickering candlelight magnified by great, tall mirrors affixed to three of the four walls surrounding her, mirrors that reflected and rereflected her image alongside Usher, casting their images far into infinity itself.

Those many mirrors served to represent what the priest went on to explain: "Your marriage is just as endless as is your image in this Temple, sealing you one to the other for all time and all eternity."

"So it has been from all time," said another one of the men. "Your life together did not begin on earth, Sister Joy—it began in heaven with your husband. Together as spirit children of your Heavenly Father and Mother. In the Heavenly Kingdom where you were spirit brethren of Jesus Christ and his brother, Michael the Archangel."

Between the two men stepped one of the women, a book held open across her palms as she said, "Only the best of God's spirit children are born to parents sealed in the Temple—as you two are now sealed for all time."

The oldest instructor explained, "As our first Prophet, Joseph Smith, saith, 'You have got to learn how to be Gods yourselves . . . the same as all Gods have done before you . . . until you are able to dwell in everlasting burnings and sit in glory.' "

"And as our Prophet, Brigham Young, says today," replied the youngest of the priests, " 'Man is King of Kings, and Lord of Lords in embryo.' "

As the eldest priest came forward, accompanied by one of the women who carried a silver bowl in her hands, he dipped his hand into the water it held, then placed it on the bald top of Jubilee Usher's head.

More sealings and anointings—it all made Gritta's head swim as these people droned on and on, moving first to Usher, then back to her, again and again, telling her to bow her head—telling her to receive a holy anointing.

This ceremony of the candles and the mirrors, kneeling before the altar and the hands of anointing priests, had Gritta's interest waning, failing to hold her interest the way the vignettes had captured her curiosity earlier in the day.

Before his descent into hell, it had been explained in one of the many instructional sessions, Michael the Archangel was placed on earth under the name of Adam—given power over all the beasts of the field, the fowl of the air, the fish of the sea. While he was given all manner of fruit borne of the earth to sustain him, he was nonetheless commanded not to eat of one particular tree that stood in the midst of the Garden.

To represent that tree, the actors had placed a small cedar in the center of the room, where she watched the characters play their parts. Fruit was tied to its branches.

"But it was not good that man should be alone," one of the narrators explained.

She nearly begged for sleep as Elohim and Jehovah had a long discussion on what should be done to end the loneliness of the archangel placed in the earthly Garden, the one they called Adam.

"They two caused a sleep to fall over Adam," one of the speakers said as the actors prepared to operate on the solitary figure. The priest then commanded Gritta also to assume the posture of sleep, by dropping her head to her chest.

Then Elohim and Jehovah went through the pantomime of removing a rib from Adam's side. When it was pulled forth, a woman appeared from the shadows. Almost immediately, however, the devil made his entrance, wearing a tight-fitting suit of black muslin, complete with knee britches, black stockings, and soft slippers. Immediately going to Eve to scrape up her acquaintance while she took her first walk in the Garden, the devil was able to woo her with his seductive tongue.

Father Adam, not being the most attentive of husbands, was completely unaware of this evil suitor, leaving his bride to the mercy of Satan's temptations. Gritta watched as Eve partook a first bite of the forbidden fruit.

As Adam reappeared, the devil fled. And Eve began to weave her seductive wiles in hopes of convincing Adam to eat of the tree's fruit. As soon as he did eat the apples, both realized their naked condition and donned aprons of white silk emblazoned with green fig leaves. At that same moment all others around Gritta put on their own aprons, while one of her attendants tied a like apron around her waist.

With the symbolic dressing complete, Elohim reappeared across the room, calling into the Garden for Adam to present himself. But Adam was afraid, explained the narrator, and took Eve to hide with him in the deepest part of the forest. Knowing full well what had taken place, Elohim pronounced a curse upon the devil—and the actor playing Satan reappeared, this time slithering about on his belly, hissing and making quite a show of it for Gritta's benefit.

"Go!" bellowed Elohim, his voice ringing off the walls of the room. "Go now and forever carry the curse of Eve!"

Escorted by her attendants as the actor playing Elohim ordered them from the Garden with Adam, Gritta left the room and entered another, representing the world of man—where new voices explained that it was the lot of Adam and Eve now to toil, earning their daily bread with the sweat of their brows.

"Yet there was given unto us the promise of salvation," a disembodied voice told her. "A path would be presented to all who would be the faithful, a path whereby everyone would be saved and returned to the State of Grace in the Garden."

Then a confusing cast of characters appeared in rapid fire, representing the ancient prophets on earth—all presaging the coming of the Savior to earth. Gritta was instructed in passwords and shown certain grips by the actors, who sat her at the center of the circle they made around her, each one with a veil over his or her face. Then all raised a hand to heaven, taking a solemn vow of secrecy, of obedience unto death.

"I swear by every means in my power," one of the elders led the others in a unified response, "that I will avenge the death of Joseph Smith, the Prophet, upon the Gentiles who have caused his murder.

"I further swear that I will teach my children to do the same.

"I affirm without murmur or the slightest questioning that I will implicitly obey the commands of the priesthood in all things.

"I swear that I will not commit adultery—but will remain faithful to my spiritual husband to whom I shall remain sealed for all eternity.

"Upon my life I vow never to reveal what has transpired in this Endowment House—for the penalty for breaking this solemn oath is disembowelment: while I am still living my bowels will be ripped from my body and my throat cut ear to ear . . . and in the end my heart and tongue are to be cut out and separated from my body. In the world yet to come, everlasting damnation shall be my portion, and visited upon my heirs."

A long sermon presented to Gritta ended that portion of the Temple ceremonies, the "Second Degree" of her endowment. At that point she was taken into still another room, where she watched the actors form a new church following the crucifixion of Christ on Golgotha. For a moment a mewling sound caught in her throat, and she sought to reach out to the actor who appeared to his disciples as the slain Jesus. But she was restrained by her attendants, prevented from seeking His succor, kept from begging His forgiveness of her sins and releasing her from her torment as the prisoner of Jubilee Usher.

With the appearance of Christ immediately after his resurrection, the oldest of the narrators changed his Temple robe and regalia from his right shoulder to his left, saying, "Those who were chosen, then joined the one true Church on the face of the earth, now and forever absolutely and in every way are dependent upon the priesthood conferred by the gods."

She was then moved forward to a curtain of muslin, where a voice demanded, "What is your name, sister?"

Again she answered, "Joy."

Hands came through holes cut in the gauzy curtain, hands that drew marks across Gritta's breast over the heart, across her abdomen, and finally over the right knee with sticks of charcoal.

"Take ye the hand of your husband," the voice commanded as an arm moved through the veil, opening the curtain for her.

It was then she saw Usher at long last and was led by him into this mirrored sanctuary, alive with the fire of candles and mirrors, men and women all gowned and robed.

The priest bent close, touched her arm, and repeated, "You may rise, sister," as he helped her up alongside Jubilee Usher.

She felt unsteady, her knees sore, filled with pain from kneeling before that altar. How she wanted most to lie down—the whole ordeal had taken hours.

"Sealed—man and wife—for all time," the priest continued, his arms and face raised to the roof as Jubilee put his arm around Gritta's waist to support her as she grew weak, wavering.

"Go forth, Brother Usher. Take ye your wife into the world and make the earth fruitful as ye have been commanded. Fill your wife's womb with children and your home with happiness. Do this as God commands, assuring that all are obedient to you, as you are obedient to Him."

Then the priest took Gritta's hand, gazing into her eyes. "From this day forth, to this man, Jubilee Usher, you belong for all time. Be faithful to him only—as you would be faithful to God—and your reward will be salvation. Should you stray from the Church, or from your bond with the man, your penalty will be eternal damnation. Nothing less than your soul is at risk."

21

USHER WATCHED ORRIN Haslam button up his britches, standing over the Indian woman. Not that she was worth looking at, even worth rutting with—but Jubilee had always found a great joy simply in watching others at their carnal pleasures, ever since the first time he spied through a crack in the wall boards, later to peer under a gap between the bottom of the door and the floorboards of the family house back in the hilly lake country of western New York.

Even before he was ten years old, he had taken to staring down through the tiny hole he painstakingly drilled through the attic's floor with his pen knife—so that he could peer into his parents' bedroom. He was finding himself thrust into young manhood so very early: having to contend with an adult body when he himself was still a child. Oh, the deliciously evil things he used to think of, the intent he felt when he used to look at girls, and the way some of those girls in the neighboring towns and villages looked back at him with devilment in their eyes.

But by watching his parents' nocturnal activities with regularity, in those early years he was able to will himself into the land of man and woman. It was as if the two who grappled on the bed below his secret peephole weren't his father and mother at all. It was then as it was now— he remained detached, the consummate voyeur.

Just as he was while he watched these men come in ravenous rotation to cover the three Indian women Usher ordered snatched from their fishing expedition a few miles away.

Nothing at all wrong with giving his men this release, Usher reminded himself as he shifted, uncomfortably aroused, on the canvas stool near the edge of the great circle where his soldiers of God took their pleasure in the bodies of these pitiable, lost souls. Pahvant Indians—dark-skinned Lamanites scratching out their miserable existence here on the edge of the great basin, where life might provide them only insects and rabbits to eat at times. Surely not the proud warrior stock of the southwest. No, these were the poorest of the lost tribe Lamanites, their skin made dark by God's own curse. Not white, clean, and wholesome as were the skins of God's chosen people here in the latter days.

These were descendants of that wayward tribe of ancient Israel—still, they served their purpose well. Usher planned for them to have a more complex role in the months and seasons yet to come as he wrested the throne from Brigham Young.

"Say, Colonel—you want any of that?" Orrin Haslam asked as he dusted off his hands on the front of his canvas pants and stopped before Usher.

He shook his head, keeping his eyes on the next man, who clumsily lowered himself between the bare legs of the squat Indian woman that Haslam had just vacated. With his pants down below his knees where he rocked himself forward, the soldier planted his rigid flesh into her without formality and began grunting almost immediately.

Only then did Usher lift his eyes to Haslam, gracing his lieutenant with a most disapproving gaze. "I am a married man now."

Haslam leaned in toward Usher's ear, whispering, "I don't figure it changes a damned thing, Colonel. Like I always say: being married ain't never gonna seal up a hole, or keep my dodger from getting hard as a cleaning rod!"

There was an unwashed crudeness to Haslam that Usher detested, yet was magnetically drawn to. He found that contradictory fascination something of great interest in himself.

"I provide the women, Major."

"That you surely do," Haslam replied, turning to watch the milling circle of men jostling for turns over the three small Pahvant women.

"I choose to take my amusement not from those low women, but from watching those of you who take your pleasure where you can find it."

"You take that'un, now." And Haslam pointed to the oldest of the three dark-skinned women pinned and struggling on the ground with their tormentors. "To look at 'er, you'd figure she was the worst of the lot. But she's so damned tight wrapped right around you—she was just about the best I've ever had my dabber in. 'Cepting for a little calf my sister was raising back to home—"

"Keep your bestial vulgarity to yourself, Haslam," Usher interrupted. "Your reminiscence of times spent with animals are of no interest, and even less excitement, to me." He glared up into the fading sunlight at the man. "You best learn that—and take heed that you don't provoke me again. It has been a long, long time since I've had to show anyone a lesson on civil or military decorum. And there's no reason it can't be you."

"Didn't mean no offense—"

"Just a reminder."

"I won't ever say no such thing—"

"The men need this diversion from time to time, Major," Usher declared with great finality, his mind going back to original intent as his eyes returned to the noisy scene played out before him. "The same way they need to be reminded from time to time who is leader, and just what the boundaries are."

"You're absolutely right, Colonel."

"If our men don't use these women up tonight—and you see that these poor, wretched souls are fed and have their needs attended to when the men are done with them—I don't see any reason why we have to be in a rush to dispose of them."

Usher watched the light of it illuminate the major's face.

"Damn right, we don't have to get rid of 'em, do we, now? Ain't all that many bitches we can snatch out in this country anyway. Not like things was down in Apach' country, Colonel. Took us a few days before we found these three off by themselves."

"Gone fishing, you said."

"Caught 'em by a stream. They hooked a little more'n they was bargaining on!" Haslam roared.

"See that you give your sergeants my order that these women are not abused to the point of death tonight. Simply make sure that they are secured and a rotation of guards placed over them come dark," Usher explained.

"We don't want 'em escaping."

"Not if your men want to take their regular recreation," Jubilee said. "Now, see that your men understand that they aren't to cut or torture these three wretches. That we're keeping them for some time to come."

"Yes, Colonel," Haslam answered, beginning to turn away into the crowd of crowing, strutting soldiers jostling with one another for position over each of the three blankets.

"A moment more of your time, Major."

Jubilee rose from his stool, straightening his coat, feeling in need of the warmth a fire could give him, perhaps some of that brandy George would pour him. As a man struggled to rise to his feet, tangled up in his own britches between the outflung legs of one of the women, Usher noticed a dark pool of dampness spread beneath her buttocks on the blanket beneath the Pahvant captive.

This matter of a man's juices, he thought. Then turned to face the shorter man who had the build of a thick oak tree. "Major, when you've seen to this matter of the women, come round before dark descends on us."

"Sir?"

"I want to discuss what our plans should be regarding the tribes in this area."

"I see," Haslam said. "Keeping them stupid of what we're doing when we take their women to use."

He shook his head. "No. I'm talking about enlisting the bands inhabiting this part of Zion to help us raise the sword of war against the false prophet."

A smile grew across Haslam's face. "You want me help get these Injun tribes to join us when we take control from Brigham Young?"

"Yes, that's the idea I've been having."

"And when I get that done—you won't mind me taking off for that mining town again, will you, Colonel? The one I told you about?"

"Not at all, Major."

"There's a gal there I'm really hankering to see again."

Usher smiled, recalling Haslam's description of the Pioche prostitute. "Certainly. But you will also be on an errand for me."

"Colonel?"

"We must lay plans to finance our war against the false prophet. I must have you return to your Chinee whore at Pioche long enough to figure out how we are going to secure the money that will buy guns and bullets, dynamite and wagons—money to ensure aid from some and silence from the rest."

Haslam licked his lips hurriedly. "I been wanting to get back to Pioche real bad, Colonel."

Usher turned to him, slapping a hand on his shoulder. "You get the

197

bands lined up behind our war on Brigham Young—and you'll get your chance, Major. Your chance to see that little Chinee whore of yours again."

Ascending Huerfano Creek into the mountains, Jonah Hook and the others had been caught near Robidoux Pass by an early snowstorm late last month. Both he and Two Sleep had recognized the change in the sky's color off to the west. The way the wind shifted out of the northwest with the hoary smell of winter in the air.

"Smell the wind, Jeremiah," he told his son, pointing. "Then look at the clouds hugging in around them peaks there."

This was the way he must teach Jeremiah about this country out here, all that he could of what Jonah had learned from Bridger and Sweete. Not that Hook hadn't already learned to read the weather when it came to predicting periods of rain or the coming of a dry spell, watching the way the critters acted before a storm's arrival, or the manner in which the wooly worms grew that told him about a hard winter on its way. But that was the valley country of Virginia, and the hardwood region of southwestern Missouri too.

This mountain West was something altogether different. And even though Jeremiah would likely head back to Indian Territory and that family waiting for him when this business with his mother was done and over with, Jonah figured it wasn't about to hurt learning the boy what he could pass on. While to some those reservations at Fort Sill and up to the Darlington Agency might not be the free West—they was still the West in Jonah's mind. A far sight farther west than most of civilization had yet ventured.

Except for the Mormons.

But Jonah wasn't counting them. Not in the slightest. Couldn't rightly bring himself to consider that pocket of settlement as civilization. Not when he blamed them all for what they done to his kin. To his life. To all the wasted years gone beneath the hooves of the horses he had ridden into the ground looking to put his family back together.

There was going to be too many lost pieces, he was afraid now, as they drew closer and closer to taking up the trail gone cold seven long years ago. He thought on Hattie, likely growed to a full woman now—hell, she was twenty years this past spring. Be having another birthday come green-up after this winter.

Hook shuddered with the cold and pulled the blanket around him a little more tightly, then held his hands over the fire they kept going day and night beneath the overhanging canopy of blue spruce. Jeremiah stirred in his sleep, went back to breathing deep. Two Sleep snored with a low rumble. Their horses hung their heads, no longer pawing at the snow and ground, their muzzles draped in crusts of hoarfrost, tiny beards of icicles suspended in a broken rosette from their lower lips.

She was damned pretty, Hattie was. Like her mother. So much had she reminded him of Gritta when Gritta was Hattie's age. Back to sixty-eight . . . there on the station platform when he put his daughter on board that train and sent her east with Riley Fordham. He had trusted his instincts about the man getting Hattie to St. Louis and into one of them fine women's seminary schools. More important, he had trusted Shad Sweete's reading of Riley Fordham. A man simply did not see the country the old fur trapper had, across all the span of years he had, and not be savvy about his fellow man. Jonah had paid attention and learned at Shad Sweete's side all he could about reading people as well as he read sign.

Somewhere to the west below them lay the long north-south expanse of the San Luis Valley. He had learned Fort Garland and Fort Massachusetts weren't that far to the south, across the Sierra Blanca from where the three were sitting out the early-winter storm. Waiting for a break in the weather when they could cut their way down out of this high country. Jonah vowed he would take them far south if he had to, if only to keep from crossing any more mountain passes at this time of year. It was a deadly choice he had made—one that could likely kill any man not near as driven as he, any man not consumed with so fiery a will to survive as Jonah Hook.

It was the same will that kept him alive in those first days, then weeks, after he was wounded at Corinth in Mississippi. The rest of the ragtag Confederate soldiers retreated out of that woods where Jonah lay among the silent dead. Their generals had pulled them back with their wounded, but left him for dead. Likely didn't know any better about him, lying like he was under the two mangled, shapeless bodies of a couple of other poor boys who had marched with Jonah out of Arkansas after their defeat at Pea Ridge. Barefoot like Jonah. All of Sterling Price's once-great army of liberation now become wolfish, rib-gaunt, and starving, like they all was when the Battle of Corinth got started.

Being hauled by railcar north to that damned prison where the Confederate boys kept dying didn't better Jonah's fate. But this was a place where the undead died slow. Not like they did when grapeshot slashed bloody swaths through their advancing front of ragged infantry. Not like they died when the rows upon rows of Union infantry fired in orderly precision at the homegrown boys in their store-bought butternut. Most wore the homespun like Jonah. Men like Hook who talked of home. Dreamed of home. Pined for those left behind at home.

As he yearned now. Here in the cold of the up-country of the Rocky damned Mountains. Brought here to this, trying to gather up the lost pieces of his life if he could. Hattie gone and likely busy with a life of her own. Maybe children of her own.

Ezekiel gone for good. Buried back to Missouri beside the sod-filled graves he didn't need for Hattie and Jeremiah no more. Only one hole left to fill in.

Jonah shuddered again, rubbing his hands and watching the frost collect at the folds of the blanket he pulled up around his cheeks. How he prayed he would fill that last hole with only dirt come the end of this search for Gritta. Too much lost already. More than any man should be asked to bear up under.

Down the west slope they'd strike Saguache Creek, so he'd been told by more than one person. That would lead them north by west. Toward Utah. How everyone looked back at him when Jonah asked the best route they could take to reach Utah—likely they all took him to be a Mormon. Heading for the holy land.

Instead, this was a holy war Jonah had taken up against the Mormons. At least the Mormons what had taken his family and torn it apart while he was off fighting that damned war that nearly cost him his life. There at Corinth he had come near laying his life down for the side that in the end finally give up and surrendered to the Yankees.

What the hell did all them good boys lay down their lives for, give up arms and legs for—if them generals was going to surrender in the end? Retreat was figured in to the way of war—a man had to retreat a time or two. But surrender? Give up your sword and guns? Ride back home stripped of your manhood and all you'd fought for? No, Jonah couldn't dream of that.

Instead he'd gone west to fight Injuns while dressed in the Yankee blue before he was finally mustered out as a U.S. Volunteer. Given his first chance in five years to go home. But—the place weren't home no more, not when he got there.

Jonah doubted it would ever be home again.

He'd have to find Gritta a place where she could grow her garden, raise her sheep for the wool she carded and spun. A place where she could sit in her rocker in the sun, or in the shade if she was a mind to. Just sit and rock while he hunted squirrels and rabbits, deer and turkey again. Remembering the way she rose from her rocker on that porch back home when she spotted him returning from the tree line, shading her eyes with one flat hand, the better to see what he was bringing home for her pots.

"How you doing, Pa?"

He looked over at Jeremiah and smiled softly at the young man who had cracked his brooding. "Doing fine, Jeremiah. Ain't time for you to wake up and tend the fire. Not yet. Get your sleep."

"All we been doing. Sleeping for days."

"And staying alive."

Jeremiah rubbed his dripping nose. "Yeah, Pa. You been keeping us all alive."

"I 'tend to, son. G'won—get back to sleep."

As his oldest son closed his eyes, Jonah laid another branch on the fire, intent on the meteor shower of sparks erupting into the overhanging canopy.

Foot-trails led off from their camp in all directions where the three of them went to relieve themselves, farther still to hunt for what they could until Two Sleep and Jonah had admitted they weren't about to find much game this high. Owned up that they'd been caught too far up the mountains while the game had been driven down toward the valleys before the early snow. So came the decision made on sacrificing the poorest of their packhorses. The ribby, galled one.

At least the meat wasn't spoiling. Not with this cold. They'd eaten most of the organs first. It was best that way, the old mountain man had taught him. The choicest portions were filled with richness that would keep them warm, keep them alive through the storm and its aftermath until the weather broke and they could beat their way downhill. Heart and liver. Then the intestines, coils of the blue gut held over the low flames and seared to crackling crispness. That horse thief's pack animal had kept them alive for better than a week now.

Maybe tomorrow, he thought. They would see what the sky to the west held for them tomorrow morning. A milk-pale pewter sun was sinking beneath a wide, thick band of violet clouds now. Tomorrow's sunrise might offer the hint of a break in the cold snap. Then would come those last warming days that showed up before winter arrived for good.

Jonah cursed those who had come and taken everything from him. The faceless, unknown man who had robbed him of all these years with his family. The man he hunted—this Jubilee Usher, who was the reason Jonah Hook hadn't yet come home from the war.

If it wasn't a war of Confederates pitted against the invading Yankees from up north . . . then at least it was turning out to be Jonah Hook's private war.

This time, Jonah vowed, he was fighting a war he intended to win.

22

GRITTA SANG AS she went about commending her spirit to God.

> *"Jesus bids us shine, with a clear, pure light,*
> *Like a little candle burning in the night;*
> *In this world of darkness, we must shine,*
> *You in your small corner, and I in mine."*

Outside the tent, autumn's early twilight had descended on these hills in southwestern Utah Territory. The air grew colder with the sun's retreat, cold enough to make her shiver and her skin prickle with goose bumps when she took off the old dress and put on this new one she had never worn.

> *"Jesus bids us shine, first of all for Him;*
> *Well he sees and knows it if our light is dim.*
> *He looks down from heaven, sees us shine,*
> *You in your small corner, and I in mine."*

Jubilee gave her the dress a few days back, and now she couldn't remember where he said he got it. It looked new, smelled it too. Not like some of the other dresses he had brought her over the seasons. Plainly they had smelled of the women who wore them before her. But this one, it *felt* new. So she had never worn it, keeping it new—until this twilight. Wanting something special to wear when she finally stepped toward God's light.

"Jesus bids us shine, then for all around,
Many kinds of darkness in this world abound:
Sin and want and sorrow; we must shine,
You in your small corner, and I in mine."

That morning when she had been digging through her worn and battered trunk, searching out some clean stockings to wear for the day, Gritta came across the dress she had worn the day Jubilee took her on that wagon ride to the long Church ceremony with the candles and mirrors. She had almost put the dress back in the trunk with the others when she remembered.

Then, standing there with the sun's first light touching the side of the canvas wall tent at dawn, Gritta held that dress up against her sleeping gown, glancing quickly at the tent flaps. She could not hear his voice. It might mean he was off in some other part of his camp. With the men, or those Indian women they had been keeping. Gritta was relieved when the three dark-skinned women no longer cried and whimpered, at least not as loudly as they had wailed and screamed the first day they were dragged into Jubilee's camp.

Better to be quiet and accept, and make one's own plans to escape for good.

"Jesus bids us shine, as we work for Him,
Bringing those that wander from the paths of sin;
He will ever help us, if we shine,
You in your small corner, and I in mine."

As she held the dress against her bosom that morning, running her hands over the fabric, spreading the long folds tucked into the bodice, Gritta's fingers ran over the small tumble of something concealed in the hidden pocket beneath one of those long folds of cloth. Her heart immediately climbed to her throat, making it hard to breathe as she turned her back on the tent flaps, but kept watching those flaps over her shoulder while she slowly parted the long drape of fabric to plunge her hand all the way to the bottom of the pocket.

Memory came to her suddenly. That room. The candles. The gown she was given to wear. The same room lit by candles where she was returned after the long day and evening of baptism and vignettes, sermons and ceremonies, washings and anointings. How she had thanked God Almighty for answering her prayers made to Him throughout that long, confusing day. For here she was allowed to put her own dress back on over the garment given her in one of the early ceremonies.

George was not there in the candlelight. Only one of the women who had played many different roles in the vignettes that day, and she sat in a chair against the wall, exhausted. Her head hung, chin to her breast, eyes closed. By the time Gritta had buttoned this dress to her neck, the woman's breathing came regular, and deep.

Without hesitation Gritta snatched what sticks she could from the small tin on the table, quickly stuffing them into the hidden pocket. All the way to the bottom. Leaving a few of the lucifers in the tin box on the table among the low-burning candles, in the event someone checked before she left.

The act made her feel like a child again, doing something naughty and hoping she wouldn't be caught. Yet still having the courage to do something naughty.

But taking the lucifers wasn't a brave thing to Gritta. Only something a naughty girl might do. The brave act would be using those sulfur-headed matches.

So she had kept her hand near that fold of fabric that spilled over her right thigh as she walked out to the ambulance, was lifted up by the men, and then sat down on the hard, springless seat for their long ride home. She tried to sleep that night while they kept on the trail and into the next day. Jubilee had been in a sure-enough hurry to return to his camp in the hills.

And by the time she got herself some good measure of sleep back in this camp, Gritta wasn't really sure if what she had experienced was a dream, or a real church. For the past few weeks, what with her confusion, she had been praying for God to show her if it was only a dream— something evil conjured up by the devil or one of his fallen angels—or if it was real and she had been baptized and dressed in strange robes and shown confusing secrets that made her head hurt whenever she recalled a fragment of that long, long day.

And she sang. That was what she seemed to remember most these days. Songs from her youth, memories of a childhood back in Virginia, she recalled. Remembering her own image: long braids tied up at the back of her head, raising her long skirts and petticoats out of the mud as she and friends dallied to play along the banks of the streams and creeks, looking for turtles and snakes. It was the songs she could remember now. But she was finding it harder and harder to recall anything after she began growing up.

Gritta brought out two of the lucifers, then flung the wedding-day dress onto the bed, away from her breasts. With her empty left hand she brushed that bruised flesh of those breasts gently. It made her head hurt again, not being able to remember when she had finally begun to bud into a woman. How she had wanted breasts for so, so long. But Gritta could not recall any of her friends in their neck of the Shenandoah Valley who had breasts yet either. Even though they were all sweet on one boy or another.

Breasts were simply what a girl got when she was ready to marry and make babies. Breasts were what she could attract a boy with, the other girls told her. Boys were fascinated by them. So Gritta wondered why Jubilee wasn't fascinated with hers. Was she not attractive to him?

It brought immediate shame to think of his being so old a man, and her such a young girl, her breasts just budding the way they were. That shame would be the power she would need to finish this walk of hers into God's light.

Slowly she opened her palm and looked at the two lucifers, then quickly closed her hand and jerked to look over her shoulder at the tent flaps. Just a noise. Something to spook a young girl, she thought. She opened her hand again and couldn't really believe she was looking at them. How dreamlike it was that she had them at last.

Last summer she had tried to burn herself one morning at George's cooking fire. Gritta had held the long hem of her dress over one of the limbs and let the fabric catch and hold the flames. As the fire licked up her dress and she felt its purifying, cleansing heat—George screamed and Usher turned just as she wanted him to.

She wanted most for him to watch her go to God's light right before his eyes.

But George and Jubilee pounced on her, pummeling her from the waist down with a towel and a coat. The stench of the burned cloth rose to her nostrils, but she felt no pain. No flesh burned. They had stopped her. . . .

But things were going to be different today, Gritta vowed. If Jubilee wasn't going to take her back to the Shenandoah Valley where she could finish growing up with her family and friends, then she would just have to show him that she was willing to die.

Placing one of the lucifers in her left hand, Gritta bent and dragged the thick sulfur head of the other across the peeled timber of the pine-and-rope prairie bed she was forced to share with Usher. Her eyes widened, her lips parted in excitement as the flame spat and caught at the head of the wooden match. Blue and yellow, dancing in concert there in the still, cold air of the tent. Gritta stared, entranced, almost hypnotized by the light she held close enough to her face to sense its flickering heat.

Then, as she watched, it burned her fingers. She dropped it, putting the fingers to her lips, and sucked on them as would a child. Grinding her stockinged foot atop the burned matchstick. Gritta finally took the second match out and quickly lit it.

Before she would give herself time to reconsider, she held the new blue-and-yellow flame against the bottom hem of her new dress. His gift to her. And now Gritta would make a gift of herself to God's light.

The cloth began to smolder, then burn. In the fading light in the tent she could see the yellow and blue licking at the dress, raking tongues of flame toward the petticoats she wore. Then she calmly blew out the match and tossed it aside.

"Not yet," she told herself in that little girl of a voice. "Wait."

She would wait until the flames climbed high enough, the dress burning enough.

Turning to glance at the tent flaps once more, she prayed Jubilee would be there, nearby, so he could watch as she took her leave of him. Just so she could see the helpless expression on his face as she left him for good. It served him right for not taking her back to her mama and papa in the Shenandoah.

Gritta waited. Watching the fire climb with darting tongues of heat that began to tell their cruel temperature against her chin and beneath her neck. But she would wait a few more moments—not like last summer when she hadn't waited at George's cook fire.

As it grew harder to breathe, painful no matter that she turned her head, Gritta pushed herself through the tent flaps into the shocking cold of the day's twilight. It was as if she were carrying a lantern, the way the ground and leafy trees around her lit up with the orange of autumn and the bright saffron of a great candle. There was the rush of air about her as the heat seemed to swell and she could no longer breathe. It hurt to breathe, so she just stopped, looking through the dancing, waterlike waves of heat for him.

And saw his face as Usher bolted toward her across the camp.

He was yelling. Other mouths were opened, yelling. But she heard no sound. Already the heat was searing at her ears. She smelled the telltale stench of burned hair and wondered if it was hers. The heat, oh the heat. And no way to breathe anymore.

Gritta collapsed, engulfed in the light.

Thanking God for taking her back to be with him. If she could not return to the shadow of Big Cobbler Mountain, she wanted to live only with God. Not too big a wish for a young girl growing into gangly womanhood, she thought.

Sensing the tug and pull on her. Feeling the unsteady, cruel blows landing about her legs and body.

Likely the contest between God's angels and Satan's devils as they tugged this way and that for her soul. She waited patiently for her soul to be released at long last.

To stop this pain. So that she did not have to worry about breathing anymore. Just a few more steps to God's light and she would make it.

If she'd never go home again, she wanted only God to take her.

A great balloon of light flared so brightly there around her as she collapsed, going limp, numb. Gritta was certain she was near the end of the tunnel the old ones spoke of.

Then it grew dark. And she smelled the stink. And all too quickly realized that it hurt all over; not an inch of her escaped the agony. Realized that she could barely breathe.

And no matter what direction she looked, everything . . . everywhere it seemed black.

"Be pleased to drop your guns, *señor."*

Jonah studied the man hard over that next moment, measuring him and the seven or eight behind him. At least those Jonah could see. They had their pistols drawn, some held a rifle, every weapon pointed at Jonah, Two Sleep, and Jeremiah. But not the one out front, not their leader. With a bit of theatrical arrogance he kept his thumbs stuffed in the crossed leather gunbelts, the butts of the two pistols slung forward of the man's hips. A wide belt of cartridges lay over his right shoulder, crossing his ample middle. His breath came in explosions that ribboned into the cold air from beneath that shaggy mustache spilling in two long points from his chin.

"If we don't?"

The Mexican shrugged, looked away, and spat. "We kill you."

Jonah shifted uneasily in the saddle. His instincts told him to make a play of it. There was still enough distance between the trio and the Mexican gunmen, some uneven ground here in the foothills, rocks, and timber—something to give them cover and make a fight out of it. Anything rather than giving up.

"You ain't thought this through, *señor*," Jonah told him. "Maybe the three of us can cut our way out on the other side of the eight or nine of you."

The Mexican smiled, looking first over one shoulder, then the other. "Eight or nine of us?" Then his dark eyes came back to lock on Jonah's. "Be pleased to make you count again."

Hook watched the bandit's right arm gesture upward. There along the nearest ridgetop appeared perhaps as many as ten men breaking the cold, clear skyline.

"I see you have more friends," Jonah said, his eyes narrowing.

"*Sí,*" the leader answered, "lots of friends," as he signaled this time with his left arm. There at the edge of the timber appeared another half dozen, each of them emerging from the shadows.

"Pa?"

Hook shrugged off his son's question, flung his voice at the bandit. "What is it you want from us?"

"I said it, gringo," he explained, moving forward on foot now toward the white horseman. "Drop your guns."

"You want guns—take 'em," Jonah said, beginning to feel less than seduced about the odds of bargaining his way out of this with anything but his life. "We got some more on that packhorse back there."

"*Gracias,*" the bandit replied, signaling forward one of those in the timber.

But the gunman stopped halfway to the packhorse the instant he saw Jonah yank up a pistol, heard the rolling tumble of the hammer lock. Hook quickly measured things on both sides of him, then straight ahead at the rest. The leader had his arms up, waving, preventing his men from shooting.

"A brave man you are, *señor*," he said softly, moving forward again brazenly, finally coming to a stop near Hook's horse. "But no smart in the head." He tapped a finger against his temple and pushed his wide-brimmed hat back from his brow at an angle. He wasn't any older than Jonah, most likely younger, though he plodded about on the icy snow under the disadvantage of a growing paunch.

"We ain't going to let you take all our guns," Jonah said, desperation beginning to cut through his words. He cursed himself for letting them ambush him like this, coming down from the mountains and that snowed-in pass, hurrying toward the valley floor the way they were heading when they got jumped. Not as watchful as they should have been. And when he decided to cut south by west, to avoid more mountains and early winter snows—the bandits made their play.

Hook had planned nothing better than skirting through some of that old, familiar country of northern New Mexico.

His eyes narrowed on the bandit leader. "Out here man's gotta have one gun left him."

Another shrug from the Mexican. "Your guns. All."

"Let him have what he wants, Pa," Jeremiah said behind him in a harsh whisper. "We can't take 'em all."

"They aim to take what's ours, son."

"Let 'em—and we can go on. Leastways we'll be alive."

The sense of it struck him like a blow from behind. Still—there were a lot of miles, a lot of years behind Jonah Hook where he had done things that didn't make all that much sense at the time, and he come out of it alive.

The bandit stepped to the side, appraising Hook's mount. "Good horses too."

That brought Jonah up short. "You ain't fixing on taking the horses too."

That cold smile crossed the dark face again. "We sell them. So you walk. Indian villages: there, there, and there," he said, pointing in the three directions. "Few days' walk." Then he turned and pointed west. "That way—Utas. Bad Injuns, *señor*. Very bad Injuns, Utas."

Hook wanted to know what the Indian thought. "Two Sleep?"

The Shoshone inched up beside Hook and dismounted. When he spoke, it was in a whisper. "We come long way for you to find woman. That long way no good to you now when you die here on this ground."

"So you're siding with Jeremiah there? Saying we should give 'em all we got—everything?"

Two Sleep nodded. "We do, they go. We walk on. One day we find woman. Never find woman you die here on this ground."

It burned in him—this rightness of what Two Sleep and Jeremiah were telling him, burned with the awful, nagging realization that it didn't feel right to him.

"*Señor?*" the bandit asked, signaling the rest of his band in from the ridge to the southwest, with a wave of his arm bringing in those from the timber off to the northeast.

"What you going to leave us, *señor?*" Jonah asked again, the edge to his voice grown metallic as rusted iron.

As he looked the American up and down, the bandit's smile disappeared. "I leave you keep your boots, your clothes. Your coat."

"That's all?"

Then he shrugged and said, "I not want you to die from the cold, *señores.*" The bandit looked at the sky and grinned acidly again. "Looks like more snow coming."

Jonah hated that smile already. Just as long as he didn't have to take off either one of his boots, he felt not quite so naked. Not that he felt all that good in the pair of old broken-down boots—but it was what he wore stuffed down in the stovepipes. At least the three of them would have two handguns between them when these bandits rode off.

No matter that it took a winter or two, Jonah vowed as he inched away from his horse and began unbuckling his gun belts, action that brought a broad grin to the bandit's dancing eyes. Jonah would find this Mexican—and make him pay for what he had taken from him.

Just the way Hook made the horse thieves pay. Just the way he was going to make that Jubilee Usher pay in spades.

No one took from Jonah and didn't come a day of reckoning.

Damn—but he hated the feel of his hips getting shet of iron and oiled leather. Like standing naked before your Creator.

Damned naked.

23

JONAH SAW THE carcass a good distance off.

Figured what it was pretty quick from the way its dark shape and bulk stood out against the white palette of the snow. An object so much bigger than the muffs of sage that dotted this valley floor.

It wasn't a good sign.

Goddamn, he chided himself. Just what the hell *was* a good sign anymore?

Three days gone now since they had watched that grinning bandit mount up his men and ride off. Watching the backs of those Mexicans, and the backsides of their horses all heading in the same direction. North.

Come a day soon, Jonah prayed again as he trudged on toward the dark mound that stood out plain as paint in a world of white—and he'd go find that greaser bastard. Gone north, or south, he'd never forget how that son of a bitch smiled back at him with such pleasure at taking near everything a man had of any worth.

Even if he had to follow that bandit into Mexico. That thought sent a shiver of dread, more so one of dreaded remembrance, down the length of Jonah's backbone like the spill of January snowmelt.

They had watched the horsemen leave, the Mexicans laughing and waving as they did, until the horsemen disappeared completely from sight. Then Jonah bent angrily to wrench the two .36-caliber Navys from his boot tops. He looked at Two Sleep. The Shoshone nodded once, emphatically. The look of rage there in those dark, flinty eyes was something they shared. Jonah tossed the Indian one of the pistols.

"What'm I gonna use?" Jeremiah protested.

"You just stay behind me, son—or the Injun," Jonah explained. "I ain't got but two guns. Till we can buy or trade or even steal our way into another."

Damn, he brooded now, looking at the carcass as they drew closer and closer to the frozen body. We could use a saddle gun, carbine. Something with some range to it.

That morning the wind rode in heavy with the bitter taste of metal to it as it shouldered out of the northwest, almost into their faces. Like sucking on a lead bullet, the way it might make a man's mouth pucker, so real was the taste of that wind on his tongue. The sky hung over them a metallic pewter as well, the sun slowly falling ahead of them throughout this afternoon's march like a dull button of buttermilk splotched against the leaden overcast. Snow. More goddamned snow coming.

It had snowed the night after the Mexicans had taken off, snowed just as the bandit leader had predicted, just as Jonah had feared. With no blankets, and only a handful of sulfur-headed matches among them in coat pockets, the three men kept moving until slap-dark made it impossible to see where they were stepping any longer. They stumbled on for a short time, scuffing against the scrub sage, spilling in the snow, finally reaching a series of hills that poked their way into the valley. There some stunted cedar and dwarf pine offered a windbreak about the time the wind worked itself up again, carrying on it the icy bite of snow.

What they could make wasn't much of a fire, yet it kept the three of them alive through that sleepless night. He would have traded one of those revolvers for a blanket, for a scrap of oiled canvas big enough to wrap around him that long, cold night. Something about these first storms of the winter, he had brooded many times in the two days since, something about the cold of those first storms: the way the icy feel penetrated to a man's bones more severe than even the horrid days of January and February. Maybe, Jonah thought, because by midwinter a man got used to the cold. But this time of the year his body wasn't ready for the beating the weather would give it.

But he vowed he'd make it.

After that brutal night they had marched on the second day. And into the darkness of a second night until they were forced to make another camp, using all but two of their matches getting a fire started as darkness squeezed down on this high land.

Finally the wind relented—and did not scatter the struggling flames or the few fledgling coals. They were able to build up the fire enough so that the three of them could sleep in rotation this second night. That was something funny, Jonah remembered. A man never really slept when he was this cold. Most everyone had heard tell of men who fell asleep in temperatures like these; most everyone knew chances were he wouldn't be waking up come morning.

Putting his arm up a few yards out from the dark object, Jonah stopped the other two. The Shoshone was already on guard too. Not looking at the carcass really, his eyes scanning the vacant horizon of the hills toward the far side of the valley, eyes moving and head turning. Just like Jonah—to pick up any sign.

"Injun pony," Jonah said quietly.

"I can see that, Pa," Jeremiah replied. "What you think I rode on all those years?"

"I was hoping . . . ," he started, then finished by saying, "I'm glad it wasn't one of ours." Jonah watched Jeremiah trudge past him, heading for the carcass.

The young man knelt next to the dead animal, put out his hand to feel the temperature of the hide, the stiffness of the flesh. "Been here for some time."

Jonah moved closer, his eyes not staying on his son or the carcass, but instead scanning the broken country dotted with scrub pine and cedar. "You got any idea how long?"

"Take a guess."

"Go ahead—take one."

"More'n a couple of days."

"But not more than a week," Two Sleep said as he came closer.

"That's right," Jeremiah said. "Been less'n a couple of days, it wouldn't be froze up the way it is. Been a week—the critters found the carcass and been eating on it."

"No tracks around it," Jonah said, squinting into the leaden light. And he saw them the same time the Shoshone spoke.

"No tracks but these," Two Sleep said, and moved off in the direction they led, walking alongside the icy shove and drag of old snow beneath the dusting of a new storm. He knelt and blew some of the dry flakes off the sign.

"Some Injun left his pony here," Jonah said, coming up behind the Indian.

"Pony was shot, Pa."

"I saw, son. We'll say someone *had* to leave the pony here."

"Rider shot too." Two Sleep indicated the way the rider had pushed himself away from the fallen animal, dragging his wounded leg off toward the northwest, into the teeth of the recent storm that had battered them two nights before. He blew some more of the new snow away from the old, icy crust below it. Traces of frozen blood.

"He hurt bad?" Jeremiah asked as he joined the other two hunched, knelt over the sign.

Jonah straightened, glanced at their backtrail, then looked at the direction the rider had taken. "That Injun probably dead by now. If he ain't dead from the blood he's lost, he's froze to death. C'mon," he said, moving away in that uneasy gait of a horseman put afoot, walking stiffly upon cold, ungainly feet beside the Indian's tracks. "That brownskin got something we need."

"What's that, Pa?"

"Look in the marks he made, hobbling through the snow, Jeremiah. Tell me what you think he's dragging with him."

A few minutes later Jonah heard his son huffing to catch up behind them, his chest heaving as he slowed his pace to match that of his father and the Shoshone.

"He got him a rifle, right?"

"The way I see it, Jeremiah. Scraping it along beside him as he limped off in this direction."

A while later as the sun was about to roost for the night at the valley's western rim, Jeremiah asked, "How far you think he got?"

"Not far," Two Sleep answered before Jonah could form the words to answer. He flung out his arm, then began to move out more quickly, leaving the others momentarily behind.

"C'mon, son," Jonah ordered as he leaned into a rolling, uncomfortable trot, scuffing up the ankle-deep snow as he tromped in the Shoshone's trail down the slope toward the line of willow and dark vegetation that bordered the narrow creek snaking its way through the serpentine hills.

Down there against the willow brush and skiffs of windblown snow, Jonah could make out the crumpled shape of a human form. Some snow lay in a drift against the windward side of him. And as Hook got closer, about the time Two Sleep came to a stop and knelt by the form, Jonah saw leggings made of thick, woolen blanket, below them the tall, fur-lined moccasins wrapped up the calves, and that blanket capote, its hood tangled with the Indian's long, loose hair.

Two Sleep was rolling the man over, twisting the rigid body slightly.

"He alive?" Jeremiah asked, still a few yards behind.

The Shoshone bent, put his ear to the Indian's chest, held his bare palm over the man's mouth and nose. "Not much. Some."

"Glory!" Jonah said in an awed whisper. "Strong son of a bitch. I'd laid odds that—"

"We gotta get him warm," Jeremiah interrupted as he surged past his father, going to the Shoshone's side. "Over there, Two Sleep." He indicated a small stand of brush where they might get out of the wind.

"Help me," Two Sleep said.

Jeremiah and the Shoshone half dragged, half carried the nearly frozen warrior across the twenty or so yards while Jonah got down on his hands and knees, feeling around in the snow where the horseman had lain.

"What you doing, Pa?" Jeremiah asked. "I need you start us a fire."

"Snow coming, Jonah," Two Sleep reminded. "Night coming. My belly empty—but I be warm you start fire for us."

"Just soon as I find that saddle gun the Injun was dragging with him," he said, growing more exasperated as he turned around and around on his hands and knees in the snow, soaking himself all the more as his hands dug frantically beneath the snow for the weapon.

"Got to the brush," Two Sleep said cryptically.

He stopped with a jerk, glaring at the Shoshone. "What the hell did you say to me, Injun?" Jonah snapped.

"Find the rifle in the brush." Then he pointed.

Shaking his head, Jonah looked back over his shoulder at the pile of brush near where the Indian had lain. "Here?"

Two Sleep nodded, then continued to break off more of the dry limbs he was collecting on a spot of ground he had scraped clear of snow.

Then Hook spotted it. The butt anyway. Sheepishly he turned toward the brush pile, pulled the rifle out. It appeared to be an old saddle carbine. Winchester.

"A sixty-six, Two Sleep."

"How many bullets?"

Jonah levered the action, found a fresh round in the breech. Then inspected the loading tube. That done, he said, "Ten. Eleven in all."

Two Sleep leaned forward and pulled the unconscious Indian's coat slightly apart. He patted over the chest, around the waist. As Jonah lumbered up, he saw that the Shoshone had found a pouch at the Indian's waist. Two Sleep stuffed his hand inside, pulled out a few cartridges.

"Good," Jonah said. He knelt alongside the horseman, said to the unconscious Indian, "Thank you."

In a moment Hook turned to Jeremiah. "Lemme have your two matches, son. We gotta warm this son of a bitch or he will die."

"Wouldn't be fair, would it, Pa?" He handed over their last two matches to his father.

Jonah took them. Put one in his pocket and started nesting some of the dried kindling Two Sleep had gathered. "What wouldn't be fair, Jeremiah?"

"Him making it all the way here, from where his horse went down. Crawling all this way—only to die of the cold, maybe the blood he's lost. Don't seem fair."

Jonah glanced once at the chest wound. The Indian had been shot in the back. High. He went back to nesting, then set the kindling down after making the dry shavings he would need. He dragged the head of the lucifer across his belt buckle. And said a prayer this fire would take only one match.

"Does dying ever seem fair, Jeremiah? No matter how a man fights it, or don't fight it—does it ever seem fair?"

The cold seemed to bite all the more when the light left the sky that night. Yet the wind quieted and the cold settled over them, the heavy, damp air refusing to stir. Jeremiah seemed to take more than a passing interest in the horseman, using his own youthful energy to rub the hands and face, the arms and legs and torso of the wounded Indian after making a crude bandage out of his own bandanna and some sage leaves he crushed. Cutting the bandanna in half, then folding each half over to wrap up the crushed sage, he pressed one bandage against the back wound, the other against the exit wound on the chest, and went back to rubbing the brown flesh in his hands to warm it.

Two Sleep busied himself moving back and forth from the fire, in and out of the light as he brought in what squaw wood he could gather for the night, and anything else he could use to form a windbreak. Jonah sat with the carbine cradled in his lap, wiping it with his own bandanna, drying it, levering and relevering the action to satisfy himself it would work without hitch when required to. And he kept looking at Jeremiah rubbing circulation into the body of that Indian.

No telling how old the horseman was—he'd always found it hard to figure an Indian's age. He was a lot younger than Jonah. Maybe a little older than Jeremiah. Not near as tall, built closer to the ground, squat and solid. Dark-skinned too—dark as any of those Comanches in west Texas, he thought. Unlike those lighter-skinned Indians farther up on the plains. Lakota. Cheyenne too.

That made him think on Shad and Shell Woman. Toote. A good woman for that old trapper. And it made Jonah dwell that night on Pipe Woman. Seven years now since he had rode off from Laramie. Rode off from her because he had to know. Seven years was a long damned time, he figured. Likely married some warrior buck winters ago. Got her some children of her own. Woman looked that good wasn't about to remain without a man for long, he thought.

And closed his eyes, listening to the crackle of the fire that illuminated the core of their little campsite inside a copse of willow, brush pulled up to deflect much of the wind. There in the middle of the long winter night, he dreamed on Pipe Woman. Content to remember her body and her willingness to have him the way a man will always remember a woman in the cold of distance and lost time.

A while later he opened his eyes, raised his head—hearing the crunch of steps—and saw the Shoshone returning, dragging his long canvas mackinaw behind him filled with brush. Jonah realized he had been asleep.

Dreaming on Shad's daughter. Wondering how her mouth would have tasted. How her brown body would have felt heaving with his as they coupled.

As the Shoshone dumped the brush and pulled his coat back on with a shudder to settle near the small fire, Jonah let his eyes droop again, gripping the Winchester tightly as he could without his hands locking up in the cold.

Was it Pipe Woman? Or was it only his need that made him yearn so much right now?

Or, he trembled, was it something that was telling him Gritta was finally dead? Out there, somewhere—she was finally dead. And it was time that he give up on finding her.

Give up on finding her alive.

Maybeso give up on finding her at all.

24

"COMB MY HAIR."

When her employer gave his command, Chung-li Chu'uan looked at him in disbelief. He stood at the door to her room, staring in at her, framed in smoky darkness. It would be morning soon. She had finished her work pleasing many white barbarians and had just crawled beneath her blankets. So cold was she.

But there he stood, silhouetted in her narrow doorway, the yellow smudge of light from downstairs behind him. Even before he had spoken, she knew it was he. The shape of him. Then with his words—a taste of home: the only one who could have spoken to her in her Mandarin dialect.

When she did not answer, she heard him sigh, his head falling forward on his chest heavily. Chung-li pulled the blanket up to her nose, partially hiding her face. If she disobeyed, he could beat her. It was his right. The others before him had. A few of the customers did.

Sex and pain—it all seemed so tangled up together somehow. Especially with the one she feared most. The white demon she feared even more than her employer.

"Why can't you just come to me sometimes?" he asked quietly, then took one step into the small room.

She caught her breath noisily. He stopped after that one step, still backlit by the lamps hovering in the layers of smoke above the saloon below.

"I ask you only to brush my hair," he said, just above a whisper.

He took a step closer—she could hear the rustle of his silk clothing. He always dressed very well, in the finest he could import from China. Chung-li knew she had no reason to complain about her clothes, their color, or the way they felt against her naked body.

Her eyes were locked on the leg that did not stand straight like the other. It was cocked in dark shadow at a funny angle. From the shoulder above it, hung the arm that was twisted almost back upon itself. Chung-li thanked the door ghost for keeping him there, the shadow ghost for making no more light—she did not want to have to see his distorted body.

"The others come to brush my hair," he said. "Why don't you come to see me? Am I . . . am I so grotesque that you cannot stand the sight of me?"

When minutes passed and she had not answered, Chung-li heard what she thought might be a stifled sob come from the shadow at the doorway. Then he slowly backed out of the room, pulling the door closed behind him. She lay in darkness again. Except for that bright-yellow splash beneath the door where she watched the shadows of his feet shuffle off.

She was sure of it now, as sure of it as any woman could be. The way he ignored her of a purpose. The way he paid her attention when he could stand it no longer. Her employer was in love with her.

Chung-li pulled the blanket down from her face, her breathing coming a bit slower now. Although she thought little of its value, she knew she was beautiful to others, especially men. This thing of beauty meant little to her, for it had only brought her brief explosions of happiness in the midst of long, long periods of sadness, loneliness, aching emptiness. How she damned her face, her tiny body—wishing that her next life would curse her to a plain form, a homely face. If only to have something more than this emptiness.

Her breasts were sore tonight. Two of the customers had bruised them. Small though they were, the nipples were a deep rose against her dusky skin, a sight that clearly drove some men crazy. She trembled with remembrance of the white demon who even spit on her breasts after he bit them to make them bleed. She prayed to the ghosts that hovered around this town in the Gold Mountain that they would prevent the cruel one from returning.

Never before had Chung-li Chu'uan been so afraid of a man. He was more than any of the other cow-eaters who smelled like the flesh of the dead animals they ate. That one was so dangerous that he might hurt her, hurt her terribly as he kept her just this side of dying. Not releasing her. That one would be capable of such torture.

Unlike the others who merely hurt her in their rush, completed their business, paid and left . . . that one who terrorized her nightmares—he would not be satisfied with leaving, nor with merely killing her. He would have to make the pain last.

Rolling over, she found the combs hurt her folded arm. Chung-li pulled both of them from her hair, one from either side, shaking out her hair. Her room still stank of the man who drank too much whiskey and threw up on her floor before he could reach the door. He had been sitting on the edge of her bed, his limp flesh in his hand, cursing it for not rising to his call. Then he ordered her to do it for him, presenting his limp manhood to her in the palm of his hand as if he were presenting her with a gift.

As she took it, he began to swoon, his head bobbing, and he lurched to his feet, Chung-li still gripping his semirigid flesh. He made it half the distance to the door before it all came up.

Now, even with the washing of soap and water, masked with some of her employer's store of perfume he provided for his girls of joy, the floor of her room still stank of stale whiskey and dried vomit. The man's memory had sunk between the boards, and there it would stay.

Like her. Trapped here in this stinking place—until she worked up the nerve to flee, or until the dangerous one returned.

Chung-li didn't have the courage to leave, and knew it. So she lived in fear each night that the cruel one would once again darken her door. She cursed herself, knowing that one day she would have to speak to her employer about her darkest fears . . . at the very least about her wanting him to do what was right by her should she die.

"If I am killed," she practiced the quiet words to herself now in the darkness of the predawn light beginning to seep over southeastern Nevada. It was like rehearsing them, pretending she sat her employer down and explained her fears to him—even though she was almost as petrified to speak to him as she was terrified of the evil white demon's return.

"I want you to do as our families do in China. As our ancestors have proscribed for us," she said, her singsong Mandarin words chopped, the high syllables sounding like a cat's mewing in her mouth, so quiet was her voice. "Remove my eyes and my heart, along with the big bones of my arms and my legs. Put them in one of your red-painted zinc-lined boxes to protect it all. This box you must send back to my family's village."

And the rest? she imagined him asking.

"You know what to do," she said defiantly in the darkness. "Just what I would do for you . . . for any of our people who died here in this land of demons."

A gold-painted coffin to burn you in?

"Yes," she answered her imaginary employer, who taunted her from the darkened doorway. "All the flesh you would cut away from my bones . . . the rest of my organs. Put it all in the coffin—and burn it in a great fire upon a pyre decorated with pink ribbons and bird plumage."

Do you wish to have the pig butchered beside your grave?

"If you so wish, my employer," she answered. "It would be a gracious act of kindness for you to have the feast there for my friends, since I have no family here. No," she thought, the tears coming for all her effort to stop them. "Do not send my box back to China. I have no family left."

I will leave flowers on your grave when the fires are all gone out. So that you can smell them as you begin your deep sleep.

"You love me, don't you?" she asked the darkness.

The darkness did not answer.

Chung-li demanded, "Why won't you tell me?"

Still, the room felt cold, and oh so silent.

"Why don't you protect me from the white demon, who will return to kill me soon?"

She sat waiting for his answer to come in that small, freezing room, waiting all the while the black changed to gray. Waiting while the gray became dawn.

The sun rose, without making a sound to disturb her great silence.

"Utas," Two Sleep told Jonah.

He squinted into the sun-washed near distance. The light tortured his eyes, making them smart and burn, so bright it was after the long passing of the storm. "They ain't got wagons," Jonah said, thinking of the Mexicans with their pair of freighters, what they likely used to haul off their stolen plunder.

"Utas," the Shoshone reminded.

"I suppose we'll find out what that means to us soon enough," Jonah replied as he turned. On foot Jeremiah was coming up behind them. Drawing to a halt, his chest heaved, hoarfrost heavy about his face with the exertion—leaning into the straps lashed to the travois that sagged beneath the weight of the wounded warrior.

That morning before dawn the three of them had put their belt knives to work, hacking down a pair of short saplings, cutting loose some stout willow limbs, tying vine and creeper around every joint the best they could. Into that woven basket they laid the wounded Indian, then looked at one another.

Jeremiah had sighed, his eyes filled with stout resolution as he said, "I'll go first."

"All right, son," Jonah replied. "You get tired, I'll take over."

"Two Sleep pull next, you tired."

Then Jonah had the Shoshone lead off, taking them north by west into the broad expanse of the valley floor, toward the foothills in the distance. Where there seemed to be a gap between the ever-climbing ranges that reached for the clearing blue of the sky left in the wake of the winter storm. Through that day they took their turns at dragging the deadweight of the Indian over the sage and through the calf-deep snow, their breath coming in raspy, raw gasps before they would give up and turn over the burden to another.

"How come you decided to bring him, Pa?"

Sorting out his answer, Jonah had looked at Jeremiah during one of those brief rests while they rotated their order in the short procession. "Only reason I'm packing this Injun along is I figure when he comes to—and by God I hope it's soon—he can tell us where we can find his band, his people."

"You figure on reoutfitting with them, do you?" Jeremiah asked as Jonah tossed his son the Winchester before stepping into the middle of the vee, where he hoisted the two saplings and leaned against their bindings to set the travois in motion with a grunt.

"They the only folks out here I figure gonna help us, Jeremiah," he said as he set off. "Mexicans gonna steal near everything we got. Mormons ain't gonna help none but their own. It's us and the Injuns. And . . ."

"And—what, Pa?"

"I just pray what Injuns we run into ain't fixing to take what little we got left." He eyed that carbine Jeremiah had cradled across his left arm.

Now that the riders were drawing ever closer, his words seemed to come back in an echo to him. Causing Jonah's finger to itch on the trigger of that carbine.

"Be quick about it, Jeremiah, and get that pistol of yours stuffed down in your boot."

Two Sleep had already done something to hide his pistol—just where,

Jonah didn't know as he stepped alongside the Shoshone, both of them watching the riders come closer, slowly, snow cascading in small showers from the hooves of their ponies. The horsemen spread out. Now Hook could count them. Thirteen. Fourteen. They were all outfitted for winter: blanket coats, the frosty halos of their breath spewing from hoods on those coats or rising beneath the fluff of coyote or wolfskin caps pulled down to their eyebrows, tucked securely over their ears, long black hair and braids reaching out from beneath the frost-covered animal skins. Feathers tied to the tops twitched in the breeze; pony manes danced as the weary animals came close enough to bob their heads when they scented the strangers. A frosty glaze encircled each pony's nostrils; tiny crescents of icicles drooped from some of the eyelids or hung suspended from the bottom of some of the rawhide hackamores.

Twenty yards out one of them signaled, and two others urged their ponies forward at a trot, kicking up rooster tails of snow.

"Easy now, fellas," Jonah said.

"Who you saying that to, Pa?" Jeremiah whispered. "Shit—I'm gonna stay easy as I can be—us outnumbered the way we are."

"You're right," Jonah replied. "Maybe it's these here brownskins I ought to convince they oughtta take it easy."

The pair of riders slowed slightly as they came up on Two Sleep and Jonah, eyeing the men on foot completely, aware of the single carbine, likely taking note of the knife scabbards hung from the belts that all three men had buckled onto the outside of their coats.

"You got idea who they are?" Jeremiah asked as he turned back around to his father, finding Two Sleep making hand talk with the pair.

Neither of the riders answered as they proceeded on past Jonah and Two Sleep slowly, heading through the snow for Jeremiah and the travois he rested on the ground.

"Keep trying to get one of 'em to talk, Two Sleep," Jonah instructed. "Especially that one in the middle—looks like he's the big gun."

Hearing one of the hunting party drop to the snow and hardened ground behind him, Hook whirled about. The Indian hurried to the travois, where he knelt to pull back the hood on the blanket capote. He yelped immediately, then stood, thrusting an arm in the air, signaling. And whooped some more in a wolf call of joy.

The other rider loped over, his pony brought to a halt in a shower of snow as the entire line of Indians screeched, their breath sent in hoary veils as they kicked their animals into motion. Yipping and *ki-yi*ing, they bolted across the last twenty yards and skidded to a halt, nearly all of them dismounting to form a formidable ring around Jonah, Two Sleep, and Jeremiah. The leader pulled his wool hood back from his face as he pushed between Jonah and the Shoshone, stopped to kneel at the travois. There he brushed his long, unbraided hair aside before bending to put an ear over the chest of the unconscious one.

When he finally raised his face, a smile flickered across it like a tentative flame licking at wet kindling. He spoke a few quick words to the others. Two came forward, lifting the travois while a third brought his pony up to pull the drag.

Jonah licked his dry, cracked, and bleeding lips, glancing again at the haunches of venison and elk that burdened nearly every one of the ponies and pack animals. He hadn't known how hungry he was. For days now really—they had nothing but snow, and that cold liquid dropping into his stomach made it knot all the tighter. Reminding him just how hungry a man could become. But nothing like the sight of that bloody meat. Why, just to chew on a strip of it raw right now, just to suck what he could of its juices—

But the leader of the hunting party stopped before him again. Speaking. And Jonah didn't understand.

So Hook made hand talk. "Speak in sign. I don't know your tongue."

"Where do you come from?"

Hook pointed, then signed. "East. Far to the east in the hardwood country."

"Who are you?"

"Two Sleep—Shoshone," the Indian explained with his own hands.

"Jonah," Hook said his name out loud. "Jeremiah," and he pointed. "My son," he told them in sign.

"Spirit Road," the Indian declared himself with his hands.

"What people are you?" Jonah asked.

"We are Utes."

Jonah looked at Two Sleep, who wore a grin. "You were right, you damned savvy bastard," he said in English. Then he looked at Spirit Road and made sign. "You know him?"

The leader of the hunting party nodded, looking back as the others got the travois lashed to the pony that would pull the drag. "This one— he's been lost for more than three nights. Separated from a hunting party. Never returned. We found his extra pony with some wagon men who passed by our village."

"Wagon men?" Jonah asked aloud—and made sign, his interest piqued. Then he glanced down, for the first time really seeing in the belt Spirit Road wore what appeared to be one of Jonah's army revolvers.

"Mexicans?" he asked in English.

The Ute nodded, and repeated in imperfect English, "Mecks-see-kins."

Jonah dragged a hand across his frosty beard, eyeing that fresh meat once more. "Your friend needs some warmth. Some food soon. We did all we could—"

Spirit Road interrupted, his hands impatient, although the look in his eyes softened. "I thank you. Come with us now so I can thank you with food and warm blankets at our village."

"This one," Jonah asked out loud, moving his cold, stiff hands once more, "this man—he is from your village, yes?"

"Yes," the leader answered as he gazed back at the travois setting out across the snowy sage. "We go now—to take my brother home."

25

H E RAN HIS hand over the oiled wood of the bookcase that rose from floor to ceiling in this house he used each winter to escape some of the cold farther north in Salt Lake City. Brigham Young had been a carpenter—a furniture maker, a true craftsman with his tools, and he admired once more the workmanship invested in these bookcases.

He had never set out to be a preacher, a man of God—a latter-day Prophet.

A carpenter. How much he dwelt on that these days as he aged, knowing that he and Jesus shared the same profession before coming to do God's work among mankind. He looked down at his hands. No longer callused the way they had been when he was a young man. But still he touched people with these hands, blessed them, let the power of God flow through him, just as Jesus must have done beside the Sea of Galilee.

But Brigham was a far different man from what he had been when he had brought his flocks west, out of the land of damnation. Now he buttoned his vests and coats around an ample, widening belly, grown corpulent. He was hard-faced, if not outright mean in his countenance, his eyes his most terrible weapon, were it not for his savage tongue. Atop his head was a graying crop of hair, and surrounding his face, the full white beard, worn without a mustache.

Young went to the window and looked out on the yard, where a light dusting of snow lay after last night's storm. The morning's light caused it to shimmer gloriously.

Brigham believed himself to be akin not only to Jesus, but to one of the oldest of Old Testament figures. Among his people Young was known as the Mormon Moses. It was he who three decades before had led the march west, that journey into the wilderness for his faithful. Although they had not wandered for as long as the ancient Hebrews, Young nonetheless sensed a swelling of pride in his breast whenever he recalled that he accomplished the same feat for his Latter-day Saints that Moses had for his. In those early years of carving out a home here in the great basin, Brigham had believed the Rocky Mountains would be a barrier to keep the Gentiles out. But it had not turned out that way.

Even more distressing to the Prophet was the notion not only that he had dissenters who had remained back in Ohio, more still who had remained behind in Missouri—but that he now had a very real threat of a challenger to his kingdom here in Utah itself.

"Usher's sent word to Lee in prison up at Salt Lake," W. C. Staines said to the president of the Church.

"That damned shenpip," Orson Pratt replied with all the bile he could muster. He had used one of the most favored references to the old Mormon order, the Sons of Dan. The Danites.

Young had his back to his two closest advisers, his hands clasped behind him as he stared out at the sun dancing off the new snow. It made him feel cold, but nowhere near as cold as did the news about Jubilee Usher.

"We should have seen that Lee was executed this past summer," Pratt replied. "It could yet be done, Brigham."

"Lee is not the root of our problems," Staines argued.

"Get him out of the way—let him be the sacrificial lamb," Pratt spoke within his great white beard that spilled down his chest. "The Federalist government will be satisfied."

Staines's eyes rolled to the heavens. "At long, long last."

"But what of Lee's sons?" Young asked.

"Now they . . . they will be trouble," Pratt admitted.

Brigham turned, nodded, then went to a padded armchair, where he settled, feeling the cold bite and chew in his joints as he commanded them to move. "So we really won't settle things when Lee is gone."

Staines shook his head. "Likely not."

Young asked, "Do we have any idea what Usher wants with Lee?

Neither of them have any power, any following outside of Usher's band of cutthroats."

"Many of them used to be your faithful," Pratt reminded him. "Men like Usher and Bill Hickman."

"The Reformation is long over," Young snapped. "Their day has come and gone. We use . . . other methods now to control apostasy."

Staines wagged his head. "Yet what do we do when a man like Usher forces his way into the Temple here in St. George and has himself married to his concubine as he did a few weeks ago?"

"Just before we arrived, I might add," Pratt said.

"It's not a holy union," Young growled. "Never will be. Are you still certain it's the woman I told him to shed himself of a long time back?"

"Must be," Staines replied. "Our man with Usher says it's the same woman he captured back in Missouri during the recent rebellion."

"And she's chosen to stay with him now?" Young asked, shaking his head in disbelief. "Being baptized in the Church, being married in our holiest of Temple ceremonies. To a man like Usher? She must be the fool."

"And perhaps he deserves nothing more than a fool for a wife," Pratt said.

"This woman is of no concern, even though Usher soiled our Temple just by entering our sacred entry hall," Staines said. "Lee's sons still cause me the greatest worry."

At that moment Pratt turned around as they all became aware of someone's arrival at the front door: voices, footsteps being ushered in. Then he said in a low tone, "No matter—we can handle the sons, Brigham. Once the father is out of the way . . . we can nip the rest of the problem easily enough."

"What is happening with a new trial for Lee?" Young asked.

"The government is proceeding nicely," Staines said.

There came a knock on the library door.

"Come in," Young said in a loud, sure voice.

One of the house servants opened the door, handed an envelope to Pratt. "This just came, for President Young."

"Thank you," Brigham said as the servant closed the door quietly. "Read it to us, Orson."

Pratt's eyes ran quickly over the page he tore from the envelope.

"Problems in Salt Lake?" Staines inquired.

Pratt shook his head, trouble crossing his face like gray across the face of a cloud. "No. It's more news about Usher."

Young turned away so the others would not see what cloud crossed his face. He closed his eyes instead of looking out the window. "What of Jubilee Usher now?"

"Our . . . our source sends word that Usher is preparing to steal great sums of money."

"Do we know where?"

Pratt said, "Very likely across the line in Nevada."

"Nothing against a man's industry," Young said, opening his eyes and watching a bird hop around on the dusting of snow, searching for a meal. "As long as Usher's murderers do not prey on the faithful while we wait to sort out just what we're going to do about him—I see nothing wrong with the man's ingenuity."

How the little things hurt anymore. At one time Brigham had ruled a feudal empire that stretched far and wide, ruled an empire every bit as big as six European monarchies.

"We all remember Jubilee Usher's years as a scalp hunter and dealing in slaves taken to Mexico," Staines added.

Pratt took a few steps forward, rattling the paper. "Brigham—it's much more than that."

"What do you mean?"

"The money isn't for his own greedy needs," Pratt answered.

Young turned around, facing his old friend, and sensed the immediate fear, that same fear written over Orson Pratt's face. "What in God's name is he going to use the money for now?"

"No," Staines replied, watching Pratt carefully. "I am sure it is for no purpose in God's holy name."

Pratt sighed deeply. "He's going to buy guns, trade goods— everything he can to barter with the tribes."

"Industrious, our old friend Jubilee Usher," Young said. "Like honey in the carcass of a lion, I have said many times."

"No, Brigham—Usher is going to buy himself into an alliance with the tribes."

Young felt his eyes narrow, that great brow of his furrowing. "An alliance?"

"This says he's preparing to make war on you." Pratt's eyes rose from the paper to gaze at the president. "He wants your . . . your Church."

Jonah was ready to move on, his strength recovered. Meat put back on his bones.

He, Two Sleep, and Jeremiah had been in this Ute camp for almost a month now. Come here about the time serious cold had settled into the valleys, and the surrounding mountain peaks lay in a mantle of white that would last until next summer. By then he wanted to be headed east, home to Missouri. By next summer he would have freed Gritta from the Mormons.

He gnawed the stewed venison from the bone, savoring the juices that dribbled into his beard. These people were a grateful lot, he had to give them that. Everything they owned they had offered to the three wayfarers—ever since that day Spirit Road led them back to the village with his hunting party.

"Pa, take a look yonder," Jeremiah had said that twilight, nodding off in a specific direction. "You see that horse the boy's leading?"

Jonah watched the animal passing them, led by a youngster. "Could be there's another horse looks just like mine."

Jeremiah shook his head. "Not with them markings. That was your horse."

"Your horse," Two Sleep agreed.

Jonah kept staring at the rear end of the animal as they moved on through the village where men, women, and children appeared from their lodges, holding elk robes and blankets about their shoulders—everyone come out into the cold to inspect the newcomers brought into camp, others rushing to follow the travois.

"If it is my horse," Jonah said, turning back around to peer at the commotion made over the young wounded warrior, "can't figure what it's doing here."

"The wagon men," Two Sleep reminded.

"Don't you remember what Spirit Road told us?" Jeremiah asked. "About finding his brother's pony with them Mexicans?"

"He never did say what happened to them wagon men, did he?" Jonah replied, pointing at the two empty freighters standing off by themselves against a copse of trees, tongues down, bereft of the cargo each had carried when the trio lumbered into the ambush days ago.

"No, Pa."

"Only way these Utes got that horse of mine—and that army pistol Spirit Road's wearing—is these Utes run across them greaser bandits too."

That night Jonah hadn't thought it possible he'd ever get his belly filled, the meat and marrow bones tasted so good. And coffee—oh, the coffee. With sugar. Why, it all made a man feel downright civilized, sitting here in a warm lodge on a bed of blankets piled atop elk and buffalo robes, leaning back against the peeled willow tripod where a backrest hung.

Jonah said, "Jeremiah, ask Spirit Road about that pistol he was wearing when his hunting band run onto us."

The youth's eyes narrowed as he whispered anxiously, "I don't know much about these Injuns—but I know that's bad manners, Pa. You're asking me to accuse him of stealing it. And in his own lodge too."

"Dammit, Jeremiah—we both know he did. Besides, he's likely proud of the fact that he stole it off them wagon men."

Jeremiah wagged his head. "I can't. Just can't. Ain't good manners."

"Shit. You lived with them Comanch' too long, son. Better you do what your father tells you."

Then he noticed that Two Sleep was talking with his hands in sign.

"Yes," Spirit Road answered in sign. "The gun I took from the Mexicans is the gun the white man asked me about."

"Tell us the story of how you took the gun," Jonah requested. "Tell us of your coup."

Smiling with satisfaction, Spirit Road cradled the small pipe he had been smoking after their supper on the ring of rocks surrounding the fire pit. "It was a good fight, though we did not want to fight when we first discovered the wagon men. Wanted only to know if they had seen my brother in their travels.

"They halted when we appeared on the hilltop, making ready to fight us. I went down with only two others to see if any of them talked with their hands, or knew my tongue. They did not."

"Is that when you found your brother's pony with the Mexicans?" Jonah asked in sign.

Spirit Road nodded. "But we were not strong enough then. My small hunting party was too weak to try attacking then. They all had many guns."

"Yes, some of them our guns," Jonah said.

The Ute's dark eyes went from Hook, to Jeremiah, and then to Two Sleep. The Shoshone nodded.

"These wagon men—they robbed you too?"

"Yes. Sometime before they came across your brother," Jeremiah answered with his hands.

"This pistol I took—it does not belong to the leader of the wagon men?"

"It was mine," Jonah explained. "Before they took it, all our guns and horses."

"All your guns—except the two guns you wanted the young one and the Snake to hide in their boots when we rode up to meet you."

Jonah had to smile, noticing the wry grin on Spirit Road's face. "Yes. All our guns taken except those two."

"You have given back my brother's rifle to him," Spirit Road said. "You should have back what is yours. All that I can gather in the morning."

"Thank you," Jonah said, filled with surprise that it would be so easy.

And with that surprise he found himself suddenly filled with a measure of shame—for these people had been gracious, welcoming, and warmly hospitable to the trio. It was only natural that Spirit Road would return what had been taken from the trio by the Mexicans, then taken from them in turn. "But you must go on—tell us about how you counted coup on these thieves."

"And killers," Spirit Road made the sign harshly. "They came close to killing my brother when he escaped from them. Badly wounded, he threw himself on his extra pony and tried running from them."

"But you said the women think his wounds will heal," Jeremiah said.

"Yes. He has suffered much. From the bullet. From all the cold. Spirit Road thanks you three for saving his brother's life. Anything that you wish—it is yours. You must stay, regain your health from your long ordeal. And wait out the hard moons of winter."

"We will stay . . . only as long as we need to rest," Jonah explained with his hands. "But then—we must go on to find another we seek—as you sought your brother."

"You seek someone the Mexicans took from you—someone who was fleeing like my brother?"

"No. The boy's mother," Jonah explained. "My wife."

Spirit Road nodded. "Family. Nothing is more important than family."

They sat in silence for long moments, each man staring at the fire until the Ute war chief spoke again. "My lodge is yours while you stay. Please, you must not think of going until you are fit and ready to go in search again."

Jonah held up his cup, had it refilled by Spirit Road's wife. "Thank you. We will drink your coffee and sleep in the warmth of your lodge . . . just as long as you finish your story of counting coup on the wagon men."

26

I F T H E F I R E S of hell ever went out, this prison cell of his must truly be as cold as hell itself would be.

John Doyle Lee leaned against the barred window in the tall stone wall as he gazed beyond at the bare, skeletal branches of the trees in his beloved penitentiary orchard. Shivering slightly, he watched a flock of black crows wing down and come to rest on bonelike perches. It was as if all the hundreds of black birds stared right at him. Looking into his soul.

I have been strong, Lee thought, determined not to allow all those eyes to infect him with guilt.

I haven't anything to be ashamed of. I haven't talked, like those government fellas want me to talk. I haven't weakened.

"By damned!" he whispered hoarsely, his raw throat aching. "I will die a man of honor rather than live one day as a scoundrel."

Shuffling back toward the tiny table beside his bed, the old man of sixty-four felt his years more in this numbing cold than at any other time. He had always remained fit, at no time in his life suffering any want of physical health. Nigh onto that dark day he had been taken prisoner by the Federals, Lee strenuously worked at the ferry. No task that called for the muscles of his back had ever proved too much. But not only had this imprisonment robbed him of activity, draining him slowly of his physical vitality and health, seeping away drop by drop—it slowly made Lee question the solid rock upon which he had based his whole life.

234

With winter fully upon this land of Zion, the aging prisoner had all the more time to devote to his journal begun that ninth day of August when he was taken from the jail at Fort Cameron in Beaver, Utah—bound for this Utah State Penitentiary. It had been just past twilight, the late-summer sky finally darkening, a time when the lawmen figured they could get away with their prisoner without causing much notice. They'd been wrong. Both Caroline and Rachel, two of his wives—along with some of his younger and grown children—had come to see him away. Besides, the street pointing north out of Beaver had been lined with townspeople— either just the curious, or those who supported old John Doyle Lee. Like Jubilee Usher.

He was there, John remembered—there to nag and prick away at Lee's conscience. To make him start questioning all that had remained unquestioned for a lifetime of faithful service.

That federal escort spent their first night of the journey in the mountains, almost as much cold piercing to the bone as this was, to his recollection. The two guards slept, as well as U.S. marshal George R. Maxwell. Lee hadn't been able to do much that cold night, rising early in the morning and shuffling out of camp to scrounge up firewood. When Maxwell awoke to find Lee warming his hands over a cheery fire, the two other guards sleeping off the effects of their frequent pulls at a bottle of corn whiskey, the marshal shook his head with a wry grin.

"I believe you're the best guard I have, John."

"You look surprised to find me here, General." "General" was what John respectfully called the marshal.

"Any other man would've taken off cross-country."

"I'm innocent," Lee had said. "I got no reason to run."

"Help me prove that," Maxwell pleaded again, as he had so many times before. "Tell me all what happened so we can prove you had no hand in planning that long-ago massacre. To prove it was those higher in the Church."

He hadn't betrayed his leaders in all those eighteen years. Lee wasn't about to start now.

When the escort reached Nephi, Maxwell transferred them to a train—the first John ever saw. From a window seat, with the lawman beside him to point out all the changes, new businesses, fields, and homes sprung up over the last two decades, they rumbled toward Salt Lake City. Home of President Young.

Settling upon his straw bed-tick now, Lee pulled a second wool

235

blanket around his shoulders. He couldn't chase away the gnawing cold on that wind come right out of the north. North—where the stench from the latrine was carried to every cell. About all he had to look forward to now was his two meals a day, writing in his journal, and any visitors who might drop by to see him. As cold as it was, Lee was no longer allowed his walks through the orchards.

The grub was good, and the coffee always plentiful with meals.

There were fourteen prisoners here now: eleven convicts and another three awaiting trial. Most of 'em for murder.

They were a jovial and talkative lot, although Lee found them all rough, even uncouth and profane most occasions. Many joined in singing along with one of their own who plucked at the strings of an old banjo, perhaps even got up to do some clogging on the clay floor. Others looked on, clapping—or stayed with their card games to pass the long winter days.

Lee felt immensely weary as he pulled out Jubilee Usher's note from the back of his journal. Dare he trust the shenpip leader? This big Danite he had known back to the early days of the founding of Zion? If Lee could not trust in Brigham Young, the Prophet himself, by God—how dare he trust in the man who swore to bring Brigham Young down?

John put the note away again. He would trust only his Maker.

"Howdy, Lee," Philip Shaffer called out as he was led past John's cell.

The middle-aged blacksmith worked nearly every day on one project or another for the prison warden. At times Lee himself had been assigned to help Shaffer at the forge. It kept Lee from sinking too low, from getting too far down in his thoughts. He wished he slept better—but not in this cold, not with those lamps the guards left burning all night.

Much better was a soothing veil of darkness when he tried to sleep. After all, his was the sleep of the righteous. But it hadn't always been thus.

Although Maxwell was still his most frequent visitor, the marshal had come even more often in those early days, trying to talk Lee into bearing witness against the others. At times Maxwell took Lee down to the city in a carriage drawn by a four-horse hitch, where John could shop for what he needed most: stomach pills, scented hair tonic, perhaps a silk handkerchief—maybe even a box of cigars and a bottle of whiskey.

"You tell your story," Maxwell reminded, "and you can return to Beaver, live with Rachel while a new trial is scheduled. It won't be like being a prisoner."

"I am a prisoner for the Gospel's sake," John wrote that sixth day of September, marking his sixty-fourth birthday. "I take great comfort that

God has reminded me the apostles, Prophets, and all the inspired old in like manner have suffered by persecutions."

What he suffered in the name of God among the other prisoners was enough—the low, vile, vulgar tongues they used in profaning God and John himself. He prayed the Lord to deliver him speedily from this sink-hole of corruption, this rank den of foul and unclean spirits.

But this was his to bear up under—just as it was his lot to bear up the burden of the massacre in silence. So that the truth might go to the grave with him. So he could hold his head high, as a man of honor when he finally stood before his God.

"I have weighed the matter over carefully," Lee declared to Marshal Maxwell back in October, "and with resignation to my fate in the future, I have concluded to take up winter quarters in this prison and here remain till I rot and be et up with bedbugs before I will dishonor myself by bearing false witness against any man."

That very day John had stuffed fresh straw into his bed-tick, swept out his tiny cell, and scalded out the boards in his bunk, hoping to drive away the progressive march of bedbugs. Ever since the day of that decision, that clarity of conscience and purpose had begun to trouble him in frequent moments of weakness. Ever since, Lee's health had begun to sink.

How thankful was he for Ed Gaines, the twenty-year-old who had become like a son. The Ogden boy in for horse theft nursed Lee daily, seeing to some of the old man's needs. As bad as he felt, John was sure he felt no worse than young Ed.

"I ain't gonna do no prison washing," Gaines told the guards and warden when told the laundry was his assigned task at the prison. "I ain't no convict. Only a prisoner waiting for my trial."

That was more than a month ago now. Eight days the guards kept Gaines chained against an outside wall, where the Ogden boy huddled against the cold stones without comfort until Lee himself closed the shutters on the window above the young prisoner. Until Lee brought a greatcoat and a blanket to lay over the shivering man in chains. Lee knew what it was to have absolute conviction, to stand up for one's own beliefs.

"John."

Lee turned to gaze at W. W. Phelps, the young prisoner who called out at Lee's cell door. "You gonna show me how to draw some more of my letters tonight?"

"I will, son. Promise."

He watched the guard lead Phelps back to his cell from his own day's labors. The afternoon sun was falling. Winter brought twilight so quickly, wrenching an abrupt end to the short days. The long nights Lee spent teaching three young men from Provo to read and write. Like Gaines, they had stolen horses, not an uncommon charge in these parts. But all three wanted to better themselves—so sat through the cold winter evenings in Lee's cell, practicing how to form their letters, stuttering as they read from Lee's worn copy of the Book of Mormon. It had become a regular class at the penitentiary, something he taught every day—even on Sundays.

Not that it was wrong for an industrious man to work on Sundays. Lee had always been an industrious man. A faithful man. A man who had put his faith in Brigham Young as well as those President Young had put his own trust in. Men like Jubilee Usher.

Usher was the sort who knew just how to shake John Doyle Lee's faith. How to raise it to question at this critical hour in John's spiritual life.

"Your sons are prepared to ride," Usher had written in his note to Lee. "They join the army of God—just as you did years ago, when the Lord called upon the righteous to raise their arms against the unholy. In days of old it was the Missouri Gentiles we were sent to smite with our sword of the Lamb. In these Latter Days—the faithful are now asked a most difficult task: to purge from our own ranks those unclean of spirit."

How was it that Jubilee Usher could step right in to widen the crack in Lee's own faith? How did the man know where John was weakest?

This was private—truly a matter between John and his God.

God would show John the way. Not Jubilee Usher. And surely not Brigham Young.

For now he had refused Marshal Maxwell's offers to turn state's witness. For now he refused to answer Jubilee Usher's appeal to support his coming war on the president and the Church as they knew it.

For now.

Night had fallen outside. In here where they had far too little wood to burn, far too little food to eat, and nowhere near enough blankets to keep themselves warm, his breath frosted before his face as he put his journal away for the night, then sank to his low bunk, his old Book of Mormon held to his breast.

Lee collapsed against the cold adobe wall, shifting the book where he held it in the folds of the blanket and opened to the Book of Omni.

Behold, it came to pass that I, Omni, being commanded by my father, Jarom, that I should write somewhat upon these plates, to preserve our genealogy—

Wherefore, in my days, I would that ye should know that I fought much with the sword to preserve my people, the Nephites, from falling into the hands of their enemies, the Lamanites. But behold, I of myself am a wicked man, and I have not kept the statutes, and the commandments of the Lord as I ought to have done.

How he hated the thought of giving comfort, much less aid, to the likes of Jubilee Usher.

Would that God take that burden from him, Lee prayed fervently as his eyes closed, brought to tears.

For here in the darkening gloom of his freezing cell, John finally understood just what role Jubilee Usher had cast for John Doyle Lee, a man who had remained obedient to the true faith, loyal to the statutes and commandments of the Lord.

The Truth was the Truth. And God's Truth was not to be denied.

John Doyle Lee had always remained faithful to the Truth of God.

Usher wanted him to be the undoing of Brigham Young.

Orrin Haslam unbuckled his gun belt, took it from his hips, then passed it across the fire to the Indian. His eyes smarted at the wood smoke in this dark buffalo-hide lodge. He watched the half-breed interpreter make hand talk for these ugly, dark-skinned creatures.

Inside, Haslam held nothing but contempt for the interpreter Colonel Usher had hired a few weeks back. The near-toothless old man wasn't worth all that much—drunk as he was most of the time. Trading his pay as soon as he got it for what bottles he could carry in his saddlebags when they set off for parts unknown. On this mission for Usher.

With skeptical eyes the war chief took the gift. Haslam waved a hand, as if to reiterate that the gift should go to the Indian. The Indian laid the gun belt, complete with cartridges and single-action Colt's revolver, in his lap and stared back impassively at the white men on the other side of the fire.

At least it was warm in here, Haslam thought as the half-breed and these ugly-faced chiefs talked back and forth in their guttural tongue and sign language. All Orrin wanted to know right now was where he was going to find a woman who wasn't so ugly he couldn't get a hard pecker over her.

All the squaws he'd seen since reaching this camp of Utes were short, squat, and near as black as the darkies down south. No woman worth getting all het up over. But one of 'em would likely have to do, he figured. He'd had Injun women more than he cared to admit: Creek and Seminole, Choctaw and others, even Apache when the colonel was raiding for scalps and Mexican gold down to Sonora years ago. That was when Haslam and others had perfected their torture of women. Seemed a squaw's pain only made the rutting all the sweeter.

But in most of these far-flung camps he and the others had been visiting in the last few weeks, Haslam hadn't spotted all that many women. Why, if he had it figured correctly, Haslam figured these bucks hid their women and young girls from the white man's roving eyes. Like they knew to keep the women hid away. All except the very old, and the very ugly—the ones who kept the fires lit and the kettles brewing while the talks dragged on.

He was sure the women and girls reappeared once the white men pushed on.

In English the half-breed asked, "He wants to know when's your white chief gonna make war on the Mormons' other white chief?"

Haslam held up two fingers. "Soon's we do two things, tell them. First off, we gotta get our hands on the money we need to buy enough guns and bullets. Second, we get our friends like him to join Colonel Usher's army. You tell them that. Tell them that's when we're riding off to make war."

The war chief listened attentively with the rest of the tribe's headmen. His eyes came back to look at Haslam from time to time while the interpreter made sense of the white man's answer.

As the lodge fell quiet, the Indian dragged the pistol from the oiled holster, rolled the hammer back to half cock, and spun the cylinder expertly. He brought it to his ear, working hammer then trigger, hammer then trigger—listening to the action of the tumbler and sears.

"He says it's an old gun," the interpreter said after the war chief signed. "But it will do for starters, he reckons."

"Tell that black-skinned bastard that this pistol's killed more Injuns than he'll ever hope to kill in his lifetime," Haslam growled sourly.

Clamping his hand on Haslam's forearm, the nervous half-breed smiled at the war chief. "Best we all watch our manners here, Major. These Utes got a big pride they ain't killed any white men in a long while. But—you go and insult 'em—they'll likely make an exception just for you."

"I've eaten the livers of better Injuns'n these—all before lunch. You tell him that, he don't think much of my gift. I'll take my pistol back and we'll go on to find another band—where the men are brave."

"Major—that's foolish talk for any man out on the prairie, especially for a man what's sitting inside a Ute chief's lodge."

Haslam tasted the gall rising in his throat—an unrequited rage for this Injun who stuffed the pistol back into the holster, then laid it down beside his thigh and gazed impassively back at Haslam. Orrin wasn't the sort to forgive little slights. Time come when Usher wouldn't need these Injuns no longer. . . .

"All right, you half-breed son of a bitch. Remember you're working for me," he snarled at the interpreter, "and if that's so hard, maybe I can stretch your goddamned neck a little just so's I can remind you it's my money fills your belly with whiskey every night."

"Thought we was supposed to—"

"I goddamned know what we're supposed to do," Haslam interrupted. "So do it! Tell this lost savage child of Satan that he and his Lamanite people will get all the spoil they want when they join us in this war. Tell them they'll have many blankets to bring home, maybeso they'll have many dresses for the ugly, fat toads they call women in these parts. Tell them they can have all the horses they steal, all the cattle they can butcher."

The interpreter clucked once. "It's the guns that war chief's got his mind set on."

Haslam glared at the Ute warrior across the smoky fire pit. "You tell him we'll get him and his men all the guns they'll need. Pistols, rifles too. And bullets enough to make every one of their ponies swaybacked. Just as long as they kill white men when the time comes that Colonel Usher wants these Injuns to kill white men. He understand that?"

As the interpreter spoke, at times seeming to search for a word while his hands danced before him, the Ute war chief dragged the gun belt back into his lap, sliding the pistol from the holster. He spun the cylinder again, pointing the revolver toward the smoke flaps.

Then, slowly, the hard-faced warrior lowered the muzzle as he brought the hammer back in the quiet interior of that smoky lodge. Pointing it directly at Orrin Haslam, without wavering in the slightest.

He heard the interpreter gulp audibly.

The half-breed's flintlike eyes darted back and forth between the chief and the Mormon. "He . . . says he's took enough Mex' scalps to do him for a long, long time. And he don't see no difference when it comes down to it—no . . . no difference taking any white man's scalp. Any goddamned white man's scalp at all.''

Haslam smiled, his face benign, though his eyes filled with hatred like banked fires. "Even my scalp? You ask that bastard that," he snarled. "Ask him he'd even take my scalp."

The fire crackled and popped while the interpreter signed. When the half-breed turned back to Haslam, beads of sweat stood out on his dark forehead like tiny, glistening diamonds. He licked his lips before he stammered his answer to the Mormon.

"Even y-yours."

27

Early Winter 1875

"I HATES DOING this for all the world, Missus Usher. Ever' time I do—hurt me bad to do it. Please, now, you forgive me? Please."

Gritta hated it too. But maybe not near as much as George, Usher's old ebony manservant, hated this changing of her bandages.

She tried to let her eyes tell him it was all right—what he was doing as he worked over her. Gritta simply couldn't bring herself to talk much anymore. Not that it hurt really, even with the new skin below her chin and on the sides of her neck—but she had learned some time ago that she really didn't have to talk anymore. All things got done in their own time, without her having to open her mouth much at all.

George's gentle, bony hands reminded her of well-oiled rope: darkened with years of toil, worn until the hemp possessed a sheen of ebony luster, knotted and gnarled as they fluttered over her bandages with the gentleness of a sparrow hen coming to rest at the edge of her nest, feeding her young.

She turned away from watching his hands on the old, crusted bandages—her eyes misting from more than the fiery torment at the healing, newborn skin he tried not to tear whenever he changed these smelly dressings. She remembered her own young—so far back now that the only image she could conjure up was that of a painted face on the rag-doll baby Usher had destroyed.

Like their child, conceived in her womb by Usher's evil seed, Gritta

243

had tried to destroy herself. Some time ago she had come to understand, come to believe fervently that the babe was far better off now than if it had survived to grow up . . . eventually to be taken from her then.

For some reason that thought hurt the way an old memory nagged like a dull-pained tooth. Confused, Gritta didn't know why she should remember children older than the baby Usher destroyed. Must be what the mind does to play tricks on itself when the hurt gets too strong, she figured out.

Only a trick she was playing on herself: these hazy, smoky, cobwebby images of a faceless man and faceless children. Like dreams. No one ever had a face in Gritta's dreams.

She closed her eyes against a ribbon of searing pain in her lower belly as George tried to loosen the crusted bandage from her upper leg.

"I see's I needs to soak it more," he murmured to her, softly laying that black hand, its back rippling with knotted veins, on her forehead.

He dipped the cloth into the pan of salted water, soaked up what he could, then held it over the bandage he gave his attention to, slowly squeezing the solution out onto the gray, bloody crust of the stiffened bandage. Letting the salt and water do its work in its own time, rather than his.

While her breathing grew more regular after the yelp of pain from those raw nerve endings that laced the newborn flesh at the inside of her thigh, Gritta concentrated on the gradual spill of tears from her eyes, sensing them tumble down her cheeks into the bandages swathed around her neck. The salt stung the red, infant flesh—just the way George's solution stung.

She even thought the old Negro mixed his tears with the water he used every time he had to change her bandages. Sure the old man cried for her. How thankful she was that someone else cried for her—the way she had cried for him the time Usher whipped the old darky. It had been George's forgetfulness with that crock—and what she had accomplished with a broken shard of it—that drove Usher to tying George's frail, bony frame to a tree and whipping him before the entire camp.

As she had listened to the darky's muffled screams pushed round a gag stuffed into his mouth, Gritta had promised she would never make another person suffer for her failure, not ever again.

How grateful she was for him, and all that he suffered for her. How ashamed it made that deep, raw spot far inside her feel for all that she had talked against, and done against, darkies ever since she was a child. Though she remembered her mama and papa as folks who never had been rich enough to own even one slave, much less a whole plantation worked by them—the Moser family had steadfastly clung to the belief that a white man had a God-given right to own Negroes. A darky simply wasn't made up to the same cut as was a white man. And just as God gave the first white man, Adam, dominion over the beasts of the fields, air, and seas—God also gave the white man dominion over the coloreds.

But could she be so sure? So sure now that the God of her youth, the God her mama taught her, the stern, Germanic God she had learned not only to fear but to trust . . . was not really the God she had learned about in the Temple of confusion? There was God and Adam, Jehovah and Michael—Jesus and his brother Satan . . . evil and good existing side by side. Born of the same womb of God.

After that day, how could she ever be sure of anything anymore?

So it was that she looked at him with her pooling eyes, studying the graying of that head as it bent low over the new skin on the leg, the raw, angry flesh where it was slower to heal.

"We put these'r clean'uns on, an' I'll be to washing out them ol' smelly'uns," he murmured over his ministrations, tossing the putrefied bandages into an empty pan.

In all the seasons gone since that summer day Usher came to take her away from all that had been before, Gritta had counted on something. At first she had counted on her dreams of a man who would come for her, to be her rescuer. It had been more seasons than she cared to remember since she had dreamed of his face, heard the sound of his voice, recalled the contentment that came of his touch. When that had been stripped from her—she had counted on her dreams of the children. But they were all gone now—along with their memories. Even the babe: taken and destroyed by Usher.

Yet in the end there had always, eternally, been her dreams of God, and righteousness, and finite justice meted out at the hand of the Lord. But the mirrors and the candles, the moon and the sun, the devil Michael and the God called Adam and not God at all . . . the voices in the darkness of that place had gone and dispelled the one dream she had been counting on to sustain her. Like a clear image on the surface of the crystal pool down at the limestone spring suddenly stirred by the hand—even her everlasting faith in God's own existence had been shaken.

All that had gone before had been taken away, dispelled on the waves rippling that clear pool. From now on she was worth very little—and all that she was worth came from Usher. Nothing seemed to exist before him. Nothing would ever exist without him. Usher was all life to her.

"Lemme take a look at that arm now, missus," George said, inching up the side of the prairie bed.

She looked at his kind eyes and, from the look on his face, knew he understood her. See, she told herself, a person don't have to speak to make herself understood.

"This'un's the worse of 'em all," he cooed at her, soaking the bandages.

Fire and infection had done its worst on the arm. It was taking the longest to heal. The stench from the oozing flesh, the very feel of that skin beneath the rotting bandages, the sight of his face when he finally removed the dingy, gray cloths—it was all enough to tell her why the arm did not move so well as he gently cradled her wrist in one hand, trying to rotate the shoulder in his other, watching her face for the faintest sign of pain. Skin so tight, so angry and oozing that she could not move it more than a few trembling inches. Feeling about as tight as her having to slip into a newborn's skin.

"Mister Usher's g'won take us away from here soon, missus. Says we going to the hills come spring. There's talk of gold mines in them hills. Talk of all the gold the mister's gonna get to buy guns and soldiers. Come spring—we be putting our foot back on the road again."

As she watched him take those crude metal tweezers to the dead skin, sloughing off her horrible arm wound, Gritta knew she had but one way to destroy Jubilee Usher. Since he was everything in her world now, since he was the reason she lived and the reason she would die . . . the only way out for her was to kill him now. Only then could she find release in death.

He had cruelly saved her from dying twice before. So the only way she could ever finish herself and escape this agony was to kill him.

Gritta smiled, even down in the pain. And began humming an old gospel song to herself.

They had to be closing in on Utah now—as much ground as the three of them had covered since leaving Spirit Road's village. Weather held for the most part. Cold, but without any of the driving fury of the early-season blizzard that had hunkered them down in western Colorado Territory with the Utes.

"When my brother did not return from his hunt, I was not worried at first," the war chief had told his story in sign, and later pantomime, that long night in his lodge. "The days were sunny, and the nights clear and cold—but I knew he could last a night, perhaps two, out in the deepening cold.

"It was not until two of my brother's friends returned to camp telling us they had seen one of my brother's ponies among a group of wagon men who they watched crossing the floor of a nearby valley. There had to be a reason that pony was no longer with my brother."

Jonah and Two Sleep had concentrated fiercely on the war chief's hands, on his words as Spirit Road related his story. For Jeremiah understanding had been much easier. He had filled in much of the tale over the following days as they languished in the Ute camp, regaining their strength, and that of their animals.

"So Spirit Road called together a war party, Pa," Jeremiah had explained. "And when they ran across them Mexicans—sure enough, there was his brother's pony."

"That's why Spirit Road believed us, was it?" Jonah asked. "If them bandits stole't from his brother—it's easy to figure they'd steal from us."

Jeremiah's head bobbed. "They took everything from the Mexicans. Wagons, horses and mules, their whiskey and blankets."

"And the guns," Two Sleep added.

Jonah looked at the Shoshone, nodding. "They've give back all what the bandits took from us."

"They didn't have to," Jeremiah commented.

He wagged his head, his eyebrows knitted in consternation. "I know that, son. So it's got me bothered."

No mistake about it—that's what had nagged Jonah ever since their second day in the Ute village when Spirit Road had returned their horses, their rifles and belt guns, their extra ammunition and cookware, their blankets and robes—everything. Such a thing didn't fit with his notions of Indians carrying off everything they could wrap their hands around, to have those Indians giving back so easily.

So for the first few days after they pulled out and put that village behind them, Jonah had kept Two Sleep watching their backtrail. The Shoshone was to bring up the rear, out of sight—Jonah grown more than merely dubious about the war chief's intentions. He had been downright suspicious.

So they slept light, made cold camps each of those first handful of nights as the trio moved west, every day covering their tracks and watching their backtrail—but all for naught. The Utes never made an appearance, not so much as a feather.

How to figure it, Jonah wondered. Warriors what gave away all that plunder they stole from the bandits—when they didn't have to. And him . . . Jonah was cut of something so different, it damned near ate him up inside trying to sort it all out: knowing he was the kind of man who wouldn't find it so easy to do what Spirit Road and his people had done.

Hook wasn't the kind of man who could give away.

But that was only natural to his way of thinking, considering all that had been took from him.

For five days now the great plateau towered a few thousand feet higher off to their left as they plodded north along the western rim of the valley scored with a tumbling procession of creeks, all spilling their runoff from the timbered, green-hued mesa striated with yellow and white and red earth, like the face of an earth-toned warrior staring down at them, painted for war. Stoic. Unmoving in its timelessness. But ever watchful with those eyes that followed their shadows as they moved ever onward to Utah.

And when he got there? Where to pick up the years-old thread of clues? That long-ago summer, seven winters past now. She could be dead now, he knew. He'd already talked to himself about that.

Still, Jonah knew Jubilee Usher was still alive. Somewhere.

The part of Hook that was a hunter, the part that would not let him rest, would not give him peace—that part told him Jubilee Usher was still alive.

And if the bastard had killed Gritta, or she had died somewhere on Usher's wanderings, sometime in that ten years plus since she and the children was took from the farm—it didn't make a good goddamn anymore. What had started out as his desire to free his children and wife had long ago become a burning need to exact his own personal measure of revenge on Jubilee Usher. Nothing more complicated than Jonah's need to take his pound of flesh. If not for what the Danite had done to young Zeke and the suffering of the other two, if not for what unspeakable horror he'd done to another man's wife . . . then Jonah was about this hunt for himself.

And himself only, if need be.

"Pa, I'm feeling the cold down in my bones," Jeremiah said as the sun came to rest atop the high plateau southwest of them. Its dying rays darkened the heavy timber on the hillsides, brought fire to the flame-hued stripes of earth. "Don't you figure we can chance a fire tonight?"

Jonah glanced at Two Sleep. The Shoshone nodded his agreement with Jeremiah.

"Yeah, son. I suppose we can chance a fire tonight. Ain't seen much sign of anything last few days."

Jeremiah wore a satisfied grin on his face. "The Utes told us the tribes would all be south of here."

"Spirit Road's band the only ones roam this far north anymore," Jonah replied. "He said most villages stay to the south, and west some now. What with the Mormons spreading out, coming in to settle and grow their crops, build their towns and churches."

"Injuns and churches—they don't mix," Two Sleep added, putting his hands together in a confusing tangle of fingers he wriggled before him emphatically.

Jonah led them off to the left up a wide draw where the timber offered good cover for their firesmoke, as well as wood and a windbreak come nightfall. The trio stopped in a long, narrow copse of trees where they could hobble and feed the horses, keeping the animals in sight near their camp. In silent agreement Two Sleep began to pull saddles and packs from the horses while Jeremiah set off into the timber to gather deadfall for the night.

As the Shoshone saw to the stock, Jonah dragged robes and blankets, saddles and cook gear over near the fire ring Jeremiah had brushed clear of old, icy snow. He hunched over the first fledgling flames he had nursed up from a glowing piece of char where a spark was caught, dropped there from his flint and steel.

"We get to one of them Mormon settlements soon, I'll see about buying us some sulfur-heads," Jonah declared as he settled back on his haunches, easing down on the spur rowels near Jeremiah. "A storekeeper's likely the man to ask my questions of—if not the local sheriff."

One by one Jeremiah laid the dried twigs he had collected onto the newborn flames as his tiny fire grew. "Will you tell me something, Pa?"

He studied his son's face a minute, trying to savvy something there in the way of a clue to Jeremiah's thoughts. "What's that, boy?"

"Want you to tell me about Mama and her churchgoing."

"What you wanna know about that for?"

He laid a few more limbs on the fire, then looked squarely at Jonah. "Sometime back I remembered how Mama knowed her Bible. Taught us the words of God, she said."

"She did," Jonah replied, taking his eyes from Jeremiah to stare into the fire. "She always saw to it you children went to church of a Sunday morning."

"But you didn't?"

He shook his head after a moment. "Your mama was religious enough for the both of us. I figured she was gonna save the two of us—all you children too—that woman was so took by the word of God."

Jeremiah slid over beside his father, placing a hand on one of Jonah's knees. "So tell me, Pa. What you think Ma . . . she feels about being took and belonging all this time to these gunmen . . . this Church of theirs?"

"Don't know how to answer that—"

"You think she's still got her religion, Pa?" Jeremiah asked, his eyes anxious and darting between his father's. "You think she still believes same as she taught us?"

How he wanted to tell Jeremiah the truth of what he felt, what he had come to believe in the last few months since leaving that little church where he lit the candle and did his praying below the bloody, carven Christ nailed onto that cross, a crown of thorns piercing his forehead, the face filled with such torture. How Jonah wanted to tell his son that he knew Gritta was dead.

But if he told him, Jonah knew now, Jeremiah would likely pack up and turn right around, heading back east for Indian Territory and Prairie Night, back to them two young'uns he left behind with the Comanche on Haworth's reservation. Jeremiah had come last April on this journey to find his mother. Jonah's oldest son had walked away from the edge of that last, lone empty grave with only one thing in mind as he joined Jonah in this search.

So Jonah knew he could not tell Jeremiah that his mother was dead. He would have to keep that buried down inside him until they caught up to Usher. After all, it was for the boy's own sake: Jonah had a score to settle with the bastard what had sold two young boys off to comancheros, off to a life worse than any death he could imagine.

Jeremiah still had enough Hook left in him that Jonah knew the boy would have something to settle with the evil that had robbed Jeremiah of his family, robbed him of his mother all these years. If there was any of himself running through Jeremiah's veins—it surely had to be that seething fury that drove Jonah on, and on. And on.

This weren't about Gritta no more. She were dead.

This was about Jonah, and Jeremiah—and what was took from them.

This was about taking back from Jubilee Usher.

No, he would not tell Jeremiah that they would likely never be finding their mother. After all, Jonah was following Jubilee Usher's trail. Always had been. And he would stay on it until he had took back from Usher in kind. Or died in that quest.

"No," Jonah finally answered his son's question about his mother still having her religion, slowly stirring the fire with a stick so that Jeremiah would not easily see the deadly fire in his eyes, a fire that might hint of some deeper truth to his father's lie. "I figure what with all that your mama's been through . . . with all that time and . . . well, I can't see as how she'd believe in much of anything anymore."

28

S HE WAS ADRIFT in a bitter sea.

It was true, just like the ancient Buddhist adage about survival in a world filled with nothing but suffering.

Ku-hai yu-sheng.

Hers was a life cast upon the waves of a bitter sea.

A life made all the more unbearable now that the white demon had returned—just as he promised through all those phases of the moon back in the Season of the Snake. Just as she had feared.

A woman must add nothing to life unless powered by Necessity—this much her mother taught her. Her lot was not to add to, nor to diminish from, what was given her by birth as a female. This was the teaching of a people who cracked open the eggshells of their own chicks, ate the heads of the unborn embryos as a delicacy, boiling a hen's spindly feet in vinegar to serve at the table of some celebration, eating everything provided by the bird—even its gizzard lining—and leaving only the gravel.

Were such demons as this white man so strange after all, she thought as he pawed her breasts with his rough hands, his red-rimmed eyes blood-shot and flecked with the fires of pent-up lust. He tore the silk crimson robe from her shoulders and bent to bite one of her nipples so hard it caused her to whimper.

"That's what I want to hear," he growled, inches away from her face with his whiskey-sodden breath. "It's been a long, long time, Chinee doll.

252

Been thinking about getting back to you—what with them ugly, brown-skinned Injun squaws—all I had out where I been since summer. But now . . . just look at you! Why, you truly been worth Orrin's wait."

Roughly he pushed her long hair back from the side of her neck and bit at the cord of muscle as she turned her head away from him.

Only an unmarried woman wore her hair long like Chung-li Chu'uan. A woman who was waiting for a man to make meaning for her life. At a wedding a bride displayed her long hair for the last time in her life.

"It fell to the backs of my knees," Chung-li's mother had explained many times in those days and weeks after the sister had killed herself in the well.

Perhaps in that way the mother tried to heal herself of so great a loss: both a daughter, and a granddaughter, in one night. Reminded again and again that her oldest daughter would never be marrying, would never have a reason to cut her hair. It was the mother's way of dealing with the senselessness of the ancient ways that gave no worth to women.

The stinking barbarian pulled on her hair, his fingers knotted in it by the handfuls. She prayed he would be quick with her—not that she wasn't used to the rough treatment . . . but prayed all the more fervently that he would finish and go. So much had this one demon come to haunt her nightmares about this land of the Gold Mountain.

This was her bitter sea to survive by herself: an employer who cared nothing for her but for the money she made him; and a white demon who cared nothing but for the pleasure he could extract for himself by punishing her flesh.

As the man yanked up the floor-length hem of her long robe, exposing the tops of her thighs and that thick black delta where she quivered in silent terror, Chung-li suddenly thought back to the weekly ritual her mother performed on all her daughters.

The demon twirled her around roughly, with a shove forcing her to bend over at the waist, then grasped her hips in two strong vises to rub the front of his canvas britches against her bare white bottom. She let her face sink into the silk bedcover, her fingers entwining clumps of the cover as she stuffed some into her mouth, hoping to stifle her cries of pain.

Glancing up just as the two roughened paws released the flesh at her hips, Chung-li caught the demon's image reflected in the smoky mirror propped up on her tall, narrow bureau. Hobbling from one leg to the other, he pulled at his boots with one hand, yanking at his belt with the other until he slid out of his pants. Kicking his britches and boots aside, he hurried back to her bedside as he unbuttoned the front of his wool underwear, from neck down to crotch. She watched his engorged flesh pop free from the faded red cloth, like the dancing tongue of a dragon flicking free of its gaping jaws.

There was no ceremony as he reached around her legs, pulled them wider before inserting his penis against her and rocking his hips forward savagely with a loud, guttural cry of his own.

She remembered the pain her mother caused them all—a mother who always preened and groomed the daughters of her family, hoping they each would attract a good young man from the village. They all had long hair then—unmarried, and waiting to fulfill themselves as a man's wife, the bearer of his children.

Her mother first combed Chung-li's hair back from the forehead, brushed smooth as a blackened silk pillow, tucking the long strands behind her ears so that it all fell loosely to her shoulders, in later years to her waist, and finally below her bottom.

Where he assaulted her now.

Then her mother took a piece of silken thread, knotting it into a circle between her index fingers and thumbs before running the double strand of thread across Chung-li's forehead. When the old woman drew her fingers closed as if she were making a pair of shadow geese bite at one another, the silken string twisted itself together, in the process catching all the little black and unruly strands along the hairline. And with one swift, smooth yank, she ripped the unwanted hairs from the flesh, leaving only a smooth, unblemished hairline—a most attractive hairline for a young woman in search of a husband.

Next came the same painful grooming at the temples, and finally the eyebrows, all cleaned weekly of the unwanted hair.

But only unmarried women—the lowest caste of all females—could let their hair grow this long, she knew.

Married women who took some measure of status from their husbands wore their hair tied behind their ears, or snarled up in a crude bun as they chopped wood or slashed their hoes down in the muddy fields. They looked like great sea turtles sometimes, perhaps more like great sea snails—these married women coming home at a crouch, their backs burdened with firewood, or babies, or laundry—everything whorled like great shells on their backs. Bearing the burdens of an ancient culture that had never changed. Stranger still was it that the Chinese did not admire a bent back—mighty warriors and beautiful goddesses stood straight as a bamboo shoot.

Even those women waiting for their men who left home, coming across the sea to the Gold Mountain. They could leave, work in the land of the barbarians, then return with their fortune. Yet it was unseemly should the men bring back any of the white demons' ways to pollute China.

She would not be going back. There was nothing left behind for her there. Nothing before her here. With no future there was still no reason to return.

As trapped as Bak Sahm was trapped. He could never return to Kwangtung Province. He could only talk of the Pearl River delta now. His eyes would never again look up at the rising terraces and steppes of cultivated land, look up at the vee'd flights of geese and ring-necked ducks. He was crippled now—not only in body, but even more so crippled in his spirit.

So they were the same in that essential way.

"Cry louder, whore!" he demanded.

Chung-li had not realized her whimpers grew loud enough to become groans of torment, cries of pain.

He pulled her hair roughly as he rocked back and forth against her buttocks, driving his hard flesh within her viciously. She had no choice now but to bend her neck back as far as it would go, he yanked on her hair so, exposing her white neck. His hands were around it, encircling her throat, squeezing down slowly to constrict her air, to impede the flow of blood.

Light-headed, she cried out, coughing at the lack of air, fighting against him—hoping to free herself. But he had her imprisoned on his terrible spear.

Her eyes glazed over as she struggled to breathe, and he pounded her all the harder, grunting all the louder as she trembled, fought against him: gratified was he with her torment and what that torment added to his pleasure.

Round moon cakes danced before her eyes. Chung-li hadn't eaten a moon cake since leaving the First City by the Sea of Lions. From there she had been brought over the mountains, down into a great desert, then finally into these mountains—brought here by Bak Sahm to service his customers with his other Girls of Joy.

All of her life was round: round doorways and round amulets worn around her neck; the round tables where family and friends always sat, preparing their meals and serving their food in round bowls that fit one inside the other—like her deepest, moistest channel the white demon assaulted, roaring now as she felt the blackness slip over her, so tight was his unrelenting grip on her neck.

Round windows and round rice bowls—everything in a circle like a talisman to warn of evil. Why had she not been warned of the demon's return?

Round and round their lives in China went in a great circle: growing food to feed the living, as well as to feed the old and the departed—those who would in turn protect the living.

Round and round . . . and in the deepening fog she saw the ghost's eyes open as the white demon behind her quivered, slowed his savage dance against her buttocks. She no longer fought, couldn't now, slipping to the silk bedcover—finally swallowed up by the nightmare behind her eyelids.

The ghost opened its eyes and stared at her fully now. This vision of a white demon she had never seen before. Dreams often carried portent—for good or evil. This must be such a dream, she decided as the breath rushed back into her throat, her flesh crying out in pain as she gasped that first breath, heaving air into her lungs at last, her tongue falling from her mouth, drool escaping down her chin to smear the rice powder and red rouge.

"You was good that time, Chinee doll," the demon said as he hurled her over onto her back and sprawled beside her—toying with her breasts. His face hovered so close over hers that his whiskey breath was all Chung-li could breathe as she filled her lungs again and again.

Blinking repeatedly, she still could not dispel the evil visage of the white demon—the one who had come to trouble her dreams so many times in the past few turnings of the moon. The eyes of that ghost so filled with evil.

"You and me, we're gonna have some fun while I'm visiting your fine town," the barbarian beside her boasted. His breath, rank with the stench of the dead animals he ate, made a frosty fog above her face in the cold room. "I've got some work to do before I'll have to pull out and go back to the colonel. We're gonna make ourselves rich—right here—one day real soon, Chinee doll."

Why did Bak Sahm allow this demon to torture her?

It was for the money that Bak Sahm did anything—always for the gold the white demons paid him.

Bak Sahm had no soul—only an empty, rotting place inside him now that he could not return home to that beautiful river delta. Only a gaping, festering void that he tried to fill with gold . . . just as the white demons tried to fill their soulless lives with gold and whiskey and a few minutes with a woman—all that gold would buy.

"Them smelters up there on the hill send off their shipments every three months," the demon told her as he sat up on the bed, swinging out an arm in a crude, ungainly circle so he could sweep up the near-empty bottle of whiskey from the floor beside her bed.

It was with those smelter shipments of gold she knew that Bak Sahm sent his own shipment of money west to the First City—from there across the sea and back to China. Each individual's payment was destined for a family back in one of the eighteen provinces, each marked for a woman who waited back at home for a man who might never return—a man who nonetheless sent home nearly everything he earned in the mines and smelters here in the Gold Mountain. When Bak Sahm had enough to pay the smelter owners for the armed escort provided during the long journey west to that First City by the ocean bay, he turned his small fortune over in the carven teak boxes. Inside rested the small silk bags—each one bearing the name of an individual Chinaman who held an account with Bak Sahm, a Chinaman sending his money home. Her employer would take his own percentage off the top of each customer's savings, shipping the rest in those chests weighted down with tiny silk bags filled with the round gold coins emblazoned with their wide-winged birds.

Like phoenixes rising from the ashes of destruction.

Yet she and Bak Sahm would not be rising from the ashes of this Gold Mountain. They, neither one, had anything to return home to.

"Maybe next shipment," the barbarian told her as he took the bottle from his glistening lips and dragged the back of his hand across his mouth. "Maybe late spring, little doll—the colonel will be ready to waylay us one of them gold shipments bound for the San Francisco mint."

He wobbled a bit as he bent over her with the bottle, pressing it against her bruised, puffy lips.

"Drink up, you little Chinee bitch," he ordered. "Drink to my success, don't you see?"

The smell of it was revolting enough, but the taste of it on her tongue made her sore throat gag, reminding her of the time one of her customers had tied her down on a table in those first days after coming to the First City—then forced whiskey down her throat until she coughed and vomited—nearly choking on the contents of her own stomach.

Chung-li retched again now, rolling onto her side as he spilled whiskey on her cheek, soiling her silk bedcover.

"You little she bitch!" he grumbled, yanking her to the side with one hand squeezing her jaws so tight that she had to open her mouth as he brought the bottle over her bloody lips. "You're gonna learn to drink whiskey with me, by damned!"

She tried to force back down the fill rising from her belly, tried at the same time to hold the tip of her tongue inside the neck of the bottle so that the whiskey would not reach her mouth. He squeezed harder and she relented, swallowing, retching and spitting up as he laughed and moved out of the way when the vomit poured out, coating the bed before she could hang her head over the floor.

"That's a good whore," he said, gasping between deep belly laughs. "Gotta learn to drink whiskey if you're gonna be my bitch, lil' Chinee doll. I pay your Chinaman good money to keep you all to myself while I'm here—so you're gonna stay right here and learn to drink whiskey."

He grabbed hold of her hair, pulling back her head, shoving the neck of the bottle against her mouth as another gush of whiskey washed in—another gush of vomit erupted and spilled over her bare breasts. She didn't care where it fell now. Hot, smelling sour of acid and whiskey.

"Ain't going nowhere till you learn to drink whiskey with Orrin Haslam. Just remember: if the whiskey don't kill you, I will, slow. Just like I'll butcher that crippled Chinaman and get all my money back what I paid him for you till I got ready to go back to the colonel."

She tried to drink—knowing it was the only way he would leave her be to sleep. Knowing he was going to stay right here with her until he left Pioche. Maybe she should let him kill her—but realized she didn't have her own sister's courage.

"You know when I leave again—I'll be back, Chinee whore," he said, plugging her lips around the neck of the bottle with glee wetting his eyes. "I'll be back with the colonel and his army—and then I ain't never gonna leave you again."

Book IIII

Redemption in
the Blood

29

DAMN, BUT HE hated the smell of those Indian camps Usher sent him to.

Lamanites—that's what those goddamned Indians were. A lost tribe cursed by God's own hand. Their skins darkened with the curse of the beast, rendered into the wilderness until they might come to the word of God. These damned Indians—descendants of the ancient Lamanites who had long ago battled the forces of Mormon.

Orrin Haslam lay in the dark, watching the icy veil of each breath halo above his head in the silver moonlight that peeked through the single, small, smoky windowpane in the whore's room. Thankful this wasn't a tiny crib, all that most prostitutes could call their own. After all, by God—he'd paid the crippled Chinaman good money for the woman, along with boarding in her room while he lollygagged these weeks in Pioche.

A better plan it was than paying out money to a boardinghouse, much less the cost of a hotel room for all this time he was Usher's eyes and ears.

Besides, Haslam enjoyed the way the Chinaman's eyes widened when presented with all that money for the exclusive use of the whore and her room for as long as Orrin needed them both.

It had been weeks already, getting here just about the time the new year turned. Eighteen and seventy-six, it was. Nearly two decades now since he had been riding with the colonel. Just short of twenty years of work on behalf of God's own Avenging Angels. Righting injustice done to the Church faithful, and sweeping the land clear of Gentiles where they could.

Mexico and Arizona Territory had been the most fun a man with a hard pecker and two belt guns could have himself. Them Apache girls near drove him crazy back then—whether they was alive, or dead, or just half-dead. He and the rest didn't care back then—hunting scalps for the colonel and to run onto sign of an Apache village. They killed what warriors they could and ran the rest off—and what women and children was left behind, all of them wounded, dying for sure—lay as the colonel's reward for a job well done.

Their scalps belonged to Usher. But those brown, bloody bodies belonged to the men gone too long between forking a whore. It got so that a lot of the colonel's soldiers didn't much care for prostitutes anymore when they reached some town. Seemed more often than not Haslam and the others found more pleasure in the wounded ones they coupled with on the bloodied ground, the kind of woman what cried out in pain and torment there in the wisps of smoke and the stench of death as Usher's army put a village to the torch.

Unmitigated violence had become the only way Orrin found any relief anymore. Blood and rape were the only things that fit together in his life. Blood and rape the only things that brought him any satisfaction—if not outright happiness. It wasn't every man who could pack along a steady woman and a nigger servant both—like the colonel himself did.

It was Usher's plan that used up the last of autumn and the early winter—going from village to village with a sizable escort of men and that half-breed interpreter, enlisting the warrior bands into the colonel's mercenary army. And with that done, Usher dispatched Haslam on this return to Pioche, Nevada.

Here he was to learn all that he could of the comings and goings at the mines south of town against the hillsides: at the Phoenix No. 1, the Hermes, the Kentucky-Ohio and Pioche-West as well as the Lightner and the Newark. Every one of them funneling its ore into the Nevada-Utah Mines and Smelter Corporation's huge belly. It was the forthcoming shipment from the NUM&SC that the colonel's army would hit. That mining outfit seemed so stinking rich, they'd likely never miss what Usher's men could lift from a puny little load of ore bound for the San Francisco Mint.

Haslam had wandered out Ely Street toward the hillsides, gone up Meadow Valley Street so many times everyone must have thought him an

NUM&SC employee. Back and forth along the tracks of the Nevada Central Railroad that plied the foot of those slopes—cars loaded with shaft timbers going into the tunnels, cars loaded with ore coming out.

He watched and listened, and engaged all who would talk. His nights he spent filling his belly with a rare beefsteak or some elk, perhaps some venison, as well as washing it all down with his whiskey before he'd trudge up the stairs to the room where the Chinaman kept the whore locked up for him.

He'd made the Chinaman do that—keep the woman locked in for safekeeping. Could you beat that? The crippled freak had been willing to do that—for all the money Haslam paid him every week. The Chinaman saw to it one of the other whores came four times a day to take the chamber pot from the tiny room, to bring coal for the corner stove and a tray of food for the whore twice a day. She needed to keep up her strength—elsewise she'd be no good to Orrin Haslam while he was in town.

When he left, Orrin was planning to take her with him. But knew better than to figure on doing such a thing just now. Oh, he realized he'd be back soon enough. Once he returned to Utah and the colonel—that is, once Usher listened to all that Haslam had learned and had his plans nailed down for attacking one of the gold shipments.

Eventually, Orrin would be back to lay claim to his share of the gold shipment, with it to help wrest the one true Church away from a sick, tired Prophet too weak to prevent his own overthrow. Damn right—Orrin Haslam would be back here soon enough! To lay claim to the Chinaman's little whore. She'd go with him everywhere then.

Or he'd have to kill her before he pulled out of Pioche, a rich man who would sit at the right hand of the Church's new Prophet.

He'd simply have to kill her.

Jonah wondered about that Christ hanging on the crucifixion tree. Carved of wood, yet so lifelike in its painted flesh so pale. Not the savior of those Mexicans who prayed with such fealty. Surely not the savior of those Indians the black-robed priests wished to save. Not even the savior of a man like him—his own hide tanned to a leathery oak color.

No, a pale-skinned crucified Christ who could not get himself down off that cross was not the savior in a land like this. Christ had not helped free Gritta. Not even helped free Jeremiah. And even God Himself would have to admit that all His powers were not enough to snatch Zeke from death's hoary grip.

That morning two hours gone after leaving their breakfast fires, they had reached the wide river. Another two hours were taken up riding south by west along the south bank of the mighty river before they gave up trying to locate a ford and found a place Two Sleep figured they could swim their horses across. Jonah told Jeremiah to dismount and quickly disrobe.

"The old mountain man teach you this?" the youngster asked, his teeth chattering as he slipped out of his britches.

"This way—you'll have dry, warm clothes to put on when we reach the other side."

The water was almost as cold as the air itself, sparkling the way it was with hoarfrost as they broke through the ice rimed at the river's bank and urged their reluctant mounts into the frigid water. By the time the trio reached the far side, the animals were all but done in from their exertion in the freezing water. Shuddering almost uncontrollably, the men quickly dressed before starting a fire. Close by the flames they sat and boiled coffee among the horses they had picketed in a ring. After drying out the saddle blankets and some of the other gear soaked in the crossing, they were ready to press on. But as cheery as that fire was, Jonah still found himself struggling to get warm once in the saddle again as the sun continued its climb to midsky.

That sun shimmered in the west now, soon to be setting. Patches of dirty snow lay iced into rimed doilies around the base of each scrub cedar, like soiled skirts brushing the ankles of every clump of squatting sage.

Turning in the saddle, Jonah looked over at his son. Bundled in his heavy wool coat, muffler wrapped around his neck, his hat pulled down over his long hair that tousled back and forth with every knifing gust of wind, Jeremiah's skin was every bit as dark as Two Sleep's. Although the young man's hair was almost as black and thick as an Indian's—it was still the streaks of chestnut-red that glinted beneath the winter sun, still the way it hung in tangled waves rather than with the obedient straightness of the Shoshone's, that ensured no man should ever really mistake Jeremiah for an Indian.

That and those eyes so blue at times it ached to look into them, a blue so translucent and deep it reminded Jonah of the fishing holes dotting the limestone hills back to home. He even swore there were times he could tell from the depth of that blue when his son was thinking back on Prairie Night, the woman Jeremiah had left behind.

Jonah wondered if his son had loved her even while she was Zeke's woman. And each time he wondered, he knew the answer. As good a man as Jeremiah had become in all those years they had been apart, Jonah realized that his son hadn't been merely following the dictates of Kwahadi custom—Jeremiah had instead been following his heart.

Maybe he had come along with Jonah and Two Sleep not only to find his mother . . . but also, in some small and unspoken way, to help another man track down that man's woman.

Now that Jeremiah must surely know about men and women, must surely have some understanding of how a man can flounder about, mired in love.

Had Jeremiah really grown up all that much in those years Jonah and his boy were apart? Or had he grown up far faster in the weeks and months since father and son had been reunited?

Not that long ago, really . . . then he caught himself. Chiding himself for his stupidity—for it had been almost a year. As close as he knew, it might be February already, the way time passed on the trail, without no calendars to mark off the days.

Almost like those weeks following Sterling Price out of Arkansas and into Mississippi. Like those lost days he spent lying on the forest floor, captured so they could load him up in a boxcar with the other barefoot, raggedy prisoners in gray and butternut and homespun all shipped north—those days shoved back to back into countless weeks and months as he lost track—in the end coming to learn he wasted something on the order of two years waiting for death to come claim him, as it had claimed so many, many more each day after endless days in that stinking cesspool of a Yankee prison.

The shadows lengthened while the sun fell before them; the blood-red land rose beneath them as if the whole earth were on fire with its setting. As if what distance remained for them to travel fell open like a fresh, gaping wound in this flesh he had to crawl across until he found her. The dark path of each creek veined the descent of the hillside, spilling onto the valley floor at their feet.

And the suddenness of the neatly platted, fallow fields leading off toward houses, barns, and corrals surprised all three of them. Jonah stopped and let the horses blow, heads bobbing, pawing in the rose-azure of twilight-coming, their breath puffing in gauzy halos within the last gold tendrils of the sun's passing. If he hadn't already counted on the certainty of his long-anticipated return, this moment might have been almost religious—for a man uncomfortable with most all that mankind considered religious: the cold, purifying air that stung the lungs . . . their icy crossing behind them now, perhaps like that journey of the Christ beneath the burden of his cross, set upon by a gauntlet of his enemies. As well as the light here at sunset. A light becoming so red in the setting of the sun that it reminded Jonah of the clarity of those blood drops painted against the pale skin of that carven, sacrificial Christ. So pale was this arid land, so red its scars in a last, momentary benediction before night fell across this empire of the Mormons.

Jonah Hook had returned to Zion.

This time he vowed not to leave without her. If he had to finish it alone, if he had to send Two Sleep back to the Wind River and Jeremiah back to his family on the Fort Sill reservation in Indian Territory—Hook felt the rock of certainty lying cold in his bowels. He had come to settle the unknown. Or die in the trying.

"You think they get this ground to grow anything?" Jeremiah asked, breaking the stillness as the air grew colder. "Dry, like it is."

"I figure these folks do just about anything they set their minds to, Jeremiah."

"Then those folks down there—they Mormons?"

Jonah didn't answer directly, but instead asked a question of Two Sleep: "Didn't know they was settling this far east, did you, Indian?"

The Shoshone only shook his head, his eyes like slits as he peered down on the settlers' houses, in the midst of even more naked, skeletal framework for more homes and what would clearly be their Church—its tall, spire-adorned steeple already raised above an unfinished roof and half-sided walls thrown up here against the late-afternoon sky, that tall, bare white spire brushing against the underbelly of crimson-tinged clouds.

Jesus still hung on the Catholic priest's cross to remind Hook of the price paid for Jonah's redemption. At the same time the Mormons' spire stood bare of all vestiges of the Lamb, so claimed the blackrobe—because Brigham Young's lost people did not worship the true Christ.

"Brigham Young."

"What'd you say, Pa?"

Then Jonah realized he had spoken out loud as he sat staring at the valley below them shrouded in winter's white. "I said Brigham Young."

"Mormon chief," explained Two Sleep.

"Then he's the one we're looking for—the one took my mother? Not Jubilee Usher?"

"No, Jeremiah. Young ain't the one took your ma. Not rightly, he ain't. That was Usher—for sure. But"—and Jonah paused a moment— "something tells me Brigham Young's the one we ought to be looking for right now."

Jeremiah wagged his head in confusion. "If this Brigham Young ain't the one who took us off the farm years ago—then why ain't we looking for the one what did—Jubilee Usher?"

He looked at his son finally, seeing the last of sunset's golden light drain from the boy's tanned face, watching the lavender hues come to take its place. "Because Brigham Young's about as good a place as any to start. I don't have any better way to go."

Jeremiah sighed, his shoulders rising, then sagging. "So—where's this Brigham Young gonna be? Where we gonna find him?"

Jonah pointed. "North of here. Place called Salt Lake."

"The place where you give up on chasing Jubilee Usher seven years ago."

"It's where I plan on picking up a trail gone cold after all this time."

With that Jonah nudged his horse off the crest of that low hill, hearing the creak of cold leather and the protests of the other horses as Two Sleep and Jeremiah put their own animals into motion, the packhorses heeling on the trio.

Lights were glowing like faint, greasy candle lanterns from many of the windows dotting the short main street of that little settlement as they reached the valley floor. Other, future streets had been staked out already by the town's founders with fluttering flags, each running north and south, or east and west from the main east-west street hemmed in by neat board-front stores and small shops, a pair of restaurants joined by a single boardinghouse.

His mouth watered.

"I'm tired of game meat, fellas," Jonah said, eyeing the small sign that hung out at a ninety-degree angle from a swing arm on the clapboard building where he reined up his horse and volved his tired shoulders.

"Gonna eat here?" Jeremiah asked.

"Food might be good," Hook said, easing down into the offhand stirrup, on down to the ground.

Young Hook peered up, then down, the street, still in the saddle. "We gonna sleep here tonight too?"

"I don't figure on paying no man for the use of a bed, son. We'll have us a bite, then ride on to make our camp some north of town."

He shifted the two gun belts around the worn, dusty mackinaw coat, his eyes sighting the inquisitive faces of those who watched with nosy interest as the trio tied off their mounts at the hitching rail.

"I suppose we do look mighty curious," Jonah said under his breath as he turned the knob in his glove and pushed open the door, stepping down one step into the fragrant warmth of the small café.

"Greetings, travelers!" a voice hailed them. "Up from the south?"

"We are," Jonah replied, turning to find a middle-aged man draped in a dirty apron he was wiping his hands on as he clambered Hook's way.

"Then you've crossed the mighty Colorado, have you?"

He looked back over his shoulder to find the other two not far behind him. "That was the Colorado, was it?"

"Yes," he replied in a distinct tongue from somewhere north of the Mason-Dixon. "Come for supper?"

"We did," Jonah replied. Turning slightly, he watched as Two Sleep entered, followed by Jeremiah, who closed the door behind them. When Hook turned back to the round-faced Yankee, he found the smile gone, replaced by a dour expression.

Leaning in so he could whisper to Jonah, he said, "We don't allow no Injuns to eat in here. Folks wouldn't wanna eat here after him. The plates and tinware and all, you understand."

Jonah quickly looked over what others filled about half the tables in the place, then whispered as well to the proprietor. "You saying you won't let him eat here, but you'll let me and the boy eat here."

He blinked his eyes, looked over the pair with Hook, and replied as quietly as he could. "Him? I don't understand, sir. I won't feed either one of them Injuns came in with you."

"Either one?" Jonah turned and looked over the pair himself, then realized that Jeremiah could be taken. "The young one—he's my son."

The Yankee smiled benevolently, seeming content with his own deduction. "Half-breed boy, is he?"

"No, his mama was whiter'n you, mister." Hook's eyes danced over the rest of the customers for a moment. "But we been out on the trail a long, long time—coming west from Injun Territory. I can see how you might mistake him for an Injun just like the Shoshone there."

"The Shoshone have been friendly to our people," the man was proud to announce. "Ever since Brigham Young led his faithful out of Missouri."

"Then you won't mind feeding this Shoshone, will you?"

His eyes flitted nervously. "I can't."

By now his mouth was watering with the aromas of grease and coffee, the pungent fragrance of fresh-baked bread wafting his way from the kitchen doorway. "Then how 'bout you telling me what you'd sell me in the way of vittles—something you can wrap up and we'll take it along with us. Seeing how you can't serve us a proper sit-down supper like them upstanding folks."

"I . . . I know all them. They're friends. They live here."

"And they're Mormons—like you." Jonah watched the eyes all come back to him, the forks and knives halt in midair. He sensed the room's silence deepen.

He swallowed. "You're not. That's plain enough to see, mister. And that's all right, don't get me wrong. But I got a business to run and I got my family to feed—"

"You just fix us some of what you're serving them, wrap it up best you can, and we'll be on our way. Won't be no more bother to you."

Nervously wiping his palms down the front of his dirtied apron, the Yankee considered his options, then replied, "Suppose that would be no trouble. We've got some venison and elk on the menu tonight. Just had it come in—"

"You don't have nothing else but game meat?"

"Got a little beef roast left."

"How much you figure you got ready?" Jonah asked, his tongue running across his lips.

"Three, maybe four pounds."

"We'll take it. All you got left. Got taters too I see."

"Yes."

"Half dozen of them."

"Yessir. Anything more?"

"Those pies—what you have in pies?"

"Dried apple. Some rhubarb."

"Gimme one of each. Wrap it all so's I can carry it back in my saddlebags. I'll gladly pay you for your extra trouble."

He was nodding, some of the consternation replaced now with a smile. "You wait right here—I'll get you fixed up shortly."

"Coffee?"

Now his eyes shot back to Two Sleep, to the kitchen, and finally to Hook.

"Tell you what," Jonah said. "Go fetch up that coffeepot and hand it over to me. We'll take it outside and have us some from our own cups while you're throwing supper together. Add the price of a pot of your coffee to our supper—how's that sound?"

"Mighty agreeable to me," he cheered as he turned away, his ample frame bustling directly for the open doorway where the fragrant aromas emanated.

In the time it took Jonah to lay his eyes on nearly every man in the place and force them to turn back to their own business, the Yankee had returned with a steaming coffeepot in hand. He handed it and a thick pad wrapped around the bail over to Jonah.

"How 'bout some bread? Any corn bread tonight?" Hook asked.

He wagged his head. "No. Just some drop biscuits. Saleratus. But my wife pulled some white bread from the oven few minutes ago. You want some of that?"

"Two loaves. Make it three."

"You fellas are hungry. Where away you bound?"

"To Salt Lake City."

"On business?"

Jonah waited a moment, then answered, "Yes. On business."

"I hope you prosper, gentlemen," the man answered, a bit of his smile returning.

"Don't know about that," Jonah replied. "I got the feeling a man what isn't a Mormon won't do well out in this country—will he, now?"

"Well," and the man swallowed, his eyes dancing around the restaurant. "Suppose not. Out here in Brigham Young's land, if you're not one of God's faithful Saints—then you're one or the other: a Jack or a Gentile."

"What the devil is a *Jack*?"

"Why—that's a Jack Mormon. A person who isn't a practicing Mormon. They're a real problem—those who have fallen away from our faith."

Jonah bent his head over the steam wafting up from the coffeepot in his hand, his mouth watering with its aroma. "I suppose that's what we're going to Salt Lake City for, after all. Going to see Brigham Young about settling a problem I've long had me with a Jack Mormon."

"Then our blessings on your enterprise, mister," the Yankee said a bit more favorably. "I pray you'll fare well and find President Young's counsel to be both wise and fair in settling your dispute."

30

THIS RECENT COLD made his joints ache like never before. It was his forty-fifth winter, so he convinced himself it would take longer for the balms to ease his pain.

Bak Sahm rubbed more of the liquefied herbs into his elbow and wrist on that withered arm, wondering why he hadn't just allowed them to cut the arm off when he was nearly blown apart by the dragon's breath many, many years before. How he yearned again for some of the devil herb, that mushroom of immortality said to take away the pain solely by taking him out of his crippled body.

Fewer and fewer were the times when he enjoyed being made a prisoner in his distorted body—times when he lay with one or the other of his girls of joy. Then it was that Bak Sahm reveled in owning a *Loh Kur Chigh,* a bawdy house and whiskey saloon where lonely men came for companionship, came to forget the hard work of the day, came to numb their minds and souls against the sameness of what lay on the morrow.

More and more it was becoming just that way with him now. Each time he retreated back into the pinkish haze of the opium he smoked, Bak wanted less and less to return from his *kwong hop*—his everlasting unity with the spirits who watched over the temporal plane.

Below him the noise had been growing since late in the afternoon as the sun began to set. It was so cold outside in the streets of Pioche and night came on so quickly here in the dead of winter that men craved little

271

else but a place where the stoves in the corners melted the icy snow into muddy slush, where gathered many other human bodies steaming, smoking, drinking—all to make themselves a little warmer in a cold, dark world just beyond the glassed doors of Bak Sahm's saloon.

While there were other places much like his up and down the streets of Pioche, his was the one most well-known to the locals—for here they could buy a better grade of whiskey. Sure enough, he didn't make as much on each drink as did the other saloons, but Bak Sahm shrewdly made up for it with sheer quantity. Especially on long winter nights such as this.

Down below voices rose and fell in an ebb and flow of anger and boasting, riding some off-key song and raging in love's torment, while more and more customers crowded in as the smelters and mines belched free their human cargo for something on the order of twelve hours before another shift was due to start.

Clamping his eyes shut against the diminishing pain in the aching elbow, Bak opened them and sighed, gazing down at the horizontal letters printed across the label glued on the jar of fragrant balm. Of late he had to use the barbarians' greasy ointment, now that he was out of that shipped from any of the street-side physicians in Kwangtung Province.

With the jar nestled in the palm of his right hand, he ran a thumb over the black, bold, horizontal letters, able to recognize some of them. Thinking how strange it was that these white demons laid down their letters across a page, from left to right, instead of writing from top to bottom, down in a column. He supposed it was because these barbarians were just that: crude savages who easily exhibited how little cultural history they had behind them. These demons of the Gold Mountain were also a superstitious lot at best—most did not believe in anything much beyond the wisdom a man could find at the bottom of a whiskey bottle, or the infinite power men could wield in the capricious explosions of their guns.

Bak Sahm had his own guns. A pair of pistols he hung from hooks on the back of his door. Another pistol he kept stuffed in his belt beneath the loose silk blouse he wore. A small pepperbox he strapped to his left forearm with one of the whore's garters, right where he could snatch it out with his good right hand. If nothing else, he considered now, by not cutting off his left arm years ago when the dragon's fire almost killed him, Bak Sahm had a convenient hiding place for a terrible weapon of his own.

Those pistols, and the two shotguns he kept handy. One hanging beneath the bar downstairs. The other right here in his room, on pegs over the door. Handiest there where he could reach for it as he threw open the door, strode out on the landing above the hazy, noisy saloon below him, light streaming in ever-moving, murky shadows through the veils of steam and cigar smoke. Whenever trouble raised its head.

It always had.

At least once a day now that it was winter and cold and every man found himself cooped up inside some small, stinking place with other men for every waking hour of work, for every hour of slumber in the boarding-houses and sleeping rooms. There was no escaping it: people crushing in on every side of a man, bumping, rubbing, shoving, and pushing—in work or at a man's play. The only escape was to drink far too much and pass out, or drink far too much and get someone else to knock you out. The worst yet was to want a woman too much—for then a man would have to feel, genuinely feel something wonderful and fragrant and soft for a few moments before he was done and had to go back to the company of men once more.

No, a woman like any one of his girls of joy only reminded a man of his loneliness, of the unhappiness come of his lot in life, of the hopelessness of his dreams.

Perhaps his curse was being born a Snake. All who had been born forty-five winters ago had been born in the Year of the Snake. Cursed were they that they all were wise and deep thinking, possessed of great charm and an uncanny intuition that could guide them, for good or ill. The ancients long had said the Snakes would be best at teaching, for they were stingy with money—and everyone knew teachers were paid very little. But worst of all, Snakes were romantics. Hopelessly, irrevocably, irretrievably romantic.

Below him the sound of breaking glass pricked his attention. Bak Sahm rose slowly, stuffing the pistol back into his belt and covering it with his blouse, closing his quilted jacket over it by slipping the top button through its hole. This way the gun's butt did not show so readily, but it was still easy to snatch the pistol free. If any situation should ever grow so bad, there was always the pepperbox. That cluster of tiny cylinders, each filled with a lead ball he could use effectively at close range.

More breaking glass and the sharp stutter scuff of boot heels and soles as he moved toward his room's door.

For some reason Bak suddenly thought again on the first time he had had his fortune told, on that very first trip taken on his own as a young man to the large village that lay near the top of the Pearl River delta. The old woman's face had looked like the inside of a dried banana peel, so wrinkled and blackened it was as she asked him to spit into a small brass cup. She looked, and studied, then swirled his spit around—before studying some more. Then with an inaudible grunt she brought forth her ink pad and rice paper. Taking the five fingers on his right hand one at a time, the old soothsayer pressed each one in the ink, then rolled it on the paper. These she held up to the sun's light at the edge of her awning, squinting at the fingerprints.

From them, and from the bubbles of saliva at the bottom of her brass cup—she told him to give up on taking the exams to become a teacher, dashing the hopes of Bak Sahm's family.

Clucking, shaking her head, she dismissed him, saying he would never amount to much and studying for the exams given each year in Kwangtung would only be a waste of time. He had wanted to let her sour predictions slide off his shoulders, but then she had warned him that unless he was careful, his life would come to no good.

"Bak Sahm!"

The first shout from one of his three bartenders shattered the noise of breaking glass and scuffling miners from below.

Unless he was careful, the old woman had warned him, he would die a wasted life: dreaming of what could never be, dreaming of holding to his breast what he could never hope to hold. Sadly, she warned him never to love, for he would love in vain.

Then the old woman had held out her hand and promptly demanded her money.

With his right hand Bak wearily turned the knob with a sigh, flung the door back into his small room, then reached overhead for the shotgun as the stench and smoke assailed his nostrils. Even the worst of his girls smelled better than this, even had she gone many days without bathing, many nights of one filthy, stinking miner after another—even a stinking woman was more pleasing to his nose than the stench that rose to it now out of the swirling smoke and throbbing, jostling mass ebbing and flowing below him in the murky light.

He glanced left, then right, finding some of the girls standing at the low rail, watching the scene in the saloon below, all in their working attire—the robes or hose and sleeping gowns. Two of them had half-drunk miners draped over them as they watched the nightly show. All for free it was. But the one he wondered about most had not come out of her door. It was closed. Bak Sahm figured the white barbarian was with her, behind that door. The stranger had paid in gold eagle coins to keep the girl his exclusive property day in, and night out—a week at a time. Already weeks had passed.

It had been a very good deal for Bak Sahm, more money than he had imagined for one woman—so it did not matter that she was not working the miners. Whatever the barbarian had her doing now behind that closed door, she was earning more than three or four times what she could if she took one boisterous, wobbling miner right after another.

Perhaps it stank more here because all the foul stench rose in waves, like heat off the desert. Perhaps he thought his girls smelled better because whenever he was close enough to smell them, it meant he was lying on top of them, coupling with them when his need grew too great, when his ache pierced him too deep. Then the smell of them grown wet with his cock moving inside them made him remember the deep, rich, black, and fertile ground that surrounded his village. How sensual it had smelled when he had plowed it with the pointed curve of his plowshare, planted his seed in the riven crevice of the earth folded back to receive it.

It was that very same way when he folded back a woman's moist, darkened flesh and rammed within his own swollen, curved cock so that he could lay within her his seed.

The first gunshot came as a surprise. He hadn't expected it so early in the night. Ducking to look through the banister at the top of the stairs, Bak Sahm watched the crowd surge first this way, then that as a second and finally a volley of gunshots rocked the saloon. For a moment it seemed every man was diving one way or the other, flinging himself out of the line of gunfire. Then he saw what appeared to be the shooters below as he crouched down on the first of the eighteen steps, hugging the banister, his shotgun poking into the gloom at the ready, the pistol's sharp hammer jabbing him in his stomach muscles.

"Go round that way!" a voice cried out its order.

One of the bartenders was signaling Bak Sahm, pointing. Seemed the man the others were seeking was evidently behind the end of the bar, in back of a table he had overturned. Bak Sahm held up his shotgun. The bartender held up his empty hands and shrugged, then pointed to the end of the bar again.

Then Bak saw what the man meant. Whoever had taken refuge down there at the far end of the bar had snagged the shotgun from him. That much he could tell, seeing a glimpse or two of the weapon's muzzle over the top of the bar littered with broken glass and puddles of spilled whiskey.

"You stay!" Bak shouted as he reached the floor and planted his slippered feet in the muddy slush. It soaked in quickly, warm—surprising him as he brought the shotgun down on the big miner he had just given his command to.

Slowly turning, the man pointed to his own chest as if in disbelief.

Bak Sahm waved him over with the muzzle of the shotgun.

"Sam! This Chinee son of a bitch here got a gun on me!"

A second miner took form out of the smoky haze, a pistol held in either hand. "Listen, you li'l yellow bastard—this ain't got nothing to do with you—"

Pistol shots whapped against the far end of the bar, some of the bullets splintering the top radius of the overturned table, a couple thunking into the solid hardwood of the bar itself. An instant later the hidden man stood for a heartbeat, his own pistol barking off three shots before he collapsed out of sight.

Two of his shots struck their targets: the first man in the chest, knocking him backward into a table laden with chips and cards, glasses and bottles, all sent clattering to the muddy floor with the miner in a heap; and the second man struck low in the gut, a painful wound that bent him in half and made him cry out, knowing his was to be a slow and painful death as he crumpled slowly to the floor, clutching for a chair back that eventually toppled over with his unwieldy weight as he went down on his face.

"You bastard!" the big miner called out, no longer watching Bak Sahm as he knelt and dived for the near end of the bar.

"Get your goddamned folks outta there!" the second hollered at Bak Sahm. "We're gonna finish that card-cheating son of a bitch now—and 'less'n you want your tenders killed when we do it—get 'em out of our way."

"You stay!" Bak Sahm repeated, his mind working heatedly at what else he could remember of the barbarians' language that would make them obey him. "Stop—"

The smoke of cigars and gunfire at the far end of the bar ignited once again with the muzzle flash of the lone man's pistol as he aimed at someone across the floor.

"I'm hit, Halley!" a new voice shouted, the man's gun flying from his grip as he spun around, clutching his wounded arm, diving out of sight behind a toppled group of tables.

"Get him this time, I will," swore the big miner as he crouched at the end of the bar.

"He cain't hit the both of us," said the other.

Then came the first cry from the far end of the room. "Only two of you left!"

Bak Sahm thought he recognized the voice.

"One of us'll get you, card cheat!"

"Not so fast, miner!" the loner roared as he rose in a crouch and snapped off a shot, then twice clicked the hammer down on two empty cylinders.

"He's outta bullets, Halley!" the big miner growled.

"But he's got the saloon's scattergun still," warned Halley.

"Meaning he can only get one of us."

Halley glanced at Bak Sahm, then turned his back on the Chinaman in disdain, a smirk on his face. "When I say go, we rush him!"

"Awright—I'm ready."

"Go!"

The big miner and Halley both lumbered to their feet and began firing at the end of the bar as Bak Sahm shouted his command, screamed out his warning into the crashing, splintering, careening noise of the bullets smacking into wood of wall and floor, ricocheting off tin and brass and iron.

But his bad, broken English was swallowed up as the man at the end of the bar stood and leveled the shotgun at the closest of his two adversaries, jerking back on the trigger. Instead of only one barrel firing, both spurted flame simultaneously. The big man catapulted back as the double load of buckshot cut him nearly in two, wild shot splintering bottles and glasses perched behind the bar, beneath that mirror and the old, smudgy painting of ducks on a blue lake, splintering the top of the bar even more as each pellet dug its own long furrow.

Bak Sahm shook his head, knowing that the man at the far end of the bar was without any way to help himself now. In his hurry to squeeze off his shot, he had instead touched off both triggers—leaving him vulnerable to the last miner.

Halley grunted as he knelt a moment over the big miner, the blood already pooling on the floor, dark and shiny in the murky lantern light. He snapped off a wild shot from one of his pistols at the far end of the bar, then rose to a crouch.

Bak Sahm's mind worked at what to do as Halley fired another shot.

"You're out of time, friend," Halley said. "Just like you're out of bullets."

"I'm gonna come out—you got me dead to rights," the voice called out.

Then two hands appeared, followed by arms. And finally the man's face. Bak saw it was the stranger from out of town. The man who did not work in the mines, nor in the smelters. The one who had no means of making money—except that he had all the money he needed. Enough money to buy a room and food and the woman for weeks on end as he drank and played cards and kept the woman in her room away from every other man who came to Bak Sahm's California Lodging House to lay with her.

"Looks like I'm gonna have to kill you," Halley growled.

"Not like this," the man said. "This ain't fair—not giving a man a fighting chance."

"Who you to talk about fair—cheating at cards the way you was." Halley glanced at the floor about him, littered with the refuse of the gun battle, the bodies of his friends who had been sitting down to a little game together with the stranger. "C'mon out here in the middle where ever'body can watch you take the bullet that's gonna kill you."

The stranger shook his head.

"You gonna shoot me, shoot me where I stand."

"Awright . . . I will—"

"No!"

In shock they both turned to look at Bak Sahm when he hollered.

Behind Halley, near the far corner, the miner who was bleeding from an arm wound had dragged himself to his pistol and was snatching it up. Bak Sahm watched him wobble up onto his knees and wheel the pistol in the direction of the end of the bar.

"Stay!" Bak shouted again, wanting to remember more of the strong words, the cursing words the barbarians used to intimidate one another when they flexed their muscle.

The wobbly miner just sneered at Bak Sahm and looked back at the stranger, leveling his pistol again . . . when the shotgun roared, knocking the man over just as he triggered his shot.

Halley wheeled in a crouch, his own pistols coming around with him. Bak Sahm watched the orange fire spit from each of them, felt the tearing burn of something across one of his shoulders as he brought the muzzle of the double-barreled fowler down on Halley and yanked back for all he was worth while he still had the strength. While he still had the resolve.

It was like diving into the mouth of the dragon again—this belch of flame, the spew of smoke from the shotgun's muzzle.

Halley flew backward off his feet, his pistols still barking. Then lay a moment flat on his back on the muddy, slushy floor. Arching onto his shoulders and hips to try rising, he found his legs would not move.

"Shit," Halley growled as he looked down at his groin, there below the bloodied, shredded shirt and coat. His pants darkened as his bladder voided. "Pissed all over myself."

Then his head keeled back on his shoulders, plopping into a puddle of melting snow and ice that spiderwebbed with dark fingers as blood dribbled from the dead man's mouth.

For the longest time no one moved and the saloon fell silent. Everyone seemed to be waiting to learn if there would be more shooting.

"Sit yourself down, Chinaman."

Bak Sahm felt the pressure of the chair against the back of his knees as much as heard the barbarian's voice right behind his ear. He turned slightly, finding the stranger who paid good gold for the woman and the room upstairs.

"Sit," he repeated, pushing down on Bak Sahm's shoulder. The Celestial settled in the chair, feeling the heat of the flesh wound in his other shoulder.

"You just saved my life, Chinaman. Someone, get me some goddamned bandages!" he shouted at the room, spurring men and women to move about once more. "This town got a doctor, don't it? Get the son of a bitch over here now. Tell him I'll pay good money to fix up my friend what just saved Orrin Haslam's life! Now—somebody get!"

They were crowding around Bak Sahm then, someone taking the shotgun from his clawlike grip as his heart pounded deafeningly in his ears, making it hard to sort out all the foreign tongue chattered at him.

"The goddamned Chinaman killed 'em both!" someone marveled.

"Ain't you seen him shoot that shotgun before?" another asked.

"Yeah," agreed a third voice, "I heard he ain't one to let get the drop on you with that scattergun of his."

Then Bak turned to soggy leaves inside. How he hated killing, coming so close to death himself as he had been hanging in that basket against the granite shoulder of the mountain years before. How close he still came to death each time he dreamed of the dragon that would one day return to his life, to finish what it had begun with the dynamite explosion that had taken half of Bak Sahm's body with it.

But he was a businessman—and this business required that he be ready to kill to protect what he had to protect. A businessman always did that. After all, Bak Sahm knew he had mouths to feed.

As someone gently stripped his quilted jacket from his shoulder, and another brought a pan of warm water and a cloth to begin dabbing at his wound, Bak Sahm's eyes climbed to the second-floor landing where the girls of joy lived and worked. They were there, on the landing, watching, reliving the gunfight with their customers, marveling at the gunplay. Every one of them.

Even the woman. She stood alone—glaring in disbelief down at Bak Sahm and Orrin Haslam.

"What you think of that, li'l China doll?" the stranger called out, flinging his voice up to the woman by herself leaning on the railing. "This boss man of yours just saved your loving man's life. All that gold I pay him each week—why, I s'pose this Chinaman does know a good business deal when he sees one!"

Bak Sahm looked away, unable to hold the woman's gaze any longer. Shriveling inside like a dying silkworm in its cocoon, feeling more shame and revulsion for himself than he felt hate for Orrin Haslam.

Even more than he felt hate for her.

31

T HEY DIDN'T HAVE any saloons in Cisco, Utah. A man couldn't beg a single bottle of whiskey out of those folks, neither.

And all the women Jonah noticed were fresh scrubbed. Not a one of them painted, with her lips rouged and smelling of perfumed water. No saloon girls would he find in Mormon country.

Now they were riding north into the very lap of Brigham Young himself.

More than once Jonah had looked back over his shoulder at those yellow streaks of lamplight dotting the darkening walls of the town's neat buildings, saffron splashes crossing the shallow, muddy ruts down that long main street where the ice again rimed with the sun's leave-taking. And each time he turned his nose back to the north, he thought to touch that cotton flour sack into which the restaurant man had dropped the beef, bread, and pies. For the longest time that sack remained warm to the touch. Cisco, Utah, wasn't.

At least not to a Gentile. Not warm to any man come here of an errand that included seeking an audience with Brigham Young.

So they rode until slap-dark that night, miles beyond the Mormon settlement, before making camp, starting their coffee fire as the cold settled down and the stars came out to prick the icy black dome of what would be another subfreezing night. Hook sliced the beef roast as thin as he could and laid the strips in his blackened skillet. Two Sleep peeled the

bark off a pair of willow branches, sharpened the ends into points he drove
into loaves of bread; the other ends he planted firmly into the hard, flaky
soil at the edge of the small fire that gave an even redder glow to Jeremiah's
and Two Sleep's tanned faces.

The meat and bread were warmed before coffee boiled—so they ate,
and washed it down with creek water guzzled out of their canteens. The
coffee done, they dished out huge slices of the dried-apple pies on the
blades of skinning knives, then settled back, each one of them surfeited
with the food of civilized settlers.

Jonah's mind stayed busy on the thoughts of settlement. If not wandering back to the Shenandoah Valley, or their farm outside Cassville,
Missouri . . . then Hook stared at those flames thinking on just how he was
going to settle matters here in the land of the Mormons.

What had once seemed so complex years before—by all rights the
hardest thing he'd ever set himself out to do—had now boiled down to
being about as simple as a man could make it. And it got itself rendered
down without his even realizing it. If anyone knew where he could find
Jubilee Usher—it ought to be the man who ruled all the Mormons. If any
man could put Jonah on the right end of a trail gone cold seven years
before, it should be Brigham Young.

The man who twenty years gone sent his Danites, his Avenging
Angels, to kill Jim Bridger and burn down his fort. Shad Sweete had been
there, clear enough. It had been Brigham Young who didn't figure there
was enough room in the mountains for the mountain men and his Mormons. So by nature Hook already despised Brigham Young. Jonah easily
hated any man who wanted that much land, that much power.

But he'd walk into hell, stand eye to eye and toe to toe with the devil
himself—if that's what it took to find Jubilee Usher.

A little west of north they had pushed on the next morning, and all
those that had followed. They crossed to the west bank of the Green River,
the great homeland to the beaver and those who once came to trap them, a
great river given birth in the snowy ramparts of the Rocky Mountains in
Wyoming Territory. And rode on to skirt the eastern rim of a huge lava
field that lay at the feet of the famed Uintahs. On north by west he led
them, searching for a pass that would allow them across into the valley of
the Great Salt Lake—no easy task when winter held its final, cold grip on
the central basin.

"Get in here, Pa," Jeremiah said, holding back the blanket door flap
as Jonah dropped the armload of pine and aspen he had kicked up in the
snow or snapped off the dead branches within reach.

They had been here three days already, forced to hunker down when a storm rumbled over them, this one given birth out of the southwest. It spent itself in the first two days, then rolled on by, heading for the heart of the Rockies themselves. Now it stank in here, with the three of them held captive under their crude shelter of buffalo robes and a blanket door lashed over tree branches. Smoky too, smoky still, but not so much that they were run out. By leaving a crack at the top of their wickiup and by lifting the bottom of the buffalo hides a few inches to let in the cold wind, they got their fire to draft and most of the smoke to rise.

But if it hadn't been for the big doe Jeremiah dropped the morning the storm settled down on them—they'd have been forced to grumble about shrinking bellies. As it was, they were now down to surviving on what little meat they could pick off the snowshoe hares they shot—that and the long, crinkling gut of the doe. Everything stayed well-enough frozen in the drift blown up against the side of the wickiup. Several times each day Two Sleep hacked away at the carcass, freeing more bone, both rib and leg. These they stuffed down into the growing mound of coals. Later the trio pulled out the roasted bones, cracked them open with the butts of their pistols or ax heads, and licked out the melted, yellow marrow that looked and tasted like creamy, fresh-churned butter as it dripped down their beards and chins.

As Jonah settled, Jeremiah said, "Two Sleep says he smells a bear."

He looked at the Shoshone, who continued to stare at the low flames. "How's this Injun smell a bear out there—when it stinks like hell in here? That's what I wanna know."

"Not all bear sleep all winter," Two Sleep replied. "Wake up hungry—fill belly again. Go back to bed."

"What you smell is one of them not going to sleep out the winter, eh?"

"Bear smell strong today."

Jonah snorted, settling his blanket around his shoulders, "Your empty belly's making you smell bear, Injun. Nothing more."

"Maybe I let you shake hands with the bear, Jonah Hook."

He turned to his son, grinning. "You listening to this, Jeremiah?"

"Don't you trust what Two Sleep smells?"

"So now he's got you believing he smells a bear, is it?"

"Two Sleep's never lied to me about nothing."

So the Injun had gone and made a believer out of his son. "Gonna let me shake hands with this bear of yours, are you, you goddamned redskin?"

The Shoshone nodded, still staring at the fire.

"You do that, Injun. You just do that. He'll likely smell better'n you anyhow."

It had taken about all he had in him, but Shad Sweete had pushed west into the teeth of winter in a hurried lope—anxious as he was to get clear of Lakota and Shahiyena country when the soldiers went looking for the warrior bands.

Late last spring, eight—no, nine moons back now—Shad had come out to Bridger's fort to ask after Jonah Hook. And now this winter's cold seemed to pierce him to the bone like never before, the way Toote's bone awl had always pierced the leather she stitched up making the elk-hide moccasins Shad walked himself out of with regularity. Trouble was, he had to trade for mocs now.

God bless her spirit—how Shad missed her. Dreamed about her too—dreamed about being wrapped up with her most nights now.

This was his sixty-fifth winter, it was, and winters were the worst of times to be thinking back on Shell Woman. No choice did he have, though, but to get clean out of that country north of Fort Russell by Cheyenne City, much less out to Laramie itself, where the soldiers were mustering and passing on through—bound for Fort Fetterman up on the North Platte. There the old Red Beard Three Stars Crook was gathering him an army to make a winter's march into Lakota hunting ground.

For the first time in many a campaign, Shad Sweete wasn't going. Not that he didn't need the work, or couldn't stand a little pay—what with the way he enjoyed having his pouch filled with smoking tobacco and a couple canteens sloshing with trader John Collins's whiskey. But this time was different: this time he wanted out of the country when the army went looking for the warrior bands. More serious now than the army had been in years.

So Shad had taken his leave of Collins's store there at Fort Laramie, gathering up the last of those letters the trader had been holding for Jonah Hook, and pushed west in the heart of the winter. If Three Stars could march his army north into the last hunting ground of the wild tribes, Shadrach Sweete could ride west over South Pass, then slip down to Fort Bridger and on to the valley of the Great Salt Lake itself. Maybe one of these days he'd get to hand over that pouch stuffed with letters from Riley Fordham out to Kansas, letters with their faded ink bearing a St. Louis postmark. Hattie likely growed to full womanhood by now.

Hell, she'd likely have young'uns of her own after all this time. Pretty as she was.

With a tug at his own longing, a hard pull at his own lonely need, Shad wondered again if Hattie truly did remind Jonah of her mother. Or if it had only been a matter of all those years that made Jonah look at Hattie and see her mother's face. All those years.

Dear God—how did a man keep on looking after all this time? What pushed a man on the way Jonah had? Or was it more a matter of something *pulling* him on?

This matter of family, and how it lay in tatters, like shreds of cloth and hide lashed to a Lakota burial scaffold, at the mercy of the winds and winter until it grew so faded and weak that . . .

Sweete's own family was much like Jonah's. Toote buried down there along the river with their son. And Pipe Woman tucked far away up north with her husband and Shad's grandchildren—north in the land of Lame White Man's Shahiyena. Where the government back east had reached out its long arm and issued an ultimatum to the freedom-loving, winter-roaming warrior bands: come in to the agencies or we're going to sic the soldiers on you, going to drive every last one of you in where you'll have to eat moldy flour and rancid bacon.

It hurt deep inside, down there in that cold place that reminded him of a stone—just to think on all that he had seen in his winters out here in the free west.

The sky was clearing a little to the south of him as he looked out from the stand of trees that sheltered the depression in the rocks he had found three days ago. The hoary storm passing on slowly.

Many more days ago back there at Fort Bridger, in the waning phase of the last moon, Shad had fingered those letters for the last time—wishing through the pain again that the Shahiyena had a language they could write down on paper, wrap up and send it far, far away to a loved one. Wishing his daughter could write as Hattie had written her father.

Knowing, though, that if Pipe Woman did write—Shad would need an interpreter, someone to read it to him anyway. Never did learn to cipher paper sign. But just in the handling of those old letters it brought him closer to days gone by, closer to the faces fading in musty memories he fought to keep alive more and more with each new day. Being close once more to that scoundrel Riley Fordham and the doe-eyed Hattie Hook. Lord, but she was the kind to make a rich man fall to his knees just to propose his undying love for her.

Safe she was, growed up back east. Jonah had made sure of that. More than Shad had been able to do for his own kin. Not that he hadn't tried. But in the end he had let Pipe Woman go the way the winds blew her, where her own heart led—north into the land of the wild tribes.

"I will worry about you," he had told her as they embraced that last time.

"I know," she had whispered against his chest. "But—in your heart—you know why I am going."

The tears had begun to creep down into his thick, white whiskers then. "Yes. Because you would rather be free . . . than safe."

She was his daughter, truly. To be free rather than safe.

To the south of him the falling sun's rays shot through the afternoon clouds like a muzzle blast—shimmering the new snow in a brilliant burst of color as the storm pushed on its way at long last. Heading east.

He could pull out again in the morning. Not all that far to the valley of the Great Salt Lake now. He didn't have much to go on after all this time—couldn't much hope the Mormons would help him looking after a man named Jonah Hook. Not that any of them would likely know just who the hell Jonah Hook was anyway.

But Shad was sure he could find out something of the one named Jubilee Usher. And if the Mormon Saints didn't know nothing of Usher, or didn't want to say—then Shad could always go to their chief. All these years out here in these mountains had taught him that much: you go right to the chief of a warrior band if'n you wanted to know something.

The Great Salt Lake was where he'd find that chief. And in that valley is where Brigham Young would know where Shad could find the Mormon war chief called Jubilee Usher.

Shell Woman was gone. And he'd not found another to take her place. Doubted he ever would. Coming to terms, was he, a little more each day now with being so alone. No one to make him moccasins, no one to warm his robes these long winter nights seized with cold—not that he didn't outright hanker every now and then for the very special feel of a woman wrapped around his pecker, warm and wet the way a willing woman would get with the right man.

But he had to admit he was getting on in winters—so old now all he really dreamed about anymore was just holding Toote while she slept, dreamed of the feel of her skin against his as the winter winds howled outside the lodge, rattling the icy skins like a gaunt, hungry wolf. Dreamed of how she looked at him with that deep, keen-edged love in her eyes, even as she lay coughing up bloody pieces of her lungs, and died in his arms.

That was what he worked his mind on most these cold nights he had left him: remembering Toote the way she had been before the winters took their toll, before the winters and a white man's coughing sickness took her from him. Stole her.

So Shad remembered.

And worked his mind on finding a way to track down the Mormon war chief.

If it was the last thing he could do for Jonah Hook—for the friend that had become like family to a lonely old man.

"Hook!"

He came awake suddenly, his eyes the only thing that moved when Two Sleep's sharp whisper penetrated his fevered dreams of having his hands around the throat of some faceless enemy. A white man. A Mormon.

"You awake, Pa?"

"I am now," he whispered back at Jeremiah. "What the hell you wake me for?"

"Two Sleep been smelling that bear all night—"

"That bear again?" Hook grumbled. "Him and that goddamned bear." He rose onto one elbow, sniffing as loud as he could to poke fun at the Shoshone, angry that the other two had interrupted his sleep—

Then his ears pulled him up short.

There wasn't another sound like it in all the world Jonah knew. That snorting, snuffling, grunting grumble at the back of the creature's throat.

Bear.

"You ever run onto a bear when you was with the Comanche, son?" he whispered now.

"No, Pa. Never. What we do?"

Across the cold blackness of the small wickiup Jonah thought he made out the shape of the Indian in the dull-red glow of the coals between them. "You, Two Sleep? What you know about bears?"

"Gonna wait, Jonah Hook. Bear come out of den in winter—this big medicine," the Shoshone replied. "Much bad medicine."

With the other two fallen quiet, Jonah went back to listening. Come each fall of a heavy, furry paw nearby, with each new snort, each new root of that grumbling snout as the bear followed its nose closer and closer to the smell of the deer carcass, Hook felt his skin prickle. And finally the first drop of cold sweat left the nape of his neck, spilling like slow mercury down the length of his backbone—an icy trace of fear.

"Ever et bear meat, Two Sleep?"

"Sh-h-h-sh, Pa!"

"Have you, Injun?"

"No. Bear meat very bad medicine," the Shoshone whispered, almost too quiet to be heard.

"We ain't got much better prospects, do we, fellas?" Jonah said, swallowing as his skin crawled with dangerous anticipation. Maybeso to screw up his own courage. "What better chance we got to make meat?"

"B-bear meat?" Jeremiah stammered.

By now he had freed the repeater from beneath the blankets, out from between his legs, where he slept with it tucked each night. "Grab your carbine, son. You too, Injun. I need you to back me up."

"No. Leave the bear go, Jonah Hook."

"Goddamned stupid Injun," he grumbled, easing forward as he got to his knees at the blanket door flap.

Two Sleep grabbed Hook's arm. "Your medicine . . . bear's medicine. You kill bear—they the same medicine after you kill."

He tried to make out the Shoshone's face in the dim red light of the dying coals as he slowly pushed aside the blanket flap with the muzzle of his rifle, wanting to believe the Shoshone was finally developing a sense of humor. "Never knew you was so superstitious, redskin. Man never has to be scared of nothing he can see. You coming to back me up? Well? Are you?"

"No."

"Suit yourself, Injun. And you, Jeremiah?"

He swallowed down hard. "I'll come, Pa."

"Good boy."

Two Sleep gravely put out his hand, held Jeremiah's arm. "All right for him stay with me."

Jonah was getting angry. "No it ain't, Injun. You're backing me up, Jeremiah."

He watched his son turn toward the Shoshone in the light, nodding slightly. As if Jeremiah was saying it was all right.

Then young Hook declared in a whisper, "I said I'd come."

Hook pushed the blanket back even farther, allowing his eyes to grow accustomed to the moon's silver light on the blue snow. Listening all the while as the creature drew closer, snuffling, pawing. Grunting in ravenous anticipation—around at the drift where they had butchered the deer carcass.

Jonah eased himself out of the wickiup on his hands and knees, then crawled to the side so that Jeremiah could come through. When he slowly levered a round into the chamber of the repeater, the snuffling suddenly stopped. Jeremiah froze, half-in, half-out of the doorway.

"C'mon, son . . . let's find the bastard—"

The smell of it was what struck him first, then the size of the bear as it reared on its hind legs at the side of the wickiup, its arms outstretched and flexing toward Jonah as Hook started to bring the rifle up.

"Pa!"

The branches and buffalo hides collapsed beneath the monster's weight as the bear crashed over them, the huge arms continuing to claw, the four-inch razors at the end of the two paws glittering like polished knife blades in the winter moonlight.

As the creature batted his carbine aside with no more effort than if it were a troublesome mosquito, Jonah heard Two Sleep grunt. The whole wickiup had come down on top of him, him and the fire pit.

That new grunt stopped the curious creature for a heartbeat. It stopped, sniffed at the hides—intrigued about what rumbled beneath him as a dim-witted creature would investigate anything it could not understand. And thereby gave Jonah his chance to dive to the side for the carbine he could barely make out in the starshine.

As he skidded sideways, the bear whirled with amazing agility, swinging one of its arms, striking Hook hard enough to bowl the man over in a heap.

At the moment he came to his hands and knees, shaking his head to clear it—the first shot split the night. The muzzle flash hurt Jonah's eyes. A grunt erupted from the bear.

He blinked, finding the creature rearing up on its hind legs, pawing the air madly.

A second shot. A third. Now the bear roared, loud enough that Jonah felt as if the forest floor rumbled beneath him. The animal staggered forward, off the crumple of buffalo robes and shattered limbs.

Now a fourth shot.

"Pa! Shoot him! Shoot him!"

As he wheeled about to search for his carbine, Jonah watched the buffalo robes heave and the Shoshone appear, arms already up as Two

Sleep vaulted into the air. He landed on the bear's back, burying the camp ax in the back of the monster's head.

Jeremiah shot again before Jonah could holler at him, "Don't shoot! The Injun . . . the goddamned Injun!"

Slowly the bear stumbled around in an ever-widening circle, one arm hung useless, the other clawing back at the cause of its pain. Two Sleep clung like a tick, one of his arms locked around the creature's neck, the other struggling to free the ax from the bear's head.

Eventually he broke it loose, swung it downward again. Ripped it upward a second time in a savage motion as the bear careened sideways over the ruins of the wickiup again.

Then Jonah's bare hand struck the cold, icy barrel of his carbine. Snatching it up, he heard Jeremiah's rifle fire again. Coming about in a crouch, Hook found the bear going down, collapsing on the Shoshone with an enraged roar, clawing, its huge jaws snapping voraciously at its quarry suddenly flung from its back.

In a spring Jonah was behind the animal as it fell atop the Indian. He fired point-blank into the back of the bear's skull. Levered and fired. A third and fourth shot before the creature no longer made a sound, began to sink. All life seemed to seep slowly out of the huge gray bulk come out of the winter night.

"Two Sleep? Where's Two Sleep?" Jeremiah screeched as he came to his father's side.

"Get this son of a bitch rolled over," Jonah growled, his own throat burning, his temples pounding with each hammer of his heart.

Together father and son were able to heave the monster's bulk aside. Beneath lay the Shoshone in a twisted heap.

"He . . . he dead, Pa?"

Jonah knelt, put his head to the Indian's chest. "No." Then he peered close at his friend's face, not knowing just what to do.

"Tell you, Jonah Hook," the Shoshone whispered in a raspy, somber voice that filled the clearing, "tell you bear is bad medicine."

"Damn—you had me scared, Injun."

Slowly, the Indian began to move, pushing some of his long hair out of his face. "Your medicine—bear's medicine . . . Jonah Hook. Goddamn bad. Now they the same medicine."

32

B RIGHAM YOUNG'S SHOULDERS sagged. His eyes closed
lightly, he felt weary—oh, so weary as he listened to the gathering
of counselors who had come when he called them upon the moment of his
return to Salt Lake. Three times now—once each week—these trusted
advisers met in Brigham's office to discuss not only matters of the First
Presidency and the Quorum of Twelve, but every man's concern with the
growing noise created down in Utah's Dixie.

Since early the past winter, Young's Indian agents among the Utes
and Pahvants had reported Jubilee Usher's men coming among the bands
to appeal, cajole, bribe, and buy the warriors' support in what was shaping
up to be a very messy situation.

If not an outright war for control of the Church of Jesus Christ of
Latter-Day Saints.

"If this isn't put to rest, our settlers will be forced to retreat from their
farms and fields," Orson Hyde complained.

John Page agreed. "Those tribes arise now, we'll lose the last twenty
years of our progress in pacifying this land."

Young took his face out of his hands and looked across the room at
Parley Pratt. "After all I did to help those tribes—the Lamanites—the lost
tribe of Zion!"

"Yes, Brigham!" said Gridley Howe. "They show their gratitude to
you by stabbing you in the back when you need them the most!"

"Then you must all understand the depth of my despair," Brigham groaned, feeling every one of his years like marble blocks on his shoulders. This coming June he would be seventy-five. "It's not so much this Jubilee Usher—I can handle him when the time comes. It's losing all the good we've done to further our interests here in Deseret."

Outside, beyond the low stone wall, carriage and wagon traffic rumbled past his offices, the Lion and Beehive Houses. His children went about their daily tutoring, his wives concerned with the operations of the households—Clara, Emmeline, Mary Ann and Lucy, Mary Elizabeth and Rhoda—seventy wives so far. As if that weren't enough to concern a man . . . now Brigham had a bloodthirsty tyrant pulling at the hem of his coat— wanting a piece of his empire. Wanting his throne next to the Almighty.

"Can't we trust in God, Brigham?" asked W. C. Staines. "Trust in God to deliver Usher—like any foul-souled apostate—to the buffetings of Satan?"

He placed his big hands, wide, stub-fingered carpenter's hands, palms down on his desk and pushed himself upright. He was a cabinetmaker whom heaven had called to be a Prophet. Standing to face the rest, Young said, "God has his own schedule for Jubilee Usher. His own retribution for all apostates who leave the Church. But I have my own plans for Usher."

"You've decided what to do?" George A. Smith asked, his clean-shaven face expectant.

Turning to gaze out the window on the wintry street below, Young sighed. "Yes. Two weeks ago—not long after I returned north from my winter sojourn in St. George—I was paid a visit by a . . . a stranger." Now he turned back to face them, sinking slowly against the window well. "A man almost as old as I—his face scarred by his many experiences, his eyes cold as the banked fires of hell, I must tell you."

"One of Usher's men—come to confess—was it?" George Q. Cannon asked, his voice rising with excitement.

But Brigham wagged his head. "No, George. Someone looking for Usher instead."

Nearly all of them rocked forward in their chairs, eager to hear the tale of it.

"Who was he?" Ira Hatch asked the common question.

"One of my old enemies—perhaps I'll explain it that way."

"By the devil, what do you mean?" Staines asked.

"An old friend of Bridger's. Jim Bridger's."

Cannon asked, "Come here with murderous intent after all this time?"

"God, no!" Young replied, attempting a bit of a grin. "Come here wanting to ask of me where he might find Jubilee Usher."

"For what purpose?" demanded Hosea Stout with sharp suspicion. "So that he might join Usher's army seeking to wrest the Church from you?"

Brigham closed his eyes a moment, sighing again, recalling the old man's face. Although not as old as Young, the visitor had looked older, so much older. All those years in the mountains, on the plains—a life lived on equal terms with the elements. Now Brigham looked around the room at his trusted friends and counselors: steadfast men all.

"No, although this man bears me no goodwill, although this stranger would likely consider me his enemy for life . . . I truly believe this visitor spoke the truth that he wanted only to find Usher—to kill him."

"K-kill Usher?" Orson Hyde gushed in a stammer. "You didn't really believe he wanted to find Usher to kill him?"

"Yes, I do."

"Don't be a fool, Brigham," George Smith chided. "We can all remember—"

"I am not an old fool," Young interrupted. "And neither was this old mountain man."

"Why, pray tell," asked George Cannon, "would this old plainsman want to kill Jubilee Usher?"

"That—the killing—was secondary: something he said he would get around to doing," Young replied.

"Exactly as I thought, Brigham," snarled Hosea Stout. "So, what was his real purpose in wanting to locate Usher?"

"He spoke so earnestly of wanting to learn about a friend he had lost track of. A man who also sought out Jubilee Usher."

"So you sent him on his way?"

"Not before I told him all that I wanted him to know," Young replied, then slowly turned and retraced his steps to look down on the muddy slush of the street below, churned with so many iron tires and plodding hooves, piles of horse manure steaming in the cold winter air. Horsemen moved up and down the boulevard.

Across the street a pedestrian was hailed by a group of muddied, unkempt travelers. He stopped, then pointed at Young's offices. The three turned, looked at the building, in fact seemed to look up at the window where the president stood. They were a rough lot, those three. Frontiersmen all. But then, his own life had been one of constant westward migration: to western New York, on to Ohio, then to Missouri, briefly to Illinois before he finally led his people west to the land of Israel—like Moses in the days of Exodus.

For a moment Brigham was seized with sudden alarm, wondering if they might be Usher's assassins. Then he scolded himself. He was too well protected these days. And besides, he thought, one of the three might prove to be the insider to Jubilee Usher's ring of apostates.

Ira Hatch asked, "You told this old man where he could find Usher?"

"Yes," Young replied, watching the trio cross the rutted, slushy street and halt at the hitching rails outside beyond the walks. Then he looked back over his shoulder to his friends and confidants. "Perhaps God will work His will in a strange way this time, gentlemen."

"If this old man kills Usher?"

Young nodded at Orson Hyde.

Parley Pratt said, "We've got enough other problems to worry about now: that damned Stenhouse's newspaper, the *Telegraph,* an evil, apostate rag if you ask me . . . and you're not doing a thing about running him out of business, Brigham!"

"T. B. Stenhouse is nothing but a troublesome gnat to me," Young said, listening—expectant of hearing the brass knocker on the door downstairs. "We've got bigger problems with this 'New Movement.' "

"By reviving the Order of Enoch," George Smith cheered, "Brigham will wrest back some control of the Church and the Saints for himself in this time of growing apostasy."

"The Order of Enoch, and the ZCMI—they are my major concerns," Young said, gratified with himself to hear the booming echo of the knocker against the front door downstairs. "Now that I am assured that it's just a matter of time before Jubilee Usher is out of my hair. What a relief that will be."

A genuine load off his mind and his heart. If anyone knew what an efficient killing machine Usher could be, it was Brigham Young. After all, Young himself had created men like Bill Hickman and Jubilee Usher. So now if that renegade Danite put his mind to raising an army of his own cutthroats, bribing the Indians into joining his mercenaries—then Usher was the man to put such a plot into motion. Still, Brigham had his own methods too. His own personal means of disposing of troublesome competition. He always had.

It was no different now.

George Cannon wagged his head. "I wish I were as optimistic as you about Jubilee Usher, Brigham."

"Indeed, let us pray you all become as optimistic as I."

Ira Hatch said, "Take it to God in prayer—"

A soft rap at the office door interrupted Hatch.

"Yes, come in."

One of Young's secretaries pushed open the door and stuck her head in, her eyes quickly looking around the impressive gathering of Church leaders to locate the Prophet. "I'm sorry, President Young—"

"What is it, dear?"

"You have some visitors downstairs."

"Yes—well, you can see that I'm busy right now."

Her eyes dropped apologetically. "Yes, I understand, President Young. I wouldn't have interrupted you if it hadn't sounded . . . important."

"Important, is it?" He turned slightly to look at the ledger book at the edge of the huge desk. "Do they have an appointment with me this afternoon?"

"No," the secretary answered. "They just showed up at our door. Come from a long way off."

That confirmed it for Brigham. "Tell them I'm going to be busy the rest of the day and evening with conferences. If they want to make an appointment to see me tomorrow—see what you can do to fit them in."

Now the secretary shuffled her feet, screwging her face up before she asked, "But I told them I was sure you wanted to see them, President Young."

This wasn't at all like the young woman. Her steadfastness, her refusal to retreat, was making Young feel more than a bit testy. "Why were you so sure?"

She looked around the room once, at all the faces, quickly—then her eyes met and held Brigham's. "They are here on the same matter of urgency as the old man was two weeks ago."

For a moment Young's breath seized in his chest. It had to be the men who had crossed the street, tied up those trail-weary horses muddied past the hocks. What relation could they have with the old mountain man?

"The same . . . same matter of urgency, is it?" Young asked, finally.

She nodded. "Yes. The one who did the talking: he said he wanted to see you right away—that he had his own affairs to settle with"—and she paused before continuing—"with Jubilee Usher."

●　　●　　●

Jonah Hook watched the procession of grim-eyed, white-faced old men parade down the long staircase past him, each one of them sternly regarding the muddy trio of wayfarers at the foot of the stairs with disdain that bordered on contempt. Next to these Mormons, he, Jeremiah, and Two Sleep were a poor and shabby lot.

Yet he met their gaze without a flinch, as the woman reached the bottom step and moved his way.

"The president will see you now."

He turned slightly to wave the other two to join him.

"No," the secretary said pointedly, her eyes filled with a mixture of fire and fear. "Just you."

"How many's up there with Brigham Young?" Jonah asked, his eyes climbing up the stairs.

"There are his most trusted counselors. What business is it—"

"How many?"

She reacted as if taken aback, answering before she thought better of it. "Two."

"Then there's three of 'em," Hook replied. "Sounds fair to me—there'll be three of us too. We'll follow you upstairs, ma'am."

"I'll see about this." With a wide sweep of her skirt, the woman whirled about and strode past the gathering of dark-coated men pulling on hats, mufflers, and gloves at the doorway landing—more than a dozen of them who had all the appearances of tarrying just so they could look over the trio a bit longer. Some whispered among themselves as they eyed the muddy travelers.

"Yes, he's an Injun," Jonah growled as he pushed past the knots of curious, stern-faced Church elders, following the woman. "The young-'un's my boy, though. C'mon, Jeremiah."

"An Injun?"

He heard that, and other whispered epithets as they followed the secretary, who swept up her skirt and petticoats when she began her climb up the stairs. At the top landing she knocked on a door, cracked it open, and told those within that three had come to call.

"Send them in, all," a voice instructed.

She turned and, without saying a word, swung open the door for the three travelers.

"Come in."

A large, round-faced man addressed Jonah as Hook entered the spacious office. He came forward, holding forth his hand.

"I am Brigham Young. President of the Church of Jesus Christ of Latter-Day Saints."

Taking Young's hand, Jonah replied, "You're the one we wanna see."

After Hook introduced Jeremiah and Two Sleep, Young indicated for them to take their seats in some horsehair-stuffed leather chairs near his desk. Two older men dressed in dark suits stood behind Young's chair as the president settled behind an imposing desk littered with opened books, ledgers, and a scattering of handwritten papers. Behind the pair stood a tall window, its borders crusted with a crazed crystalline maze of frost.

Shuffling his red-flecked boots on the thick rug spread beneath his chair, Jonah arched forward uncomfortably. It had been so long since he had last sat in such a chair, since he had last been within so grand a room. If ever he had.

Brigham Young broke the anxious stillness as he leaned forward amiably. "I'm told that you wanted to see me."

"I come here to talk to you, yes," Hook replied. He took his hat from his head, digging his hand back through his long hair in deep furrows.

"You said you had business with Jubilee Usher."

"I'm looking for him."

"What makes you believe I would know where this Usher is?"

So this Brigham Young was going to spar with him some—that was it?

"I figured he worked for you, for many years," Jonah began, his eyes leveled on Young's. "He was one of your loyal officers. Now, I'm just a simple man, President Young. But it makes sense to me that you'd know where—"

"Usher worked for me long ago. Yes."

"Long, long ago," added one of the other two, quickly, as if in apology.

Young nodded. "We've had no dealings in many, many a year."

"You're saying you ain't heard one word of his whereabouts?" Jonah asked. His eyes touched first one, then the other of that pair standing behind Young's chair. Then he again gazed at the Church's president.

"No, I'm not saying that at—"

"You wouldn't have seen me if you didn't have no idea where I could find Jubilee Usher," Jonah interrupted. "I'd be out on the street if you didn't have something to talk to me about."

Young straightened his tie, smoothed his laundered shirt. "Even though I know little of you, Mr. Hook—you seem to be a most uncommon man."

297

"Just ordinary. Used to be a farmer—before the war."

"I, myself, used to be a carpenter—like Jesus Christ Himself," Young said. "A carpenter . . . before God called on me to join . . . gave His call for me to *lead* His church."

Jonah nodded impatiently. "You know where I can find Usher?"

Young grinned, then it was as quickly gone. "A most uncommon man you must be."

"I'm looking to find Jubilee Usher—to settle a matter with him."

"A . . . *personal* matter?"

"It is. That."

"Perhaps we can do some business, Mr. Hook."

"Don't need to do business with you. Only need you to tell me where I can find Jubilee Usher."

"Like I was trying to explain—perhaps we can help one another," Young pressed on.

"You help me by telling me where Usher is," Jonah began. "And how am I going to help you?"

Young leaned forward, his forearms planted on the desktop. "I know where Jubilee Usher is."

Jonah grew irritated at the senseless chase. "What I gotta do for you to tell me where I can find him?"

"Perhaps I can explain it by asking if you know an old man by the name of Shad Sweete?"

His eyes widened, his jaw went slack. Turning to glance at Two Sleep, he found the Shoshone's face crossed with incredulity.

"S-Shad Sweete, you said?"

"Yes. I take it you know him."

"I . . . yes, I sure do. What the hell is that got to—"

"Then you surely are the one he told me was also looking for Jubilee Usher."

"He . . . Shad Sweete told you I was looking—" Jonah was stammering in disbelief. After all these years. "I ain't seen Shad in more'n seven winters."

"He came through, saw me—like you, he said he wanted to find Jubilee Usher."

"And he said I'd be coming through?"

Young wagged his head. "No. He did not tell me your name. He only spoke of a man who was also looking for Jubilee Usher. Wondered if you had been here, if I had met such a man of your description. Said it had been some time since . . ." And the president turned sideways to one of the two others.

"Since the fall of sixty-eight, the old man explained," added the man behind Young.

Jonah nodded. "Yes. He would be an old . . . old man by now." He turned to Jeremiah, a smile warming his face as he told his son, "Shad Sweete is still alive, Jeremiah. That ornery, ol' strap of saddle leather is still alive! Can't hardly believe it." Then he whirled back on Young. "How long ago did he come through here and see you about Usher?"

"It's been almost two weeks now."

That sense of immediacy to it, this sense of drawing close to the old man once more, if not drawing a close to his years of stalking Jubilee Usher—it all rushed through him with the fire of adrenaline pumping into his veins. Jonah fought down the impulse to leap to his feet in joy—a sensation he had not allowed himself in so, so long. An emotion he hadn't experienced since he looked down from the gallows on the face of Captain Lamar Lockhart, Frontier Battalion, Texas Rangers.

"You say two weeks?"

"No more than that."

"And you told him where he could find Usher?"

Young nodded. "Told him all I knew—where Usher was said to be."

"Where's that?"

"Ah, Mr. Hook . . . I first need to know that you'll help me."

"But you told Sweete where he could find Usher."

"Not before we two struck a deal," Young said. "And I believe this old man Sweete is someone I can trust to honor his end of a bargain."

Jonah's lips drew back in a thin, grim, bloodless line. Finally he said, "What Shad Sweete says he'll do for you—he'll do. Count on it being done."

"Then . . . I take it *you* trust the old man to find Jubilee Usher?"

"What he sets out to do, by damned—that old man will do," Jonah snapped, a ball of sentiment rising in his throat. If he wasn't careful, his eyes would begin to sting.

Young eased back in his chair. One of the men behind him crossed his arms confidently, all three of them now wearing benign smiles.

The Mormon leader asked, "So I can take it that Shad Sweete will do the same with Jubilee Usher as you would—should you find him?"

"You mean . . . kill him?"

Young instantly smiled, his eyes dancing as he quickly lunged forward, his hands clapping enthusiastically. "You will follow Shad Sweete?"

"All you gotta do is tell me where he is—and I'll follow him into hell if I gotta."

"But first—you and I have to strike our bargain."

"What you want out of me?"

"Only the same thing I asked of Sweete."

Jonah stood, placed his palms down on the desk, rocked over them toward Brigham Young. "And what did you bargain for?"

"I want proof that Jubilee Usher will no longer be a problem for me."

"You want proof?"

"Sweete said he'd bring it to me."

"Proof," Jonah said, his eyes narrowing into slits. "All right. You'll have all the goddamned proof you need—and I'll bring it right here and lay it on your desk. Now, tell me where will the old man find Usher."

"Will you guarantee me the same as Sweete did, Mr. Hook?"

He leaned a little closer to Young. "Just told you I'd bring you your proof. Damned right I will." As if they'd been sprinkled with pickling salt, Jonah felt his insides tightening up as he watched the Mormon leader's face. "Where's Shad Sweete headed? Where the hell is Jubilee Usher?"

"Then we have a bargain, Mr. Hook?"

Jonah stuck out his hand, trying desperately to keep it from trembling as Brigham Young swept it up in his. They shook.

The president smiled widely within his full beard, his eyes sparking with great enthusiasm. "I'll tell you where Shad Sweete will find Jubilee Usher . . . then you can tell me why you and the old man are both looking for Usher."

His eyes quickly flicked over the other two behind Young. "Sweete didn't tell you?"

"Only that he was a friend of yours—and you had a score to settle with Usher. That's why he was going to help you."

"Shad is a friend," Jonah replied, sensing the rise of sentiment. He glanced at Two Sleep. "One of the few I had in my life."

"What score must you settle with Usher?"

Hook swallowed, took a deep breath with the remembrance. Hard with its saying. "He took my wife."

Young slowly sank back into the tall chair. The two behind him seemed to ease a step forward on either side of him, as if not wanting to miss a word of the exchange. "Y-your wife . . . the one he kidnapped years

ago? Then she's the woman—the woman with him in the Temple and all
. . . she's the one—"

His throat seizing, Jonah interrupted. "The one . . . the one
what?"

"The woman Jubilee Usher married."

33

NOW HE KNEW she wasn't dead.

That much for sure—from the lips of Brigham Young.

Jonah scolded himself again for ever letting the Shoshone make him jump at shadows. All that nonsense about the bear's medicine being his medicine now. All that hoodoo talk right on the heels after Hook had figured out on his own that Gritta couldn't still be alive. So now he chided himself for even starting to believe Two Sleep. Superstitious claptrap.

Gritta was alive!

At least as far back as last autumn. Six, no more than seven, months ago. That would've been about the time he was finally accepting her death.

But now he knew he would find her . . . find her alive, by God!

Whatever it was made him ride into that valley of the Great Salt Lake, whatever it was pointed him toward that Mormon leader—Jonah Hook was a grateful man . . . no matter whose God had a hand in it.

Just so he could take her in his arms once more, stroke her hair with his fingers, wipe the tears from her cheeks as he had done so often in their short life together—then tell her it was all behind them now. To pick up where they left off . . . and go on as best they could. Like none of these goddamned years ever happened.

To let it all be put to rest. The way he filled in those three graves back to that cold Missouri valley. Once he filled in Gritta's . . . it would all be behind them.

And he could take her back home, where they'd both go back to working the land. Finish out their days together plowing and planting—just as they had done before the war came, before Usher showed, before all hell tore them apart.

Iron County. Beaver County. Cedar City. Panguitch. Nowhere near as far south as St. George, though. North and west of there, Brigham Young had told him. Toward Nevada Territory, more than likely.

"Is there anything else I can do?" the president had asked when Jonah turned to go, snugging his wide-brimmed hat back on his head. "Do you need anything for your journey? Anything at all?"

Hook turned back to stare a moment at the big-boned, portly man rising behind his desk like a grim-eyed monument. "Only . . . to know your folks gonna trade with us, us not being Mormons."

"By all means!" Young said, landing back in his chair, dragging forth a small ledger, over which he moved a pen he dipped in an inkwell. Ripping the page from its binding, he held it out to Hook. "You show this wherever you may stop in Deseret. Wherever you are in the land of God's Saints, Mr. Hook, you will be well received, that I promise you."

Without reading it Jonah took the paper and stuffed it inside the flaps of his shirt. Touching the brim of his hat, he turned on his heel to leave.

"Mr. Hook—you know Usher has a formidable army with him: cutthroats, murderers, rapists, and the like."

Jonah halted at the door, looked at the three of them. "What you want to say to me?"

Young shrugged, a pudgy hand scribing the air in small circles before him. "Just that . . . there's only three of you."

"How many did Shad Sweete take with him when he left here to track down Usher?" Hook asked.

Young's brow knitted in some confusion at the question. "Just himself."

"There you have it," Jonah replied. "It don't matter how many gunmen Jubilee Usher has him. Fact is, as far as I've learned in my life, President Young: no goddamned army is going to stand up agin a man what's in the right and keeps on coming."

The Prophet's composure changed. Enthusiastic once more and smiling, he touched his brow with his fingers and said, "By the Lord's providence: I believe you three and that old mountain man will make just the army to bring Jubilee Usher down."

"He took my family from me," Jonah said. Tugging on the bottom of his heavy coat before he patted the butts of the pair of pistols he wore in gun belts, he added, "These here is all the Lord's providence that bastard better be reckoning on when I come to send his soul straight to hell."

"For the time being, my work here is done," the white demon said.

Bak Sahm nodded, watching the face of the man whose life he had saved.

Orrin Haslam turned slightly to the table beside him, where he slowly unwrapped the weapons he had hidden in the folds of a threadbare, army-gray blanket. "These . . . are for you, Chinaman."

"Me?" Bak said.

Painfully conscious of dragging the left foot, he inched forward, peering down at the gifts of great surprise. Slowly, he reached out his good right hand to stroke that checkered wood on the wrist of the shotgun. Caressed the Damascus pattern of the breech and barrel.

"It's the finest two-shoot shotgun I could find in your piss-hole dung-heap of a town, Chinaman. But it's far better'n that old bird gun you used on them goddamned dead miners. But—hell—you shot straight enough that day, didn't you, now?"

Some of the demon's talk he caught, just a portion did he understand as the barbarian rattled on. Bak Sahm next touched the carbine.

"That's a repeater," Haslam explained, taking up the rifle. "Seventeen-shot repeater. Lemme show you how to load it."

The white demon went on to take a handful of shells from one of the boxes on the table, demonstrating the loading tube and the levering to load and eject cartridges.

Then Haslam held the carbine out to Bak Sahm, his eyes flicking once to the Chinaman's distorted left arm. "Here, now—you try it. See how that barking lady feels in your hands."

Taking the rifle to lay across the frozen crook of his left elbow, the Chinaman held it no less reverently than he would accept some ancient icon passed down across the centuries by his ancestors. Running his hands over the walnut stock, sensing the fit and finish of the breech to the wrist, caressing the oiled sheen of the barrel. This particular smell of the white man's weapons—so different a smell did these guns have now from the odor they had once the oil became superheated, mingled with the acrid stench of burned powder.

But for now Bak Sahm gazed at the carbine as if it were a work of art—

as worthy of worship as was any holy carving made in the likeness of a guardian spirit.

Perhaps, truly—this weapon of the white demon would now become Bak Sahm's new guardian spirit.

Planted fields, streams and rivers, the top of a mountain and the spread of every valley, down to each fish pond or village well: everything had its ghost, its demon, its own spirit. Spirits controlled air and earth, water, and even fire. Surely these fire-breathing weapons would be controlled by fire ghosts.

Why, Bak remembered, the good fortune of a man and his family, even the entire village itself, rested upon the goodwill they engendered from the ghosts who ruled their nearby world. Ghosts ultimately more powerful than any faraway Mandarin ruler. In fact, the forces of pirates, robbers, and petty landlords were nothing when compared to the people's belief in the forces of those spirits ruling their daily lives.

Still, the wars always came and the men would protect the women and children in the fortified places, the *wai*—a place garrisoned by the boys and old men who served as the last bastion to watch over the wives and mothers and little ones while the fighting men went out to meet those who sought to plunder the villages dotting the great Pearl River delta.

If his people had had such weapons as these—Bak Sahm thought—no evil would have visited his village. His people would not have been cursed, forced to pay tribute to petty warlords.

"Put it to your shoulder—see how it feels, Chinaman. Go ahead."

Haslam gently pushed a hand beneath the weapon to get Bak Sahm to bring it to his shoulder. With his right hand gripping the carbine's wrist and by hoisting the crooked left arm from his shoulder to support the barrel, Bak snugged it into position. His left arm was bent so that the hand lay back nearly to the trigger guard, to give an adequate rest on which to lay the weapon, to sight down that long blue barrel.

"Work the lever," Haslam said. Then he impatiently yanked the carbine from the Chinaman, worked the receiver several times at his own shoulder. "See if you can do it like that." He handed it over to Bak Sahm.

At first it was a struggle, holding the carbine securely enough atop the crippled left arm while his right hand rolled the lever down and forward to eject an empty cartridge and insert a new shell into the breech. After a half-dozen tries at it, Bak Sahm found a way to grip the receiver tube below the barrel down in the crevice of that left elbow tightly enough that he could work the lever without the carbine rolling out of his control.

"You'll get quicker soon enough, Chinaman," the demon said, grinning, proud of himself. He tapped some fingers on the boxes of cartridges. "Don't go running out of shells too soon when you go to practicing how to shoot that gun."

How his mind ached to hear the purer Cantonese—rather than struggling even after all these winters to learn enough of the demons' talk. This was such a hard language, especially with the many different manners of speaking the barbarians' tongue.

As he had been shown, Bak rolled the action open and inserted a brass cartridge. Then, slowly, he brought the loaded rifle's muzzle up and around, pressing it squarely against the second button on Haslam's shirt.

The demon grinned, his dancing eyes mocking Bak Sahm. "Go ahead. You got the balls to pull that trigger—go ahead, Chinaman."

He studied the white man's smirking face, wanting to prove Haslam wrong . . . struggling to make himself pull the trigger. But for what? Because the white man had paid for and used the woman for many, many nights? Was that enough to kill the demon?

Would he pull the trigger if Haslam had injured his pride? Would such an offense of etiquette be better reason to kill the barbarian? Not in a fit of heated senses was it ever accepted. But to pull the trigger here, now— merely because Haslam might have ridiculed him?

But the demon hadn't ever brought Bak Sahm shame. Not that Bak Sahm could attest. Unlike others who had come and gone through the winters—Haslam had not made jokes at Bak's expense. He had not been among those who repeatedly imitated the Chinaman's lurching hobble across the barroom floor, as some miners and visitors to Pioche did. Never had Haslam made others laugh in their drunken glee by tucking the left arm up in a tight, angular crook, the wrist frozen for all time. Some men had—and Bak Sahm had learned to ignore them. As he likely would have ignored Haslam. But as much as he loathed the man come to buy the woman for weeks on end, Haslam had never ridiculed the Chinaman for his walk, for his near-useless arm, for his singsong Mandarin difficulty in speaking English.

Haslam hadn't even pulled on Bak's long queue the way practically every newcomer did—at least if they weren't warned by others never to commit such an act. Those who did were asked to leave and never return to his establishments. The few who could not believe they were being thrown out of a saloon for pulling on a Chinaman's hair were shown the door at the double-eyed business end of that old bird gun Bak Sahm had used so effectively the night the miners were about to kill Haslam. Indeed, those who pulled Bak's queue could never again darken the door of his House of Joy, his saloon, nor his shop next door where he not only sold the merchandise the town's miners coveted, but especially the articles most wanted by the Chinamen who invested their lives in the mines and smelters of Pioche.

They, like Bak, were *k'e-chia,* the guests, or literally "strangers" who migrated from their home to a new place. None of them were *pen-ti,* or natives to this land. So Bak made sure he brought in all manner of goods and clothing from China—those items that would make strangers feel more at home here in the land of the Gold Mountain. In Bak Sahm's island of quiet civility, the Chinese laborers spoke their own language to their own kind, ate their own food, and talked of a faraway home. Here Bak Sahm operated a spiritual sanctuary for the coolies—relieving anguish over being so far, far away from loved ones.

In his shop Bak also functioned as a middleman who would ship the American coins back to wives, parents, and families in China for each man come here to make his fortune as a hardworking coolie. To do so, he had to ally himself with the *tan-chia,* the boat people who operated the vessels that sailed from the port at Canton across the Sea of Lions to the Gold Mountain. With mighty, many-legged centipedes and scrambling, leather-winged dragons plastered on their canvas sails, they legally transported much cargo, while illegally smuggling opium, for it was three times as profitable as tea and herbs and silk—all of it was the same to the *tan-chia,* who took their healthy cut of the monies sent home to families waiting in China.

Bak shook his head, lowering the rifle. He did not smile when Haslam laughed. For a moment the barbarian looked like a statue Bak Sahm had seen many, many winters ago in China—the likeness of *chao-i kung-so,* the Luminous Unity. So cheerful were the demon's deadly eyes, but for the moment.

Then they narrowed, as Bak found the rifle heavy, laying it on the table next to the shotgun.

"Don't you ever point a gun at me again, Chinaman," Haslam snarled in a whisper, almost like the hiss of the huge tree snakes that coiled around limbs and branches above the delta's floor. "I'll give you count this time that you didn't know—but one chance only. Next time you do point a gun at me, I'll have to kill you . . . just the way I killed the miners who said I was cheating at cards."

He blinked at the demon. "You come back?"

"Me? Coming back?" Haslam asked, his mood changing in that instant. "Soon enough I hope."

Bak watched the demon's eyes slowly rise to gaze up at the second-floor landing, to that door behind which the woman lived.

The Chinaman asked, "When?"

Haslam smiled as his eyes came back to Bak Sahm. "Maybe before you know it. You'll miss my money, won't you?"

When Bak Sahm didn't reply, Haslam went on. "I'll bet you will. But when I come back—the men I'll bring will keep your girls busy from sunup to sunup, Chinaman. You get that whiskey shipped in here for us, like I said. 'Cause there's gonna be some celebrating when the colonel's army gets here. And when we come—the colonel and Orrin Haslam gonna make you a rich man. A real rich man."

From all that Haslam told him of the colonel and his army, it sounded as if those demons had their own Triad Society: with tenets based upon the immutable bonds existing among Heaven, Earth, and Man. In China the Triad had risen to prominence by a bloody usurpation of power from the ruling Manchus, rolling over far-flung provinces with their rebellion, installing puppet lords in every village and hamlet. From the powerful, ruling Triad eventually emerged the six tongs that controlled much of Chinese life in the barbarians' Gold Mountain.

But no tong ruled in Pioche, Nevada. The gold companies ruled here. The smelters. The very power of the shiny metal. What power it came in to displace was the only control any man held over another. Here there was no spiritual power. Only the raw, unadorned power of sheer might.

Like that which came from the business end of a gun.

"You saved my life—and I'm grateful," the demon reminded. "So I'll give you your life in return, and a warning too: don't ship none of your gold with the spring smelter shipment."

He watched Haslam's eyes, not sure he understood all the man said, all that was meant. "Gold to go home to China."

"You got me? Wait till summer to ship it."

Shaking his head, Bak said, "I must."

Haslam chuckled, shrugging. "Just say I warned you, China-man. Warned you about losing your gold. And about pointing a gun at me."

Bak lurched toward the bar nearby, signaling the bartender to pour him a glass of the whiskey that burned his throat. He tossed the amber liquid back and swallowed, for this once enjoying the stinging lick of fire all the way into his eyes brought to tears with the taste of the demons' fermented corn.

"No guns. No pointing," Bak agreed, his throat raspy, raw from the burn as he finally turned clumsily to look at Haslam.

"Right down to those miners we killed—there ain't a man what's pulled a gun and pointed it at me that's still alive," the demon said. Then his face went long. "Well, there was one pointed a gun at me and lived, Chinaman. And you'll get a chance to meet him. He's the only one."

"One? One only?"

The demon's eyes nearly closed as he said it: "The colonel."

Bak watched the white man turn, sweep up his saddlebags and bedroll lashed in a gum poncho from a table, swill down the last of his whiskey from a glass before he filled his empty hand with his Winchester repeater. Haslam tapped the shapeless brim of his hat with the carbine's barrel, then swept out to the hitching rail in a rattle of spur rowels, leaving the door wide-open in his wake, both doors left to creak on the winter breeze that swirled a skiff of icy snow into Bak Sahm's saloon.

Yes. He had to start thinking about putting together his shipment of gold coins to China. All the coins deposited with him by the Chinese mine and smelter workers in the nearby mountains. Have the boxes made and painted red, trimmed with gold leaf—each family's name emblazoned on the top. Each small box to go safely inside a large chest addressed to the Triad headquarters in Canton. That was pressing business now. To get his gold shipment ready to accompany the smelter companies' westbound caravan.

Bak Sahm pounded his right hand down on the bar. Obediently the barman poured another double shot of the amber liquid, set the dark bottle down, and stepped backward, folding his arms. The Chinaman drank it all, eyes shut to clench out the tears. Corn spirits.

Ghosts and corn spirits.

Like his distaste for Orrin Haslam, his distaste for dealing with the evil ones, his distaste for the very failure of his own life . . . this whiskey reminded Bak Sahm of his curse.

Then the Chinaman's eyes crawled ultimately toward her door upstairs.

She—who had brought him so, so much wealth.

Yet caused him so, so much pain.

34

'THE COLONEL—HE says we'll be stopping for the night soon,"
George told her.

The old Negro talked to her in that way of his that had long
ago convinced her he must have had children, perhaps even grandchildren, before he hooked up with Jubilee Usher. For the old slave
spoke to her as a parent would a child, turning his head, shuffling
his body partway round on the ambulance driver's seat to reassure her
throughout the hot afternoon. Saying something to her just about the
time she would begin dozing off with the jolting rock and lurch of the
ambulance.

By late in the morning, and by the middle of every afternoon, Gritta
Hook would become enough accustomed to the painfully jarring ride in
the ambulance that she could almost will herself to sleep atop the pallet of
blankets and quilts George and Jubilee Usher had padded around her for
their portion of the journey that day. They did not travel far—that much
she knew: setting out well past sunup, and stopping for the night well
before sundown. And, Usher always preferred a long layover for noon
while the sun climbed high. It seemed as if he weren't in a real hurry to get
them where they were going.

No, this wasn't the sort of traveling they had done years before down
in the deserts with their towering pancake or spidery cactus that frightened
her as she peered out at the landscape from the tent flaps after dusk. Such a

hot and despairing land that was—growing so cold so quickly with the falling of the sun.

Almost like her heart now, Gritta thought.

Now that she had given up. Gone cold where she at one time burned with despair of being set free.

No more. To return to what? Her child gone. Unable to recall any of what had gone before. Nothing of who had been there for her before. The cold had settled in.

Although her brow beaded with tiny diamonds of sweat, Gritta felt cold. She was certain it was the new skin, pink as a newborn babe's. But that was difficult to think on: babes, children—since Usher had killed their baby, her child. She had done this to herself, to take revenge on him.

To take revenge on her own body and soul—to send it straight to hell for what she allowed him to do to her.

In all this time after the fire . . . all that painful, new skin growing up and down her legs and hips, over one side of her belly and a breast, covering one shoulder too. But as new as was her pink skin, as tender and raw as it felt at times, tight and quite a size too small—Gritta realized somehow that she had healed for the most part. At least healed on the outside.

"I'm taking you to a town," he told her the night before they set off on this journey that took them away from the rising sun each morning.

She knew that much—knew enough to realize they were going west, ever farther west. Something tugged, tightened, drawn taut within the core of her—as if it were lashed securely around something that lay behind her in its direction: east. Something behind her in time: and she was wrenched all the farther from it with every new mile.

"A town," he explained as he lay with her, the sweaty expanse of his fleshy frame beside her, brushing her tender, new, and pink flesh.

"We'll camp this time near the town," his voice droned on in that darkness of their tent.

Outside drifted the quiet murmur of horses, mules, men moving about. A harmonica and distant laughter. Sounds so familiar. Reassuring sounds.

"I can take you to see dancers kick up their heels—a long row of women, each with a different-colored dress on. And I'll take you shopping for a new dress once a week if you want. So we can go dancing—and you can kick up your heels."

His voice was almost dreamlike: not spoken in primary colors any longer, but almost soft, and in its softness, pleading for some sort of forgiveness.

"I never gave you a honeymoon. So this will be ours to share after all these years together . . . now that you're finally my wife."

Gritta recalled rolling away from him that night, remembered how he rolled toward her, draping his great, powerful arm over her. Unable to escape the feel, the smell, the very aura of him. No matter that he lay flesh to flesh.

"There'll be lots of music for you to listen to. Pianos and fiddlers. Not mouth harps and squeeze-boxes like some of the men play here in camp. Real music for you to tap your foot to and sway back and forth in time. Just think of it—those dresses, with the long gloves to match, and we'll go stepping out each evening to some new entertainment house or another. Stepping out in a new pair of velvet boots with buttons that go all the way up to your knees."

Boots didn't have to go up to her knees, Gritta knew. All her dresses already reached her ankles—hiding her scars. She didn't need such velvet boots. A real bother, when the boots that laced up to the top of her ankles served her just as well.

For the longest time she hadn't been able to wear any boots at all.

"We'll fix your hair up with ribbons—brush it over to the side and hold it in place with combs and bright ribbons," he went on. "No one will be able to tell anything about your ear or how you lost your hair on that side of your head. No reason will you have to feel ashamed—for you'll be the belle of the ball."

In all the time lost and gone behind her since last autumn when she watched the flames licking their way up her dress, when she drank in the smoke and breathed deep of the heat—Gritta had felt the stubble of burned hair grow a little where it could. Where it did not—why, that was scar tissue. George kept the bottom of a brass kettle polished for her to use as a mirror. No more did Jubilee allow looking glasses around her. They could break—into shards that could cut flesh and do her harm. So the old Negro had come up with the brass kettle—a little dented in places, distorting her image some . . . but she could see most of what she wanted to see these days anyhow.

She could see enough to recognize a lot of the damage to the side of her neck and ear, the scar tissue where the hair would never again grow back. Enough to see how she could brush her hair over the new, pink flesh.

"Doesn't that sound like something we're both due?" he asked her in the dark, thrusting his body against her buttocks. "To go to a town together after all this time. The two of us . . . Joy."

He used that new name of hers again. Gritta wondered why she hadn't grown used to it in all this time. If it was truly her name, then why, oh, why . . .

"The two of us going in, arm in arm, entering someplace filled with happy people, all jumping with noise and celebration, rolling with music and flowing with liquor for man and woman alike. A place where people can dance and shout, and shoot out the lights if they're of a mind to. Where we can drink and be merry with them—after all this time: don't you think you owe that to me, Joy?"

She didn't answer. She couldn't. Gritta hadn't spoken to him in so, so long. Hadn't even said a word to George in . . . she could not remember now. Instead she communicated with the old Negro with her eyes. And right now her eyes were spilling tears on the musty sheets beneath her cheek.

"It's what I want for you, Joy," he said to her, his lips brushing the back of her ear. "To go to a town—and take you to someplace happy. Where people are merry. Where there is *life*. So much life that I can at last see you smile."

She felt his flesh growing hard quickly, its mass pressing against the back of her thigh. He lifted her top leg, shoved his rigid flesh inside her, then began pumping his hips against her savagely while she cried.

As certain as she was about anything anymore, Gritta knew she would never smile again.

The moon had risen full three times, taking on the color of a yellow squash, since the white demon had left her. For those first few days after Bak Sahm found her bleeding, bruised, and battered, squatting in the corner of her room, Chung-li Chu'uan had allowed him to care for her.

Clumsily he lifted her like a child in his one good arm, against the bent and crippled wing, murmuring that she weighed no more than a child—so he was able to get her over to her bed, as he explained, although he was not as strong as he had been in his youth. She hated herself for feeling sorry for him, sorry for the way he struggled with her. But Chung-li could not help herself.

Perhaps he owed her this, she had thought those first days that ran into weeks as he nursed her. Yes, perhaps he owed her all of this for what ruin he had brought her.

"The dragon god can appear in different shapes," Bak Sahm read to her one night from the old book he said was the only possession he brought with him all the way from China.

She had looked, briefly, at the yellowed pages bound inside a thick leather cover of faded blue—each page covered with its up-and-down writing she had never learned to read—and glanced ever so quickly at the picture inked on one page: a mighty thunder god.

Bak Sahm went on that third night after the white barbarian had taken his leave, reading to her while the noise swelled in the saloon below them, reading each night after he had fed her the greasy soup he could pour between her swollen, battered lips. Tenderly pressing the spoon against her teeth and tipping her head back, as one might feed a newborn.

Chung-li let him feed her, clean her, take the bedpan from her room each morning. She did not care. If she died—so much the better. Then her ghost would stay here to haunt him: to remind him that he had brought this horror upon himself. Bak Sahm cared more about gold than he did about her.

"Dragon gods can appear in the shape of a youth, or an aged man. As a lovely young girl, or an ugly old hag. As a rat, or snake, a tree, or tool . . . even a weapon: sword, knife, or bow. Any weapon. But no matter what shape it takes, the dragon god is intimately connected with water. It is a rain lord and therefore the thunder god who causes the rain to fall."

She glanced once more at the page with the picture of the thunder god dancing with one foot pirouetting upon a very small earth. Then she peeked at Bak Sahm. His lips were clenched in a tight, thin line as he stared at the page—fallen silent for some reason.

"L-like an avalanche of r-rocks," he said to her, his eyes finally finding hers. "A rain of r-rocks."

Bak Sahm blinked and returned to his reading as a man would who had regained control of himself. She did not know what he meant by a rain of rocks. It was a strange thing to say. But then—this man was very strange. Not only was his body shaped funny, but his thoughts were misshapen and contorted as well.

"There are sea dragons that send storms like the wind gods and may be appeased with offerings. These sea dragons are guardians of treasures, guardians of great riches."

Again he seemed to drift off in his own private thoughts, his eyes not reading the page below him, but staring off into the middistance of her tiny room.

Bak Sahm licked his lips and said, "There are dragons that hide the great treasures of the earth, dragons that hide the great riches of these mountains, Chung-li. I know this. You must not think that I don't. I know all too well about the thunder god which protects the gold found in the bowels of the earth dragon."

She closed her eyes, hoping he would either continue to read to her, or go away. She was growing tired again.

"In an ancient Chinese work the story is told of a dragon that appears in the shape of a little girl who sits at the entrance to a cave in the mountain. She sits there playing with three pearls. When a man appears, the child flees into the cave—and reassuming its dragon form, the thunder god puts the three pearls of great treasure into its left ear for safekeeping."

Chung-li breathed deep, held it, trying to picture the dragon taking shape from the body of a little girl, but could not.

"The enemy of man—a snake—can become a dragon after many centuries," he continued his reading. "The *Shu i ki* says that after five hundred years a water-snake changes into a *kiao*. A *kiao* after one thousand years changes into a *lu'ng*. A *lu'ng* after five hundred more years changes into a *kioh-lu'ng*, and another thousand years into a *ying-lu'ng*. The greatest dragon of them all."

He looked at her, watching her for several moments. She could feel him staring at her, even though Chung-li kept her eyes closed. Finally she heard him sigh and begin reading once more, doing what she had willed him to do for her as she sensed her body drifting off to sleep.

"This dragon dwells in pools, it rises into the air to form clouds, where it thunders and brings rain to flood the rivers, flows to the oceans— controlling the tides and causing the waters and seasons of man to ebb and flow."

Bak Sahm shifted his weight on the side of the bed beside her. Chung-li wanted to move away from him, but she dared not. Didn't know if she even had the strength right now. She had lain with him long, long ago. Her mind stretched the way a weary, unused muscle would stretch—trying to recall how it had been to lie with him atop her, desperate for a moment to capture the thought of him with his crooked arm and that twisted leg moving on top of her smooth, naked body.

For the briefest of moments she held the image, let her thighs relax as he read to her—sensing his hot flesh within her, his warm mouth on hers. But as suddenly the image disappeared. She realized he had never laid his mouth on hers. As much as she wanted him to in her mind-picture, Bak

Sahm had not kissed her. She struggled to conjure up the image once
more.

"The dragon was in the early days, just as it is now, the god of water,
thunder, clouds, and rain. He is the harbinger of blessings and the symbol
of the holiest of men. As the emperors are the holiest of beings on earth,
the idea of the dragon as the symbol of imperial power is based on our
ancient conceptions."

When her dream vision eventually returned, Chung-li found Bak
Sahm beneath her, stretched out on the bed, his one good arm raised, its
hand stroking first one breast, then the other, as she moved up and down
on his eager flesh where she had herself pinned to him atop the silk covers
spread over her bed. His twisted leg, nor his crippled arm—neither ham-
pered their enjoyment of one another.

"The Chinese 'dragon well' is usually placed inside a deep mountain
cave," Bak Sahm read more to her as she worked hard, concentrating so
hard on sensing someone come to bring pleasure to *her* body—not merely
using her flesh to take his own pleasure.

It was a good dream, a pleasing vision—this watching of the image
she had conjured by listening only to his voice. Focusing on herself, on her
own pleasure at long last, Chung-li had made herself wet, made herself
warm. Seeing her nipples grow hard in the dream caused them to grow
hard now beneath her silk night robe.

Was it her need? Was it his stories? Was it Bak Sahm's voice?

"When the yellow dragon, born from yellow gold a thousand years
old, enters a deep place, a yellow spring dashes forth, running in all
directions through the bowels of the earth. It is these yellow springs that
become the layers of gold buried deep within the darkest regions of the
mountains."

Eventually she became aware of the quiet—realizing he was no longer
reading. Chung-li cracked an eye open into a slit and saw he was studying
her.

"Are you all right?" he asked.

She turned away. Her face flushed with hot embarrassment, wanting
to hide her smile.

"I was worried," he said sympathetically. "There for a moment: you
were making such . . . such strange noises, as I'd never heard you make
before—and you were moving some, just a little, as if you were . . . well, I
thought you might be in some kind of pain."

She waited, keeping her face turned toward the far side of the room
where pegs were driven into the wall, pegs on which hung her few robes.

"In China the season of drought is the long months of winter," he finally went back to reading from the old work titled *Yih Ling*. "They are supposed to sleep during this dry spell so that they may preserve their bodies."

Chung-li wanted to preserve her body, hoping that someday it might truly bring her the happiness it brought her in her dreams. Long the same happiness it had brought the men who used it for their own pleasure.

"Dragons begin to stir in the spring," Bak Sahm read more, his voice soothing. "And soon they will fight one another. The Chinese have always welcomed dragon battles after the dry season. Thunderstorms break out. Rain pours down in torrents. If a number of dragons engage in battle, and the war in the air continues longer than desired, the rivers rise in flood and cause much destruction and loss of life."

She enjoyed this wet, warm sensation—a new feel between her legs. So unlike the hurried, painful experience that was the way with the men come to cover her. She yearned to have it continue, to have it increase in fervor, burning as she was whenever Chung-li focused on the thought of herself seated on top of Bak.

"As the emperor himself was closely associated with the chief dragon god," he explained, "it was feared that social upheavals and wars might result . . . all in consequence of the failure of the priests and the emperor— as the holiest of priests—to control the dragons. The dynasty might be overthrown by an unruly and ruined peasantry."

She kept her eyes closed, listening to his voice. And wondered on his continued fascination with dragons. Dragons, opium, and the powerful shooting weapons of the white demons—these were what fascinated Bak Sahm.

They were not what fascinated Chung-li Chu'uan.

"Among the most curious beliefs entertained concerning dragon battles in ancient China is one that no mortal should watch them. In fact, it was not only very unlucky . . . but absolutely perilous for human beings to peer into such celestial mysteries."

Bak Sahm cleared his throat, and for a moment she thought he might be finished reading to her. But he went on reading, and she was glad for the sound of his voice. It was a poem from the book that he held on his lap.

When they fight, the dragons do not look at us;
Why should we look at them when they are fighting?
If we do not seek the dragons,
They also will not seek us.

317

He was quiet for a long time, so quiet, and for so long, that Chung-li grew tempted to peek to see if he hadn't left the room without her knowing. When she opened one eye into a slit, he was still sitting beside the bed—staring at the old book in his lap. Again he had a strange look on his face: something that reminded her of pain, of fear, yet with some determination etched around the corners of his mouth. She wasn't sure of anything more than that, for she looked only from the one eye, and that a mere slit.

With a sudden blinking Bak Sahm focused on the page below him and began to read again.

"When the Chinese dragons fight, fireballs and luminescent pearls fall to the ground. These pearls give promise of abundant supplies of water in the future."

Then he stopped and looked at her. Chung-li slowly closed the slit, not sure if he had caught her watching him from her clenched eye. Would he know what she was feeling, by looking at her face?

"If we do not seek the dragons, the ancient stories tell us," Bak said softly, "then the dragons will not seek us. But—what of those of us who already tempted the dragon? What of us already known to the dragon?"

Though she did not open her eye to see for sure, Chung-li was sure her employer was crying. She could hear it in his voice, roughened, snagging—the way one of her silk robes would catch on a rough length of lumber in the saloon floor below.

Bak Sahm whispered hoarsely his question she could not answer. "What of us who have already dreamed of battle with the dragon? Haven't our dreams already spelled our doom?"

35

" 'LOVE YOUR DUTIES, sisters,' so saith the Prophet, Brigham Young."

Jubilee Usher looked up from his reading. "There were times in the past, in those days gone by when I truly believed President Young was anointed by God's hand, Joy."

The woman watched him strangely for a moment; then he turned away, his long black hair falling forward as he bent over once more, a single shaft of a finger tracing the lines he read from the book on his lap.

" 'Love your duties, sisters. It is for you to bear fruit and bring forth, to the praise of God, the spirits that are born in yonder heavens, and to take tabernacles on earth.' "

George stood behind him, his old arms slowly undulating with a large fan made of starched paper that had been painted with a gay scene of a time long ago. Now faded, the fan served only to stir the afternoon air in the tent where Usher read to her as if the Negro were not there at all.

"Tell me, Joy—for I have long wondered: why do the Gentiles tolerate prostitution, but decry the Saints' polygamy?" Usher asked of her.

He watched her face, as if truly waiting for an answer. But she did not speak. It had been too long now that her tongue had refused to move, even to sing the old songs he thought she likely remembered from her childhood. He missed that almost as much as anything else—not having the sound of her voice, her singing.

"What makes the worst of womanhood? Would someone tell me that?" he demanded as the thoughts sprang to his mind like water issuing from a rock.

He wanted to save her from eternal damnation. To make her one of God's chosen. To make her a Saint. So Usher preached to her—even more fervently than he preached to his men three times each week.

But with Joy he preached and read, read and preached every morning before they set out on their journey west, every evening when they went into camp early. It was this life-and-death struggle for her soul that was of concern to him. He would reach Pioche soon enough as it was. Far more important was this matter of saving her for all eternity. Sealed to him was she. Joy must not be one of those Gentiles cast into the lake of fire beyond hope for all time.

"Is it better for these women, these harlots who ply their trade in the saloons and brothels, to have many husbands each night? Far better, isn't it—that they should marry one man . . . even unto several women taking one God-fearing man as their husband in kind . . . or they should die the horrible death of a sinner cast out of the garden."

Taking up his china cup, Usher held it out at arm's length. George immediately laid down his fan and poured more of the cool water from the crock pitcher into Jubilee's cup. As the Negro resumed fanning them, Usher offered her the first drink, holding it beneath her face where she would see it. But she said nothing. Made no gesture at all. Only continued to stare at her hands clasped loosely in her lap.

Jubilee took a long drink himself, then set the cup aside on the small folding table.

"Jesus had plural wives, you know," he stated with the certainty of bedrock faith. "Yes—it's true. Mary, Martha, and even the whore, Mary of Magdalene."

Leaning forward, Usher lifted her chin with a finger, gazing into the blue of her eyes. Eyes he swam in, feeling lost in so many times. "Although Adam himself, even Jesus, took plural wives—I want to assure you that I have found the one woman who will be my *only*. For all time, you and you alone, Joy."

Outside the shadows lengthened, the air beginning to cool. The camp went about supper preparations, horses watered and picketed on the good grass for the night. His officers moving among the men to remind them of the need to clean weapons after the hunting they had done that day. Soon enough they would reach the Pioche mining district of Nevada

Territory—and then Colonel Jubilee Usher would be ready to raise the Sword of Laban against the smelter operators. To take from the Gentiles what rightfully belonged to this army. Usher's Danites, his "Sons of Dan."

As it said in Genesis:

Dan shall be a serpent by the way, an adder in the path, that biteth the horse heels, so that his rider shall fall backward.

Those men who cooked their supper, cleaned their weapons, made their music in this evening camp—they would be Usher's serpents in the path, the adders who would await the gold shipment headed west to the mint in San Francisco. His Sons of Dan would rise up and strike. All for the downfall of the false Prophet, all for the glory of the Church.

Haslam was east. Perhaps even having taken up the way back to Pioche already himself. Sent by Usher on a return to the Indian bands, Utes and Pahvants, who had vowed to join Usher's army. He had taken with him not only a sizable escort, but one of the wagons laden with what Usher could find in the way of gifts: just enough to whet the palates of the chiefs and old men, enough to let them see that Usher's word was good—that he would come through with far greater riches once those brown-skinned Lamanites had helped him snatch a fortune away from the Gentiles.

They were a doomed people anyway, Usher always told himself. That spiritual leap of logic he had learned from Joseph Smith, heard espoused from the tongue of Brigham Young.

Now, the Gentiles . . . they were to blame for their own misfortunes. They had the opportunity to change, to hear the Word and become Saints—but they had not.

Taking from the Gentiles, even taking the life of a Gentile, was justified—for they were the unholy who had not converted although offered the chance for eternal salvation.

Usher looked up, his thoughts totally gone astray from the lesson on Mormon womanhood he had been teaching her. At this very moment he could sense the burning in his own bosom—again confirming that he was being touched by the fiery finger of the Lord God, again convincing him of his own holy righteousness as the *chosen one.*

His eyes narrowing, Jubilee said, "Hasn't Joseph Smith's Book of Mormon itself said, 'God Almighty will visit the unclean with the fires of His greatest indignation!'?"

Something was coming over him again, moving him with a physical power—uplifting him in all its glory. Usher stood, his eyes shooting back and forth between the Negro and his wife. "Even unto the old days when Brigham took up Joseph Smith's mantle—didn't he also talk repeatedly from the pulpit against the Gentiles, raising his voice in favor of clearing Zion of all the unholy? Didn't Brigham Young time and again preach that a man who killed an apostate Mormon or a godless Gentile was truly nothing more than an instrument of God?"

Drawing his own long knife from its riveted leather sheath at his belt, Usher said, "That man's role in the murder of a Gentile is no more than the knife God Himself wields, no more than the bullet God Himself fires into the breast of the ungodly."

He held the blade up to what fading light drenched the western wall of the tent in a rosy orange. "See to the lamps, George."

For almost twenty years now, ever since the Church's Reformation, there had remained intact this belief among Brigham Young's faithful that murder was at times one of a Mormon's righteous duties. A belief which held that murdering Mormon apostates and enemy Gentiles was no longer a sin in the eyes of a jealous God.

As the Negro laid the fan on the bed and shuffled toward the oil lamp in the corner, Usher said, "Like Brigham, I too would prefer a dead Saint to a living sinner. It has long been we Sons of Dan who are chosen to save those who have not the will to save themselves. To kill even unto the throne of the Church itself."

How many, many times had he killed in the name of the Lord—taking as much pleasure as did Almighty God in this purification rite—each time he shed another's blood, repeating the same ritual litany: "O Lord, my God—receive their unholy spirits. It is for Thy kingdom that I do this."

There were those who went among the unclean—among Lamanites and Gentiles all—to bring the Lord God's written word to them. Men like Abraham, Joseph, and Moses. And ever since the ancient days of Israel, there had been the mighty right hands of God, men like David, Aaron, and Joshua. The strong, like Jubilee Usher, who knew when the hour came to unsheathe the sword.

"The time has come," he murmured as he slid the long knife back within its scabbard, "for judgment to be laid to the line and righteousness to the plummet."

"Colonel Usher?"

Jubilee turned on his heel and pulled back the tent flaps to find one of the men. "My supper prepared?"

"It is, sir."

"And my prisoner? You've secured him the way I instructed?"

The man's eyes rolled as he glanced over his shoulder quickly. "The boys did just as you said. They made that cross you wanted."

"Have they planted it in that open glade by the stream?"

Jubilee watched the man's prominent Adam's apple bob as he spoke. "It's ready, Colonel. That big cross for him—everything . . . ready when you are."

Smoothing his damp shirt and refastening the collar button through its hole, he said, "First, my wife and I will have our supper. Only then will I punish the guilty, scourge this sinner."

Having let the flaps fall, turning back around, he drank in a healthy draught of the cool of evening's approach, enjoying the swell and fall of lamplight on the tent walls. Usher stepped over to the woman, took up her left hand, and held it as she rose to her feet uncertainly.

"Appears we must exercise your limbs a bit more each morning and every evening, Joy," Usher told her. "I so want you ready and able to enjoy your trip to the mining town. Nothing would disappoint me more than if you weren't ready to dance and dance and dance."

With her on his arm he left the tent, halting just past the flaps to appraise the tall cottonwood cross erected in the nearby meadow. Then he looked over the faces of those who stood in the immediate area, savoring the fear etched on some, finding on others an eagerness to get on with the evening's sport.

They know what to expect from me, Usher thought. The fearful ones. The rest are hungry for the blood, eager for the pain.

It was strong men like him who would shove aside the old priests and resurrect the power of God's Church.

While God gave His written word to some—it was to Jubilee Usher that the Almighty gave His sword.

The soggy skies of late winter had reluctantly given way to a wetter spring and now even that was slipping away into summer.

For most of it John Doyle Lee had been helpless, able only to watch the seasons change. He yearned for the freedom to plant, to harvest, to work the soil. He had waited through the agony of seeing another new year begin while the government readied his second trial.

How he had missed Rachel down at Moenkopi, Caroline and her family alone at Panguitch. Both Polly and Lavina held on at Skutumpah while Emma continued to raise their children at Lonely Dell. It was not for himself, but for them—the women and his children—that he prayed beside his musty cot every morning, where he knelt every night before slipping between the two thin blankets allotted him. Daily devotions—the time he could talk to God—were all that kept him from slipping away.

"Keep thy hand over them, Lord," Lee begged. "You may ask sacrifice of me—but shelter those I love."

With spring came a new U.S. deputy marshal. Benjamin L. Durham suggested that Lee might decide if he wanted to go east with two or three guards, mainly to visit the Centennial Exposition in Philadelphia. There, Durham explained, Lee could give public lectures.

"I'll help you write up a short story of your life," the marshal said. "And you can sell photos of yourself, signed of course, for a dollar each. Just think of the thousands you can earn in no time."

"I don't need thousands of dollars," Lee told him.

"What about your debts?" Durham prodded. "What you owe your attorneys? Your personal debts gone unpaid since you've been imprisoned? Think of your family, Mr. Lee. Think how much help that money could be to them. Think of them."

Lee had brooded on it, hard.

Durham pressed him. For some reason the deputy marshal was persistent about making plans to go east by the beginning of spring. "It will be good for you to get out of Utah for two or three years."

"Two or three years?"

"I think I can get it arranged. Get you . . . away from here where emotions are running against you."

"Who wants to do me ill?" Lee had asked. But both the warden and Durham would not say. Only that things weren't looking favorable if the government won their request for a second trial.

"You come back after that time spent in the east—you could be well off, Mr. Lee. Quite comfortable. Your family. Heirs."

So he brooded on it more. But as good as it sounded—the thought of going east and earning money for talking about his life, lecturing on the Mountain Meadows massacre and the lives of Mormon polygamists like him—the less he favored the whole idea. Being away from his wives and children because he was in prison was one thing. Being away from them of his own choosing was entirely another.

In his journal Lee wrote:

> *I am loath to accept liberty & favours from those not of my*
> *religious faith. But what can I do. I am here in their hands & am*
> *powerless. Near 18 months have past since my arrest and confinement*
> *. . . I have tired with all the energy of my soul & body to call fourth*
> *aid from those who would stand by me, but as yet have failed to elicit*
> *their sympathy.*

His letters to Brigham had gone unanswered—even though the Prophet lived and worked less than an hour's ride from where Lee waited out the soggy spring days in prison. The only one who had promised to help was Usher. Besides his grown sons, Usher alone had remained steadfast to Lee's plight. But here in the valley of the Great Salt Lake, Jubilee Usher could not help John Doyle Lee. It was up to Lee to get himself released on bail.

"We must get you returned to your home," Usher had written. "Then we can be of service to one another, Bishop Lee."

Spring came, cold and wet, but with it the prospect of planting in the prison fields. He was assigned three others to help him in selecting seed potatoes. The four planted their crop in the freshly turned earth. He began to fill the pages of a third ledger journal following his arrest and confinement.

Then came the surprise.

That eleventh day of May, Warden Greenwood came to him at the edge of the muddy field Lee worked with a weeding hoe. "John, you can be released on a bail of fifteen thousand dollars."

"The money—where . . . where did it—"

"It was brought to us by your sons this morning."

Lee shook his head, unable to fathom where they could have gotten that sort of money. And this—his release, his freedom—it was almost too much for him to believe, too much to trust.

"I . . . I can go home?"

The warden nodded. "You have to reappear at Beaver in three months."

"August?"

"Yes."

John turned, looked over his fields, feeling the tug of this righteous season pulling at something within him. As much as this hoped-for freedom was all that he had dreamed of, the smell, the moist, fertile give of the earth beneath him was every bit as real as anything had ever been real for John Doyle Lee.

He turned back to the warden. "Mr. Greenwood—if it's all the same to you . . . would it be all right if I finished my planting before I go home?"

36

"T HAT MORMON GOD-TALKER is no different from any man who wants to get rid of the likes of us," Jonah grumbled in exasperation.

Jeremiah asked, "You figure Brigham Young lied about Jubilee Usher—just to get rid of us?"

With a shrug he answered, "Can't figure, son. We ain't run onto a sign of Usher or his outfit in any of the towns where Young said we could narrow down the chase."

For the better part of three months they had been scouring the country southwest of Young's City of the Saints.

"Concentrate on the country north of St. George," Brigham Young had told them. "Between St. George and Beaver."

That was more than a hundred miles of road strung between austere hills and rough-cut ranges, a land scarred with a thousand places where Usher could hide his small army of thieves and cutthroats.

"My best guess would be that Usher keeps in that unforgiving country west of the road," Young had disclosed before they headed south. "It's country crossed by few white men, and even fewer trails."

But for all their searching, any sign they came across proved itself old. Any trail not heavily used in the past two weeks would get obliterated by the recent rains that hammered this country every afternoon and into the early evening as spring bled away into summer. In the midst of one of those sky-belly downpours, Two Sleep had stumbled onto an old campsite in a meadow where the grass had been close-cropped by more than a hundred head of stock, the ground crisscrossed with the telltale scars of iron-rimmed wagon wheels, pocked with the dead-eyed black rings of abandoned fire pits.

And at the edge of that meadow stood a crude cross made from two peeled cottonwood logs both more than twenty feet long, bound together in a rough X, an end to both timbers buried securely in the earth. Hanging from the weathered timbers was a naked form long picked at by the carrion eaters.

"Who you figure he was?" Jeremiah asked.

"No way of knowing," Jonah said, mesmerized by the empty, sightless sockets in the skull draped in very little flesh, tufts of hair clinging tenaciously to bone here and there. Only enough of it all to tell this had been a man hung here to die.

"Spikes in hands," Two Sleep said, pantomiming as he turned back to the two white men who still sat atop their horses, staring at the grotesque sight. "In feet."

"He was nailed to that goddamned cross?" Jeremiah asked.

"Just like the Bible says they done to Jesus," Jonah replied, his eyes narrowing, throat constricting with the sudden taste of his breakfast shoving up against his tonsils. His breath came hard, remembering the sight of the padre's Jesus nailed to an upright cross.

Here was something more crude, its crucified victim spread-eagled to the extent of his limbs as his flesh was pierced, nailed to the cottonwood timbers.

Jeremiah turned this way, then that, peering around the meadow. "What the hell was this place?"

"Only bunch Brigham Young says he knows runs with this many men down in this country has to be Jubilee Usher," Jonah answered.

"This was their camp?"

"Yeah. Likely as not."

At last Jeremiah hunched over his saddle horn, leaning forward to rub a sore tailbone. "And him, Pa?"

"Some poor soul who crossed Jubilee Usher."

All three fell silent, staring at the carcass left to rot, left to the predators, as birds called from the nearby trees ringing the huge meadow. The air had grown warm, and the close-cropped grass was alive with the buzz and hum of winged insects. The scritch-scritch of many-legged

onlookers from the brush seemed almost deafening in the summer stillness.

"It's real, Pa."

He turned to look at the oak-brown face of his son. "What's that?"

"Jubilee Usher and his bunch."

He looked back at the corpse. "You'd know that better'n me, Jeremiah. I never laid eyes on the man. He's been like a ghost. Tracking him
all this time's been like a dream. Never nothing solid to go on—nothing I
could really get a holt of."

"This . . . this is something solid, Pa. He was here. That's why I said
it's real. This hunt for Ma. We're going to find her."

"Your ma."

"That Mormon said he heard of the blond woman with Usher last
fall," Jeremiah said, swallowing hard as he did. "She was alive then.
Chances are she is still."

His shoulders hunched involuntarily, as if collapsing in on his scarred
and much-wounded heart. "Married off to Usher."

"She can't be, Pa. Not when she's still married to you." .

How he had prayed Jeremiah was right over the past weeks as summer
made its grand entrance onto this southern land. But try as he might, the
doubt still clung there, like a bit of tenacious rust at the bottom of a cast-
iron skillet—something that would simply not come clean. Too much
time, a part of him always reminded Jonah. So much time that he wasn't all
that sure anymore if she still counted on his coming for her.

Maybe she had given up—and had consented to marry the bastard
who had come to claim her more than thirteen summers before. Gritta was
tough, as tough as any woman came. That's why he had married her, loved
her more and more every day of their life together as she bore their
children and hitched the mules, made their meals and drew the water . . .
every one of the little insignificant tasks that went into Gritta's life on their
farm. Small things that he had rolled over and over in his mind all these
years they had been apart.

Wondering if she had rolled them over and over in her thoughts too. If
she had memories of their time together. Or had they dimmed, like the luster
from some shiny new thing grown old and cloudy with the drag of time and
wear? Had she given up on him—and grabbed hold of what she had?

He wouldn't blame her if she had, Jonah had decided of recent. But—
he would keep on coming anyway. Gritta was alive. He knew it now. And
maybe, just maybe, he could make her fall in love with him all over again.

One day soon. When he found her again.

As he had long ago in the shadow of the Shenandoah's Big Cobbler Mountain.

If he could find her, Jonah swore, reining his horse away from the cross and the carcass covered with bird droppings—then he could make her love him again.

He circled the meadow slowly, thinking on that: on what it would take for a man growing old to make a woman love him. Easy enough for a young man courting a young woman. But this was going to be something harder.

How was he going to convince her, after all this time, that he'd been looking for her all along, that he'd never given up?

So he asked himself then as he found the remnants of the deep, rain-washed wagon ruts stringing west out of the meadow camp on that most recent of hoof-pounded roads: how in the name of heaven was he going to make Gritta ever believe in him again?

There was a baker's dozen of 'em. Them and the two young boys the gunmen had took down near the settlement at Marble Canyon just south across the territorial line in northern Arizona.

From there they turned on their heels and nearly backtracked. Curious, Shad Sweete had followed them north into Mormon Utah, across the great Colorado River, riding north by west after skirting around Lee's Ferry near the mouth of the Paria River. Weeks ago down there he'd learned even more of the man he'd taken up tracking. That had been a land where he soon learned the Usher family had friends—there in the land of John Doyle Lee. His children. His grandchildren.

And for a time Sweete wondered if he was a grandfather yet. Thought on Pipe Woman up north with Charcoal Bear's Northern Cheyenne and the Medicine Hat. It pained his heart too goddamned much to think that Shell Woman never would get to bounce one of her grandbabies on a knee . . . he worked hard not to think of young'uns again.

Besides, there was work to be about.

The task at hand wasn't at all like stalking game, he had decided some time back. Hell—there was a passel more sense and reason to the way an old six-by-seven bull elk moved across familiar, even new, territory than the way Jubilee Usher left sign of his passing. Decades gone now Shad had come as a young man to understand that the way to track down his quarry was to learn all he could about the critter, even come to respect that critter and its ways.

That was just the problem that gnawed at Sweete now with tracking Usher. He wasn't all that positive he'd not make a mistake following the Danite's spoor. He was old now, maybe got a mite hard of hearing and dim of sight over the years. But even more than all that: there was simply no way Shad was ever going to respect this two-legged, man-killing beast.

Summer came early to country this far south. Of a time before the Mexican War he had wandered on down to Taos, like many another man come to the Spanish settlements, every last one of them drawn like bees to the hive, craving the potent corn liquor and the dusky, bare-bosomed *señoritas.* Of an autumn a long, long time ago, he had even come this far southwest with Bill Williams and Pauline Weaver—two of the wiriest hivernants a man could ride the river with. That was back to the waning days of the beaver trade, when the trio of hardpanned trappers vowed they would search farther and higher still, bent on finding the mythical, elusive streams where a mountain man could discover a hidden cache of pelts— beaver a'plenty, glossy hides as big as a Hudson Bay horse blanket.

The three of them never had, and the following spring Sweete rode off alone, on the backtrail that took him to Shell Woman in the north country.

After something on the order of two hundred miles now, for the life of him he still couldn't figure why the gunmen had laid on to the young boys the way they had. The towheaded pair were riding tandem, headed south on an old draft horse for Marble Canyon, when they met up with the baker's dozen, not long after Shad had caught up with the gunmen himself. From atop a ridgeline Sweete watched one of the Danites slap the workhorse on its flank, sending the lumbering animal on its way, before the gunmen continued on their way with the boys firmly lashed to one of their packhorses.

No mistake about it, he'd decided. These were the ones John Doyle Lee's son said Shad might join up with so he could throw in with the colonel's army. Sweete had other plans for the moment. He'd just follow, long as this bunch seemed to be of a purpose—for he figured that these kidnappers would likely lead him to Jubilee Usher.

And once Sweete found Jubilee Usher, he'd find a way to free Gritta Hook. If nothing else, he could get her back to St. Louis for a reunion with Hattie. The girl'd be a growed woman by now, surely capable of taking care of her mother until Jonah showed up. If he ever did show up.

A trusting, plain-faced, ruddy-skinned one, that son of John Doyle

Lee was. And he had quickly assumed the old frontiersman was nothing more than a killer looking to hook up with the colonel.

"For a time, years back, I run with Major Wiser," Shad even told the suspicious, doubting Thomas. "The pay was always good. I figure I could use some steady money again."

"Ain't heard nothing of Boothog Wiser in . . . in a long time," the young man said, his face still a mask of suspicion.

"Going on seven—maybe eight winters now. He got killed over a game of cards."

He smiled at the old mountain man. "That Wiser—he always was one for gambling. That, or the women."

"The devil finally got his hands on Major Wiser, I s'pose—one way or the other."

That had done it—Sweete's mention of Usher's favored right-hand man who Jonah himself killed back in Kansas in the gun battle that freed young Hattie. Years gone behind them all.

Lee's son gurgled free of most that he knew. "More'n ten of Colonel Usher's men was just here, seeing to my pa—recent let go from prison up to Salt Lake City. The colonel sent 'em down with word he wanted Pa to join up with his army," the young Lee explained.

"Just what I aim to do, son. You tell me where."

"You're welcome to stay the night. Likely Pa would enjoy talking to any friend of the colonel's."

"No, but thankee just the same. I best be heading out myself like them others. You say it ain't been long since they rode off north?"

He shook his head. "Not more'n a day. You can catch 'em, you get hard after it."

"If the colonel wants your pa come join up with him—them fellas say where your pa's s'posed to find Usher?"

This time he nodded, pointed off over Sweete's shoulder. West of the lodestar. "They said Usher's moved out of Utah to raise him some money—the money he'll need to set the Church back on the Lord's path after Brigham Young and his kind gone and ruin't the true calling."

"Which way out of Utah?"

With a shrug he said, "Just like I'm showing you. West—into Nevada Territory is what them others told Pa. Told us come join the colonel in some mining town where all the folks is pulling silver out of the hills by the bucketloads."

Shad had watched the young man squint, staring down at his scuffed, worn boots.

"But I can't for the life of me think of the name of the place—but for sure you can catch up to them others. Only a day ahead of you, 's all."

"I'm obliged, son."

Touching the gentle upward curve of the wide, floppy brim of his sun-baked hat, Shad tapped moccasins against the horse's flanks and set off.

He'd run onto their trail easy enough, and dogged it until he found the bunch wheeling round to the south. Strange of them to do such—until they nabbed the boys. Only then did the gunmen point their noses back to the northwest. He'd follow them all the way into Nevada. Not that he gave a damn about those two young'uns. Shad had enough to worry about right now, haunting their backtrail as they pounded their horses through the growing heat of each summer day. With each day crossing this spare, open, broken country frying beneath a white-eyed sun—Shad was once more reminded why he stayed in the north country. Hot as it was, this far south he figured he couldn't be more than a few steps away from hell itself.

He'd follow this bunch into hell, if it led him to stand eye to eye with Jubilee Usher.

Man got to be as old as Sweete, he had few priorities in life. With his wife gone some time now, and his daughter among her own people, living a life of her own . . . with the hell gone out of beaver and buffalo robes, along with the army harrying the wild northern tribes until the white man would have them all on those spirit-robbing reservations soon enough anyway . . . why, there wasn't much excitement left for a man who had just about seen it all. From setting foot across a wide stretch of country where no white man had set a moccasin ever before, to watching the first white-topped Conestogas lumbering past at a snail's pace along the Holy Road for California and Oregon itself.

But every day this bunch of gunmen moved another twenty-five or so miles closer to Jubilee Usher.

Shad didn't have nothing else to do, but right what wrong had been done to a man he'd come to love like his own son. Wasn't nothing Sweete could do for High-Backed Bull now. But there was this one last thing Shad could do for Jonah Hook.

If it was the last thing he was going to do in a long, long and glorious life—Shad was going to stand eye to eye with the elephant this time.

With nothing else to live for—Shad Sweete wanted only to see the rabbit-eyed look on Jubilee Usher's face as the Danite butcher felt the first cold brush of death's call.

37

I N T H I S H O T T E S T of seasons how he wished he could molt his skin like the snakes, peeling his uncomfortable covering of flesh back over itself until he pulled fully free of it and the heat.

To the white demons of this land it was early September. To Bak Sahm it seemed as if summer had never relinquished its furnace grip on this high desert, even here in the mountain country.

But now that he had completed his preparations for those contracted shipments going back to the eighteen provinces, all it seemed he could think of was getting away to the cool of Echo Canyon, maybe even the hard climb it would take for a horse to carry him up the slopes of Highland Peak southwest of town. Whichever he chose for an escape from the heat for a few days, Bak looked forward to leaving Pioche in a way he never had before.

Most of the summer had been taken up with his painstaking labors in building the small wooden chests, complete with hinged tops, each one carved with the likeness of a curled dragon, its wings spread, fire steaming from its nostrils, ready to strike. As each new chest was constructed, Bak painted it in a deep red that reminded him of the color of blood when it first flowed, blood first touched by the air. Over that crimson he carefully illuminated the dragon's every scale, every frightening feature, and described intricate borders along the edges of the box in an expensive gold-leaf paint.

Many of his girls of joy helped him next by placing the soft red velvet lining to the inside of the boxes, where would lay the gold coins he was shipping back to the First City, from there across the Sea of Lions to the various tongs in Canton and the Pearl River delta. Come at last to Chinese soil, an individual chest would be dispatched to a specific family, destined to cross the many provinces, off to a far-flung village.

This was gold sent back when a father, a son, a husband, could not yet return from the Gold Mountain. The money, emblazoned with the white barbarians' great and powerful bird, its wings spread, would go a long way to soothing the pain of absence.

With the chests completed, each one filled with a single man's monetary shipment, then secured with a wrap of gold braid that he sealed with a dollop of thick wax—Bak Sahm could then think about leaving town for a few days, leaving the drinking house and store, leaving his girls for a few nights while he wandered off into the high places for solitude and peace, to lie beneath the tapestry of stars and try to sleep without a return of the dragon dream.

Struggle as he did, Bak found it hard not to think on the white demon and his colonel . . . and their army of thirsty, hungry soldiers, each one eager for repeated visits with his girls of joy as well as the town's other prostitutes who served as queen bees drawing the drones to such hives as the Fashion Saloon, the Capital and Pavilion, the Brick and the Crystal. When that army reached Pioche to erect its camp on the outskirts of town, the barbarians lost no time in streaming from watering hole to watering hole, testing the strength of the whiskey in each, ascertaining the luck at every gambling table, rotating through the last of the working girls until they decided upon a few favorites.

It was but a matter of days before the white demon brought his "colonel" to the California Lodging House.

The first night Bak saw the tall barbarian, the colonel was standing at the bar beside the white demon as twilight gave way to inky darkness and the coal-oil lamps spewed their feeble light-and-shadow dance across the smoky barroom below the landing where the Chinaman stood frozen, his chest unable to fill with air. He gripped the railing, afraid he would fall as he took in the monster's profile, his long, glossy, oiled hair spilling like a black raiment across the shoulders of a gray wool coat that nearly reached to midleg where his creamy buckskin britches were neatly stuffed into gleaming lamp-blacked, knee-high boots. It amazed Bak that on those boots there lay no pale crust of mud; indeed, not even the merest film of dust.

To either side of the tall man stood those who clearly revered the colonel—yet each of them looked the vagabond: plainly marked by the long ride on a dusty, muddy trail that brought them to Bak Sahm's gaming saloon. Instantly he knew the colonel would stand out in any crowd, especially the shadowy clientele who frequented the Chinaman's place.

Forcing himself to move from the railing, Bak steadied his body over the first step, holding tight to the banister as he rocked forward on the crippled leg. At that moment the colonel turned, drawing himself up to his full height, and brought his black eyes to bear on the Chinaman—having caught sight of Bak Sahm in the smudged mirror behind the bartender. The eyes, the smooth, polished features of the colonel's chiseled face, the wild sweep of his waxed mustache, froze Bak in midair above that first of twenty-four steps.

After a long moment of suffering the intensity of the colonel's steely appraisal, the Chinaman knew he must go on. Knew this meeting was fated—understood that whatever had brought this imposing demon to Pioche had already embroiled Bak Sahm himself.

Destiny must play itself through, he decided. Man has little, if anything, to contribute.

Beside the huge man stood the demon Haslam who had again paid good money for exclusive use of the woman. He was saying something to the colonel, raising himself slightly so that he could whisper into the tall one's ear amid the raucous noise of the barroom. Yet their four eyes never strayed from the Chinaman, the colonel nodding slowly in response to what Haslam told him. They watched every snaillike move of Bak's body as Bak Sahm finally looked away. Rolling to the side ever so slightly, he eased himself down onto the same step where his strong foot first rested. Then he repeated the process, step by step, ever downward, descending to the main floor through the murky layer of yellowish alkaline smoke.

He was trembling slightly as the colonel presented his hand. They shook, the huge, immense monster of a man painfully polite—never allowing his eyes to wander to Bak Sahm's crippled leg, much less his contorted arm. A few pleasantries, some cheerful banter, then talk of how the white demon had boasted of his beautiful China whore . . . then Bak Sahm made excuses to leave, his throat gone dry standing there in the ominous presence of the man's bulk. Just gazing up at the colonel, Bak felt the giant would all but make two of him.

Unsteadily, he tottered away toward the back rooms, making his apologies—eager, relieved . . . prayerful to escape the dragon's aura that radiated unmistakably all around the colonel. Perhaps it was the long black mane. Or—yes! It had to be the eyes. No other creature but a dragon could possess eyes like that. Still, this man, this apparent mortal being, possessed the most evil eyes Bak had ever seen.

Perhaps it was, as he had first feared moments before at the landing, that a dragon could take on any form it desired. Even that of a man.

The only thing he could take pride in, Bak understood, was being able to recognize a dragon in disguise. No man could be that tall, possessed of that slippery, reptilian smoothness . . . and those eyes, were he not the dragon of Bak Sahm's dream.

The Chinaman pushed through the first of the two doors. Closed it behind him. His hand trembled on the second knob. Twisting it, he hurried into the dark, close interior, where the sweetish smell assaulted his nostrils, spurring his head to reel as it became hard to breathe. So heavy was the air with the smoke of the opium pipes that he sensed an instant relief, as well as a certainty that his dragon dream was no longer that.

It had instead become Bak Sahm's nightmare.

After camping for weeks at the edge of town, the colonel's army had pulled up their tents and departed within the space of two days. The residents of Pioche had watched them drift off in pairs or small knots of riders, each taking a different road out of town. A few headed north, but most to the other cardinal directions.

Even the white demon named Haslam. He had left, although Bak had gone for himself to look at the colonel's camp from a nearby hilltop—and found several tents still erected: several white barbarians well armed and evidently left behind to watch over something or someone. The Chinaman had been sure they held prisoner the black-skinned demon he watched passing in and out of a large tent's flaps . . . until he saw her. Such fine, light hair tugged by the breeze, it seemed to radiate the autumn light with a strange luminance all its own.

Eventually Bak had retreated from the hilltop and returned to town— glad that the dragon army had abandoned the country, delirious that Haslam had gone away with his colonel. Bak even allowed himself hope that the white demon would not return for the woman.

As quickly he scolded himself: to wish misfortune to befall another man was to bring that misfortune upon one's self, so had he learned long ago.

Wishing such as that had called forth the dragon from the mountain-side years ago . . . come to take most of the use of an arm and a leg—like an ominous warning to Bak Sahm.

Instead of wishing such misfortune on another, Bak turned to his dream pipe that night as he did every night after the colonel's army marched away in small tatters of their gathered greatness.

But instead of dreaming of the delta, Bak Sahm was once again visited by a terrible vision.

No longer a dream . . . what dragon Bak Sahm saw now in his opium smoke was now a nightmare.

Over and over again Jubilee Usher ran through the plans as he led a handful of his faithful northeast from Pioche toward the rendezvous point. There Haslam's Indians had been waiting for the colonel's arrival, waiting to join up with the various small bands Usher had scattered across the compass— his idea being to throw off any man who just might be keeping an eye on this army's movements.

From Echo Canyon they moved slightly east of north, then struck out due north along the eastern slope of the Wilson Creek Range, where the nine-thousand-foot peaks looked down upon the formidable array of white and red horsemen pushing ever onward in orderly formation, the Pahvants thrown out on either flank and far ahead for each day's march. Haslam and a half dozen of his own always rode the backtrail—in the event some curious soul might decide to dog the heels of Jubilee Usher's army of liberation.

Jubilee had done all he could to disperse his soldiers to the four winds to prevent suspicion on the part of the mine and smelter owners who grew nervous each time the day drew closer when another shipment would push north from Pioche, bound for the tracks' transcontinental railroad. The fifteen high-walled wagons, their bottoms reinforced with sheet iron riveted to thick cross members of bar steel in order to support the great weight demanded of the freighters, each groaned behind a twelve-mule hitch. Four accomplished teamsters were assigned to cajole and curse and whip each team north on its journey. A hundred well-trained, superbly armed gunmen formed the escort that rode along each flank of the wagon train in two neat columns-of-twos.

In all the years those mine and smelter owners had been shipping their wealth north to rendezvous with special railcars kept on a short siding for that specific purpose, there to await the arrival of the next westbound freight that would pull the fortune in gold and silver on to San Francisco's mint—there had never been the slightest intimidation of their system, much less a problem. Not a single ounce of the precious ore had been lost. In all those years, in all their experience, no one had ever been able to pull together a force large enough to challenge the might of that hundred-man armed escort. And, so everyone back in Pioche believed, likely no one ever would.

At least Jubilee Usher grinned again—now that he had found himself this superbly brilliant way in which to finance his ascendancy to the throne of the one true Church of God.

Baker Cunningham, likely the best tracker and trail dogger Jubilee Usher had in his employ, had spent the better part of two months riding over this trail north, back and forth to learn every mile of the road. And when he had returned, Cunningham unsettled the colonel with his appraisal of Usher's plan of attack.

"You ain't gonna hit that wagon train and its escort between Pioche and the rails."

"Why not?"

"No place to ambush 'em," Cunningham replied, slicing himself off a sliver of chew. "They'll always be out to the open. Where those wagons can fort up and them riflemen can make a stand of it."

Usher ground his hands together. Not this close—not to have all his plans fail now! "Where, then?" he growled at Cunningham. "And when?"

"What I think we oughtta do is hit 'em west of the place they link up with their railcars, after they've hooked up with the westbound that makes a short stop to take them on."

Usher had nodded—while the wagons and railcars and escort were all sitting on their thumbs: brilliant! "So you're thinking of hitting the escort before it gets hooked up with the freight headed to California?"

But Cunningham had another shock for Usher. "No. Easy as it may sound on the face of it, Colonel—I don't want to see us attack them while they're hunkered down there waiting for the freight to come in from the east."

Calmly as he could that night in camp some fifty miles north of Pioche, Nevada, Jubilee Usher had asked, "Why in the devil's name shouldn't we hit them sitting on their hands? They're like fish in a barrel. Squatting down, waiting for the engines to come through."

"That's just what I don't like about it," Cunningham admitted. "That bunch is always prepared to hunker down if need be."

He had sighed, nettled at the scout's delay. "Just where in God's creation, then, Cunningham?"

"Not long after the engine hooks up and pulls out of that siding where they'll be—just east of Connors Pass."

"A pass . . . you mean a mountain pass?"

The tracker smiled. "That's right, Colonel."

"Excellent," Usher had gushed. "And you've considered what your plans are for snatching that shipment from the train?"

"You'll leave a small force behind in the hills above the track siding."

"Yes," Usher agreed. "They can hit the teamsters once the railcars are hooked up and the train has moved on out of earshot with those hundred riflemen."

"Exactly," Cunningham said. "A dozen of our boys can make quick work of those mule skinners . . . then wait with the wagons until we send back a rider to hurry them on up the pass to help us off-load the ore."

Usher's eyes had narrowed. "How do you figure to stop that freight rolling west to California? Even in a mountain pass."

"To climb a mountain, Colonel—a train can't do it any different than a horse or mule. Means that the tracks work their way this way then that, on up to the pass."

"Switchbacks?"

"That's right, sir," and his hand inched back and forth slowly, gradually climbing. "We'll go find us one of them switchbacks where the turn is treacherous, where the engineer's got to slow way down to make so that heavy load don't rock too much as he grinds up the steep grade."

"And that's where we'll hit them."

Cunningham smiled. "I'll tear up some track, drop a big load of timber across the rails—something that'll get that goddamned engine stopped right where we want our Injuns to ride down on the train."

"Yes! Turn those Utes loose on that escort. And when they're done with those men—not a white man west of Salt Lake City will be blamed for that attack and robbery."

The scout's smile now turned to evil glee. "Not with what them red sonsabitches can do to a God-fearing man's body with a knife and a few minutes of idle time!"

Usher had to grin with delight. It sounded like a damned fine plan Cunningham had seen his way through.

Jubilee turned back to his tracker. "Timber? And rocks big enough to hide men and horses behind?"

"All you'd ever need, Colonel. That pass is over seven thousand feet there."

"Splendid. I want you to call Haslam in here."

Minutes later the scout returned with Orrin Haslam.

"Cunningham said you wanted to see me, Colonel?"

"Yes." And Usher proceeded to lay out his new plans for attacking the ore shipment after it was off-loaded onto a westbound freight.

"If they got away on schedule," Haslam said after listening through the litany of details, "that wagon train can't be no more than five days behind us."

"Which should give us plenty of time to reach the siding, where we can leave a dozen or fifteen men to await the wagons."

"And be sure they understand their goddamned orders," Cunningham growled. "Understand they ain't to move down out of the hills and rub out those teamsters until that train's long out of sight."

"I'll see to that myself," Haslam said.

"At the same time," Usher went on, "the rest of us will follow Cunningham on up the pass to set up the ambush, and ready our surprise for the day all that precious wealth comes rolling our way."

Jubilee turned, signaling the Negro over.

"Colonel?"

"Bring us three cups, George. And a bottle of that brandy I had you put away when we left Pioche."

Haslam swallowed hard, licking his lips. "Just the same to you, Colonel—I'd prefer some whiskey myself. Can't speak for Cunningham here."

"Me too," the tracker agreed. "Whiskey . . . other'n that brandy."

Usher smiled harshly at the slight both gave him. "We'll drink what I say we drink. And brandy it will be. Whiskey is for drinking—and something as fine as an aged spirit is for celebration, gentlemen. We do have cause for celebration, don't we now?"

Haslam nodded as George reappeared with the handles to three tin cups suspended from the fingers of one gnarled hand, a bottle in the other. He and Cunningham took a cup and held it out, waiting while George poured some of the brandy into the colonel's waiting cup.

"To the success of our enterprise, gentlemen," Usher said, holding up the cup in a salute. "And to the return of our beloved Church to the path of God!"

"To success," Cunningham echoed before throwing back the brandy, its thick cascade of fire down his throat causing him to sputter.

Wary now, Haslam drank slower, the potency of the brandy making his eyes water. With a raspy throat he repeated Usher's toast, "To the return of our Church, Colonel."

Usher sensed a genuine jubilation as it seemed the brandy coursed through his veins with warmth. "Gentlemen, I can all but feel Brigham Young's throne beneath me already!"

38

T RY AS HE might to keep his mind shed of them, questions about those two youngsters nagged Shad Sweete all the way north from Arizona Territory into Brigham Young's Utah as he dogged the backtrail of a small band of gunmen who eventually rode into a mining town in southeastern Nevada to rendezvous with Jubilee Usher's army.

Over and over he told himself it didn't amount to a hill of bear shit what Usher planned for them two boys—Shad damn well had more pressing business to attend to himself. Closing in on Usher, waiting out his moment to free Jonah Hook's woman, escaping east with her: that's what wore heaviest on his mind.

But try as he might to keep those lads out of his thoughts, Shad still struggled to figure out what purpose the youngsters would serve. Time came when he believed he had it all sorted out: the horsemen were welcomed back into a camp of wagons and tents, horses and gunmen, gathered near the hills outside that prosperous, rowdy mining town. A place that called itself Pioche, Nevada.

Now Shad never had any use for gold seekers. In fact, to his way of thinking things—it was their sort that had ruined the mountains. Oh, for certain there was them that said it was the farmers, settlers, families, that brought in white women and plows, that made a place for preachers and barristers—some who claimed it was the sodbusters who ruined the West. But far as the old fur trapper figured it, those sorts of folks stayed to the valleys where they could farm, and therefore they really did no harm to the sort of country where Sweete's breed roamed.

But these gold seekers . . . they invaded *his* mountains. Because of them the Sierra was overrun with the sort that dug and tore and ripped apart, only to spit back out whatever tailings they had yanked out before moving on to do the same thing someplace else. That someplace else turned out to be down to the Cripple Creek country in Colorado a decade later. Up to Montana Territory along Alder Gulch. Over among the hills hemming in the great Snake River too. No, it weren't sodbusters the likes of Jonah and his family that spelled an end to what Shad Sweete loved most. It was miners in his mountains.

With no small measure of disgust, the old man had swallowed his pride when he figured he'd be staying in these parts awhile—and after a week or better without catching sight of Jubilee Usher in that camp of a hundred or more men, Shad darkened the door of the Dexter Livery Stable.

"Something I do for you?" the blacksmith asked, then turned toward the old man, a look of sudden surprise crossing his face mottled by heat, smeared with soot and a three-day growth of black beard.

Even at his age the trapper still cut an impressive figure, tall as he was, with that white mane of hair spilling well past his broad shoulders, his mustache and beard stark against a face tanned to the color of oiled saddle leather.

He eyed the younger man, who stood beside his forge stripped to the waist with the heat of the day and the fiery hell of his work. Sweat glistened on the thick, swollen bands of muscle as he gripped a hammer in one hand, tongs clutching a glowing hinge plate in the other, both poised over the large anvil perched atop the huge cottonwood stump.

To Shad it felt like begging. "Looking for a way a man might make a dollar or two."

"Passing through?"

"Might be here for a bit longer, things work out."

He looked back at the hinge, its reddish glow fading. The blacksmith plunged it back among the coals of his tender, set the hammer down, and with that right arm began to pump the handle on the huge bellows above the tender into a wheeze, coaxing the coals hotter and hotter. "What sort of work you want to find, ol' fella?"

Shad enjoyed watching the licking flare of flame, the puffs of black soot, the rhythmic stoking of the tender with gusts of air. It had been a lifetime since last he worked with iron and fire. "I figure a man gets to be my age, he's done just about everything. Some better'n others."

"Anything against loading wagons?"

"S'pose I can at that."

He dragged the tongs back out of the coals, laying the glowing hinge atop the anvil. Brought the sixteen-pound hammer down three times with sharp, ringing strikes. "You work a mule hitch?"

"Like I said," Shad began.

"I know," the blacksmith interrupted, "you done everything." He struck the hinge at least a dozen more times while Shad waited, growing impatient, turning to gaze out the door at the southwestern sunshine that midmorning. "Head up McCannon there and cross two streets over to get on Meadow Valley. You'll run onto a road south off Meadow Valley that will take a man up the slope to the company operations."

"Company?"

Beads of sweat glistened like diamonds against the flushed face flecked with dark soot. "The Nevada-Utah Mines and Smelter Corporation. It's them that hires any man wants to work in this country. They might could use you to whip some mules when they take their next shipment of ore north to the railroad."

"They haul all that gold and silver north? What about thieves?"

The blacksmith snorted. "Not with the army them mine owners keep around to ride along with the freight shipment. All the way from here until the ore reaches San Francisco and the federal government buys it. Never been anyone foolish enough to try hitting one of those shipments."

Shad watched the man strike the hinge twice more before he plunged it into a bucket of water with a steaming hiss. "Army, is what you said." Sweete's mind squeezed on it the way he would wring out his wool longhandles beside a stream.

"Guards. A hundred hired guns. Because there's so many of 'em—no one's ever tried so much as to look sideways at one of them shipments."

"Damn right. A *army*," Sweete repeated, looking at the patch of sunshine spreading toward his moccasins from the open double doors. Then, as if struck with sudden inspiration, he gazed back at the blacksmith. "They're hiring drivers for that next shipment, you say?"

With a nod he said, "You don't find work there—and that's something steady for the next couple of weeks, understand . . . you come on back here. I can find a big fella like you something to do help me out around here for a few days. Wouldn't pay near as much as the company gonna pay you for slapping the ass of a mule all the way north to the rails and back here again—but it might make you a few dollars so you can mosey on some more."

"I'll go see about working on that ore train," Shad replied.

"Just figured you to be the type to mosey, more'n a fella looking for a steady sort of job."

That had been the day Shad fit another small piece of it together in his mind.

Before the company's wagon bosses he had proved himself capable enough with the animals, showing his prowess with the hitches—and had awaited only the date of the ore train's departure. Certain was he that should Jubilee Usher stay back in the shadows and refuse to show himself in the sunlight, at least the Danite renegade would one day make his grand entrance when his gunmen made their play for the fortune in gold and silver to be hauled north.

It took an *army* to guard that ore train. And the prospect of tearing that fortune from just such an armed escort was the only damned thing that would keep an *army* the likes of what Jubilee Usher commanded back in the nearby hills. What other reason would so big a band of gunmen have to hunker down near Pioche, Nevada?

Then, late of an afternoon the day before the train was scheduled to depart, Shad again saw those two boys. Sure there at the first, certain they were the same two youngsters the gunmen had kidnapped down in Arizona. But the more he looked them over at the sunny street corner of Bush and Dry Valley, the old man couldn't swear by it. As much as the two looked ringers for the pair hauled along with the horsemen he had followed north, Sweete began to doubt.

These two he spotted now wore the finest of clothing, the newest of boots—their cheeks scrubbed to a rosy glow. And all the more unsettling, they were in the company of a fair-haired woman whom they treated as only children can treat their mother.

So he had watched them on the streets of Pioche, moving in and out of the stores and sun-drenched shops, one boy on either side of the tall woman, who in turn was escorted by an old black man, his wool suit shiny at the elbows and knees from years of wear. For sure he followed them and studied her—as he brooded on how he was going to get Usher by himself when the time came. Somewhere—he would get the bastard alone, maybe in some confusion . . . then try his best to keep from killing the Mormon outright. Shad had vowed he'd do his best to keep Usher alive: to save him for Jonah. If there was one man who deserved to kill Jubilee Usher, it was Shad's friend, Jonah Hook.

If . . . if Jonah was still alive after all these winters.

So if things hadn't worked out for Hook to track this bastard down, it would be Shad's certain pleasure to even the score for his dead friend. Or, if Usher gave him no other choice, Sweete would kill the Danite leader, personal. And later on just have to make his apologies to Jonah for gutting Usher himself.

They were on the way now. All those wagons, and mules, and mule whackers like him. Along with their escort strung out along each side of the ore train. Plodding through each day beneath the baking sun, rolling across one blistering valley after another, pushing north for the past week. This sort of work gave a man a lot of time to think, and remember those two young boys. To remember his own son.

And to think on that tall, fair-haired woman. Which always made him remember Toote's merry laugh, the way she wrinkled her nose when he made her laugh. The way she made his whole body smile what with the way he felt when he was around her.

Across the last four days before the ore train was to depart Pioche, Shad had watched Jubilee Usher's camp grow smaller each time he crept into the hills overlooking the gathering. Each day more and more of the gunmen tore down tents, saddled up, and moved off in different directions. Sweete was sure they were going to rendezvous farther north.

Still, as many as they were, Shad didn't figure Usher's men would stand a chance against the armed escort. Outnumbered, likely outgunned too . . . Jubilee Usher's army was one day soon going to try jumping this escort and come off short for it. For all Shad's thinking on it—there wasn't a way they stood a Chinaman's chance of making good an ambush along the trail.

Shad's only worry as he rocked high atop the plank seat of the high-walled Pittsburgh freighter was that Jubilee Usher might just have sent his men north to strike the ore train without him. Which would mean that Shad was making this journey for nothing. Usher might have stayed back in Pioche. And Sweete wouldn't get his hands around the bastard's neck.

So he couldn't worry about those boys no more. From the looks of things, they'd likely found their mother, no doubt—and were living the good life filled with fancy clothes, rich food, and even a Negro servant to tag along behind them and their mama.

What Sweete had to work his mind on, as the mules pulled his wagon north to the rail siding where Shad came to believe the ambush would take place, was praying Jubilee Usher would be along for the attack.

Praying the bastard wouldn't miss the chance to be there when his gunmen rode down on the wagons and the armed escort—rode down on an old frontiersman who was waiting to finally look the very soul of black evil square in the eye before he pulled his trigger.

And blew that face into all eternity.

His tracker Cunningham kept some Indian scouts watching every mile the ore train made through the long, hot days as summer clung tenaciously to this basin country between the Ely and Egan mountain ranges to the west, the Wilson Creek and Snake ranges to the east. Each day found one of the warriors riding in with a message for Usher—Cunningham's way of updating the colonel on the progress of that ore shipment.

Most of his men were already on their way west toward Connors Pass, long gone from the rail siding when Cunningham himself rode in with the remaining scouts.

"They're coming, Colonel."

His pulse quickened. "How far?"

Cunningham twisted around in the saddle, then said, "Can't be more than two hours behind us, maybe three at tops."

As the sky to the northwest began to darken like the summer underbelly of coming doom, the train's armed escort appeared to the south, most every one of them particularly nervous as they and the teamsters rode in to await the engines said to be coming from somewhere in Utah. While the wind came up, rank with the smell of autumn thunder and hail, they labored in shifts to off-load the ore into three waiting boxcars . . . then settled down in the growing cold of the damp air, watchful for that first puff of telltale black smoke along the eastern horizon after the steam engine would make its descent from Sacramento Pass into the valley where the escort had pitched its camp along the rail siding.

"Train's coming!" came the first shout from the ridge to the east.

Word quickly spread that gloomy afternoon, raising every man's spirits.

Spewing a long column of black into the deepening gloom of that sky quickly washed of summer blue, and hissing streamers of dirty white steam from the bowels of its boiler into the thickening summer mist of the afternoon storm, a belching engine finally showed up a day late. It ground to a halt, wheezed, then achingly backed onto the siding, where its wood tender clattered against the first of the three boxcars. The train men coupled the freight to the tender in a fevered hurry to be out of the weather when the call was given for the escort to climb aboard, among the extra cars where they had just led their horses into cramped stalls. With a screech and a grunting chug, the train lurched away as the mist gave way to the first cold blast of a driving thunderstorm. The engineers wasted no time dropping their sand on the rain-slickened tracks, spinning their huge iron wheels atop the thin ribbons of iron rail before they were able to heave themselves off the siding onto the main line, slowly, agonizingly gaining speed for the climb up the Connors grade.

Jubilee Usher had chuckled smugly—certain that both the Central Pacific men and the escort as well believed they were most vulnerable sitting still in that valley between the passes. How simpleminded they were, he thought: to figure that once they pushed away from the siding, they would be safe, able to roll on comfortably and without concern with their precious cargo all the way west to San Francisco.

The colonel had chosen to stay behind temporarily with the men detailed to make quick work of the teamsters before he pushed on—hoping to follow the rails west quickly enough so that he could also get in on the fighting when the Pahvants attacked the train itself.

He watched from the hilltop as the train churned its drive wheels faster and faster, the engineers knowing full well they would have to make a strong-hearted run at the coming climb that would take them all the way up to Connors Pass. And with the fire tender's trail of smoke nothing more than a distant thread on the western horizon beyond the foothills, Jubilee Usher turned and nodded with smug satisfaction to the four who sat behind the crest with him.

"Each of you remembers the plan: make sure your men have a target before we open fire. I want every one of us to cut down one of those teamsters and guards with the first shot. Don't let a one escape our first volleys. It's surprise I demand—just as I have demanded surprise from Major Haslam and Cunningham's Indians when they strike the train. First shots follow mine."

Two nodded, two grunted their agreement as the four moved off through the crevices in the rock formations surrounding the wagon camp, where a few of the teamsters were already trying to start fires in the rising wind, others hurrying to drag kindling and wood out of the pelting rain, under the cover of wagon bellies.

Usher gave the four what he felt was time to spread out among their gunmen, then eased down on his belly, dragging the repeater into his shoulder's notch, resting his cheek along the stock.

He couldn't help smiling as the one he had figured to be the leader of the escort left behind with the teamsters dropped a load of firewood beneath one of the wagon's canvas possum bellies. As the man started to straighten, Usher squeezed the trigger.

The signal for all the rest to commence their attack.

Through the curl of muzzle smoke that was just as quickly whisked away on the misting breeze, the Mormon watched the teamster suddenly snap erect upon the bullet's impact. His knees buckled as the surrounding hills exploded with gunfire. The mule whacker collapsed onto his face, scratching his leg for the pistol he wanted to get clear of his holster. Usher saw that the man was dead before his face smacked the damp ground.

Here and there among the wagons, the teamsters and what escort was left behind were all diving—those few who hadn't been dropped on the first volley. There couldn't be more than a handful that they'd have to weed out, Jubilee thought, once they worked their way down the hillsides into that teamster camp. All the rest lay where the bullets had found them: at campfires, at a tailgate pulling bacon or beans from the wagon, dropping harness from the backs of the weary mules.

Already Jubilee was waving his men down from the hillsides into that teamster camp. Once there, they would make quick work of the four or five who kept up the barest of resistance.

Like frightened jackrabbits, he thought. Wishing he were close enough to see the fear in their eyes as they were cut down. Close enough to smell the fear oozing from their skin as death seized them each one by the throat.

Death was so much more a magnificent creature when viewed up close. Close enough to stare it eye to eye. Close enough to have it excite his nostrils with its stench. His heart beat fast, his skin prickling with goose bumps, his breath coming hard. Adrenaline dumping hot into his veins. How he wanted to wade in the blood again. At the same time sensing again the intense longing to impale the woman on his manhood.

Firing his pistols, Usher lumbered down the slope into the smudges of gunsmoke clung in damp streamers to the bluffs around them—aiming at what targets presented themselves behind the wagons or among the frightened mules.

Heady, utterly intoxicating this feeling was—more powerful than any elixir man could ever himself create. For taking the life of another man was, after all, the work of God Himself.

How exquisite this bloody season! How divinely delicious the killing.

"In the name of the Everlasting God—kill them!" he shrieked above the tumult and gunfire, the cries of men and animals. "Butcher every last one of these heathen Gentiles!"

39

S HAD STOOD WATERING the scrub growth in the narrow ravine
when the first volley roared from the surrounding ridges.

That rattle of gunfire was enough to cut off the best man's piss—right
then and there.

Something inherent in his marrow screamed out its certainty. Sweete
knew who it was as he whirled about, stuffing himself back through the
woolen underwear, back into his leather britches secured with antler buttons. Yet he discounted that certainty as nothing but stupid foolishness.

And became thankful that old habits proved themselves hard to break.
With him into the mouth of the narrow, brushy ravine, he had carried the
two gun belts, looking for a peaceful place where a man could relieve himself in privacy back in the brush. There were no shadows that afternoon,
what with the clouds, and the mist, and the way the wind had flung its
temper down upon the land as a child would hurl a flat stone across a piece of
water. Those two old cap-and-ball revolvers along with the .45/90 Sharps
he had leaned up against a brace of scrub before he loosened his britches and
let out that first sigh. Of late he was working up to admitting his kidneys
were getting old, especially with the pounding that big Pittsburgh freight
wagon had given him on the jarring trail north from Pioche.

Now, his Sharps was nowhere near being a repeater like them Henrys
and Winchesters, to be sure—but an old plainsman like Shad Sweete who
of a time was weaned at the breast of one-shot muzzle loaders could fairly

make that big-bored buffalo gun sing out a steady tune. It were repeater enough for any man.

He blinked, staring through the gunsmoke. Trying to sort out the cut of this Injun fight. A man always kept his guns close by, Shad thought—no matter what errand called out its urgency.

Crouching at the mouth of the ravine, Sweete cradled the Sharps across his left elbow and slid open the breechblock, assuring himself of a cartridge. He doubted he would need the Sharps for the work at hand. The long-range weapon might better serve him later, to hold an enemy at bay should he have to make a run for it to flee the warriors.

But that's just what surprised him more than most anything. His instincts had been right at the first whack. Something had told him it was Usher's men—and sure enough, these were white men who were firing down on the last of the teamsters taking cover under the wagons or among the nettled mules. Not Indians . . . this ambush was the work of white thieves.

Through the swirl of movement thirty, maybe forty, yards away, Shad caught a glimpse of the man. It could be no other—as tall as the bastard was, the way his coal-black hair lay in disarray over the shoulders of his wool coat glistening in the rain-drenched air. In and through and among his men the tall one moved with the grace of a cat. Shad could only admire that agility, as big as the man was. As old as he was too.

Stuffing the pistols back in their holsters, he wrenched the Sharps to his shoulder, blinking in the mist. Finding the tall man at the end of his front blade notched there, down in the half-curl buckhorn rear sight. Sweete squeezed down on the back trigger, setting the front to take a hair's touch, then immediately moved his finger to it as Jubilee Usher turned, seeming to stare right at him, then whirled back around to prance off to another part of the fight just as Shad eased back his trigger finger.

His powerful rifle sent the soft lead bullet careening through the chill air, smashing through a wagon's sidewall. With all the noise reverberating off the far side of the canyon, with so much whine and hiss of lead scorching the air around them, no one paid any attention at all to a stray bullet from a lone rifleman in the brushy mouth of a nearby ravine.

Somehow he'd have to keep track of the black-coated bastard until he had a clear shot at him. Not that Usher didn't deserve to die. There was no doubt of that—but only one man really had the right to say how the Danite leader was to have his life rubbed out. Many times before this afternoon, Shad Sweete had vowed he would do his best to take

Usher alive so that one day real soon he could hand him over to Jonah Hook.

Sweete could wing the son of a bitch. Go on and drop him with a good wound if Shad couldn't get close enough to knock him out. With the bastard tied over a horse, Sweete planned on tearing off with the Mormon. Back to the east to find Jonah. Nothing wrong with that plan . . . except as the firing died, Shad realized he wasn't going to get a chance to get anywhere close to Usher, much less be presented with a clear shot. Not the way the tall son of a bitch kept moving, hollering orders, darting in and out among the wagons, through the wounded mules set out on picket pins to graze.

"That's the last of 'em!" a voice cried out across the campsite.

In a situation like this a man couldn't be too careful. He had no way of knowing just how many of Usher's gunmen were in on this ambush. But as quick as they had made work of the teamsters and what guards had stayed behind, Shad supposed there were twenty, maybe as many as two dozen of them.

"Make sure none of them escaped!" Usher bellowed, waving his two shiny pistols about in the air expressively.

"You ain't changed your plans about the bodies, have you, Colonel?"

Shad listened to the big man laugh before he replied, "Of course not, you simpleton. Strip the bodies, every one. Scalp and mutilate each carcass the way I've taught you. It must look like an Indian attack."

"Still don't understand why we don't take credit for taking this shipment, Colonel!" a new voice complained.

"Because once I have what I want from that train—its gold—the Indians who help us hit the train are going to be hunted down as renegades by every lawman and the government too: wanted for butchering these teamsters and the crew aboard that freight climbing toward the pass."

A high, reedy voice cheered, "Where I wish I was right about now, sir!"

"Soon enough," Usher replied, turning to gaze west. "Up there Major Haslam is preparing to make so much fodder of the rest of the escort as I speak."

"We finish up here, Colonel—we going to mount up so we can get in on the attack the major's making on the train?"

"Once everything is done here to my satisfaction, then we'll hitch up the mules and take these wagons up the pass."

One of the wild-eyed pack shouted, "So we can off-load that fortune from them boxcars!"

"Then we gonna burn the goddamned train!" cried another.

Swallowing down his revulsion, frozen with his rage at what he watched, Shad waited through their butchering those white bodies, through the whipping of the mules back into their traces to get them hitched to the high-walled freighters, until the old man watched the last wagon rumble noisily past the mouth of the ravine before he poked his head up and assessed how the land lay.

There wasn't a living thing left in that dusty bowl Usher's butchers were leaving behind. Not a single horse nor mule. Certainly no man was left alive after the crazed mutilation. Each bone-white carcass lay mute against the darkening, muddied ground, each bloodied body spattered by the hammering rain that worked relentlessly to wash the crimson pools into muddy, rippled patches.

Lurching to his feet, the old man set off at a bound over the glistening scrub and pooling wheel ruts, racing for the gate on that last wagon before any of Usher's men turned to discover him. His moccasins soaked and slickened, his old muscles nearly done in from the fire of adrenaline, and with his breath down to nothing more than painful, clawlike seizures that attacked his chest, Sweete reached the tailgate and grabbed hold with his left hand, heaving his Sharps onto the loose canvas cargo cover at the same time he lunged forward, snagging hold of the tailgate with his right hand. Lumbering ungainly behind the jostling, jolting wagon, he clumsily snaked his way onto the lowered tailgate. The clomp of mule hooves, the rattle of iron wheels and the squeak of running gear beneath all those empty boxes, thundering together with all those jubilant voices, were more than enough to cover what sound a solitary man might make in shimmying out of sight under the wagon cover, out of the rain and on this ride up Connors Pass.

In that darkness beneath the oiled canvas his heart seemed to swell in his throat, tongue sticky from want of moisture, his hands clutching that Sharps he might well have to use to bring down Jubilee Usher.

The rocking of the ungainly freight wagon, combined with the rhythmic patter of the rain on the oiled canvas bedcover eventually lulled the old man to dozing as the gunmen rumbled on up the road toward the ambush. It seemed as if he'd been asleep only minutes when the first distant explosion awoke him.

Dynamite. As untrained as his ear was to such a thing, wasn't many men who would have trouble knowing what had caused that rumbling roar as its echo thundered down the slope, its low roll washing on over the wagons Usher was leading toward the pass. By now the rain had slackened off some. If he used the muzzle of the Sharps to lift the canvas just so, Sweete could make out the background rattle of faraway gunfire. Usher's army was having a time of it.

Sounded like the majority of that escort wasn't about to make it easy for the Danites. Shad brooded as he lowered the canvas, jolted out of position, forced to secure himself a new purchase between the two wagon sides, bracing his two legs and one arm as the wagon box careened back and forth atop the running gear.

The hair on the back of his neck bristled. A sense of cold dread spilled like January ice water to the base of his spine.

He heard Injuns. Nothing else like it in all the world. No mistaking those sounds that could curdle a man's blood to gnat-shit: war whoops and the screeching of brownskins. A fella what had lived his whole manhood among the mountains and crossing these plains ought to know the sound of red niggers worked up to a good fighting lather.

Swallowing down his first impulse to fling back the wagon cover fully, Shad struggled to contain the curiosity he realized just might kill him. For the longest time the gunfire continued unabated, drawing closer and closer: on occasions growing in volume and density, later falling off and fading as if withering. Like any fight between white men and Indians, this had the fury of a thunderstorm's journey, swelling or sinking with the rise or ebb of the wind. Then it sounded as if he had been hauled squarely to the middle of the fray.

As the wagons lurched to a halt, nearby voices grew louder—shouts, orders, cries of the wounded—these too taking up the gunfight. Skittish in their traces, the mules jolted forward a few yards after Shad heard the driver leap out of the footwell. The mules jerked, rocked to a stop, then lurched forward a few more feet a second time before clattering to rest. He listened to the weary animals blow with a shuddering jangle of their lead chains. Hoofbeats faded off, then the ongoing gunbattle swallowed up the pounding of many boots across the soggy ground.

When he finally dared raise the canvas shroud the width of one eyeball, not a soul could Sweete see. But up the slope toward the pass, drifting over the top of that deep, glistening black-green of the rain-soaked trees, streaked tattletale against the purplish blue of the bruised sky of a stormy afternoon, there rose the unmistakable oily smudge of a black streamer. On up the track, around a bend in the railbed, is where they must have the engine stopped, where Usher's men jumped the train—having likely blown up some section of the track. Then sent those cursed Indians down on the escort, who were forced to fight back from the boxcars like fish in a barrel.

Sweete flung himself to the ground as another sharp blast erupted. This one wasn't as loud nor did it rattle the ground as the first. Likely just a single stick of dynamite. Not a whole goddamned fistful of it. Usher was the sort who would try anything he could to pry loose those hired guards who were giving his men and the Indians a fit of it. Shad figured the Danite leader would do everything he could short of blowing up those boxcars where the fortune in silver and gold rested—just beyond his reach.

Down the naked slope toward a thick border of brush Shad lumbered, past it into a stand of trees. Another small blast of dynamite shuddered through the forest above him. Out there where the wagons stood on the naked ground at the bottom of the rail line's elevated roadbed, there wasn't a damned thing a man could use for cover. It was clear he'd have to make it from here through the timber and the huge boulders that long ago had tumbled off the ocher and yellow, red and dun-colored ridges where the scrub cedar gave way to the taller pine.

Sweete was rewarded for his hard-fought struggle through the broken rocky ground once he peered over the edge of ridge that gave him a view of the gunfight continuing only some fifty feet below him. Where those Indians came from, or what they were, he had no idea. But in among those damned brownskins stood white men—all of them, red and white, firing a concerted, deadly fire into the boxcars, where fewer and fewer puffs of smoke could be seen. One by one, minute by minute, Usher's men whittled down the powerful armed escort paid to guard that precious shipment never to see the mint at San Francisco.

Then the Danite leader's bulk was in the forefront, shouting something over the gunfire. His murderers and the Indians gradually ceased their fire. Shad watched Usher turn toward the boxcars with a dramatic flourish.

"We don't have to kill you all!" the Mormon said to the men left inside the railcars. "It's not you we've come for."

There couldn't be that many left, and the ones who were still holding on, Shad knew, had to be surrounded by the dead and dying scattered all around them.

"Throw down your weapons—and come out with your hands where we can see them."

"If we do—you'll let us go?" asked a voice from the first car.

His voice was quickly countermanded by another man in the second car. "None of us giving up. You hear that, mister? None of us."

"You'd be smart if you did give up," Usher hollered. "Those who want to save their hides can come out now. We'll let you go your way."

The nervous voice asked, "Got your word on it?"

"You have my solemn vow," the Danite leader replied. "No guns. No horses. You'll just have to return south on foot."

"No one's coming out!" the commander in the second car shrieked.

Shad could read the desperation in the man's voice. Very likely he could be the only one left in those boxcars who realized Usher for the low-down, gut-bucket liar that he was, realized they were all going to die. Just a matter of choice now: take your chances pinned up in the railcars like this, or give up and venture out to be cut down by the attackers.

"This man doesn't speak for all of you, now!" Usher countered.

"You hear me? Them sonsabitches'll kill you if you go out there!"

"I'm coming out!"

"Me too!"

Jubilee Usher stepped backward toward the side of the railbed where most of his gunmen inched forward as the first one of the escort shouldered the heavy, iron-riveted door open, muscling apart a gap big enough for him to step through.

"Lay your weapons down!" Usher ordered.

The guard dropped his carbine, snagged loose his gun belt, and dropped them both onto the railbed below him before leaping to the slickened gravel below. He got to his feet and held his hands up as another handful squirted through the crack in the door one at a time.

From the third car another half dozen emerged as well. Until there were no more than fifteen spread out along the tracks, their hands raised, peering at their enemies—both white and red-skinned. No more protest was heard from the second car as Usher turned and spoke quietly to one of his men, then quickly retreated behind the thick cordon of gunmen.

Once he was ten yards behind them, Usher whirled about to bellow, "Open fire!"

Those who weren't dropped where they stood as the Danites' guns exploded dived for cover beneath the railcars, or dragged themselves behind the bodies of the dead and seriously wounded, struggling to get away from the terror-filled lead hail as Usher waved an arm, signaling the Indians in for the close-quarters kill.

Uncontrollably, Shad's throat constricted, his belly gone sick as sour meat while he watched those Indians swoop down on the dead and dying with the knives and clubs and bloody tomahawks. Smashing, and slashing, cutting and pummeling bone and sinew, blood and flesh to a pulp.

Sweete turned aside, anxious to find a crevice through the rocks that would give him some cover as he crept down to the spot where the Danite leader stood. A pitiful, weak return of gunfire spat from the boxcars as the sun lowered itself behind a darkened, overcast sky, turning the scene even gloomier.

"See? Didn't I tell you?" Usher was heard to ask in his booming voice above the renewed rattle. "They'll figure it was these heathen Pahvants who are responsible for the attack on the train—for stealing this fortune. What with the way we left those bodies down in the valley at the wagon camp . . . just what we'll do to the bodies of those we leave here."

He was out of earshot by then, working his way through the rain-slickened boulders, down through that narrow crevice where he fought for purchase with each footstep in his gummy moccasins. Most places in the rock he had to turn his great bulk sideways to squeeze himself through the opening. And by the time Sweete emerged from the opening in the ridge wall, he found more than two dozen horses, which Usher's gunmen left tied to the cedar and scrub pine while they laid their ambush.

If he played things right, the animals would give him more cover. Some of them shied and whinnied when he suddenly appeared whole from the rocks. Clucking to the nearest ones, Shad tried to sense the wind. With his nose testing the damp breeze, he inched away to his right, downwind of the horses, his back hugging the rocks as the mist thickened. It served to dampen a lot of the sounds from the skirmish—yet still he could hear the muffled cries of the wounded, the screeching blood lust of the Danites and the Indians.

Along with making out the soggy bootsteps of someone drawing near. Shad stopped, clamping his breath in his chest—waiting.

Jubilee Usher himself stepped in among the horses, his gigantic frame moving first this animal, then another aside, as if he were looking them over, searching for one in particular.

Passing the Sharps over to his left hand, Sweete drew the rain-slickened butt of the old Remington from its holster and hammered it back.

"Don't you dare twitch a hair on your ass, you murdering son of a bitch," Shad snarled as he pushed himself away from the rock wall.

Usher froze in his tracks. The horses were instantly restive, anxious around him. Though the Mormon's arms did not come up, Shad realized he had the bastard dead to rights where he stood.

"What . . . what is this?" he asked as he turned to appraise the old mountain man.

Sweete's eyes narrowed with this first real look at the Danite. "Damn, but it's been a long time I been waiting to see what's behind them snake's eyes of your'n."

"Seems you have me at a disadvantage, sir. Do we know one another?"

Jogging the Remington's muzzle, Shad replied, "Raise 'em, Usher. Shove both your hands up where I won't get so nervous about shooting you."

"Just who the hell are you?"

"Someone's been on your trail for a long, long time."

Then he watched Usher smile and take a step forward, a second step as the mist became a light rain. The wind whipped it against their faces. Usher took two more steps until he was barely more than an arm's length away. Sweete held on him steady.

"I aim to have you find a horse what can hold you for a long ride," Shad began to explain. "I'll get one my own self."

"And then what?"

"We're slipping out of here."

"Just like that?"

"Just like that," Sweete answered. "I don't count on having to cut my way out. Just you—only one I want. Now, get yourself a horse . . . that big'un . . . there. You can ride that—"

"Drop your gun!"

The snarling voice hit him like a bolt of electricity, the way bad whiskey troubled his tortured, tired belly anymore. A heartbeat later Shad felt the jab of a gun's muzzle between his shoulder blades. And the disembodied voice repeated its deadly warning.

"Swear I'll drop you where you stand, you don't lose that pistol—the rest of what you're packing too."

"Here, stranger," Usher said as he reached out and took the Remington pistol from Sweete's drenched hand. "Let me help you with that. An old man like yourself shouldn't be carrying all this weight around with you."

Orrin Haslam watched the old man he had the drop on stand there like he was frozen when Usher came up to take his pistol away. Likely he was cursing himself. Which made Haslam chuckle as he rubbed the shotgun's muzzles up and down a few inches of the stranger's spine. Meanwhile Jubilee Usher stuffed the first of the man's pistols behind the buckle of his own gun belt, pulled out the second revolver, then yanked the Sharps from under the old man's left arm.

"Good of you to drop by when you did, Major," Usher said.

"The boys had everything under control," Haslam replied. "I saw you head back here, so I thought I'd come back to have a smoke myself while the Injuns finished with the bodies."

"So you found me and our stranger here."

Orrin nodded. "Yeah—who is he?"

Usher shook his head, staring at the old man. "Don't know."

"You got any idea who the hell he is?" Haslam asked. "Where'd you come from, you son of a bitch?" He shoved his prisoner forward about a foot with a savage ram of the shotgun and chuckled as the man stumbled forward on the slick ground.

"Yes, I'd be interested in knowing that myself," Usher agreed as the man picked himself out of the mud. "You're not from the train. And not from the guard at the teamster camp . . . unless . . ."

While Haslam kept that shotgun in the stranger's back, Usher studied the man up and down carefully, pulling open the flaps to his worn, threadbare canvas coat, checking him for more weapons.

"Now," Usher said with a long sigh as he stepped back from the stranger and the rain came up with every renewed gust of cold wind, "as I asked you before: just who the hell are you?"

Haslam prodded the old man once again, the shotgun's muzzle hard by the stranger's backbone. "The colonel asked you a goddamned question!" he reminded. "This is a double-barreled shotgun, sawed off to fifteen inches. It's gonna make a hole in you big enough for me to shove a skillet through and catch rainwater, you don't answer us, and *now*."

"Major Haslam is a bit on the itchy side, stranger," Usher said with a malevolent smile. "Take that big knife from his belt too."

As Orrin reached in with his left arm, sweeping the big skinning knife from the beaded scabbard, the colonel said, "So as was explained to you— I don't want to lose my patience. Do you work for the mine owners?"

"I'm just a mule whacker."

"Ah. One of the teamsters," Usher hissed. "How convenient. How'd we miss you?"

"Nature called me out of camp."

Usher smiled, his teeth gleaming in the twilight. "How fortuitous for you."

Then the colonel suddenly shoved the second of the stranger's revolvers into the fleshy underside of the old man's chin. Haslam noticed that they were all but both the same height. The stranger might be slighter, but not by much. Their prisoner was a man who might truly be an equal in physical might to Jubilee Usher.

"Let me put my question this way—so we both understand what I'm dealing with here," Usher said quietly.

Beyond the trees and boulders the firing had ceased. Only the muffled yelping and screeching of the Indians was heard in the distance now. Here the rain pattered against the rocks surrounding the trio, slapping the saddles on the backs of the horses.

Usher leaned his face close to the stranger's. "Tell me why you want me."

"It don't matter, Colonel," Haslam said a moment later after the stranger didn't answer. "Lemme just kill him here. Leave him with the rest—"

"No," Usher interrupted. "I must know why this one wants me. Why *I'm* important to him."

The prisoner surprised Orrin Haslam when he said, "I promised myself I'd find you someday, Jubilee Usher."

That rocked the colonel back on his heels, so he could get a good look up and down the stranger. "No. You don't look like any dirt-grubbing sodbuster to me. Besides—you're too old."

The man snorted. "Too old to be the husband of the woman you stole back to Missouri?"

Haslam saw how that stung the colonel. Orrin swallowed hard, his finger itching on the trigger as his blood thumped in his ears like thunder, figuring Usher was going to kill this old man and he'd be robbed of the pleasure of watching the stranger get cut in half with the shotgun.

Finally Usher asked, "So you're telling me . . . you were her husband years ago?"

The prisoner shook his head. "No. But I come to help him find you."

The colonel's eyes shifted left and right. "He's with you?"

"No," the stranger answered firmly. "Not just yet. But—he'll be along soon enough."

With a growing smile Usher replied, "Yes, Major—we're going to keep this one alive. Do not hurt—"

"Shit, Colonel!"

"Don't give me any trouble on this, Major."

"Yessir," Orrin replied, disappointed. "But what the hell use is this'un to you anyway?"

"Just more bait, don't you see?" Usher replied as he drew the pistol away from the stranger's chin, swung it back in an arching blur, then savagely brought the barrel down alongside the old man's temple.

Orrin watched the stranger's knees buckle, give way, and collapse, the side of his head opened up in an oozing wound that the rain splattered as the old man crumpled to the mud beneath a horse's hooves.

"Yes," the colonel repeated. "He'll be all the more bait when that heathen Gentile sodbuster from Missouri comes calling."

40

WHISKEY, NOW MORE than anything, would stoke the fire within. Whiskey to warm him, keep him from freezing.

Across the last few hours of their agonizing ride to reach this Nevada mining town Jonah had brooded if he shouldn't just stop and make camp. Instead he had pushed on—driving himself and the other two, driving their animals. Just as Jeremiah always complained: Jonah was always hammering at things—shoving, lunging, heaving at things without letup. Such was about the only sort of talk Jonah found he couldn't cotton to from his son.

Hook let such talk pass without comment because—no two ways about it—Jonah figured it likely was true.

Now, with the black of the sky being squeezed down to an inky ooze between night's cold fingers all around them, it made a man hanker for changing his ways—as if Jonah Hook ever could. He sat there in the cold out front of the place, hungering to wrap his insides around some cheap, potent whiskey, figuring he was what he always had been . . . and doubted he could ever be anything else.

Sliding wearily down from the saddle at long last into the frozen slush of the rutted street passing before the California Lodging House, Hook doubted he would ever again be a farmer. Not with all that he had scratching round down in his craw. Sure, he could get her back, take her home to Missouri like he planned a hundred thousand times all these

363

winters wasted fighting Yankees and dying slow in a blue-belly prison, summers wasted fighting Injuns and dying slow tracking down Mormons. Didn't seem odd to Jonah that he doubted now, doubted most everything, doubted mostly if he could ever make a go of farming like they'd done before, in those days rich with their youth.

He sighed, his fingers aching with cold inside his leather gloves as he tied off the horse, then one of the pack animals beside it at the gray, weathered rail. Too damned much took from him over all this time. Simply impossible, he had decided, not possible that none of it would ever be returned. The years, those miles . . . and the son he lost down to Texas.

The woman too—possibly the very same fair-haired woman some folks back to Utah was saying they'd seen with Jubilee Usher's outfit just this past summer. A person had to look quick, one older woman told Jonah—quick as light in a mirror and you'd catch a sight of that fair-haired woman. Jonah figured he could trust what the old gal told him: she ran a rooming house, so kept her eye on such things in her little corner of the world. Besides, she claimed she'd caught sight of the woman more than once.

"You was close enough to see her eyes?" Jonah had asked.

The old woman leaned back to gaze at him like she thought him crazy. "Heavens no! Not a soul ever got that close to Usher's camp before he pulled out with every one of them gun-toting, high-strung throat-cutters of his."

If someone had only seen the eyes—Jonah brooded ever since—seen that light in the fair-haired woman's eyes. Then he'd know for sure.

No matter if the old woman hadn't seen the eyes, maybe he could trust her word—if for no other reason than she wasn't Mormon, wasn't one of them.

"If you can't believe it was Ma—just how many women do you figure Usher's packing along?" Jeremiah had asked him as they cleared the last outbuildings of that small Utah town called Gunlock.

"Might be her, son."

"Damn right it's her," Jeremiah had taken to growling. "Damn right that son of a bitch got my ma with him."

There were times like that when even his own son looked at him like he thought Jonah wasn't playing with a full hand. That was all right—no man who'd never rode the trail Jonah Hook had taken these last nine-some years would ever have call to judge him. What some called sane was just quiet, safe living. And what most called crazy—why, that was just having the vengeance to go after what was yours to begin with.

After all that was took from him. Never again to have most of it back. No matter how it come out when he finally got his hands around Jubilee Usher's throat, most of it was still gone for good.

Slowly he eased his saddleman's hips onto the muddy boardwalk in front of the saloon. Jonah's bones ached with the cold of winter coming to this high land. But nowhere near like the pit of him ached for all that could never be replaced. Never be took back, never would belong to him again— no matter what he did to Usher to try quenching the fires of his own rage.

Two Sleep grabbed hold of Jonah's elbow, held him there on the muddy street as Hook was about to push through the isinglass front doors into the watering hole.

"They let Indian drink?" the Shoshone asked, his dark eyes shiny with a soulful thirst.

Hook peered through the door he had open, regarding the smoky interior. With his free arm he waved up the street at the long cordon of other saloons in this part of the mining town and answered, " 'Pears to me this'll be one of the few places gonna let a flea-bit blanket Injun like you drink some whiskey. You telling me you've got a powerful thirst like me after all, redskin?"

The warrior wiped a worn, greasy glove across his wind-chapped lips, his iron-flint eyes glancing in at the doorway, then off to one of the two front windows where murky lamplight spilled onto the boardwalk, as faded a yellow as wolf-piss on old snow. "Injun thirsty."

All three of them turned at the shuffle, the noisy clatter of human bodies, the foreign tongue. Down the walk hurried a half-dozen hunched forms, their forearms clutched at their middles, their shoulders rounded against the cold wind, heads bowed politely as they passed the trio, each a'sway with a long braided pigtail. The first slipped past Jonah through the saloon's open door, held it for the rest as all hurried in.

Jeremiah's eyes narrowed. "W-what was they, Pa?"

"Don't know for sure, seeing how I've never laid my eyes on one myself," Jonah explained. "But they looked like what folks told me was Chinee."

"Chinee?"

"That's Chinamen. From someplace long, far away." He looked at Two Sleep, found the Shoshone's eyes following the last of the Chinamen into the watering hole. "I tell you I spoke the truth, Injun: they serve whiskey to those Chinamen, they sure as hell gonna sell whiskey to the flea-bit likes of you, Injun. C'mon, Jeremiah.''

Inside those clapboard walls the place stank of bodies retreating from the cold of the wind, a festering humanity thrown together of this early winter night. No place better for a man to go with what he had left of waking hours but inside. Steaming clothes, unwashed bodies, the damp, sodden air, as crusted mud and frozen slush slowly melted underfoot, puddling on the floor. Very few in that crowded room turned to regard the trio of newcomers. Most sat their chairs if they had one, while some squatted against the walls where they drank in silence, still others shoveled food from tin plates and trenchers with their belt knives or grimy fingers. Two dozen or more leaned elbow-to-elbow down the long bar scarred and nicked with the path of bullets, patrons who kept two bartenders on the move with bottles and glasses, forever mopping up with their dingy rags.

Always find out what's above you, he'd learned years before.

So Jonah's eyes were drawn to his left on instinct, to the stairs climbing to the second-floor landing that stretched across that side of the drinking house. A long banister ran past a row of narrow doors.

He swallowed hard and willfully tore his eyes away, forcing himself to think on nothing beyond the burn of cheap whiskey. He would try again tonight to drown the savage woman-hunger in him with the coarsest corn liquor he could force down his gullet. If he was lucky, he might damn well pass out—and by the time he came to again . . . the woman-hunger would pass.

At the bar he paid for a bottle, wrapped one hand around its long neck, and fingered up the three glasses the barman slid toward him. Nary a complaint voiced about the two with Jonah: the old Indian, and the young one who looked every inch one. When a few feet of bar opened up down by the wall, Hook led the others into the breach, where he plopped everything down and yanked free the cork. Jonah felt warmer just pouring that amber liquid into the three greasy glasses.

"To the end of this trail," Jonah said as he held up his brimming glass to the other two.

They clinked. He watched Jeremiah's face register the torment of cheap drink as the youngster poured the corn liquor past his lips. Jonah put his own glass to his lips and tossed it back just as he caught sight of some new movement from the corner of his eye. Setting the glass on the bar to pour himself another, relishing the burn the liquor made in his belly, Hook watched the barrel-chested man step out the door onto the landing, pulling suspenders over his shoulders. For a moment the man leaned against the railing, regarding the scene below him.

Jonah followed the man's eyes as they came to rest on the far corner of the room. There in the shadowy darkness at a large table, surrounded by empty chairs, sat a lone Chinaman. Damn, but this town seemed to have its share of them.

The two of them, Chinaman and the barrel-chested cock rooster, looked one another over, until the Chinaman went back to staring at the glass he cradled between his hands, gazing at the bottle beside them. Above the pungent tobacco haze and a gauzy layer of smoke leaking from the woodstoves, the big man started down the stairs, crossed the floor, then edged among those at the bar until he stood beside Hook.

How he wished it was Usher, Jonah thought as he turned back to his glass, refilling it. Just the way Hook had come to regard about every white man he ran across in the last few years. Especially here in this Nevada town—where he was told they might just run onto word of the Mormon raider.

This one beside Jonah was strong as an ox, but not near tall enough. Besides, this man had long, curly, unkempt hair. Usher—Hook had learned years before from Riley Fordham—was nearly bald on top.

"You're new to these parts," the stranger said without so much as looking at Jonah while he took hold of the neck of a new bottle slid before him by a bartender. "The three of you."

Hook glanced up briefly, at the side of the big man's face, then turned away to throw back the fiery whiskey so that it struck his throat with severe intensity. "We're new."

Now he felt the man's eyes on him, sensed them move on to Jeremiah and eventually the Indian.

"Passing through? Or you looking for work?"

Then he looked the stranger's face over. And answered, "Never done any mine work. Don't plan on staying long, besides. Moving through. Looking for someone is the only thing brought me here."

"Don't say," he replied, bringing the bottle to his lips and drinking long from it, noisy in his guzzling.

Jonah measured the man's eyes, the impassive steel in the man's face, looking for something there that might let Hook know he could ask. Then he just went on ahead, like taking that last and hardest step off the limestone cliff above the deep spring's pool near the home where he grew up in the shadow of Big Cobbler Mountain. The pool where boys came of age swimming naked and starting to talk about girls. Jonah felt about as naked now—stripped near bare of just about everything. Nothing to lose.

"One I'm looking for's got a band of riders with him. Likely some wagons and at least one old army ambulance along. Not hard to miss. Heard he'd come this way. You hear tell of that bunch in this part of the country?"

The stranger licked a transparent droplet of whiskey from his lower lip before answering, a gleam come to his eye. "Fellas like that—them wagons and all—true enough, they wouldn't be hard to miss."

"No, they wouldn't . . . if that bunch passed through here."

"You said you followed 'em here?"

Jonah nodded. "Any sign of 'em? Maybe you heard tell of something?"

With a shrug he put the bottle to his mouth and drank. Hook watched the stranger's throat work the whiskey down in long, slow draughts. He was thirsty, Jonah thought, waiting for his answer. Likely worked up that kind of deep thirst upstairs straddling one of them fat and fleshy white-skinned crib girls. Jonah hadn't been with a white woman in . . . hell, he couldn't remember how long—

When the stranger interrupted. "This fella you're looking for— what's he to you? What brings you to look him up?"

"Usher's his name. A murdering thief," Jonah replied, turning sideways at the bar, gingerly pulling back the flaps of his mackinaw to expose the two hog-leg holsters, their butt-front .44's like a pair of worn brown hooves.

The stranger glanced down, then back into Hook's eyes with an even brighter gleam bordering on approval. "Score to settle with this Jubilee Usher, you say?"

Resting his left hand on a pistol grip, Jonah said, "Didn't say his first name—how you know him?"

"Easy, friend," the stranger replied, his face drained and sheepish. And he shrugged. "Near everyone knows that bunch you said you tracked all the way here. Ain't no mystery to the one leads 'em either. Every man knows who Jubilee Usher is."

Jeremiah suddenly leaned in to ask, almost grabbing for the front of the man's dirty, tobacco-stained shirt. "And where we can find him?"

With a genial bob of his head, the stranger answered, "Out of town. Southwest along the hills. They're all camped there—been for some time now."

"Easy to find?"

"Pretty hard to hide that many riders, their horses—camp that size." His eyes lost some of their sheen as he leaned in close to Jonah as if to confide. "You ain't told me why you want this Jubilee Usher, stranger."

"He took something of mine."

"You lost money at cards?"

Wagging his head, Jonah replied, "Never was one to gamble. No— Usher's got something what's still mine."

"You ain't no lawman, I can figure. Maybe a bounty hunter from somewhere—this Jubilee Usher got a price on his head, that what brought you on a long ride?"

"No. Ain't no bounty hunter. This here's something real personal."

The big smile returned to the stranger's face. He looked over at the far table in the shadows where the lone Chinaman sat as he said, "If it's something all that personal, I can show you where Usher's camp is, you want me to."

Jonah drained his glass again, emptying it before he poured himself another. "S'pose that'd be right neighborly of you. But why don't you tell me what it's to you—what corner you got on helping us?"

"You're lucky tonight, stranger," the big man replied, eyes dancing with devilish delight. "You just happened to bump into the right fella, I suppose. That tall bastard owes me too. I'm the sort plays at cards. Usher's took a lot of gold off me that I'd like to get back some way if I can."

"You show us where this camp is," Jonah said, easing his hand off the pistol's grip, "you can have all of him that's left over after I get done."

"I'll show you," the stranger replied. "You fixing to go tonight?"

Jonah considered on it, his belly twisting like an oiled rope into greasy knots. Better not to let this one out of his sight. Not make any delay to it. Now that he was but a handful of miles from her. So damned close to Usher.

"We're gonna eat first. Finish our whiskey too," Hook replied. "After midnight—you'll find us here, ready to ride out there with you."

"Good," and he nodded. "We can be in position come first light." Rubbing his nose, the stranger turned to glance at the lone Chinaman in the corner, then turned again to gaze upstairs.

Jonah thought to ask, "They got whores up there?"

He turned slowly around to face Hook. "Yeah," and he smiled. "Good ones too. Feeling like you wanna thump one?"

The tug in his groin made him purse his lips, remembering the feel of a woman's moistness clasped around him so tight he was sure she never would let him go. Then Jonah wagged his head. "No. It's a woman I'm looking for . . . but not their kind what's upstairs. One woman only. I hear she's with Usher."

The man's eyebrows raised like a yank on a window sash, a gleam returned to those eyes again. "That woman with the hair like corn-straw?"

Hook appraised him eagerly. "You seen her your own self?"

"Damn right I have. What's she to you?"

"The one I lost long . . . long time ago."

With a low whistle the stranger said, "By God, you do have a score to settle with Usher, don't you, mister?"

"You come get us by midnight, like we planned. And tomorrow before sunup, I plan on getting into that camp to finish some old business. How many you figure Usher got with him out there?"

Smiling broadly, the stranger looked over Hook's shoulder to Jeremiah and the Indian. "Not more'n the four of us can handle."

"You sound certain of that."

"We hit 'em afore they're out of their blankets—you snatch back that woman . . . even things up with Usher . . . and in the meanwhiles, I can clean him out. We both ride away happy men. Right?"

Jonah brought up his glass. "Here's to making ourselves happy men." He held out his right hand. "My name's Hook. Jonah Hook. Didn't catch your'n."

The stranger clasped Hook's securely, pumping it with eager, happy satisfaction. "Jonah Hook, you say? Well by doggy—I'm sure glad to meet you, Jonah Hook. Mine's Orrin Haslam. Damn—but I'm looking forward to riding into Jubilee Usher's camp with you!"

She listened to the sounds of them sleeping, the gentle rise and fall of their breathing in the cold darkness of the small tent where Usher had provided a bed for the boys. Against the far wall were the two chests where she kept their clothes, their toys. The youngsters didn't have much else.

No matter, because it was still more than either one of Gritta's sons had had for many, many years.

Jubilee Usher had seen to it that the boys were returned to her a few months back. An uncomfortable, strained reunion that had been. Nothing unusual about that—what with all the time they had been apart.

After that it had taken weeks for the boys to warm up to their mother again, to get to where they would let Gritta hold them against her, to let her read them stories each night before they drifted off to sleep wrapped up in their bed in the tent always pitched right beside the one where she slept with Usher. Most every night now she came here, slipping through the tent flaps to peer into the darkness—not really seeing them among the shapeless tumble of blankets and comforter, more so hearing them as they slept.

Gritta found herself believing more and more every day, counting on it more and more every night.

Usher's heart must be softening—to return her sons to her. Maybe he really did love her as much as he had professed for so, so long. His heart softening after he had taken their babe from her arms and burned it, after she had paid him back by burning herself—Usher relented and he returned the boys to her. Boys every bit as young as they had been when Usher first rode into their valley.

Dim, watery memories flooded her teary eyes—images of a cabin and the fields beyond where a man plodded behind the team of mules. Two young boys moved behind the man. Into the long rows of steaming earth they dropped seed from the burlap sacks strung over their shoulders.

Jeremiah and Ezekiel.

It had taken a long time for her to remember their names. To remember their faces. Tow-headed, wide and frightened eyes—Usher presented them to Gritta. Saying it was his wedding present to her—to give the boys back because he loved her so.

How she so enjoyed stroking their hair as she held them against her, laying their heads there in her lap while she told them stories of long ago, or softly sang them lullabies until their breathing became as rhythmic as it was here in the darkness now.

Rarely did she let the boys out of her sight. Gritta had learned her lesson long ago. They had been taken from her by someone Usher said he had caught up to, said he reclaimed the boys in a bloody fight and brought the pair back to her. She wouldn't let them out of her sight again. Not even when Usher took her to town for some shopping. She even refused to leave them at night when Usher wanted to take her in to town where they would glide across the floor of one of the town's dance halls, or to see a traveling troupe of entertainers from San Francisco visiting the Brown Opera House. She simply would not go without the boys—and Usher relented. George kept them with him in the ambulance, where they slept on a pallet of blankets while she danced. Usher loved her and understood how much the children meant to her.

371

No matter how confused she was, how afraid the boys were—Gritta loved them totally. So she tried to ignore the doubts, the voices, the tangled snarl of memories of time and place and even the distinct, individual smells of her children as they had huddled close to her in those days before they suddenly disappeared. Like a torn hank of a spider's web clinging to an upper corner of that valley cabin, some small shred of her sanity clung tenaciously to her every waking moment.

It made her remember how she had been as fearful of Usher as the boys had been of her at first. She couldn't blame them.

After George saw her back to Usher's tent, Gritta knelt before her trunk, intent on finding something new for the boys to play with come morning. She found nothing there, so bent over to pull back the top to one of Usher's trunks. In the tray she found the long loops of strange necklaces he had worn without fail so many years before. Gently she raised them into the soft, muted lamplight—grisly scapulars of shrunken Apache ears and bony fingers . . . shriveled, blackened flesh . . . mummified scalp locks and penises . . . shrunken tongues and women's breasts. Dried, stiffened— amulets marking a long chapter of her own frightening life with Usher.

She shuddered, at that moment coming to realize that each of these revolting ornaments was not obscene in and of itself. Instead they all served as grotesque reminders of how God had doomed her to live out her days with Jubilee Usher: Satan's evil seed.

Gritta ran her fingers over the shriveled, rawhide-tough skin of a scalp, its long black hair spilling from the domed cap of flesh. How powerful this amulet of horror must be to Usher, she thought: how he revered these sacred ornaments the way ministers and preachers and men of God worshiped their religious icons. Many were the times she had watched him take these objects from their trunk, handling them as if they were holy relics, donning each one and them all with no small ceremony on those special occasions.

A shrunken tongue—slashed at the root from its victim's throat by Usher—caused Gritta to brush her own tongue back and forth against her upper teeth. Simply to feel its presence in her mouth, to reassure her. She hadn't spoken for so long . . . until she began to coo and sing, call out and talk, to the two boys.

For so very long there simply had been nothing worth saying at all— especially to Usher—until he rescued the boys and returned them to her. As if a great slice of her own life were brought back from the brink of the grave, as if some small wedge of her existence had been miraculously resuscitated: at long last Gritta spoke. But spoke only to her children.

"Jeremiah and Zeke," she whispered now. To say only their names, as if in a prayer of thanksgiving.

Otherwise she remained as mute as her living death would make a corpse consigned to a cold, dark grave for all time.

"Jeremiah and Zeke . . . and . . ."

Tears came. Gritta could not remember her daughter's name. Knew she had a daughter. Then, squeezing down on her memories, not sure if she really had a daughter. Everything so watery anymore, so fluid, her sense of real and myth, tangible and mist all leaking from her mind like a thin soup from a crack in her favorite blue crock.

No matter, she decided with great certainty. She had her boys. No matter that God Himself had decided the price she had to pay for getting them back was living out the rest of her years with Michael, the Fallen Angel, Lord of the Netherworld.

Long ago Gritta had discovered that here on the frontier as hard men push relentlessly against the savage wildness—the holy and the profane existed in a delicate balance.

At times God's almighty and holy hand would seize the day.

But more times than not here in her own wilderness, Satan's brutal, bloody paw brought down the night.

At the end of every day, she knew, there would always come the night.

41

"F OLKS LIVE IN these parts call the place *Golgotha*," Haslam whispered to Jonah.

Hook nodded. He'd heard the word before. Couldn't remember where. But it had been a long, damned time ago.

"See there," Haslam explained in a hush, pointing into the inky, predawn darkness at the canyon's gray wall rising above the dirty strings of canvas tents stretched out below the coming roll of the daylight. "Can you make out them eye sockets, the nose hole, and that big cave where the mouth would be on a skeleton's head?"

"I can see it, Pa," Jeremiah replied. "Rock wall looks just like a skull."

Haslam nodded eagerly, grinning toothily in the ashy light. "The boy's got it, by God. That's just what the place means in the Bible."

"Bible?" Jonah asked, his stomach flopping as he turned to look at Haslam, alarm rising like gorge at the back of his throat.

"Golgotha," Haslam repeated the word. "Means 'place of the skulls.' Where the Jews crucified Jesus on the cross."

Jonah wagged his head. "My wife was the one always read the Bible," he replied in a hush, then glanced past Haslam at the Shoshone, who was studying the abrupt fall of the land, the dark clots of timber that dotted the creek bottom between them and Usher's camp.

"You look careful enough when the light comes up—you'll see Usher's got him his own crucifying going on over there," Haslam explained, pointing an arm across the distance. "There by the cave what's the skull's big, grinning mouth. Usher's done it just like they nailed up Jesus, by God."

Jonah squinted, straining his eyes in the darkness to make out some faint object swimming in the distant half light at the side of the cave entrance. "What that black-hearted bastard's doing to one of his own don't mean a thing to me. I'm only here to claim what's been took from me."

Like a carnival barker eager to gather and secure an audience, Haslam rubbed his gloves together. "Lookee careful, fellas—and you'll see just what a bloody bastard that Usher is. For sure, for sure."

"You gonna come in there with us? That's the only thing I want to know," Hook growled as he whirled on Haslam.

"This ain't none of my affair," the man replied, holding his hands up in a helpless gesture of futility. "Me? I got a warm Chinee whore back there in town waiting for me . . . and some hot breakfast too. This here's your business, boys. But—I brung you here, and that bastard owes me gambling's dues, so I'll just wait back yonder with the horses till your business with Usher is over and then I'll come get what money's mine. That is . . . if that sets all right by you, Jonah Hook."

Hook nodded once, turning back to regard the entrance to the cave again, looking over the three irregular columns of tents, a dim glow radiating in waves from all those untended fire pits. "Sets by me. G'won back to the horses now. Just wait there till we're done. Then you have what you come for."

"My money," Haslam answered. "I want all my money." And the man shuddered. "Damn, but I seen Usher put a few men up on a cross like that'un over yonder by the cave. Hell of a way to die, that is."

Jonah didn't look at Haslam as the man talked on, as if he refused to slide back down from the lip of the ridge where the four of them overlooked Jubilee Usher's camp. So damned close now—it didn't matter, nothing much else mattered now. The adrenaline surging through his veins was like liquid fire, igniting Hook with a passion he hadn't sensed in years. In its place there had been only doubt, and fear. Lots of both in all those seasons chasing down the wind. Doubt, and more than his share of cold, gut-crimping fear.

"How many, Two Sleep?" Jonah asked as he looked over Haslam's shoulder.

"Three," the Shoshone answered, holding up both hands.

That meant at least thirty.

"Shit. They ain't no more'n fifteen down there now," Haslam quickly asserted.

"How you know?" Hook asked.

"Word says Usher's sent some of 'em off for something no good."

"Sure of that?" Jeremiah asked.

He looked over at the younger Hook. "Sure as I'm sitting with the three of you. That ain't bad odds—you come down on them sudden like you're planning—now, is it?"

"What's on round the far end of that ridge over there, down beyond where the cave is?" Jonah asked, for the first time noticing a wispy trail of smoke rising from the distant end of the bluff. It could be smoke from cook fires.

"Nothing," Haslam answered with a shrug.

Jonah's gut itched. "Two Sleep—you go find out what's over there before we go in shooting."

Haslam twisted suddenly, grabbing the Shoshone's arm while his eyes flared at Hook. "You gonna wait too long and your surprise gonna go up in smoke," he warned.

Shrugging off Haslam's admonition, Jonah nodded to the Indian and said, "G'won, Two Sleep. I wanna know who the hell's camped other side of that draw."

Jonah watched the Shoshone slip off into the darkness, then looked back at Haslam's face, his brow wrinkling as he gave orders to his son. "Jeremiah, off down to your left is a coulee I want you work your way down. Careful as a Comanch'. Where the ground starts to rise again, there by that far line of tents—you hang back in the brush. The shooting starts, you take everything gets flushed out."

"Just like them horse thieves back to the Nations."

Hook nodded. "That's right. Just like the horse thieves."

"Right, Pa."

Jeremiah inched back about a foot, stopping suddenly. He pointed. "Pa! Look there."

Jonah stared across the rugged floor of the ravine, trying to make out some movement. Two small figures had emerged from the flaps of a tent pitched near the cave's mouth. Together they edged over to some brush and with some watchful caution stood there in the coming light, watering the bushes.

"Just a couple of boys, Jeremiah. All you got to worry about is watch out for 'em when the shooting starts. Don't wanna kill no young'uns."

Jeremiah looked hard at his father. Then nodded. "All right. I'll do my best. Still . . ." And while his voice faded in the chill of that morning, he did not move. Instead he rubbed the barrel of his pistol against his lips as he studied the far side of the ravine.

After a long moment passed, another figure emerged from the tent nearest the mouth of the cave. This one emerged in a swirl of cloth. A dress. In the pale light of coming morn, her hair as luminous and fair as corn silk.

Jonah's mouth went dry.

He watched the two youngsters turn when the woman waved them over to her. She clutched them to her as she turned back toward that skeletal face, her arms around their shoulders, all three trudging up the slope toward the cave, past the foot of the crude cross, where Jonah at last made out the naked body of a man in the light that ballooned like a bubble rising beneath clear water.

For an instant he glanced off to the east. Enough light to make their play and still possibly get away in the sudden confusion, escaping into what remained of the predawn darkness. Simply to get her out of that cave and onto the back of one of the horses down there in that camp. They'd sort things out later.

In the hush of that dawn Hook said softly, "Jeremiah, your mama's still alive."

The young man nodded. "We gonna get her now, Pa?"

"We gonna do that, son," he replied, flicking a look at a wide-eyed Haslam. "Or we don't leave without her. Now g'won—get on down there like I tolt you."

Jonah watched his son swallow hard as he pushed back past Haslam, like Jeremiah was having trouble keeping down his cold breakfast wolfed in the darkness better than an hour ago back along the trail where Haslam led them up to this low ridge. Hook waited for his son to scoot back down from the top of the bluff, disappearing into the wide, dark maw of the coulee.

Pulling one of the pistols from its holster, Hook rolled the cylinder to check each chamber. He stuffed it back into the holster, pulled the other revolver, and made certain it was fully loaded. Then he pointed the weapon generally in Haslam's direction. Something he could not deny ran cold in the marrow of him, something earned of all the years on this trail come to a sudden end here above the ridge—something now warning Jonah that he did not want this stranger at his back.

"Didn't you tell me you was going down yonder to wait with the horses?"

Haslam looked down at the muzzle of Hook's pistol. "Yeah. I did say that."

"Better scat," Jonah suggested, waving his pistol down the slope in the direction he wanted the man to take. "I don't figure it's going to be all that safe here with me much longer."

For a moment he did not move. Then Haslam smiled with those teeth the color of pin acorns, starting to inch backward as he again glanced down at the hole in the muzzle of Hook's revolver. He nodded. "I gotta 'gree with you, Jonah Hook. Looks of things now—soon enough it ain't gonna be safe with you here at all."

The sun first brushed with warmth the top of his head where it hung, a bearded chin collapsed against his bloody chest as he grasped at fevered moments of sleep in the cold like a man would clutch at limbs and vines that snapped, failing to prevent him from tumbling into a bottomless cavern.

Tortured, every inch of him. Stripped naked for days now. Left to hang on this crude cross each night the sun went down.

Warm.

Shad sensed the sunbeam's caress on his bare skull. That bare bone where Jubilee Usher had scalped him days ago. A man didn't have to die losing his topknot. Winters without end trapping the mountains had taught him that much. With a glimmer of some inner fire, Sweete recalled ol' Scratch. How his friend had survived his scalping to one day take his honey-sweet revenge on the red nigger what stole his hair.

With an agonizing cry from the thick bands of muscle strapped along each side of his neck, Sweete raised his head slowly, so very slowly, to face the coming of the sun as it appeared at the bare ridgetop. Felt it instantly on what was left of the flesh on his forehead, on his blood-crusted eyelids where the insects came to cluster and crawl in the heat of the day, sensed the very rapture of the sun's warmth across his swollen cheeks and the broken nose.

Painfully, he parted his puffy and cracked lips, silently mouthing the words to the ancient Shahiyena morning prayer. Waiting in exaltation for the great life-giver's warm blessing to work its way down his neck, like a healing balm pouring over the gaping, oozing wounds on his chest and across his belly where Usher had burned him with fire pokers, where the Mormon had operated with a sawbone's precision to peel back lengths of skin the way the Comanche could.

He nearly choked on the dryness in his throat, trying to laugh at his own stupidity. Should never have come down south, he scolded himself. Down here to Ute, or Apach' country . . . down this far into the belly of hell itself.

But it was here he'd found the woman. He'd seen her, most every day. She didn't know who the hell he was—didn't have no idea he was her husband's friend. The woman had no way of knowing what Jonah meant to Shad neither. Couldn't know how Shad ached for what had been took from Jonah Hook. His boys gone.

That proved to be a pain worse than anything Jubilee Usher had come up with in his exquisite torture, no matter what the Mormon could devise to make Shad slowly bleed a little more every day as he hung from the huge spikes, nailed and lashed to this cottonwood cross raised near the mouth of the cave where the sun arrived each morning to warm his cold, crusted, riven skin for what he knew must be just one more sunrise. Knowing what Usher had done to Hook had to hurt far more than any physical agony Sweete had to endure.

Children. What sweet joy little ones brought to a man's life.

Still, the hurt Usher had visited upon Hook might be matched only by the emotionally gnawing agony Shad suffered again this sunrise—once more realizing he would never see his own grandchildren. Never to cradle them in his big hands. Never could he whirl them round and round and round in his arms as together they danced before the sun—the great life-giver that returned without fail each morning of his torture to gift him with one more day. Another sunrise come after a long night of agony, brooding on what pain Jonah must be feeling: simply because Hook did not know what Shad knew.

She was alive!

Grandfather! his fevered mind cried out in jubilation. *Jonah's woman is alive!*

How he'd tried to call out to her, but couldn't make his tongue work. Nothing more than guttural grunts as his battered lips flapped painfully. Knowing no one would ever make any sense out of what he mumbled around the root of his tongue—all that Usher had left him days ago. Sweete again recalled how he had refused to give the Mormon any satisfaction when Usher pinned his head back, shoving a peeled cottonwood stake between Shad's teeth to force open his mouth before ramming a sharp sliver of a willow branch through the end of the tongue, brutally yanking its length from between the old man's swollen, cracked lips. When the Mormon began slowly, slice by slice, to sever it from Sweete's throat.

There arose that cold ache deep in his marrow that he could not remember her name. After all those nights Jonah had talked so endlessly of her, told of their farm and children, spoke time and again of all their dreams together, admitted how warm she was of a winter night beneath the layers of blankets beside him . . . and now Shad could not remember her name. Able only to remember Shell Woman. Toote. Able only to conjure memories of her face, the feel of her breast in his hand, how it tasted in his mouth—feeling again the tangible, cold, cast-iron pain of watching her die.

He couldn't tell Jonah's woman he was there to rescue her. Couldn't tell her she would have to save herself now—that he was good as dead nailed up here. Some Injun bands always was good at torturing a captive . . . but this Mormon wouldn't have to stand in no Comanche buck's shadow.

The sun reached his upper legs where Usher had run the sharpest of knife blades down the length of both thighs, opening up the flesh, delicately laying back the layers of skin to expose the purple muscle the way the Shahiyena marked their enemy dead. Shad fought to keep those muscles from giving way on him, forced to stand against the pain of the holes riven in both feet where Usher's men had driven a huge iron spike through one instep held over the other, driven deeper still with that sledge hammer to bury itself in the soft cottonwood platform anchored high on Usher's crude cross.

Sweete fought down another wave of nausea. Nothing in his belly any longer. Not even bile. His body ready to die, near all his body closing down.

But not his will. Not Shad Sweete, by damned! He wanted Usher to be standing before him when he finally closed his eyes—wanted to see the look on Usher's face when Shad won.

It hurt to remember that the fair-haired woman didn't look at him much anymore. And when she had, it was with pity in her eyes, with shame for his nakedness, shame at his torture. No, she didn't look at him at all anymore. But the two boys did—wonder in their eyes.

Yes! Look at me, you pups! See what a man is made of that he can hold on to life even after all that's been took from him!

Look at me, Usher! his mind cried out. You haven't won! Jonah Hook is coming for you!

The ache of missing Shell Woman was like a crude file drawn across cold cast iron: grating, aching with each rise and fall of the file across the crude, battered surface of his heart.

A weighty ache like the pain of knowing he had failed Jonah. Failed his friend in this last act of love. Here sensing in some way that he too had become bait for Usher, to draw Hook into the trap. Hung here, knowing that Jonah Hook wouldn't be able to refuse this challenge.

He hoped his friend was somehow dead already. So that Usher wouldn't have his ultimate victory. So that the Mormon could not take the last shred of everything from Jonah Hook. To take Jonah Hook's life.

He was aware of voices below him. Through the swollen eyelids he gazed down, finding a group laughing at him, poking burning brands against his leg wounds, along the gaping slash of riven flesh across his belly. They were starting on him all over again this new day. Shad remembered the taste of a first cup of coffee in the morning. How nothing had ever tasted so sweet as savoring the thick, hot liquid brewed over an open fire on the south slope of a hillside overlooking the Bayou Salade, camped there with Scratch and Ol' Bill and Mad Jack and all the rest of them free hivernants.

Nothing had ever tasted so goddamned sweet as that . . . except . . . except for Shell Woman's mouth.

Damn you, Jubilee Usher! Jonah Hook is coming for you . . . you gut-eating digger son of a bitch. Jonah Hook gonna come for you!

Shell Woman, his mind whimpered. I'll be coming . . . be with you soon.

"But you said we wasn't leaving without her!" Jeremiah bellowed in a low rasp.

Jonah gripped his son's arms in a vise, ready to slap him. But he didn't, knowing instinctively the youngster suffered the same agony as he at pulling back. Retreating.

Like Sterling Price's battered barefoot southern farmers had been forced to do at Pea Ridge. Like all those divisions of Confederate infantry had done at Corinth, Mississippi. Leaving him with the dead among the groves of trees shredded by grapeshot.

Two Sleep had returned from scouting the camp at the far end of the ridge, his face etched with the undeniably bitter news: more tents, along with an Indian camp—a few lodges, and many, many brush and blanket wickiups. Could only be a war camp. He had spotted a handful of women come with their men. But mostly warriors who for some reason had thrown in with these Mormons. Camped in and among the rest of Jubilee

Usher's cutthroats. For some goddamned reason—those Injuns had turned renegade.

"We come to get her, Pa!" Jeremiah whimpered, sagging in resignation.

How he hated that look on the boy's face. Knowing what pain he caused Jeremiah, feeling the gorge rise in his own throat as he owned up to retreat.

"Listen to me: I ain't come this far to get ourselves killed before we can get your mama out, son," he explained, shaking Jeremiah's shoulders slightly. Then he pulled his son against him suddenly as Jeremiah turned his face away the moment tears began to spill onto his tanned cheeks. Jonah gave the young man his dignity—not forcing Jeremiah to show his father or Two Sleep his tears.

"What now?" Jeremiah said, backing away when he had composed himself.

"We go back to town—see the law. Maybe it's time we tell 'em the story about your ma and Usher," Jonah said, grasping at straws, his mind turning hope over and over, looking for some reason to believe.

How he wanted Jeremiah to sense some hope, even though Jonah himself had little belief that the sheriff or marshal or any duly constituted authority would rise to do a damned thing against a small army like Jubilee Usher's.

"And if they don't help?"

Jonah stared at the ground, brooding on Jeremiah's question while he listened to the shuffle of hooves of the nearby horses. "Then we come up with something, son. Maybe we go in at night."

"Tonight?"

"I don't know if we got time to set plans."

"Tomorrow night. Tell me we'll get her tomorrow night. Tell me, Pa."

He wanted to give that much to his son. "Yeah, Jeremiah. By tomorrow night."

Turning fully on his father, Jeremiah reached out and grabbed hold of the front of Jonah's coat, saying, "We come get her tomorrow night. Or we don't leave again."

"Yes."

"Say it, Pa!"

"Yes."

He jerked on the front of Jonah's coat. "Say we're gonna come tomorrow night—"

"Tomorrow night . . ." Jonah repeated, nodding slightly as he looked into the welling eyes of his son. "I promise you: we ain't leaving without her."

Hearing Two Sleep's birdcall, Hook turned, finding the Shoshone back at the top of the ridge above them, signaling. He pushed Jeremiah ahead of him and together they reclimbed the wide cracks in the rock, bellying up beside the lone warrior at the top rim.

Ashen-faced as the aging Shoshone could be, Two Sleep pointed down, across the ravine to the cave entrance. "My old friend."

"On the cross?"

The Shoshone nodded.

"Friend?" Hook swiped the blur of tears from his eyes and blinked them several times, fighting to focus on the naked form as the sun came up, the bubbling light pushing the shadows down heartbeat by heartbeat by moment, shadows retreating inch by inch down the tall form of the old man.

Suddenly—Jonah swallowed hard. Recognizing. "N-never thought we'd see him again."

For both of them Shad was an old friend, Two Sleep's memories harking back to the days of Bridger come among the Shoshone. Back to the days Jonah first came to the west to keep the talking wire up, keep the freight roads open—to try holding back the wild tribes of the plains.

At the very same time Jubilee Usher was ripping Jonah Hook's family from their farm back to Missouri, tearing Jonah Hook's life asunder.

He shook his head, wrapped in webs of disbelief. It hurt unbelievably—like his head had never hurt before. To realize he now had more than Gritta to rescue from the Danites. The old man too.

Shad Sweete and the old Injun were undeniably the best friends a man could ever deserve. Both had taken up Jonah Hook's quest as their own—both had willingly accepted the possibility of sudden death implicit in that quest. Yet neither one had ever asked anything in return but to ride along and help a friend put his family back together again.

Perhaps because—only in that way—both would find a healing forgiveness for themselves. Forgiveness for what each of them had failed to do in their own lives, failed to do in the bosom of their own families.

Jonah licked his dry lips, his mouth parched. He hungered for a powerful, numbing drink in the worst way.

The odds against them were all but insurmountable. Yet between now and tomorrow night he vowed he'd come up with something. If he didn't—at the very least Hook swore he wasn't leaving this ground a second time.

"Jonah Hook," the Shoshone said quietly, holding something out in the worn palm of his glove.

A circle of wrapped rawhide: a little larger than the Indian's hand, filled with twists of sinew woven like a fisherman's net, a small hole left open at the very center.

Looking down at the object, Hook asked, "What's this?"

"Dream catcher."

Taking it, confused, he turned it over, over again. "What for, Injun?"

"I make it for you. Time now you have it. Now you wear it."

"Made it for me?"

"After the bear."

He wanted to laugh. Not because anything was funny—just to release his sodden despair at leaving his woman, his friend, this place. "Shit. That goddamned bear again. All that talk—his medicine now my medicine."

"Dream catcher: it keep all bad dreams from getting through to you." The Shoshone ran a finger around the outer circumference of the woven sinew net. "Only a good dream can get through the middle. There."

At the very center, that tiny hole. "What's my dream?"

"You get your woman. Is your dream, Jonah Hook. This your dream catcher."

It all made him feel damned uneasy. This talk of something bigger than he. Something he would never understand. "More hocus-pocus bear medicine, eh?"

Two Sleep shook his head emphatically. "Down there. Usher. His men. Those warriors I see. All them, Jonah Hook. That bear's medicine, your medicine now."

"You figuring I'm going to die, that it?"

Instead of answering yes or no, the Indian tapped the dream catcher, then slowly closed Jonah's fingers around the object. "You remember. Dream catcher made of bear's hide protect you now. Keep you from all bad dreams."

A cold shudder of dread made him tremble as he gazed into the cold black flecks of the Indian's eyes. "All right," Jonah whispered, dropping the dream catcher down the neck of his wool underwear. He patted it where the object rested against his chest, perhaps only to reassure the Indian. "I'll keep it right here. Safe."

"Yes, you safe now. Powerful mystery—these dreams." Two Sleep looked around them at the walls of the canyon, sighed. "Bear's bad medicine all around us. But Jonah Hook safe now."

He patted the Shoshone on the shoulder. "Safe now—safe when we come back for those two we're leaving down there."

Jonah turned, started back down the ridgeline as the sun began to outline objects below . . . then stopped, taking one last look at the bloodied, naked friend strung on that cottonwood cross.

Two people he loved were down there. As much as it hurt to leave this morning . . . Jonah Hook vowed he was not abandoning them—knew that when he returned tomorrow night, there would be no retreat.

There would never be another retreat for a man who had nothing else to lose.

42

ORRIN HASLAM HAD failed in his first attempt to get the farmer to suicidally attack Jubilee Usher's camp.

As much as he itched just to shoot the son of a bitch himself and get the goddamned thing over with, he knew Jubilee Usher would have his head for it. Usher wanted the sodbuster for himself.

And Orrin was going to give the colonel what the colonel wanted most.

Usher wanted Hook to come to him. Where the woman would watch it all happen right before her eyes.

"It's part of the divine plan, don't you see, Major Haslam?"

Orrin really didn't see—but he did understand that if Usher had to send him with some men into Pioche under orders to take Hook, chances were damned good that Haslam wouldn't have a prisoner to bring back to the colonel. Chances were he'd be left with delivering a dead man to Jubilee Usher. And then, Orrin Haslam knew, there would be 100 percent odds of a second cross planted in the ground outside that cave at Golgotha.

He shuddered at the thought now, remembering how the old man clung to life that very morning as Orrin watched the trio mount up and ride back toward Pioche. From a far ridgeline Haslam had waited, watching with boiling distress as the three pulled back in retreat. Just as he had feared, that goddamned Injun had found the rest of Usher's men, and them Pahvants too.

Licking his lips now as the light faded from the sky on a most aggravating day, savoring the taste of the whiskey as he waited for the Chinaman to come down the stairs, Haslam thought on how he had climbed back into his saddle and raced back to Usher's camp, where he was shamed to declare that the colonel's plan had gone awry.

Usher was fuming. "Don't tell me you've got a better idea how I'm going to get that sodbuster to deliver himself to me!"

"Something better than Winkham's plan," Haslam said.

"Yes," Usher said quietly, brooding. "His idea of having most of the men camp just beyond the ridge with the Indians didn't work at all, did it? I suppose none of us foresaw that the farmer would have the skills to see through our ambush."

"Just send them all away, Colonel."

Usher had turned from the fire where his nigger was cooking a late breakfast. "Send . . . send them all away?"

It was Orrin's turn to fume. "This is between you and one goddamned sodbuster, for Christ's sake!"

Usher wore a smile. "Yes."

"Keep a handful of us here to take care of the other two."

"Yes."

"Get the others packed off—go anywhere—but far enough away to make it look good. And I can tell that farmer you're staying behind."

"For what reason?" Usher asked.

Haslam shook his head. "I'll come up with something . . . some reason why the rest has gone on and you're staying behind. Staying behind with the woman . . . staying behind to finish off the old man there." He pointed at the naked body, bearded chin collapsed against his bloody chest. He was in wonder once more at how the son of a bitch clung to life.

"Yes," Usher whispered with some glee as he strode slowly around the cook fire. "It just might work." Then he suddenly whirled on Haslam. "When?"

"Tomorrow?"

"They won't come tomorrow. They'll come at night."

Haslam nodded. "Just like they come before daylight this morning."

"Yes. Tomorrow night. So we need to hurry, Haslam: pass the word among the men and those Lamanites that they are to move north a day's ride to a new camp, where I'll join them in less than a fortnight. From there we will plan the beginning of our campaign against the false prophet. By

Christmas, the New Year at the latest—I want to sit on Brigham Young's throne."

"Did that rider you sent back ever return with word on Lee?" Orrin inquired. "We could use that old man and his boys when we go up against Young's faithful."

He watched Usher's face go long, drain to gray.

"The sons of my old friend tried to get their father to flee to Colorado, even down through Arizona all the way into Mexico, where he could live out the last of his days."

"A second trial?"

Usher nodded. "Now Brigham Young has conspired to make John Doyle Lee his scapegoat. Ancient biblical law, it is—this requirement of sacrifice to a jealous God:

> *"And Aaron shall lay both his hands upon the head of the live goat, and confess over him all the iniquities of the children of Israel, and all their transgressions in all their sins, putting them upon the head of the goat, and shall send him away by the hand of a fit man into the wilderness;*
>
> *And the goat shall bear upon him all their iniquities unto a land not inhabited: and he shall let go the goat in the wilderness . . ."*

Haslam shook his head in disbelief. "They're gonna kill Lee?"

"He mounted no defense, Major. Wanted not one witness called this time. Once John Doyle Lee saw that the Church had abandoned him . . . when he saw that Brigham Young himself had turned his back on his faithful servant—Lee put his faith in a jealous God."

"Death to Brigham Young!" Haslam had cried. "He betrayed a good, faithful man!"

"The judge asked Lee how he wanted to be executed, and he answered that he wished to be shot."

"Then that is how Young will meet the devil!"

"No," Usher remonstrated. "I have plans to take the false prophet myself."

"Just as you want to take the farmer?"

"Exactly. I want to poison Brigham Young . . . kill him slowly, exactly as he has slowly strangled the life out of our one true Church of God!"

"That what you want to do to the sodbuster?"

Usher nodded. "A fitting death, this poisoning, don't you agree? So that the woman can watch him die a little more every day: to make them both pay for all those years she clung to hope that he would come for her. At long, long last—she will see that I am her husband. She will see that I have conquered!"

As the sun began to fall that autumn day, Haslam rode back to Pioche, finding the sodbuster's horses tied outside the saloon. Over a bottle of whiskey he told the trio of what he had witnessed after they abandoned Jubilee Usher's camp.

"You'll get your chance again soon enough. They're packing up."

The farmer looked at him with disbelief. "Leaving?"

"Usher's army."

"Injuns too?"

Haslam nodded this time, glancing superiorly at Two Sleep. "Why, you wasn't worried about a few Injuns, now, was you? Not when you can get your hands on the man took your woman."

"Where they going?" the younger Hook demanded, wiping whiskey from his lips, his eyes glazing with the effects of the liquor.

"Heard it myself not long ago. One of Usher's men got himself liquored up and got loose-mouthed about their plans to pull out for the north—riding back to Utah."

"We gotta move quick—"

"Hold on," Haslam warned. "Word is Usher ain't leaving right away."

Hook hunched forward, elbows midtable. "He's staying behind?"

"What I'm told. So . . . if you want Usher yourself. And the woman."

"Ma," was all the younger one said before he was silenced by his father.

"If you want to settle this thing yourself," Haslam repeated.

It hadn't taken much more to convince those men—in as much pain and confusion as they were. A simple lot, Haslam had decided even before he took them out there the first time. A most simple lot, he reaffirmed, as he convinced them to make a second attempt on Jubilee Usher's camp. Hardly worth calling this trio of fools "enemies." Gentile fools.

He had ordered supper, some beef roast with boiled potatoes and gravy. And a bottle of rye for himself to celebrate. Some pink bitters on the side. Tonight would be the last he would spend with the woman in that room upstairs. Come morning when he damned well felt like it, he'd crawl out of her bed. They'd get dressed and come down here for breakfast. Or lunch. Hell, maybe even wait until supper if he wanted. It made no matter—wouldn't be no reason to hurry, especially.

As long as he got her back to Usher's camp by nightfall. There to wait out the hours of darkness, knowing the sodbuster and the other two were coming before daybreak.

Haslam caught sight of the door opening upstairs along the landing. Across the throbbing saloon he watched the Chinaman come out of his room, close the door behind him, then stop at the railing when he found Haslam at the far table where the Chinaman himself usually sat each night. The pitiful cripple hobbled along the landing, hovered above the top step a moment, then desperately clutched the banister as he began his descent down the stairs.

Orrin stuffed his hand into his left pocket, where he had the leather pouch filled with coins. Likely more money than the Chinaman ever seen in his life. His fingers moved slightly, reassured by the presence of the pepperbox nesting beside the pouch. With his right hand Haslam pulled his coat back behind the grip on the revolver that lay just forward of the hip.

And smiled at the Chinaman he was about to make very rich.

It was the Season of the Boar. Only a season of change. Not a season of ill winds.

But when the white barbarian offered to pay hard money to take the woman away, Bak Sahm realized not only that things were about to change for all time, but that they were about to change for the worst.

"We go upstairs," Bak told Haslam after the demon made his offer to buy away the Girl of Joy. "Business talk in my room."

"I figured we'd stay right here," Haslam pouted. "See? I'll even put my gun on the table. You ain't got nothing to fear from me."

Bak studied the man's face, glanced at the pistol Haslam thunked on the table, then gazed back into the barbarian's eyes. As if he had always been able to read anything in the face of these white demons. No Celestial could. It was as if the barbarians' souls were empty, devoid of spirit, vacant of a dream. Better to talk business in private. Always better.

Especially when a man had to refuse the offer of a lot of money. Funny that these demons believed there was a price on everything, Bak thought as he turned his back on Haslam and started across the crowded, bustling floor for the foot of the stairs. He would not even look back. If the demon wanted to talk—he would follow. He would follow because Haslam was the sort of barbarian who believed there was even a price that could buy another man's woman.

He waited for the demon to enter his small, austere room, then shut the door behind them, indicating a chair beside the table where Bak painted his wood chests. A chest nearing completion sat at the center of the table, its gilt-trimmed top rocked back on its brass hinges, the interior partially padded in the deep, blood-red silk.

"Say, now—I seen these before, Chinaman," Haslam said as he settled in the chair, leaning an elbow on the table to run some fingers around the gentle rise and fall of the padded silk lining the inside of the small chest.

When one talked business, one always came directly to the point. "I cannot sell the woman."

"What's the matter?" the demon said with a cold grin. "I'm not giving you enough? That it?"

Looking down at the barbarian's right hip, he saw that the big pistol once more rested in the holster. Bak decided to try a different tack. "She will not go with you."

"S'pose we give her a chance to tell us that, face-to-face."

"She is mine," Sahm protested, sensing the pressure, feeling the flush of anger come of frustration, his mind struggling to get his words right in the demon's language. "San Francisco, I pay for her. She belong to me. She say nothing about business."

"Here," Haslam said as he took the skin pouch out of a coat pocket. Opening the drawstring, he poured some of the coins into his right hand. These he let fall through the gaps between his fingers into the silk-lined box, where the hard money landed in utter silence. "Is that enough to buy your whore?"

"You have her for the night. Keep for many nights, all right," Bak said. His leg began to ache deeply. He wanted her to rub it for him, using some of the pain-relieving balm. He would not be able to sleep tonight if she did not.

"I'm leaving soon—gonna take her away from here, Chinaman."

"No. You enjoy her here. Then go away. Go away for all time, you better."

He watched Haslam slip his left hand back into the coat pocket where he had extracted the coin pouch, and realized there would be a gun there. Instinctively Bak Sahm knew he was dealing for his life here. Not just for the woman. But also for his own life. What was the true worth of one whore? What was the ultimate worth of his own life now—what was its value after living on borrowed time for all these years? So it surprised him that it should come to this. Bak had not expected it; he was totally unprepared for this situation—not with the dragon dream that had haunted him for all these borrowed years. This demon Haslam was not the dragon he had dreamed would kill him.

He wanted to hope as he watched the hand that perhaps his dream was still correct. Perhaps no matter what the circumstances with that hand, this barbarian would not kill him.

The pouch came out in the demon's palm. "There's more in here," Haslam said, pouring a few more of the coins into the box. "What the hell—you can take it all." He emptied the pouch.

Bak stared at the small mound of gold and silver coins. It was more wealth than he had ever handled for any one man before—more than he had handled for any ten men.

"Why, with all this money—you can go to San Francisco and buy yourself another whore, Chinaman."

He wagged his head, wobbling and unsteady on his one good leg and the hickory cane. Bak had begun to sweat, his head aching with a sharp pain piercing him at the temples like a pair of hot tongs pushing inward, attempting to meet somewhere behind his eyes.

"I cannot," Sahm said quietly, inching backward toward the bed, afraid if he did not sit, he would surely collapse and fall as the dizziness threatened to overcome him. It was this way with the advent of every dragon dream. Warning him of the monster's coming. Slowly his fingers felt for the reassurance of the cold steel he carried within one of his loose sleeves.

"You can take the money or refuse it, Chinaman. But either way— I'm leaving with the woman tonight."

"You go away. She is mine," he said, sinking to the edge of the bed, his vision blurring, his ears roaring with the explosion that had crushed him beneath rocks so many seasons before. It was as if his ears were buried in layer upon layer of cotton.

"You foolish shitbag. I'm buying her—"

"Go away now," Bak tried to say with as much stony ice as he could.

Although he could no longer hear the demon, Haslam was clearly laughing. Rising from the chair, the white man pulled his big revolver out, ever so slowly, and spun the cylinder before reholstering it as he turned toward the door.

Then turned back to look at the man on the edge of the bed. "Keep the money, Chinaman. You earned it."

Bak pulled the knife from the sleeve that enclosed the withered left arm by the time Haslam reached for the door's knob.

"Leave my house."

Cracking the door open slightly, Haslam turned, his mocking laughter filling the room—but his expression suddenly changed when he saw Bak Sahm's long, deadly stiletto.

"A pretty knife, Chinaman. What you fixing to do with it?"

"Go from my house. Now."

"I aim to do just that. But I'm taking the woman with me."

"Go alone."

"Keep your money and buy another whore you like," the demon growled as if losing patience with a domesticated animal. He turned on his heel, pulling the door open.

Bak Sahm drew his good arm back—

as Haslam whirled in a crouch, sensing that Bak was about to hurl the knife at him. The demon's coat flap came up in a puff of smoke, a second puff, then a quick third by the time Bak Sahm felt the tongue of fire penetrating his chest, another torment in his belly. A third along the top of his right arm.

He slid slowly to the floor, unable to stay on the edge of the bed. Landing, he wanted so badly to crumple to the side, but dared not. With all his strength Bak willed himself to sit up, choking on his warm blood, thinking only of staying rigid, so that he might sit upright against the side of his low bed.

Grinning, Haslam turned quickly to peer through the crack in the door, then closed it. And reached around to pull the long stiletto from the wall. He leaned an ear against the door and listened. Then dragged a heavy chest across the jamb to block it and came over to kneel near the China-man's feet.

"Told you I'd have the woman—either way. Man like me don't take to being told no, you should've understood. It was better you just take your money and forget me. Take your money and forget *her*. Get yourself another whore to wet yourself in. She's going with me . . . and look at you: you're going to bleed to death right here."

Bak gazed up into the demon's eyes as he knelt before the Chinaman. Seeing clearly, the ringing in Bak's head gone for the moment. Feeling Haslam tear open the folds of his quilted silk jacket. He sensed the tip of the stiletto as the demon cut through the silken cord that secured his quilted trousers around his waist. Haslam slashed at the cloth brutally, laying the Chinaman bare from his waist down to his knees.

"Always wondered if you Chinee was any different from a white man," the demon muttered with a grin, his cruel, twisted mouth just inches away from Bak Sahm's face as he peered into the Chinaman's glazed eyes. "The woman ain't no different down there—s'pose it makes sense you wouldn't be either."

Bak tensed, the dizziness returned as he sensed his scrotum and his penis being gathered into the demon's hand.

"Way I figure, you won't be needing these no more anyhow, China-man," Haslam cackled. "Not since I'm taking your whore."

It was more as if he felt a cool rush of air between his legs than any hot pain. Then, a number of heartbeats over time, he felt the icy numbness turn to a searing heat as warm liquid puddled beneath him, seeping against his bare thighs.

"Lookee there, Chinaman," Haslam jeered, holding the bloody flesh right before Bak Sahm's misting eyes, "I got your pecker and balls."

Fighting down the sour taste rising to the back of his throat, Bak sensed the holes in his body, felt the fluids draining from him, oozing right out onto the floor where he sat in that warm puddle.

How would he ever again . . .

Haslam stood, straightened, dangled the Chinaman's limp manhood from the fingers of his bloody left hand. "But I'll leave it here for you—so before you die you can remember how good it was to poke a woman with what you once had to poke her with."

Through the swelling haze of red waves of coarse, burlaplike nausea, Bak watched the demon toss his bloody heap into the unfinished chest on his worktable. It made a sodden clap, followed by the distinctive tinkle of cold money as it struck the pile of gold and silver coins.

"Ain't never been a woman worth dying for, Chinaman," Haslam said as he yanked up the window sash.

By the time Bak Sahm overcame the last acid heave of his stomach, the demon had disappeared from the room. He sat in a pool of his own blood and vomit, feeling as light as a slip of rice paper. The breeze wafting in through the open window frightened him—not so much because it tormented his ugly, gaping castration—but more so because he was afraid if the breeze blew hard enough that he would blow away. His soul become almost weightless.

Bak closed his eyes, fighting to hold on to the vision of her, the feel of her stretched out beneath him, the smell of her rich moistness in his nostrils. Wanting so badly again to have the taste of her scented breast in his mouth, against his tongue. As tightly as he squeezed his eyes, straining to have a vision of her—the dragon dream still thundered around the periphery of a shrinking tunnel.

No longer could he see across the small room, so Bak closed his eyes again—squeezing hard, struggling mightily so that he could sharpen the fading vision of her that swam before him in the deepening mist.

Yet forced still to fight the snorting, roaring, thundering fire and torment as the dragon drew closer along the wall of the ever-shrinking tunnel.

Nearer, ever nearer as his dragon dream closed in . . . ever more suffocating as the dream wrapped tightly about him.

43

Early October 1876

H E SAW HIS enemy.
   The man he had tracked for nearly ten years. Across more seasons than Jonah cared ever to remember.

His moment finally come.

"That him, Jeremiah? Can you remember?"

Young Hook studied the big man who sat in a chair at the dancing fire near the flaps of the dirty wall tent. At his back a Negro pulled a hot towel from a large tin pan and wrapped it over the big man's face.

"Looks to be . . . hell, Pa—I can't tell from here. Been a long time."

Hook laid a hand on his son's shoulder, his mouth turning up slightly at the corners. "It's all right—'cause it has been a long, long time, Jeremiah."

"Sun's bound to come up over that ridge soon," Jeremiah told his father.

Jonah looked off to the east, recalling how the three of them had skirted what was left of the Indian camp in the darkness that followed moonset. All three of them were eager to learn if it all was true about Usher's men pulling out—true that the Indians were dispersing with the Mormon army. Only two lodges remained, squatting like dark cones in the murky light of that coldest time of the day when night has not yet begun to consider yielding itself to the ashen gray of predawn. In the deepening indigo of that starless night Jonah reined up and stared across the foggy distance at one of those last two lodges. Something nagged him, a discomfort that forced him to recall. Unable to remember, he shook his head and moved on. Clustered around that pair of lodges sat the skeletal domes of wickiup frames stripped of their blankets and buffalo robes. Abandoned. Gone as well were the tents that had lined the foot of the ridge two days before.

He wanted to believe, wanted to hope, his heart leaping like a trout fracturing the surface of a high country pond. The odds had been narrowed. No more than a matter of minutes, a matter of nothing more than a few hundred yards left in what had been an endless quest.

The trio had led their horses back through the brush until they tied the animals off and began their ascent of the ridgeline across the ravine from the cave. In the coming light Jonah finally counted four tents—all that remained of what sat beneath the cottonwood trees two days before. A pair of tents staked down near the bank of the narrow creek that cut the hollow of the canyon. And two others huddled close to the mouth of the cave, starkly white below the grave, gray face of Golgotha.

"Place of the skulls," he whispered again, straining to make sense of the crazy swirl of ground fog that wisped up in frosty layers from the icy creek. He turned to Two Sleep and asked, "Can you see our old friend?"

The Shoshone nodded.

Hook trusted that old Indian's eyes much, much better than his own. "Same place he was?"

"Yes."

"Can . . . can you tell if . . . is Shad still alive?"

It took a long time before the Shoshone answered. Then he looked at Jonah to say, "Not always good to be alive."

Hook's belly flopped, fluttered like a rainbow trout hurled onto a streambank by a bear's paw, left to struggle futilely there in the wet grass. "Y-you saying . . . Sweete's dead?"

Two Sleep shook his head. "He moves."

Jonah finally let the breath gush from his lungs. "There's two of 'em we're taking outta here with us. Your job, Injun—I want you to cut the old man down when we go in there."

The Shoshone's flint-dark eyes flicked over to Jeremiah. Then he nodded without making another sound.

Jonah nodded once to acknowledge the Indian's unspoken question. "I'm going for Gritta. The woman." Again he turned to the east to watch the layer of rose growing along the horizon behind the ridgeline.

"What about me, Pa? What you figure on me to do?"

His heart swelled again as his eyes came to rest on his oldest son. With his gloved hand Jonah stroked the side of Jeremiah's face, unable to speak for a moment as he recalled the child's birth in that cabin back to Missouri. Remembered how the youngster had yearned to work the mules, plodding behind the plow for that first time. Remembered how both Jeremiah and Zeke had waved that last time Jonah had walked off to join Sterling Price's army that was sure to drive the Yankees right out of Missouri for good and all time. And remembered the look of peace that crossed Zeke's face as the youth died in his father's arms, Jeremiah huddled there beside Jonah, tears streaking the paint and dust furring his cheeks.

Here in the dark Jonah recalled Jeremiah's words beside the pitch-black grave they left open as they were about to set out to take up Usher's trail, set out to find the woman.

"She'll always be my mother. I owe her just as much to try as you do, Pa. But I ain't really asking you, Pa. I'm *telling* you what I'm going to do. With you . . . or without you: I'm going after my mother."

Then and there Jonah had taken his grown son into his arms, hugged him fiercely. At long last to hold Jeremiah as he had never held him before. As a man.

He had quietly told Jeremiah, "Son, let's go find your mother."

So now Jonah struggled to find his voice before he said, "Jeremiah— you got the most important job of all. I want you to cover our backs. Me and the Injun's."

"That's it? Cover your backs?"

"Listen, son: I figure I made a lot of mistakes before—figuring I could do all this on my own. Almost got us hanged down in Injun Territory—"

"That's all in the past now."

"Listen to me, Jeremiah. We're going into something I don't know if we all will come out of. Only way we will is if one of us watches out for the other two. Way I see it—if it ain't Shad Sweete or this goddamned Shoshone here watching my backside . . . there's only one other man I want to cover me while I go free your mother."

"M-man? You said, man?"

Jonah nodded.

"I hear you right . . . you calling me a man, Pa?"

"Damn right I am, Jeremiah," he said, a sour ball of sentiment clogging his throat. He angrily swiped at one eye with a glove. "Now— you gonna watch our backsides or not?"

Jeremiah glanced over at Two Sleep before he looked back at his father, put out a hand to touch Jonah's cheek, wiping away the narrow path of a solitary tear. "Don't you worry about nothing—not with me covering you."

Hook swallowed, fighting that sour ball. So many miles. So damned many winters. And now she was less than a few hundred rods away. As he sat out that night, waiting for this dawn—it hadn't seemed real in many ways. But now as the light came up, while the sun broached the far side of the earth, Jonah could once more see his old friend, nailed and lashed, naked, to Jubilee Usher's cross before the skeletal rock wall. It came real to him, all too real.

Shad had done this for him. Gone in search of Gritta his own self.

Right now Jonah believed he owed Shad almost as much as he owed Gritta. About as much as he had ever felt in debt to any man.

"We go," Two Sleep instructed, as soft as the whisper of the fog that lay like a gently shifting ashen blanket down along the creek bottom.

Jonah nodded, shifting to one knee in rising—then stopped as something across the ravine . . . a flicker of movement . . . just the hint of something . . . He held out a hand to stay Jeremiah when he saw Shad's cross disappear behind the line of leafless trees that hugged the creekbank.

"Wait."

From their place at the lip of the ridgeline, the trio watched only the murkiest of shadows finally take on substance and detail as a golden-rose light began to streak across the eastern sky.

Beyond, the Negro finished shaving the seated man. When the tall one stood, wiping his face with a towel, Jonah knew it could be no other. Just the sheer size of him.

With a signal, Jubilee Usher brought figures forward from the murky shadows: a half dozen of his men struggled to carry the great cottonwood cross down the slope from the mouth of the cave into an open glade beside the creek. In the growing spread of soft light, Jonah saw the small clearing where they were headed as Usher took up position in the front of the procession. There a mound of dirt had been shoveled out of the hard ground. Beside it, a hole.

Faint shreds of voices floated to the top of the ridge where Hook lay watching, mesmerized—fearful for what those men now intended to do with his old friend impaled, imprisoned on that cross. Usher waved as his voice drifted up through the frosty air, ordering, pointing, commanding the six who bore Shad Sweete. Clumsily they set the base of that great cottonwood cross into the hole, and with a heave brought it upright. The cross settled. As three of them steadied the tall beam, the others quickly shoved rocks and earth into the hole, stomping the cold earth with their shovel-backs and boots until Usher commanded them to step back.

He inspected the work at the base of the peeled timber, then held out a hand to one of the men who laid something in the open palm. In the new day's light Jonah caught the flicker of polished steel.

"Gonna cut him some more," he growled as Two Sleep inched forward, an angry sound issuing from the Indian's throat.

But instead of beginning more grisly work on his impaled prisoner, Jubilee Usher turned, raising his face to the far ridge, and flung his booming voice like a cannon shot at the trio across the ravine.

Just as if he knew the three were there—lying atop the rock, watching what was yet to come.

Her touch at this moment was all that he had ever wanted it to be.

Always before she had lain beneath him, complying without assisting, her body not even resisting. Lo, the many times he wished she had shown him even that emotion. Some feeling, any passion at all.

Her voice touched his ears as softly as the moist breeze coming off the great Pearl River delta. "If you can hear me, look at me."

Bak Sahm's eyes fluttered open. Blinked. Straining to focus. The tunnel shrunk so narrow now. Little light could he glimpse at the end— exactly like the tunnels they bored through the high mountains to lay the iron rails for the white man's *poot poot.*

Yet, narrow as the tunnel was, by twisting his head slightly, he saw her. It wasn't just her hands, she caressed him with her eyes. The woman held his face cradled gently in her palms. Her eyes down near his, just inches away. He noticed they pooled with tears as she studied his face.

Don't hold me too tight, he thought. You might crush me. So light, he knew he was made of rice paper—she might easily crumple him into something they would have to discard.

"I don't know what to do . . . how to stop the bleeding," she whimpered to him in the gentlest Cantonese.

Bak tried smiling. "There is nothing to do now." He wasn't sure at first if he really had spoken the words, or merely thought them.

But she shook her head, reaching down to tear off a thick wad of her long gown she stuffed between his legs. That done, Chung-li drew Bak's thighs together more tightly.

The woman explained, "I have called for help."

"How . . . how did you?"

"The white barbarian came looking for me," Chung-li replied. "I knew the instant I heard the gunshots from your room. I knew and hid."

"Where?"

"It does not matter," she said, placing a finger against his lips glistening with frothy blood. "Others told the demon I ran away when the shooting started. He went to look for me."

"That one will return."

"Not soon. They told him I fled in a carriage—riding to the north."

With a cough Bak realized he wasn't able to see much anymore. Not even her face. The tunnel's aperture was collapsing in around him. He had stolen all these years from the dragon. After all this time the dragon had returned for him at last. Bak Sahm knew he should have died in that explosion of rock and dragon's scales peeling from the side of the mountain. With that knowledge, he had reveled in all these years like a thief spending a fortune he had stolen.

Yet here on the precipice of his great becoming, Bak felt like such a pauper—having lived all this stolen time without her. Without the sound of her voice.

"I love you, Chung-li."

"You always have, Bak Sahm."

Choking, he spat out some of the thick, pasty blood. "And I always will."

"I am here with you now, Bak Sahm."

"Why didn't you love me?"

"It is not an easy thing to explain: I could not let you love me, just as I could not love you."

Growing more dizzy, his head sank against her upper arm, where she cradled him against her shoulder. "Why?"

"I was not worthy of anyone loving me," she replied softly against his ear as she pulled his head against her breast, laying one hand over the bloody, wheezing hole in his chest, another over the bluish hole in his belly, oozing just above the groin where she had stuffed the silk of her torn gown, the figures of gulls and dragons encircling a huge, rising phoenix quickly stained with his dark blood.

"You were all I ever loved, Chung-li."

"I love you, Bak Sahm. Do not go away."

"I . . . I can't help . . ."

"Don't go, Bak Sahm. Stay with me. Stay!"

He heard her shriek his name. Heard her repeat over and over and over again that she loved him now, had loved him always, that she always would. Heard her shrill whimper as she cried out her shame for not telling him before.

With the last remnant of strength Bak rolled his head so that he could gaze up into her eyes, then tried moving his lips, but no sound came forth. Her tears spilled upon his face.

"Thank you for your forgiveness, Bak Sahm."

He smiled at her, wishing he could truly see those eyes that cried for him. All he felt were her tears, until he sensed her breath against his cheek, struggled to draw that taste of her mouth into his nostrils.

Drinking in the very essence of her this one last time as Bak Sahm heard the loud, leathery flap of the dragon's wing, swooping down from the riven sky to carry him away.

"Hook!"

Jubilee Usher bellowed out the sodbuster's name, then felt the sound of it rock back over him time and again as the name reverberated from the towering ravine walls. That lucky son of a bitch, Usher thought.

"I want you to watch what I'm going to do to your friend, Hook!"

Turning back toward the pitiable figure draped on the cross, Usher reached as high as he could with the tip of his knife blade, pricked the old man's cold skin and started drawing the weapon down the chest as slowly as a surgeon making an incision. As slowly as a hunter was in making that first, careful opening of his fallen quarry.

Blood began to bead, then flow, along the thread of skin riven open by the narrow blade. From the top of the chest down to lower belly, Usher made one after another of those long vertical incisions until it appeared the old man had been striped with war paint glistening in the new sun.

Only thing wrong was that the old man was withstanding more and more pain as he drew closer and closer to death. His victim barely squirmed anymore fighting off the agony that Usher visited upon him now after day upon day of torture. Jubilee liked to extract the pain, the agony, himself— see it in his victims' faces. As he had grown so accustomed to with the Apache, with the poor Mexicans, with any of the Gentiles who had stood in his way . . . even with any of his own men who dared question, dared even to doubt Jubilee Usher's anointment to stand at the mighty right hand of God.

Again Usher hurled his voice at the far wall of the ravine where Haslam had told him the three would be. "You see how easy it is to make a man bleed—to make him bleed slowly, Hook?"

Even after all this time, Jubilee thought, turning round to his victim. Still alive, even after all this time. Lord—would I like to have an army of men as strong as this old man.

Through the brush and trees where his men hid along the slope toward the cave he watched the first of the Pahvants emerge at the edge of the clearing. They sat a moment atop their ponies as if to determine the course of events, then slowly dismounted and tied off the animals before more than a dozen spread blankets and robes on the frosty shards of autumn-dried grass and squatted to watch the white chief's show.

All the better to have an audience, Jubilee cheered himself as he turned back to the work at hand.

With the tip of the knife he drew a short horizontal incision between two of the bloody vertical lines, then pricked up a tab of skin, holding it between the fingers of his left hand. Now Usher worked the knife deftly, slowly pulling the long strip of skin upward from the body until he reached the top of the chest. Standing on his toes, he slashed with the knife, freeing the inch-wide strip from the old man's body, for the moment enjoying the quiver it gave his victim: that raw flesh laid bare to the frigid torment of the morning's breeze.

The two ends of that long strip of human skin he held out in his hands, raising his arms to their full length above his head, sensing the amazing elasticity of human flesh as he displayed it for the sodbuster and his companions.

"I'm no stranger to this, Hook! I've done it countless times before. But never—I must hasten to add—with more pleasure. Amazing material: this human flesh. The primitives of this land"—and he used the knife to point at the crescent of Indians seated and standing at the upper end of the clearing—"these savages use the flesh of animals to make repairs, to reinforce their bows, to tie river stone and sharpened shards of metal to tree limbs—thereby making clubs and axes. But it took me—a man delivered to this land by the hand of God Himself—to show the savages that the best . . . the very best flesh to use for such construction of the weapons of destruction is, in fact, the flesh of one's enemy."

Usher used the knife to point to the old man. "Behold, Hook! My enemy! Your friend!"

Suddenly Usher's knife slashed sideways through the air, just above the level of his own head. The long black wound slowly widened, gushing blood, suddenly spilling its first greasy-white coil of gut. Into his left hand he pulled a length of the warm, shuddering viscera before slashing through it with the knife. He held up the moist clump of tissue in his open left palm for all to see.

Around him his gunmen and the Pahvants gasped at the suddenness of his savage act. What did his audience expect? Didn't they realize he was going to give them a show worthy of a great and powerful man?

Usher whirled, holding the end of the intestine so that it dangled from his outstretched arm. A bloody, purplish-white tissue glistening in the sun.

"You see, Hook? I'm going to slowly take something from this pitiful old wreck of a man . . . inch by inch, part by part, breath by breath—until you come down from hiding and fight me just as you have always intended to do."

Turning his head a moment, Jubilee gazed back up the slope to the cave where George stood behind the chair, the towel still draped in his clasped hands. The old Negro had his head bowed, his lips moving, emphatically wagging his head side to side—almost as if the man were praying. To what God, Jubilee Usher did not know.

"George!" he hollered, waiting to continue until his nigger raised his head. "Release the dogs!"

Waiting until George nodded, turned soddenly, and hobbled away, Usher stood before the cross, admiring the bloody gobs of gore that splattered onto the bare ground beneath the cross. Then he heard the dogs coming. Jubilee whistled as he saw the three of them bounding his way from the mouth of the cave. Huge stag hounds these were—his pets—like his children. No, more than children, so he had decided long ago, for children would never be as obedient as these creatures of terror.

"C'mon! C'mon—here you go!" he called out to them as they drew near, ears flapping, jaws snapping, snarling at one another for position—tongues lolling.

Usher held up the still-warm viscera, its blood dripping down his palm, onto his wrist, darkening the cuff of his freshly laundered shirt.

"Which of you wants this?" he asked the dogs, then whirled about, dangling the long coil of intestine even higher to shout to the far ridge across the ravine as the dogs scampered, pawed, growled at his feet, noses buried in the blood spotting the dust, raising their jowls hungrily, their wet nostrils flaring with the smell of raw meat. "These are beautiful creatures, Hook! Already they've come to enjoy the taste of human flesh!"

With the last word Usher hurled that length of the old man's intestine high into the air. The three hounds followed the flesh with their hunters' eyes, watching the arc of its flight, sensing where the greasy coil of bloody gut would fall with their preying instincts, all the while biting and nipping at one another as the viscera tumbled down through a shaft of morning sunlight. One set of jaws leaped higher than the other two, snatching the raw meat out of the air—but as that dog came down, the other two were there to try tearing what they could from the victor's jaws.

Usher turned away from the snarling, grumbling tussle. "Easy, my children," he shouted so the trio could hear. "There's much more where that came from."

Lifting the old man's left hand by the index finger, Jubilee drove the sharp knife down suddenly—then flung the freed finger toward the animals.

"There you go, my pets! Another tasty morsel."

As quickly he held up the old man's second finger and severed it from the hand, tossing it to the hounds, who crunched and devoured the digit, bones and all.

A third and the fourth, then the thumb he flung toward the animals, whose jaws were lathered with blood, frothed with gore, their eyes flecked with lust as their master fed them fresh, warm flesh.

"You see, Hook! It does not take much! Come down! Come down and face me! It is what you want more than anything! Even more than the life of this old man! Dare I say it: you want to face me even more than you want the life of your woman!"

The gunshot surprised Usher.

In the reverberating waves of its fading echo Jubilee quickly patted over his chest, his belly—just to make sure he had not been shot.

The ravine fell strangely silent as he slowly realized he had not been the target.

44

Early October 1876

"JESUS GOD," JONAH Hook exclaimed under his breath as he crouched there—stunned, watching the dogs snarl and fight over the coil of raw meat from what had been Shad Sweete's belly.

He swallowed hard, his empty belly having nothing to hurl up against his tonsils but the acidic sting of bile. With difficulty he swallowed it down, the taste of it burning its remembrance all the way back down his gullet.

It came clear as rinsed crystal to him that there was only one thing left to do.

He glanced at Jeremiah. The young man had his head raised, staring at the sky. Mouthing unintelligible words to some God somewhere up there. Comanche words. For the moment Jonah felt abandoned by his son.

Quickly he whirled on Two Sleep—finding the Shoshone staring at the newborn sun emerging beyond the red horizon: his arms outstretched, chanting. Both of them praying—and for what?

"Damn you!" he cried out to the pair of them. "Damn you both!"

So he had to do it alone. They would call out to their God. Supplicate their greatest of powers, asking—even begging—for help. But not Jonah Hook—hell no. He hadn't come this far not to know that in the end what a man had to find was only what piece of God still remained inside him.

Falling to his belly at the extreme lip of the ridge, he rolled onto his left shoulder, brought the big-bored Sharps buffalo gun up, and yanked down the lever, rolling the breechblock down and open, exposing the maw of the breech. From the wide leather belt he had strapped over the pistol belts buckled around the outside of his dirty canvas mackinaw coat, Jonah pried loose one of the long brass cartridges, his eyes beginning to smart.

The sting of bile returned to his throat. As much as he had wanted to kill Jubilee Usher, as much as he had dreamed of just how he was going to do it—Jonah had never imagined it would end like this.

Into the wide breech he shoved the cold brass cartridge bearing the 550-grain lead bullet. Then snapped up the lever and rolled back onto his belly, flat—legs spread out from his body at an angle. The way he had killed buffalo from a stand nearly a decade before.

"You gonna kill that bastard now?" Jeremiah hollered behind him, his own rage finally come to a boil. "You finally gonna do it, Pa?"

Instead of answering, Hook laid his cheekbone along the oiled stock, still blinking to clear the salty sting from his eyes. He pulled on the back trigger, setting the front one to a hair's touch.

For a long moment, two or more heartbeats' worth, he held his breath, consciously willing his eye to clear. Sensing the rising breeze on his cheekbone, Jonah charted his windage. Muttering under his breath—realizing that he was forced to shoot down in elevation—Hook reminded himself that he'd have to hold low on his target. Slowly, his right eye cleared as he drifted the front blade across the stark whiteness of his target.

And froze. He couldn't fire. Knowing it simply couldn't be finished like this.

"Shoot 'im, Pa!"

Jonah swallowed against the bitter gorge clogging the back of his throat.

"Shoot that son of a bitch now!"

Blinking his eyes clear once more, Hook swore he would pull the trigger this time—no matter that long ago he had vowed he would one day kill Jubilee Usher with his bare hands, choking the life from the bastard's throat. To watch him struggle for air, to see his eyes bug out, to see the man's fear seeping out of his every pore.

As Jonah swung the sight picture with that front blade down to rest within the notch at the bottom of the back sight's curved buckhorn, he stopped, not believing what he saw. Then moved the front blade a fraction of an inch higher; a moment later he raised it a little more, the sight picture climbing hair by hair until he was dead certain of what he saw at the ravine's bottom.

"Jeremiah—"

"Pull the damned trigger, Pa!"

"Look through them field glasses you got."

"What?" the young man whined with exasperation. "What the hell you want with—"

"Just take them goddamned field glasses and look at . . . look at the old man."

Behind him he heard his son shuffle close across the rocky ground, coming to a rest at Jonah's shoulder.

"Want you to tell me if you see what I think I'm seeing, Jeremiah."

There was a moment of quiet while Jeremiah cranked the wheel, adjusting the cloudy, leather-wrapped field glasses.

"The old man, Pa . . . your friend—"

Jonah didn't have to look for himself. As if he heard the old man's voice welling up from the cold recesses of his head, issuing from under the layers of years of dust and cobwebs, he was certain.

Go 'head, son. I'm good as dead already.

Hook closed his eyes and finally relented, letting the tears come. Lowering his head, he allowed them to flow now, hot and salty, as he choked on the words. Wanting to be completely certain before he did what could never be undone.

"Tell me, Jeremiah—tell me if the old man really is looking up here . . . looking up here at us."

Pull the trigger, Jonah Hook.

"Seems to be, Pa. Like he knows someone's up here. And . . . he's—I can't figure it, but the crazy old man's *smiling.*"

Angrily raising his head from the rock, even more confirmed in what he had to do now, he bitterly swiped at the tears, clearing his eyes.

That's it—c'mon now, son. Do this last favor for me: just pull the trigger.

Jonah wagged his head as if trying to loosen something that haunted him in the hollows behind his eyes. He looked across the ravine for himself. "That's right, Jeremiah. He's smiling. Smiling 'cause he knows I'm up here. Knows it's me. Usher ain't the only one knows Jonah Hook's up here. That crazy old man been hanging there, taking all that Mormon bastard can do to hurt him . . . and he's smiling up here at me now because ol' Shad knows it's me gonna help him."

Jeremiah wagged his head, asking, "Help him? Help him how?"

"Only way I can help him now."

Shad Sweete was staring with those glazed, all but sightless eyes across that narrow canyon. Jonah couldn't be more certain of it. The old man knew Hook was come to help. Knew Jonah was come to deliver him as sure as Hook had come to reclaim his woman.

And in the core of him on which was written that silent code of love, Hook knew what had been asked of him: this last act of true friendship. If a man could not lay down his own life for another, then he must surely be prepared to take the life of a friend who was all but dead.

"The one you called Shad . . . Shad Sweete," Jeremiah said softly. "I can't believe it—but he's smiling while Usher is hacking off his fingers. You . . . you gotta drop Usher now!"

Easing his cheek back down on the stock, Jonah drew in a long breath that helped erase the sting of bile on the back of his tongue. Always before he'd killed in anger. Never had he considered killing out of love.

Pulling again on the back trigger, he remembered he already set it. Carefully he inched the finger to the front of the trigger guard, took another breath, and let it halfway out. Held it in his chest.

"Shoot him, Pa—the bastard's daring you to put a bullet in him."

I ain't never asked you for too much as a friend, Jonah.

Squeezing his eyes, Hook blinked a couple of times to clear a swirl of dust the breeze twisted past the lip of the ridge. Lowering the muzzle to take in the whiteness of his target, he gauged the amount of drop in elevation from where he shot to where the bullet would impact against the target down on the canyon floor beside the icy creek. For a heartbeat he allowed himself to look at the familiar face. The big man's flesh covered with welts and blood, bruises and torn hide. As much pain as he had to be in, Jonah lay there mesmerized by that smile.

You're the only one be able to make a shot like this.

God, how he didn't want to remember Shad Sweete this way. Wanted to remember the old trapper full and vital, reveling in life. The sort of man who took what was dealt him and smiled on through all his pain. A glorious, generous man who had nothing more but to offer up his own life to a friend's quest.

Hook vowed he would remember the smile. Just the way Shad was smiling now as the sun cleared the far rim of the ridge and drove the shadows from the side of his face. That big, goddamned smile.

Quickly, before he lost his resolve, Jonah lowered his sight-picture down the neck. Farther down the bloody chest. Lower still to allow for the bullet's natural path. Because he was shooting downhill, he held on the bloody rivers that streaked the old trapper's lower belly—held right there on that gaping maw of bloody bowel squeezing out through the edges of the wound. There, if he figured right, the bullet ought to strike the old man in the chest. Through the heart.

Strike true, old friend. Shoot center.

"Can't believe he's smiling, Pa."

"Smiling at me, Jeremiah."

"How . . . how come he's—"

"Made peace with his Maker," Jonah said. "And he knows in the marrow of him I can do no less by him."

"Then—ain't . . . ain't you gonna kill Usher?"

Thank you, Jonah. Thanks, my good friend.

Sucking in another breath, he let it halfway out, eased back on the trigger, eased back, back gently . . . just the way he had held his babies when they first emerged from their mother's womb . . . the way he had cradled little Zeke, in those lost years grown to be a young man as together they sat crumpled on the bottom of that snowy arroyo out on the trackless-ness of the Staked Plain, held and rocked his son as his youngest breathed his last.

So much pain endured. So goddamned much pain—

The sudden jolt of the buffalo gun surprised him. Just the way it was supposed to. The breeze nudged the muzzle smoke away quickly as he strained to focus across the distance, across the shards of sun streaks, what distance lay between him and his old friend.

Watching, Jonah saw Shad's body tense backward as the big slug flattened against bone, tore through muscle and sinew, his head driven back to strike the top of the cross as the huge, naked form was shaken in its ropes, reeled a prisoner on those three iron spikes. Then slowly, slowly the head fell forward, the grizzled chin collapsing to the breastbone, where a dark, shiny, puckered hole opened up.

In the silence of that canyon, Hook could hear the feral sound of his enemy beginning to rise. At the foot of the cross the tall, black-headed Danite leader made a low growl in his throat.

"See . . . see how I done, Jeremiah. Want to be sure."

The Mormon leader turned in a slight crouch, his shoulders hunched, entire frame tense, his hands carved into a pair of trembling claws he held before him as the growl rose into an unearthly shriek.

Jeremiah shouted, "You didn't get him! Usher's still standing!"

Angry at his son, Jonah whirled, ripping the field glasses from Jeremiah. Through them he peered down into the canyon. For a moment he watched Usher shake both fists at him, shouting, hurling his orders to his men and the Indians, turning again to fling his foulest oaths at the far ridge. Then Jonah inched the glasses over to peer at the naked, crucified body.

He had hit him just above midchest.

"Thank you, God," he whispered under his breath, fighting down the cold seeping through his own bowels. And realized he had just prayed for the first time since he had knelt at the candlelit altar in that blackrobe's church.

You done good, Jonah. No less'n I'd done for you.

Hook raised the field glasses an inch, barely more, looking at the old man's peaceful face to be certain of what he had just completed. Such peace come of death. Always before in anger or in hate, in desperation or to save his own life. Never had he killed . . . because he loved another.

He couldn't remember anything tougher. It had been the hardest thing he had ever asked himself to do.

The old, bloodied body slumped within its rope bonds, suspended against the crude iron spikes driven through his feet and hands. Freed at last from Jubilee Usher's torture. Even in death Shad Sweete smiled. Peace come at long last.

All the way down through the crevices of the rock Jeremiah grappled with what his father had done. How his pa had the chance to finish things and let it slip through his hands. He could have shot that bastard—but instead Jonah killed a man he claimed to be his friend.

Hook and Two Sleep prepared to move out as the shot's echo disappeared down the depths of the canyon.

"They're coming for us now, son. We better get off the ridge. Up here, where they can surround us."

His heart was hammering again. "Where?"

"Down there," Jonah had said, pointing. "Follow the Injun. We're going down there to get your mother."

By the time they made it to the foot of the red-and-yellow rock wall, Usher's men were waiting. At close range. None of the three would be moving much from these clumps of brush and boulders at the base of the wall now. Couldn't cross any of that open ground sloping away to the creek bottom where the timber was alive with gunfire and shouting. The angry voices of white men, the savage cries of Indians.

If any pale-skinned man trapped here at the bottom of this canyon knew the import of those Pahvant war cries, what they shouted to one another—it was Jeremiah Hook. Not that he understood their tongue. A Comanche warrior didn't have to know a foreign tongue to understand that they were working each other up, puffing up their medicine—calling out their dares and battle challenges to determine just who among them would be coming in to make a suicidal dash to count coup on the enemy.

Over the last half hour or more—the time it would take the sun to cross something less than the distance of two lodgepoles, Jeremiah had watched the gunmen and their Indians slowly work their way through the brush in a ragged crescent. That much was for sure. From time to time as he waited for a target, he glanced across the open creek bottom at the tall, peeled cottonwood cross. At the naked, bloody body of the old man strung there for Jubilee Usher's torture. He had taken part in the Kwahadi torture of Tonkawa and Lipan prisoners. He had mutilated the dead in battle. The Comanche were warriors. War was war.

But as far as Jeremiah Hook was coming to realize—there was nothing more savage than a man who maimed and killed, inflicting pain and death in the name of his God.

"How many cartridges you got left for that Winchester?" Jonah asked his son.

Tugging the belt around on his waist, Jeremiah counted. "Twenty-two."

"Any more?"

He patted his pockets, shook his head. "Only my pistols."

"All right," and Jonah nodded, laid a hand on his son's shoulder. "Save the last bullet for yourself, son."

With what he had left of resolve, Jeremiah tried to smile while the noose around them drew tighter. That thought reminded him. "You remember when we three was standing on that hangman's platform, Pa?"

Jonah's voice sounded harsh. "Yeah. Never forget."

Jeremiah figured it wasn't the sort of thing his father wanted to remember: how Jonah had nearly cost them all their lives out of nothing more than his eagerness to take back in turn what had been took from him.

"Remember them nooses around our necks . . . how we got out of them, Pa?"

"Wish right now I had your—"

The bullet smashed through the brush, ricocheting off the rocks behind them, and a shard of lead smacked into Jonah's shoulder, spinning him around in a heap. Crumpled a few feet away.

"Pa!"

Diving to kneel over his father, Jeremiah pulled back the flap of Jonah's coat to expose the wound. He wouldn't bleed to death from it, but that shoulder was all but useless now. Maybe even worse still: there wasn't an exit wound. Jeremiah remembered the vision of the Comanche women stuffing their pounded herbs and the leaves they had soaked in boiling paunches into the open wounds of their warriors. Right now how he wished he had paid more attention, to remember how to care for such a wound.

In thinking of the Kwahadi women, he carelessly recalled Prairie Night—after trying so to keep her memory at bay. At this moment, bending over his father's bloody shoulder, hearing the gunfire and the war cries . . . it hurt to know he wouldn't see the woman again.

"They're getting too goddamned close, Jeremiah!" Jonah growled, trying to raise himself on his good, right elbow. "Push 'em back! Forget me! Shoot—goddammit!"

"We don't stand a chance, Pa."

"We stand a chance—shoot at every puff of smoke you see!"

"Pa, we're good as gone—"

"Then go down fighting!"

"But . . . my ma over there!"

Like he was slapped, Jonah seemed to smart at the remembrance. Trembling as if attempting to control his private rage, Hook snagged hold of the front of Jeremiah's coat, pulled his son's face near. "We was close, boy. Ain't nothing to be ashamed of when we die—'cause we was damned close."

Jeremiah sensed a flicker of hope as he stretched out his arm. "She's right across the creek."

Jonah's eyes welled again as he struggled to rise. "Then go get her, Jeremiah. I . . . I can't—you go get your ma."

He laid the Winchester down across his father's chest, then leaned over to take Jonah's face between both his hands. From somewhere inside him, someplace left untouched in more years than he could remember, Jeremiah was suddenly overcome with the simple beauty of that touch, that closeness, that intimacy between him and his father. The Comanche were not a people who touched—much less one man touching another. And it was damned certain he hadn't learned such a thing from his father, this man whose eyes he gazed into at this moment.

This act, this plain and purely beautiful act of cradling his father's face, of bending low to kiss Jonah first on one cheek, then on the other—it could have come from nowhere else but something of his mother that still rested deep within Jeremiah Hook. The heart of Gritta that lay at the core of her children.

He leaned back, slowly releasing his father's face, seeing the tears glazing Jonah's eyes.

"I . . . I truly liked that, son," his father said with some struggle. "Jeremiah, I love you."

"I love you too, Pa."

"Now—you heard me—go get your ma."

Jeremiah dragged a hand beneath his nose and nodded, turning away as he yanked up the Winchester. He took no more than a single crouched step as he saw Two Sleep hurled through the brush to land on his hands and knees, the side of his face bleeding. The Shoshone shook his head, as if coming to his senses—while a half-dozen men broke from the edge of the brush behind Two Sleep.

"Don't try it, boy," a voice snarled.

Half of them were Indians in buckskins and blanket coats. The rest were white men. For a moment Jeremiah studied the man who had called out, couldn't be right, couldn't be sure. "Haslam?"

Orrin Haslam had his carbine leveled at Jeremiah's chest. "That's right. Now, just you drop your gun and we'll walk on across the crik real peaceable to meet the colonel."

"Usher?"

"He's waiting for you three."

Turning slightly to glance back at his father, who raised himself to a sitting position, Jeremiah found more Indians emerging from the brush, their weapons trained on Jonah.

"Don't move, Pa. They got us."

"You're a smart lad, boy," Haslam growled. "Get that old Injun up and let's march cross't the crik. Rest of you bring that sodbuster the colonel wants to meet."

But the only ones to move in were the eight white gunmen who approached Jeremiah, Jonah, and Two Sleep. The Indians remained still as stones, their dark eyes darting back and forth between their prisoners and the one of their number who stood near Haslam.

"You heard me, Injun!" the gunman barked to the warrior. "Get them prisoners across the crik!"

The lone Indian shook his head emphatically.

Jeremiah studied the one who refused Haslam's order. His breath caught in his chest—recognizing the Ute war chief they met a winter gone now. The older brother of the hunter they had saved from freezing, shot by a comanchero's bullet.

"Spirit Road?"

"Jeremiah."

Orrin Haslam couldn't believe it when the goddamned Pahvants' war chief called out the name in clumsy English. "Y-you know that son of a bitch?" he asked.

"I know," Spirit Road answered.

With a growing smile the gunman said, "Well, now, ain't this cozy? Don't make no matter now: let's get 'em moving over to meet the colonel."

"No," the Ute said evenly.

It turned Haslam's belly to have a savage like this refuse his order. Just who the hell did this red bastard think he was—this godforsaken Lamanite?

Haslam did not know the import of the message as the war chief's eyes touched the eyes of each of his warriors ringing that small piece of open ground. What did make Orrin grow edgy was watching the savages inch backward toward the brush. Must have been given some silent signal from that big red bastard.

"Major!" Usher had called out from across the creek.

Haslam flung a glance in that direction to find the colonel standing alone at the foot of the cross buried at the edge of the open meadow. It was because of Usher that Haslam had been forced to hurry back from Pioche without the woman. He had been granted the colonel's permission to hang back in town after seeing that the sodbuster was on his way back to Golgotha—just long enough for Haslam to buy the whore and bring her back to Usher's camp. Then that messy business with the Chinaman had forced Orrin to flee town. He tried—and in his hurry did not find the whore—told she was running off on the north road. For the time being Haslam had been forced to make himself scarce in Pioche, kept from following his China doll.

What was of utmost importance for the moment was to get the sodbuster dropped into Usher's lap. Once and for all.

He would go back for the woman when he had time, follow her north if he had to, when this matter with the colonel and Hook had run its course. But the whore! His China doll! For years he had put Usher's desires before his own. And for years that poverty had eaten at his craw.

Haslam flushed with sudden anger, feeling himself trapped like an animal with no escape—his guard hair up. "All right, Chief—get your red asses moving now!"

"Jeremiah Hook."

At another guttural mention of the name Haslam whirled to his left to find a young warrior striding across the open toward the sodbuster's son. The savage held up his right arm, weaponless.

Hook's son looked away from Haslam to hold up his right arm in greeting. This boded no good.

"Get away from him—now!" Orrin bellowed.

"Friend," the war chief attempted to explain. "Jeremiah friend. Like you, Orrin."

Haslam shook his head savagely. "No! Not like me! Not like me at all!"

He started across the open ground for the young warrior heading toward the sodbuster's son, glancing once at Jonah Hook where the sodbuster still sat wounded beside the boulder. With the muzzle of his carbine Orrin motioned violently as he neared the young warrior. "Now—get off with you! Back, back!"

He stopped two feet from the young warrior. Haslam took his eyes from the sodbuster's son, seeing there some flicker of recognition of what could likely happen between them when he jabbed the muzzle of his carbine into the Indian's ribs. "Told you—you red son of a bitch—back off!"

The young warrior was shoved a clumsy step backward, glancing once at his older brother in bewilderment, glancing once more at the sodbuster's son in the coming flush of rage.

Haslam didn't recognize anything but Jubilee Usher's wrath. "Let's get across the creek."

"Major—what's the holdup with your prisoners?"

The last thing he wanted to do was anger the colonel. "Move out." He swung the carbine again to gesture across the creek bottom.

"No," the young warrior refused.

Turning to Jeremiah, Orrin growled, "Move. Keep your goddamned arms up . . . hands where I can see them."

From the corner of his eye Haslam watched the young warrior inching back toward the sodbuster's son, holding out his empty hand.

In a whirl Haslam turned on the Pahvant. "Son of a bitch! I warned you!"

With the muzzle of the carbine nearly touching the red savage's chest, Haslam pulled the trigger. Watched the force of the impact drive the red bastard off his feet, hurled back into the brush. The sodbuster's boy dived, trying to catch the Indian as he fell.

Then a lanyard of fire raced through his lungs, through his belly, hell-flecked tongues of it. Blows strong enough to spin him around and around as Haslam watched the clearing erupt in smoke and orange licks of muzzle flame. Every one of them firing now: the savages at Haslam's men; his soldiers back at the red sonsabitches.

His ears no longer echoed so loudly with the hammering of his heart as Orrin Haslam watched the war chief coming his way. Slowly, he realized the firing had died off. Now he was able to make out nearby the yelps of glee and fiendish delight these savages reveled in. Remembering bloody and brutal images—what these Lamanites had done to the bodies of the escort when Colonel Usher had captured the train.

Feeling sodden, weighted down as if he were sitting under a pile of rocks, Orrin smiled up at the red bastard when the war chief stopped over him, putting a moccasined foot on Haslam's gun hand. Slowly kneeling, the goddamned savage pulled a butcher knife from his belt.

This red bastard is going to . . .

Smiling, Haslam spat, flinging blood and flecks of his riven lung into the savage's face as the war chief came to rest beside the Mormon and laid the knife's edge across his throat.

It was cold, suddenly very, very cold. And immediately he heard a strange, eerie gasping suck of sound. Perhaps the soughing of the wind that made him feel so damned cold.

Then Orrin Haslam understood as the coldness came to take him. He had no idea his last breath would ever sound quite like that.

45

Early October 1876

H E S W O R E H E could feel the icy lump of lead snarled in his shoulder muscle. Like some cold, metallic thing burrowing inside him at the heated center of his wound.

Enough raw pain to make Jonah grit his teeth when he yanked his greasy bandanna from his neck, padded it over the bluish, puckered hole, then pulled his shirt back over the bloodstained dressing.

Damn—the same shoulder wounded in that dimly lit watering hole back in the early winter of sixty-seven . . . Abilene, Kansas. He rode away from that one with Artus, the bullet gone clean through.

But this was more like the leg wound that had crippled him at Corinth while the rest of them pulled back and left him with the others who couldn't retreat, the dead. Left him for the Yankees to run across in that grove shredded with canister and grapeshot. No blue-belly doctor gonna come near him with a knife—Jonah cut the bullet out himself.

Now this bullet would have to come out.

Wincing, Jonah stuffed his left hand down the waistband of his britches, drew his belt up a notch tighter—and swept up the first revolver that had tumbled to the ground when he was hit. Slowly he crabbed toward Jeremiah as the firing withered, then suddenly exploded in one last mad volley before the thicket on this south side of the stream fell silent.

Across the open ground he watched the warriors stand behind the brush where shreds of gunsmoke clung, watched only Spirit Road emerge

418

cautiously at first. When the Ute finally raised his carbine in the air, a chorus erupted from the trees that ringed the battlefield. All was color and raucous commotion as the Utes sprang into the open, dashing about the meadow like water striders on the placid surface of a summer pond. They dragged the dead and the wounded from the places where Orrin Haslam's men had fallen, gleefully gathering the enemy all in the open before they began their grisly work.

Hook swallowed with difficulty, squinting as he turned away, not sure he wanted to watch. Not that he hadn't seen enough of . . .

He suddenly became aware of the far side of the stream—and like a fog burning off beneath the emergence of the morning's sun, Jonah remembered. Shaken to his marrow into remembering, as Jubilee Usher emerged from that grinning, gaping cavelike mouth of the skull . . . emerged with her. The old Negro trudged in an ungainly hobble behind them, pawing at Usher, pleading with the Mormon, trying his best to keep purchase of the woman's other arm—dragged along as the Danite pulled them into the open.

Jonah sickened with fear. Now that the Mormon had seen Hook himself kill Shad, Jonah knew the Danite leader just might possess the sick sort of courage that would drive him to kill Gritta right there in front of him. If for no other reason than to keep her from Jonah.

Now that Jonah had shown he would sacrifice a friend—the Mormon just might sacrifice the woman.

A few yards away two young boys stood in terror at the flaps of a dingy canvas tent, watching mule-eyed, mouths gaping, clutching one another. Who were they, he wondered . . . Usher's boys?

They didn't matter. Likely more victims—like Gritta. Like his children. Like Shad.

Trying to roll his shoulder forward, Jonah found he could force movement from it, but that movement hurt him like a solid blow.

To come this close . . . after all these winters . . . Jonah felt sick suddenly—his head dizzied as he peered across the canyon floor. Forced now to watch Usher's profane drama as the Danite dragged the woman into the open, stopping near the foot of the cross at the moment the yellow orb bubbled fully from the top of the ridge, flooding the canyon floor in sudden light.

Usher dragged one arm from his heavy coat, then changed the arm looping around Gritta's neck as he pulled the coat off the second arm and flung it behind him at the Negro, who stumbled and lay sprawled in the broken, brittle, autumn-burned stubble of trampled grass.

The Danite cried out, "Do you see her now, farmer?"

Jonah squinted, shading his eyes with his right hand clutching the revolver. He saw her.

"She isn't your wife anymore. This is a new woman. And she belongs to me—ordained by God. Married to the one true Prophet of God's holiest Church."

The sound of boots behind him. Jeremiah asked, "Is it . . . is it really Ma?"

He turned as his son slid up beside him at the edge of the clearing that dropped gently to the streambank. On the far side of the creek stood the cross, and Jubilee Usher.

"That's . . . her, son."

"It don't—she looks so tiny, Pa. So small."

Jonah nodded. "You was young. Small yourself when you was took from her. You wouldn't know her now."

"Will you, Pa? Will you know her after all this time?"

He looked into his son's eyes as Two Sleep came up at a crouch. "Jeremiah, I'd know your ma anywhere."

Jubilee Usher bellowed out again even while directing the last half dozen of his gunmen who remained alive. "Are you there, farmer? You saw to it your old friend is gone now—killed him yourself. Maybe she's next. You wouldn't want to do that. I don't think you could, farmer. But—hear me! I'll kill the woman myself if you don't show yourself now!"

"You wouldn't!" Hook shouted, the terrible truth of his greatest fear forcing free the words. "Damn you! But in your own twisted way, Usher— you love her too. You didn't keep her alive all these years if you didn't. So I know you want to keep her for yourself—almost as bad as me wanting her back!"

The Danite laughed low, no humor in its echo—that mocking sound reverberating from the canyon walls. "Still—there's one thing you didn't figure on, farmer. I just might want you more."

"I counted on that. Counted on it hard."

"Come. Come, farmer. Come and save her if you can."

Jonah turned away, yanking up the pistol, snapping the hammer back to half cock, spinning the cylinder as Jeremiah came up to touch his wounded arm.

"Never thought this day'd come, Pa. Not really."

"I knew it would. I believed. Only thing that got me here."

Like an emotional tearing away, Jonah turned from his son to study her—distressed to find Gritta so changed. Yet the same woman still. He held his gun arm out, stepped from the brush into plain view. "I'm here, Usher."

Across the creek the Mormon grinned, moving the woman forward a step beside him, the muzzle of his pistol rammed under her jaw. "You know my name. And soon—the masses will bow before the very sound of that name. God's Prophet on earth!"

Glancing to his left as Spirit Road came up beside him, on his right stopped Jeremiah and the Shoshone. "Just a matter of tracking you down."

He held his arms out. "You found me, farmer."

A great, great weariness seeped up through his legs. "I . . . I just come to take the woman home."

Usher laughed crazily, throwing his head back and showing his tonsils as he bellowed lustily, "You want nothing else, farmer? Just take the woman and go?"

"No," Jonah answered, the years of weariness here galvanized into the rage he had nursed on one long, lonely winter after another. "I come for you too."

"So . . . we arrive at the heart of the matter, don't we?" Usher shoved the woman forward abruptly. "My God has brought you to me. Delivered you unto me for sacrifice, farmer. To redeem my bride. She is mine. The woman is *mine*. Now you are mine as well."

"She ain't yours!" Jeremiah hollered, wheeling on his father, gripping his shoulder. "Pa—you're wounded! Let me go—should be me goes to kill the bastard."

Two Sleep restrained young Hook's arm as the Shoshone's eyes met Jonah's.

Hook said, "Man like that, son—he'd eat you alive."

"And you? Just look at you, Pa." He wagged his head. "You got one good arm." His strong jaw squared. "I can take him. That size don't mean a damn thing to a Comanche warrior."

Jonah patted Jeremiah on the shoulder with that hand clutching the pistol. "This is for me to do. One day you might understand that. No matter I win or lose right here, right now. I figure you'll come to know what I'm talking about one day. Years to come you'll realize a man ain't

421

never gonna win what he wants most of all . . . unless he's truly willing to risk everything to get it. Unless he's willing to lose it all to get what he wants more than anything."

Turning to Two Sleep, Jonah said quietly, a sudden serenity come over him, "Injun—you watch over him. If I ain't around, you see to him. Get him back to the Nations. To his family."

"No, Pa!"

The Shoshone gripped Jeremiah's arm. "I do, Jonah Hook. For you. For Jeremiah."

Jeremiah almost whimpered, "Pa?"

"Stay put, son. This is my hand to play out."

"But, Pa!"

"Said to stay put!"

He turned his back on Jeremiah, filling his chest to fling his voice across the creek and the open ground between them. "You don't stand a chance, Usher," Hook said as evenly as he could. The pain in his shoulder nowhere matched the pain of looking at her: finding her so changed. So worn and weary.

"What, farmer? You say I don't stand a chance?" Usher laughed. "Just because those damned Lamanites have once more forsaken the God of their deliverance? Because those Indians have decided to bite the hand that has fed them?"

From the corner of his eye Jonah watched Spirit Road silently signal what remained of his warriors back into the thickest of the brush, left and right along the streambank. Hook figured they would disappear to find the five or six Usher had left. Yet he cared little for all the others—Utes or Mormons—Hook's mind clutched only at Usher and the woman. Clung to the thought the way a starving man would think only of gorging on food after the long, racking agony of hunger. Such a man didn't think on making himself sick. He thought only on filling that gnawing hunger that has driven him, nearly consumed him.

"One thing I do know about you, Usher: you want me too."

"Yes," the Mormon replied, dragging the woman to his side, stepping out from behind her as he brought the pistol from her neck and pointed it across the stream at his enemy. "I want you very bad, farmer."

With the nearby explosion of shots, Jonah watched the Mormon twist and jerk. Usher jammed the pistol back against Gritta's neck.

Fearing it to the soles of his feet, Hook hollered at Spirit Road, the Utes, to stop their fire.

"The woman—no danger!" Spirit Road yelled over the fading echoes of gunfire rattling off the canyon walls.

Jonah warned, "Don't shoot at him—the big one."

With a wag of his head, and a knowing look in his eye, the war chief replied, "The big one—Usher—he yours."

"Yes, he is mine," Jonah replied.

Spirit Road came up to Jonah, touched the white man's wounded shoulder. "The woman? She yours?"

"Yes. Mine too."

Turning, the Ute flung his voice over the creek, calling out to his warriors in his tongue.

"I think he says to them the big one is yours," Two Sleep explained. "Says because the woman yours."

One by one, the Utes appeared from the brush, two of them dragging a dead warrior from the timber, another two carrying wounded into the open.

"Usher?" Jonah asked as he turned to Spirit Road, his eyes searching the Ute war chief's. "The big one—he is . . . alone?"

"Big one yours now. No more guns to help him."

When Hook looked back across the stream, he found Usher slowly retreating from the foot of the cross where Sweete's bloody, battered, riven body hung from the nails, suspended from its hemp cords. Jonah tasted the bile at the back of his throat as his gaze once more leveled on the Mormon.

Usher shrieked, "Seems you have evened the score somewhat, farmer!"

"Said you wanted me, Usher. Still want me now that you ain't got your bushwhackers to pick me off?"

"More than ever, farmer!"

"Let her go—and you can have me. Let her come over here."

Usher peered down at Gritta. "You won't win her back. Why should I let her go?"

Hook swallowed hard, his heart pounding. "Because she never was yours, you bastard."

"And when I defeat you—kill you—string your intestines from tree to tree to tree around this meadow . . . when I drape the branches of these trees with your arms and legs that I'll rip from your body with my bare hands—will she be mine then, Gentile?"

"She never was yours, Usher. Never gonna be."

"No!" the Mormon screamed. "God joined us in His Church's holy Temple—"

"God brought me here to get her back!" Jonah cried out as he stepped down the bank toward water's edge.

"Pa! You can't! Your shoulder!"

Jeremiah dragged Two Sleep from the brush behind him as Jonah turned slightly, gesturing angrily for them to stay where they stood. "Dammit—stay back."

"I can't let you cross over there without me—"

"You rode this far with me, son. But no farther. It's mine from here on."

"She's my ma!"

"And she's my wife."

"Mine now, farmer!" Usher bellowed. "Say, is that your boy, farmer?"

"I'll come—"

He whirled on Jeremiah, flinging his anger at any target now. "You stay! Goddammit—you're a man now so you best understand this. You're a man—you chose to take care of your brother's family. Go back and make it your own family, Jeremiah. You'll never know just how I'm . . . I'm so goddamned proud of you for that, son. You made that family your own. Made that woman your own too. That man in you got to understand."

His eyes damp, Jeremiah finally nodded. "I'll wait here."

"I asked if that really is your boy, sodbuster?"

"Yeah—I'm his son!" Jeremiah screamed across the open ground as Hook moved away. "You tried once to kill me—sold me off."

"How well I remember that, you little son of a bitch. Why—tell me wherever did you come from?"

"The ones you sold me to . . . the Comanche took care of them."

"Comanche," Usher repeated, nodding knowingly. "And your father there? How did he—"

"He come for me, found me."

"Just like I found you, Usher!"

For a long moment the Danite leader turned his head to gaze up the slope at the two young boys, at his Negro servant. Then finally he again looked down at the woman, stroked Gritta's matted hair with the barrel of his revolver. "So—all these years—what took you so goddamned long, farmer?"

That smacked his gut with as much cold as the bullet had sent a tongue of fire through his shoulder. He saw her staring at him. Jonah struggled to speak for a moment, then sniffed, dragging a hand under his nose as he fought to find an answer, to explain more to her than anybody. She was staring at him.

Jeremiah spoke first. "He was finding the rest of us, Usher!"

"This I see, young one. Well," and Usher brought the pistol from Gritta's hair and shoved it again beneath her jaw, causing the woman to cock her head to the side. "Are you coming, farmer?"

Filled with a fierce pride for his son, Jonah turned from Jeremiah to look at his enemy across the creek. "I'm coming."

"Leave the rest over there."

Glancing quickly at Two Sleep and Spirit Road, letting them see the steel in his eye, Jonah finally gazed back at Usher. "They'll stay on this side."

When Usher shoved Gritta across the open ground, flinging her into the Negro's arms, something inside Jonah was yanked, like a section of wound cable snapping taut. He stepped down off the bank, breaking the dirty slick of ice that crusted the borders of the shallow stream. The Mormon's servant dragged the reluctant woman back up the soft slope toward the edge of the trees near the left side of the skull's mocking mouth.

Usher turned back on Hook. "Lose the gun!"

Cracking more of the ice-rime at the water's edge, Jonah emerged from the stream on the north bank. He stopped on the frosted grass, now slicked with melting frost. Keeping his eyes on Usher, Hook shoved the pistol into its holster. Slowly he fought the coat from his good arm, dragged it from the wounded shoulder already stiffening in pain, swelling in protest at the lump of lead still lodged against a bone. Every time he volved the arm, Jonah tasted the rising gall at the back of his throat, a pain threatening to hurl bile against his tonsils. A grating, metallic pain like fingers raking across the uneven surface of a crude iron pot.

Stuffing his own pistol back into the holster over his left hip, the Mormon slid a long-bladed knife from the scabbard at his back. It caught the morning's rose light.

His eyes tearing in pain, Hook blinked, bringing out his own belt knife, half the size of the Mormon's. Hook's was a skinning knife—not a man-killing weapon.

With a dramatic flourish the Danite bent at the waist, sweeping the ground with the long knife as he bowed elegantly.

"Then—by all means, farmer . . . come meet your doom!"

"*Pa!*"

He started up the north slope toward his greatest enemy. "Stay back, Jeremiah!"

"You heard your father!" Usher ordered as he rocked forward on the balls of his feet, beginning to wag the big knife back and forth before him in great loops. "You can only watch now: watch your father die."

"I can hit him from here, Pa!"

"No!" Jonah flung his voice back over his shoulder. "Tell him why, Two Sleep. Tell him I didn't ride all these years just to watch this black-hearted son of a devil's whelp die in front of me with someone else's bullet in him. Tell Jeremiah that I didn't dream of getting my hands around the neck of this bucket of whorehouse slop every night across every last one of those years just to watch someone else drop him in his tracks with a bullet."

Usher grinned malevolently. "You want me very, very bad—don't you, farmer?"

"Two Sleep, you explain all that to Jeremiah for me—"

"He don't have to explain it to me, Pa. If you . . . should he . . . I just want you to know that—if that bastard kills you—I'm coming over and finish the job you started."

Hook turned to look at his son, for what might be the last time. "You take your mama home, Jeremiah."

"I'll take her back. Just like we talked."

Jonah turned back to face the man who for over a decade had been his enemy, his reason for being.

"You're here at last, sodbuster."

"I'm here, Jubilee Usher: come to take my revenge on you. To take my revenge even if I have to follow you into hell to do it!"

Usher closed within two yards, striding down the slope in a ground-eating gallop. "*Hell* is just where you're headed, Gentile!"

Jonah lunged furiously—driven into action by the sudden closeness of this enemy he had stalked across so many winters. The Mormon side-stepped, throwing out his boot to catch Hook's ankle. Jonah spilled onto his left shoulder, sprawled on the ground in a pained heap that sent shards of icy metal slivers through his chest, deep into his bowels.

The Danite stood nearby, waving his knife at him, laughing. "Is this your best? You make this all too easy, farmer!"

426

As he struggled to his feet, Jonah fought down the acid that laced his tongue with fire. Swallowing to control the waves of pain, he swiped the dust and brittle grass from his eyes, smearing the melted frost across his face in a muddy streak.

"Come. Come for me, farmer," Usher taunted. "Get on your feet and finish what you have prayed to your God to do."

"I have prayed," Jonah said quietly as he struggled up, came forward, his knife held out between them. "Prayed for more days than any man should ever have to pray without an answer."

"Your God is mute, farmer," Usher said as he lunged and swiped past Hook's useless left arm, opening a bloody gash in Jonah's striped shirt. "Your God will never answer you. While mine is a jealous God. A God that takes revenge on all who do not fall down on their knees and worship Him. God Almighty puts you in my hands!"

Feinting left, lunging forward on that leg, Jonah suddenly whirled to his right in a complete circle, dragging the knife in a savage blur across the Mormon's hip, sensing resistance; then in an instant the blade slid free.

Usher grunted, slapping his left hand over the wound that immediately began to soak the immaculate shirt, darkening the ruffled cuffs. More ruffles lay against the throbbing arteries of his neck, trembling against the swelling neck cords.

"You were lucky there, farmer," he said, his voice edged with fatigue. "But—I tire of playing with you. This has quickly become wearisome."

Not prepared when Usher flung himself toward him, Jonah found his knife arm shoved aside as his enemy hurtled him off the ground. Back he flew, crashing against a rock shelf, the air hammered from his lungs.

He rolled onto his knees, struggling for a breath, each one like a sliver of ice in the side of his chest as he fought for air. Sensing the piercing, tearing of flesh inside. Choking, gasping, he knew something was wrong— terribly wrong. And began spitting up the yellow bile he was no longer able to swallow down.

Blinking his eyes clear, Jonah heard the Mormon coming behind him. Yet for that crucial moment he did not turn toward his enemy. Instead he turned away, raising his eyes misting against the pain in his shoulder, flooding against the torment in his chest—and looked at her.

Gritta's eyes—so icily vacant—stared back into his. Expressionless as her face was, it was those eyes that had so long ago looked deep into his soul. Those eyes that had so very long ago convinced Jonah that the two of them had belonged to one another across the centuries, belonged to each other across lifetimes. Even unto eternity.

And should it end here, should it end now . . . she would have seen him come for her. He had kept his promise.

Savagely twisting like an animal caught with its paw crushed in an iron trap, Hook led with his knife, catching Usher in the softness of the gut at the moment the tip of the Mormon's knife blade pierced the tough muscle and sinew stretched across the flat of Jonah's shoulder blade. Loosening those thick cords of muscle that had screamed with brilliant streamers of fire that awful winter morning at the bottom of a snowy arroyo beside a Comanche village on the mapless Staked Plain.

The morning he lost Zeke.

With a gasp Usher shuddered and withdrew a step, then took a second step as his bloodied left hand clutched futilely at the wound.

Fighting the tears of pain, Jonah swiped at his eyes with the back of the knife hand. Able then to watch the Mormon's face blanch in its first real show of doubt, its first sign of genuine fear. Slowly, Hook looked down that immaculate white shirt, gazing at the bloody fingers of the Danite's left hand where the first puff of purple gut bubbled.

Usher fought, clawed with that bloody hand, then vainly with both hands as he struggled to stuff the first shiny glob of pinkish gut back into the wound.

"My . . . m-mine . . . ," Usher burbled.

"That's right, you son of a bitch," Jonah growled, finding something within him that allowed him to stand against the pain that rose like an evil thing within his broken chest to pierce the nerves behind his eyes, spread a meteor shower of sparks from his vision as he fought to keep his balance, fought for breath to utter his oath. "That's your belly I opened up."

"Come on, farmer," the Danite said stoically, a thin streamer of blood oozing down from the corner of his mouth, a dark streak against the ashen gray of his skin. "We must finish this. Let the woman see me kill you as it was written by the hand of God."

Jonah watched the Mormon keel slightly, stumbling backward a step, then another before Usher straightened. He lowered his head wearily, his eyelids drooping halfway like lamp-blackened hoods over the dark fires they contained as they focused on Hook.

Hook was shaking in great gushes of pain. "You're done, Usher."

With a violent wag of his head the Danite suddenly lumbered forward a step, shakily raising the knife in the bloody right hand. "In my arm rests the power of the one true God Almighty! By His hand has He this day delivered you to me!"

As Hook watched the left arm come away from that bloody wound when Usher started forward atop shaky legs, Jonah felt his own knees turning to water as the Danite's shadow reached him. Feeling the great power of his enemy's rush, Jonah collapsed on those watery legs—cursing himself. Vowing not to fall farther as Usher reached him.

The Mormon's knife glinted down from the icy blue winter sky above them. The color of Gritta's eyes.

Jonah drove his knife up, up farther, up and across the path of a rib, from breastbone all the way to that soft flesh beneath the arm that had cradled the Mormon's riven gut.

In that long and terrible moment he winced, feeling the Danite's blade slowly pierce his thin cotton shirt, sensed the edge of that weapon as it slid along the top of the wounded left shoulder that Jonah thought could hurt no more than it already did. He waited breathlessly for the coming pain while a cold breeze rattled the dry-leafed, skeletal trees ringing the open ground that sloped away to the creekbank. In the deafening silence that followed the passing of that breeze, Jonah raised his face to the sky, sensing the sun on his skin, the cold air caressing his cheek as the great shadow inched to the side.

He looked at the Mormon's face as Usher began to tumble to the side, his big knife spilling from his grip and out of reach across the broken shards of frost-drenched grass. The surprised look captured on that craggy, seamed face, the wickedness in those chertlike eyes still glowing with their unquenched evil.

Now pain raced on down Jonah's shoulder, the moment Usher grunted, striking the ground. For another heartbeat Hook squatted there on his side near his enemy, staring into the man's face as Usher grinned malevolently back at him, his right arm fumbling against the folds of his bloodied shirt. As if reaching for something. Perhaps his gut that spewed onto the grass, steaming.

From the corner of his eye, Jonah caught her moving. A step at first, then another. Gritta inched down the slope toward them.

Usher grumbled, "She's mine, farmer. Nothing you can do ever . . . ever will change what God has joined. Can't change that."

He watched her as he listened to the Mormon's words, blinking his eyes. Hook hadn't been this close to her since that morning he had walked off down their dusty lane to join the other dirt-poor farmers who were marching north to fight with Sterling Price, leaving homes and families to keep the Federals out of Missouri, out of their lives. It had been nothing less than a whole lifetime since he had seen her.

When his eyes came back to Usher, Jonah's breath suddenly seized in his broken chest. The Danite had pulled a stubby pepperbox from inside his bloody shirt. There it glistened in the hand drenched with Usher's gore. All those barrels pointed at Jonah.

"She's mine, farmer."

Several yards behind the Danite, Gritta moved with ease, as if she did not move on feet at all. In one swift motion as she came forward, she knelt, sweeping up the big knife that had tumbled out of the Mormon's hand, and kept on coming down the slope.

Against all that his pain-riven body refused to do, Jonah clambered to his knees, held up the one arm—his mouth moving but no sound coming forth . . . become afraid for her, afraid the Danite would turn his terrible pepperbox on her—needed to warn her.

"She's all mine. When I cut you in half—" Usher choked, coughing up some more fluid before he wiped his mouth with the back of his white sleeve and went on. "When I cut you in half with this sweet, powerful little weapon, farmer."

"No!" Jonah shouted at Gritta, lunging toward the Mormon at the same instant.

The pepperbox spat yellow fire, belched smoke. A burn along the side of his head, another finger of fire across the cheekbone and ear where the cold breeze struck the fiery furrow seeping ooze as he spilled backward.

Smoke clearing, he blinked the shards of volcanic light from his eyes. Through them Hook saw her pounce across the last few feet of shattered, brittle grass dampened with the morning's frost and the Mormon's blood to land on Usher's back, shrieking like a nightmare's unearthly apparition. Into her left hand she quickly gathered most of his long stove-black hair that ringed the smooth, bald flesh atop Usher's head, yanking back with an inhuman strength to expose the great muscular trunk of the Danite's neck.

He still grinned at Jonah. "Like I told you: she's mine, farmer."

In the next moment Jonah looked up from Usher's face. Found Gritta's eyes locked on him. Pulling the head back, she had a knee braced against the back of the Mormon's shoulders, bunched beneath the tumble of her dirty skirts.

In all the fury those eyes contained, there remained the faintest of question as she stared at Hook still sprawled on the ground, his head buzzing with a sharp, icy noise. It was as if she were looking at his face, studying him, searching to find something she could recognize, something she could remember. Something to grasp and hold on to with all her might in a spinning world gone upside down on her.

The Mormon's eyes rolled back in his head as he looked up at the woman, then came back to rest on Hook as he growled, "She always will be mine." Bringing the pepperbox up again, stretching out his arm until the weapon was all but two feet from Hook's face. "I'm sending you straight to hell, Gentile!"

Jonah looked up from that circle of deadly steel eyes to look into Gritta's face. And, wordlessly, he nodded to her.

With all that inhuman strength surging through her small body, Gritta cried out as she dragged the knife across the Mormon's throat. Jonah watched her face, saw her revel in the feel of its release as the first explosive gush of warmth spilled across her own cold flesh the moment the deadly knife laid Usher's flesh asunder, opened from ear to ear. As the second great artery burst, erupting in a great pumping froth, Gritta hurled the Danite's head forward savagely.

Usher's breath bubbled. Hook watched the Mormon fight to speak, mouthing wet, garbled words. Unable to curse his killers, it was now left to his eyes to speak their evil. Until they fluttered, froze open, and glazed over in death.

For a long time neither she nor Jonah moved. Instead they stared at one another in the eerie silence of that clearing beside the ice-slicked creek warming beneath a new sun. No sound could he make out but the metallic grate of pain inside his head.

Jonah fought to stay awake, so tired. As if he hadn't slept in years. So damned many, many years.

Gritta was the first to finally move, slightly, gazing down into the Danite's frosty, open eyes. She rocked forward to balance one knee against his back and with that bloodied right hand she began the long incision at the nape of Usher's neck, up across the smooth, shaved skin of the wide brow, down past the other ear and back around the nape of the neck. The long gash complete, she struggled with this last act for an agonizing moment.

In utter awe, frightened by the stranger he watched, Jonah stared at the woman who yanked, tugged, fought over the dead Mormon's upper body, shifting her knee so that it pressed against the side of Usher's head.

Those cold blue eyes. Her eyes. He had never seen such evil in a woman's eyes. Never, never before such evil in Gritta's eyes. As if the black light that possessed Usher's lost soul had here in the end come to possess her too.

Then Gritta rose in triumph, stood with the trophy at the end of her outstretched arm, dripping its blood, its gore, on the body of Jonah's greatest enemy. Through the metallic pain in his head, Hook heard a sound begin low in her throat, rumbling, like some animal chewing off a limb to free itself from a trap . . . a sound that rose to take form as a hideous shriek as she shook the scalp at the sky. As if shaking some amulet or icon before God Himself.

As that terrifying cry of hers rocked back from the canyon walls, eventually fading into icy silence once more, Jonah's greatest fear became that Gritta's evil cry of triumph would be the last sound she would ever, ever make.

In the sudden, renewed quiet, the woman stared at the scalp for a long moment, her blue eyes simmering with unrequited evil. Finally looking down at Usher.

And in the passing of a bird's wings, Gritta's eyes once so coldly marked by the fires of hell went soft once more as they crawled to gaze into Jonah's.

When they met his, Hook felt a shiver of cold pass over him like nothing he had ever suffered. He stared into eyes gone vacant, all in the passing of a puff of smoke on a cruel wind. Gone distant, in retreat . . . in the sudden, all-too-quick awakening from her terrible dream.

Her soul flown from the windows of those eyes—as if Gritta had disappeared that moment within herself once more.

For now, and for all time to come.

Epilogue

Late Summer 1908

NATE DEIDECKER RAN his fingers through the long black hair sewn so it hung suspended from the rawhide-wrapped wheel. "With your wounds I imagine it was some time before you were able to fashion this . . . make this scalp into—what did you call it?"

"A dream catcher," the old man replied. "But I didn't make it."

"Don't tell me Gritta made it."

With a wag of his head Jonah said, "No. Two Sleep did. Then he give the scalp back to Gritta."

It was, after all, Nathan thought, her scalp. She was the one who took the damnably grotesque thing from Usher.

Then Deidecker asked, "What became of him—the Shoshone?"

Jonah sliced a thin sliver of chew from a plug as dark as molasses and placed it, pocketknife blade and all, into his mouth. When he had the knife folded and stuffed away deep in his patched canvas britches, he explained, "Him and Jeremiah, 'long with Spirit Road's warriors—they done what they could to patch me up first off, and while they was chewing roots and pushing all kinds of leaves into the holes in my poor ol' flesh, Two Sleep got Jeremiah to help him."

Still in awe of the climax to Hook's quest, Deidecker asked, "Got Jeremiah to help bury Jubilee Usher?"

"Hell no," Jonah growled, testily. "Them two cut Shad down from the Mormon's cross. Looped a big rope under the old man's arms, pulled them big railroad spikes loose the best they could and slowly let the body down to the ground. Two Sleep brung over his own buffalo robe where he laid Sweete. Tied the body up tight with some rawhide whangs."

"Just the way you said the Indians do it."

He nodded, his jaw quivering with emotion. "Just the way Shad would want it done. Like he done for his own boy."

"You buried him there?"

"No. Me and Two Sleep talked on it some that same day. Finally figured out a special place for the old man—a place that Shoshone said Shad really loved. Clear up in the flattops, in the Wind River Mountains." Jonah pointed southwest, toward country over and beyond the Big Horns.

"You brought his body all the way back to Wyoming?"

"I'd want a friend to do the same for me."

"Yes," Deidecker replied. "A last, final request. So—you didn't bury Usher's body."

"Once the Injun and Jeremiah had Shad down and his wounds cleaned, his body wrapped up for our trail back to Wyoming—them two decided to raise the Mormon's body back onto the cross, right where the bastard hung Shad."

Deidecker's face lit with glee, visualizing the amazing image he could describe for his readers. "They put Usher on his own cross?"

"Yep. Tied him up there, beside that creek in the canyon."

"And you just left him there when you rode away?"

"That's right, Nate." He sighed. "Rode away with Gritta and them two boys."

"You bring those youngsters here to Wyoming with you?"

"No. Neither the woman nor me was in shape to raise 'em—give 'em what they needed right then. 'Sides, by the time we got back to Pioche, the boys wasn't so scared of us no more. Talked a little and told us their families was down to Arizona. We left 'em with the sheriff, Jake Johnson was his name. Johnson said he'd get the young'uns on back to their folk. Things was just quieting down some about the time we come through—seems there'd been another messy saloon killing. Sheriff Johnson figured the Chinaman saloon owner was killed by one of the Mormons—but he really didn't have no way to prove it, 'cept on the word of one of the Chinaman's whores. Not that Johnson ever did put much stock in her whole story . . . but, she was the sheriff's only witness. He said she up and disappeared. Nobody's ever heard tell of her again in that part of Nevada."

"But you got the old fur trapper back to Wyoming."

"Buried proper."

"Yes, buried proper," Nate repeated, scratching at his notepad. "What of Two Sleep? Did he ever go back to live with his people again on the reservation?"

"Wind River?"

Deidecker scribbled furiously on his notepad. "Is that the name of the reservation where Two Sleep returned?"

Jonah put an old, veiny hand on the newsman's wrist, preventing Deidecker from writing. "Two Sleep come here with me and the woman."

With what beautiful symmetry life sometimes reveals itself, Nathan mused.

"Yes," Deidecker said absently, considering, looking over the yard that stretched away toward the endless foothills rising into the gray, granite spires hulking above them. "But when did the Indian move on?"

"Never did."

"He stayed with you and Mrs. Hook?"

"Yep."

"How long?"

"All the rest of his years." Jonah gazed down at the top of the old dog's head, scratched under its chin as the animal's eyes slipped to half-mast in feral pleasure.

"You don't mean he's still alive?" he asked with a sudden surge of excitement. "Can I meet him?"

"The Injun's dead. Passed on peaceful, Nate. Been almost ten years now. Damn," and he spit into the yard, keeping his face turned away so that he could drag a sleeve under his nose, angrily stuffing both hands into the pockets of his britches. He kept his back to Deidecker as he spoke. "God*damn* but I miss him."

With a sudden sharp pang of sadness, something that allowed Nate to sense the regret the old man must feel, Deidecker came to Hook's shoulder. "Where . . . where is . . . where'd you bury him?"

Jonah pointed. "Up there on that little hill."

Nate looked. It wasn't far. A couple hundred yards perhaps. That at most. But with the tall grass stirring in that summer breeze slinking off the icy glaciers, the newsman couldn't make out a gravestone. Not that he really expected to find a Christian cross over an Indian's grave—not after Jonah told him about their stop at that church in Trinidad, but . . . something.

"I don't see a . . . anything—"

435

"I just buried him, Nate. Him and me—we already talked about it. Asked him long time before he died what he wanted. To go back onto the reservation to be laid out. Or up in the rocks of the high places like ol' Shad. Didn't want neither one he said," and Jonah's voice cracked as he struggled to regain control of it. To make his words come out even. "He said he wanted to stay close to me and the woman. We was his family now. Can you believe that goddamned redskin said we was his family now? Can you beat that, Nate?"

Jonah turned slowly on Deidecker, his eyes pooling with tears as he gazed directly at the newsman. "Well? Can you beat that goddamned red son of a bitch wanting to be buried right up there on that bare hilltop?"

Unable to find his voice for a moment, Deidecker fought to hold down the welling of his own emotions. He turned slightly, afraid the tears might overtake him, a little embarrassed for this strong man, this man enduring enough to last the years of pain and search. A man strong enough to cry in front of a total stranger. Nate felt a little embarrassed for Jonah Hook, but feared most that he would get overwhelmed himself.

"You see, son," Jonah said quietly as he turned to settle onto the first step at the front porch, "an old farmer like me is the only kind what really knows. The ground is in my blood. Not just under my fingernails. But it's in the air I breathe, the food I eat. The land feeds you. It sustains you. Then—eventual—it comes time for every man to pay back the debt he's built up . . . and the land claims you back. You was born of the land. And in the end a man is laid back to rest out all eternity under a thick blanket of that land."

The old hound rose from the yard, stretched, and waddled up so he could lap his muzzle atop Hook's knee. There the old man scratched the dog's ears again, then gazed up at Deidecker.

"Nate, I s'pose it takes a man like me to understand what power the land means to an Injun like Two Sleep. What the land means to all Injuns. It's what most of us was fighting for against the Yankee Federals. The power of the land is what them redskins fought so hard to keep too. It's the land what gives us birth—the land what claims us back again when we grow so tired and can't rise up no more. When a man has to lay himself down for the last time."

Nathan sat writing, scratching his lead pencil across the pages of his writing pad furiously—attempting to adequately catch the wording Hook used to explain his connection with a time, his bond with a place, perhaps what was both a mythical time and a mythical place. If he did capture it just the way Jonah Hook said it, Nathan knew he had a winner. A long-running series that would undoubtedly catapult him to national fame.

"You know, Nate," Hook continued, interrupting the newsman's reverie, "a bunch of folks came down from Sheridan last month and spoke a bunch of big words around a monument they put up not far from here."

Deidecker looked up at the old, deeply tanned face etched with seams. "A monument? To you?"

Hook snorted, his eyes grown a bit softer, like the downy breast of a ring-necked dove come back to its roost. "Hell, no. They threw up a big, tall monument of washed river rock, all stacked up tall as can be down the road there—cemented together to stand for all time on top of a place called Lodge Trail Ridge."

Absently, Deidecker turned to look off in the direction Hook had pointed. "Why there?"

The old man wagged his head. "Where a wild-eyed army captain back to eighteen and sixty-six figured he could take a hundred soldiers and march right through the wild tribes gathered up on the Tongue and the Powder and the Rosebud and the Bighorn. Injuns what hunted all this country."

"Who was that officer?"

"Fetterman."

Nathan nodded. "Yes. He got himself killed. I remember hearing the story many times. But—I still can't figure the significance of Fetterman getting a hundred men killed on that Lodge Trail Ridge to what you've had to say."

Hook shrugged, gazing down into the old dog's eyes with nothing short of total love for the animal. "Nothing more but what that ridge is the place a lot of folks figure the whole godblamed Indian wars got started."

"So they put a monument up there—last month?"

"Third of July," Hook replied. "The next day was all the hoopla over the Fourth."

"You went for the festivities—the monument dedication?"

"No," and he wagged his head. "Heard all about it, though. The fort's old commander came back. Carrington. Folks said he was decked out in his old dress-blue uniform, said he gave a sort of speech out there on the ridge. Him there—and a handful of the old soldiers what come back to hear what Carrington had to say, and see that monument for themselves. Scarce more than a corporal's guard there was left to come back to Wyoming—but all of what did come back made that climb back up the ridge to remember the hundred soldiers the Sioux and Cheyenne swept away that cold, cold winter day"—Hook brushed one open palm quickly over the other in plains sign language—"the time when the army started this goddamned war that ended up taking us a quarter century to get finished."

"Sounds like you're pretty bitter about the way things turned out," Deidecker replied softly after a moment of reflection.

It took even longer for Hook to reply. "No. I ain't got no room inside me for no bitterness, Nate. Maybe just a few regrets is all."

"I can understand that, Jonah. How it ought to have been different for you."

"No man's got a right to ask for no more than he's ever given a chance to get on his own." Hook stared up at the peaks as the sun fell toward them, where that bright-yellow orb would impale itself in the southwest come sunset. "God will take care of the rest. A man does what he can to help God the best way that man knows how. To fight the devil the best way he knows how. But in the end, out here, God has to do the rest."

Deidecker found himself squinting, as if he hadn't really heard the old man correctly. "I'm afraid I don't follow—"

"Out here, Nate . . . in this land out here, this frontier that ain't no more—a man what comes here finds that there's always been a struggle between the purest of good, and the purest of evil. Not like nothing there is back east. Maybe it has to do with all the open space. Where time and place, good and evil, all tumble over and over on one another."

"Wait," Deidecker said anxiously, scribbling key words down on his pad and quickly flipping to another page before he lost the train of thought. "You're talking about your life as a battle . . . a battle of good against evil?"

Hook nodded. "Isn't any man's, Nate?"

Deidecker eventually nodded once, wrote a half-dozen more words down on the pad before he continued. "Tell me if I've got this right." Then he peered up at those gray, granite monoliths that shed their immense shadows down upon them as the sun sank ever farther toward the west. The way Jonah Hook watched every last sundown in this silent land. "You're telling me: the sacred and the profane are inextricably bound one to the other. You're saying that neither the sacred nor the profane can exist without the other, that neither one can exist in a vacuum. In the emptiness left without the other."

Jonah started nodding first, then finally turned to Deidecker. "I think

438

that's what I wanted to say. Yes. Especially here on the frontier. What we got left of it. What little there is way up here, way out here. Why, with the way folks is crushing in—this wild, free land is dying. And, every day this wild, free land dies . . . Jonah Hook dies a little more too."

Over his shoulder Nate heard the woman's footsteps. He turned slightly to watch her emerge from the open door and come to her rocker, where she settled, arms and hands in their accustomed place to begin her easy roll on the porch where the bows had worn their tracks over the years in this scene played out every sundown. Every last twilight. She watched the sun ease off this wild, free land . . . just like the old man did. Every last night.

Turning back to look at Hook, Nathan found Jonah smiling at his wife. A gentle gaze, something soft and warm around the eyes. Then Deidecker looked back at the sunset. The sunset Gritta watched.

"Nate—a man can't really know what is sacred . . . no matter what all the preachers and God-talkers . . . no matter all them Bible-thumpers and folks out to save the souls of others . . . not a goddamned one of 'em. No man can really know what is truly sacred—until he has lived through what is wholly profane."

The silence that night grew into something tangible and profound. Jonah cooked supper in silence. The three of them ate in silence. And then the old couple disappeared sometime after moonrise, gone off to bed. Leaving Nathan alone with his thoughts, and this great land.

They didn't talk until the next morning when Jonah pushed past the curtain in the doorway to find the newsman folding his clothing in the early light, stuffing it all within his one carpet bag with the leather handles thick as a man's swollen thumb.

Hook pulled a suspender up onto his shoulder. "You figure we talked all we need to talk, Nate?"

He studied the old man's face a moment, then turned back to buckle the strap on the bag. "I know all I need to now, Jonah. Enough to know a windbag when I meet one. Enough to know a real hero when I meet one of those too."

"You . . . you ain't gonna make me out to be a windy ol' half-assed loon, are you?"

Nate fought down the sting of sentiment rising in his throat. Of all the others he had interviewed over the years, he had never been this close to feeling the clutch of shameless sentiment overpowering him. He shook his head. "No, no I won't do that, Jonah."

Hook smiled. It struck Nate that it was the same gentle, warm smile he had seen on the old man's face at sundown the evening before. And Deidecker felt proud, right proud to earn one of those smiles from the old man.

"Tell me—about the Utes, Jonah." He picked up his bag and moved out onto the porch as the woman pushed aside the blanket that covered the doorway to the back room. She stood there a moment as Nate stopped on the porch. Her eyes fell to his bag, to the coat he had draped over his arm. Then Nate looked back at Hook.

"They rode with us a piece. After Spirit Road's warriors took what they wanted from the bodies, took all they wanted out of Usher's tents. Then rode with us until they moved north to gather up the rest of his war party that was still with some of the Danites. From there Spirit Road said they was going to head back to the plateau country in Colorado Territory."

"Did you ever learn what became of Jubilee Usher's Danites—his Avenging Angels—after that?"

Hook glanced at the woman, who stood as still as Lot's wife at that blanket doorway, watching the two men. Then he looked back into the newsman's eyes. "Didn't ever know for sure. Some say the Mormons finally took care of 'em themselves. Wasn't long after . . . after we got back to Wyoming that the government finally executed John Doyle Lee. March seventy-seven is the way I remember it. Took Lee out and shot him on the same ground where him and the rest butchered those Arkansas emigrants twenty year before."

"Brigham Young's people took out after Usher's Danites, broke them up?"

With a shrug the old man studied his boots. "I heard talk come out of Utah—mostly from Mormons traveling south of here. Said the trouble got started just after Brigham Young hisself died the next year."

"In seventy-seven?"

"Yes. Lots of talk—rumors mostly: Mormons said their Prophet was poisoned. Lots of Mormons claimed he died at the hand of some of Jubilee Usher's faithful taking their revenge."

"But that's nothing but rumors." Deidecker waited for an answer, studying the old man's face, his eyes, for a clue.

"S'pose it's just talk, Nate. No one ever proved anything one way or another about how Brigham Young died for sure." He turned his head, whistled toward the barn. "Only thing I know for sure is how he got men to do his bloody bidding for him, men like Jubilee Usher—all in the name of God."

"How Usher in turn got men to do his own bloody bidding."

"Yeah," Hook replied, whistled again in the direction of the barn, expectant of the dog. "No matter what folks say, truth is that some of those who rode with Usher likely would have stayed together. Could have kept on with what they believed was their mission ordained from God. Ain't hard for me to believe they one day took their revenge on Brigham Young—the man they figured was a false prophet."

"The man they could ultimately blame for Jubilee Usher's end. If it hadn't been you, then it might well have been Brigham Young who brought down the curtain on that blackguard's reign of terror."

Deidecker turned away and took two steps to the edge of the porch, where he stopped as Jonah came up beside him. His eyes quickly found the woman back in the cool morning shadows of the cabin. Still standing there at the blanket doorway. "You took Gritta back to Missouri?"

The old man shook his head. "No. Jeremiah and me decided there was nothing left back there for her. Figured we could let Hattie know soon as we found a place to spend out our days."

Deidecker swept a hand in an arch across the yard. "Here?"

"Yes," he answered. "I knowed this country a little from my time with General Connors. When I was scouting with Bridger."

"But that was seventy-six," Nate said. "The great Sioux war was in full swing. The army's campaign to end it all, once and for all."

With a nod Jonah answered. "Time we finally got here, ol' Ranald Mackenzie had hit Dull Knife's village of Cheyenne down south of here a ways. November it was. Had 'em a hell of a fight. But—the Injun wars was all but over for this country. The soldiers had the wild bands on the run from there on out. While the army was cleaning out the wild bands, we found us a place to put up outside Fort Fetterman for that winter."

"The four of you—with Two Sleep and Jeremiah?"

Hook wagged his head. "No, Jeremiah rode south alone, back to Indian Territory."

"Back to his family."

"Prairie Night. My two grandbabies. Come green-up, Jeremiah showed back up with 'em."

"They come to stay?"

He shook his head sadly, a gray grief returned to those eyes. "No. Just to lay over the spring and summer. To help his pa raise this cabin for his mother."

Down the two steps off the porch he went, then turned—Deidecker looked it over once more when he reached the ground. "A fine, fine place you built, Jonah."

Hook ran a hand up a peeled pine that supported part of the front porch. "It's a place a man can live out his days with his woman. This is country where the water's so cold it'll set your teeth on edge. And there's quiet here. Lots and lots of quiet. Enough silence for a man what's been through all that I've seen. Quiet enough for us both."

Deidecker looked past the old man at her, finally asking, "So when did Gritta come to recognize you again?"

Jonah looked at the newsman for a long time before answering, his face quivering ever so slightly, as if the old scout were fighting for control of it before daring to speak. "She . . . Gritta ain't never . . . she's never showed me she knows who I am."

In his belly he felt a sudden and immensely cold sadness for the old man. "I'm . . . sorry, Jonah. I didn't have any idea. After all this time."

When Hook turned his face away, to stare up at the distant, towering bulk of Cloud Peak become a golden rose with the new light, Deidecker caught but a glimpse of the saddest look he had ever seen cross a man's face. Something new, something he had never recognized on the old scout's face, which heretofore had remained hardened, a mask to what lay within.

"One day, Nate," Hook finally said. "One day soon she'll be healed and come back from that place where she's gone . . . that place where Usher drove her to take refuge. So the best I can give her is to be here when she does come back."

Deidecker swallowed hard, a ball of sentiment threatening him again. He gazed at the woman, who settled to her chair and began to rock, as if she were completely unaware of the men and their words about her. "God bless you, Jonah Hook."

"It'll be soon, Nate," the old man continued. "She'll finally know who I am. Real soon, she'll know—she'll remember I come got her from Usher. Realize it was her husband come got her, brung her home. Maybe tomorrow, Nate. Maybe tomorrow morning when she wakes up."

It was hard breathing around the rancid ball of sadness choking him. Deidecker nodded, forcing the words out. "Yeah, Jonah. Likely tomorrow. Come morning—she'll finally know it was you who came to rescue her. She'll know Jonah Hook brought her home."

The newsman turned away and shuffled off, unable to think of anything better to do, anything he could say, his shoulders quaking slightly. Jonah followed at the young reporter's heels.

"Hattie come out to visit us the next year. Seventy-eight. Lord A'mighty, was she ever a beauty! And her new life? That's something too. Jeremiah come up that summer too. Like a family reunion. Brought his family—and a new baby. Gritta loved holding all them little'uns." Hook stopped a minute, his lips pursing as his eyes pooled. "God, how I hated Usher for taking the young'uns from her. Almost as much as I hated him for taking her from me."

"That . . . that why you did everything you could to have the children come back so often? Bring the grandchildren?"

With a nod the old man turned away, blinking in the sun's light to clear his eyes. The dog loped up and sat at his knee, tongue lolling as Hook ran his bony fingers along the animal's muzzle.

"The boy—he'd gone back to Missouri that winter before Hattie and him brought their families out to see Gritta."

"Jeremiah filled in the last grave?"

"Just like him and me talked. He took Prairie Night and the young'uns back there with him. They cut back the weeds under that big oak tree. Planted some wildflowers on Zeke's grave. After couple of days they turned back for home."

"You ever . . . go back there? Your homestead in Missouri."

He shook his head. "Nothing for me there." Then turned a moment to glance at the woman in her rocker on the porch. "Nothing for neither of us there. Not no more."

Deidecker flung his bag into the back of the single-horse hitch.

"Here," Jonah said quietly as he put a hand on the newsman's arm and started them toward the barn. "If you don't wanna stay for breakfast, least a cup of coffee . . . I can help you with your rig."

"I'd like that, Jonah. Like your help very much."

They were quiet together, an easy sort of silence that needed no filling with idle talk as the old man stroked the muzzle of one of the old horses that wandered in from the paddock for a brief rub before Hook pulled the harness from a nail in the barn wall. Quiet through it all until the newsman finally stood beside the front wheel, his arm perched on the dashboard nervously, not really sure of what to say now that departure was imminent. Then he held out a hand.

Jonah took it in his, suddenly pulled the newsman close into an embrace. Into Deidecker's ear Hook whispered, "Hope you don't mind, son. This hug we're having. I . . . I don't get all that much opportunity to have someone get their arms around me much anymore. The children—both of 'em got lives of their own. Back east. And . . . Gritta . . . Gritta . . ."

Nate heard the old man sigh, his voice drop off as he stepped back, let go of Deidecker's hand, quickly glancing at the woman.

"Gritta ain't much a one for hugging these days. Likely natural, ain't it? What with getting old, I s'pose. But it feels good now and again, you know?"

Nathan felt the tears coming. "Yes. Understandable, Jonah."

He swiped a sleeve under his nose. "So you know just about all there is to know about this ol' man's life now, Nate. Write it good. Make me proud of you. Proud as I'd been of Zeke. Always thought he'd rise up and make something of himself, like you done. With proper schooling. He was a smart cracker, that boy. Just like you—he'd made something of himself."

Nathan turned quickly as his eyes pooled, and clambered into the buggy to take up the reins. He turned one last time to look at the old man standing there in the yard, the old dog seated beside his leg, and asked, "Jonah, if I ever would . . . send you a letter—will you read it?"

"I can read a little," he answered. "Yes, Nate. I'll read it."

"If I come . . ."

"There'll always be a place at Jonah Hook's table for you, son. I'm damned proud to know you."

Nathan watched Hook take a step back. Watched the old dog resettle beside his dusty boot. "I'm . . . I'm goddamned proud to know you too, Jonah Hook."

Then Deidecker savagely brought the strap leather down on the back of the rented horse and felt the sudden lurch of the livery as the animal set the rig into motion, turning those front wheels into the narrow ruts, rumbling out of the yard to begin his descent through the foothills that would take him back to that wide, dusty, north-south road stretched between Buffalo and Sheridan—the growing metropolis where he would spend a night having supper with Will Kemper and catch the next train east to Omaha.

He had a story to write. The sort of story many men never found in an entire lifetime, much less got the chance to write about.

Deidecker had rocked the single-horse hitch some distance down the rutted trail before he eased back on the reins, stopping the horse. Turning around one last time to look back at the old man, Nathan found Jonah Hook still standing in the yard, that old dog patiently waiting at the knee of his canvas britches shiny with age and wear.

Beyond the man and dog, back over Jonah's shoulder, on the porch the woman still rocked, and rocked, and rocked endlessly—not watching the newsman's departure, not even aware he had gone, staring only at the sun's new light turning Cloud Peak and the rest of the granite spires of the Big Horns into rose-colored monuments to the soul-crushing silence and space and wildness of this land, each immense gray peak scraping at the raw underbelly of the morning blue like a wild beast's claws tore at its helpless prey's most vulnerable weakness.

Seeing both the man and the woman there beneath all that wide sprawl of wilderness, too much for any one man to comprehend, Nathan Deidecker felt suddenly overcome with what he had been fighting all morning.

So he began to pray for the old man: to pray that the silent, wild-eyed old woman truly would one day do just what Jonah Hook so desperately believed in, what Jonah clung to with a faith most people reserved only for their God.

As the tears finally came, Nate wondered for a moment if he would write the story, that growing doubt become undeniable, become tangible at last. Or would he simply put his notes away in a box somewhere in his boarding-room closet? Perhaps even burn them when he got back to Omaha. And in thinking even that—Nathan Deidecker knew he could not write the story. Knew he *would* not. Never would anyone know of the pain Jonah Hook endured. No one had the right.

To cry here for the first time in his adult life—it did not matter. There was something supremely human in what he had just experienced. Nathan had felt more in the last few days than most men are blessed to feel in an entire lifetime. The old man had taught him that: by the richness of his passions, through his love and his hate. To feel, and to laugh, to feel and to cry.

Goddamned good to have this cry.

Not fighting the tears that came as he turned to lash the horse into motion once more, Nate knew the old man and woman had the right to live out their lives as they each saw fit: Jonah in his world. Gritta imprisoned in hers.

God, Nathan prayed, if you can answer prayers—answer that old man's. Bring her back to him. Let her know Jonah came for her across those miles and all those years. Came to bring her home.

Dear God, if you do answer prayers: bring her back to him one day soon.

Amen.